DEBBIE MACOMBER

Then You Came Along

mira

Recycling programs for this product may not exist in your area.

ISBN-13: 978-0-7783-8613-1

Then You Came Along

Copyright © 2022 by Harlequin Enterprises ULC

Father's Day
First published in 1991. This edition published in 2022.
Copyright © 1991 by Debbie Macomber

Same Time, Next Year
First published in 1995. This edition published in 2022.
Copyright © 1995 by Debbie Macomber

For questions and comments about the quality of this book, please contact us at CustomerService@Harlequin.com.

Mira
22 Adelaide St. West, 41st Floor
Toronto, Ontario M5H 4E3, Canada
www.Harlequin.com

Printed in Lithuania

MIX
Paper from responsible sources
FSC® C021394

**Also available from #1 *New York Times* bestselling author
Debbie Macomber and MIRA**

Midnight Sons

Alaska Skies
  (*Brides for Brothers* and
  The Marriage Risk)
Alaska Nights
  (*Daddy's Little Helper* and
  Because of the Baby)
Alaska Home
  (*Falling for Him,*
  Ending in Marriage and
  Midnight Sons and Daughters)

This Matter of Marriage
Montana
Thursdays at Eight
Between Friends
Changing Habits
The Sooner the Better
Three Brides, No Groom
Summer Breezes
  (*Fallen Angel* and *The Way to*
  a Man's Heart)
Seaside Springtime
  (*For All My Tomorrows* and
  Yours and Mine)
Fairy-Tale Forever
  (*Cindy and the Prince* and
  Some Kind of Wonderful)
Perfect Partners
  (*Rainy Day Kisses* and
  Love 'n' Marriage)
Finally You
  (*All Things Considered* and
  No Competition)
Winning Hearts
  (*Laughter in the Rain* and
  Love by Degree)
Finding You Again
  (*White Lace and Promises* and
  Jury of His Peers)
A Second Glance
  (*Shadow Chasing* and
  Yesterday Once More)

Longing for Yesterday
  (*Reflections of Yesterday* and
  Yesterday's Hero)
The Night We Met
  (*Starlight*)
Time for Love
  (*A Friend or Two* and
  The Trouble with Caasi)
Their Perfect Match
  (*Promise Me Forever* and
  Adam's Image)
Married in Seattle
  (*First Comes Marriage* and
  Wanted: Perfect Partner)
Right Next Door
  (*Father's Day* and *The Courtship*
  of Carol Sommars)
Wyoming Brides
  (*Denim and Diamonds* and
  The Wyoming Kid)
The Man You'll Marry
  (*The First Man You Meet* and
  The Man You'll Marry)
Orchard Valley Grooms
  (*Valerie* and *Stephanie*)
Orchard Valley Brides
  (*Norah* and *Lone Star Lovin'*)
An Engagement in Seattle
  (*Groom Wanted* and
  Bride Wanted)
North to Alaska
  (*That Wintry Feeling* and
  Borrowed Dreams)

Debbie Macomber's
  Cedar Cove Cookbook
Debbie Macomber's
  Christmas Cookbook

CONTENTS

FATHER'S DAY

One

"I can't believe I'm doing this," Robin Masterson muttered as she crawled into the makeshift tent, which was pitched over the clothesline in the backyard of her new home.

"Come on, Mom," ten-year-old Jeff urged, shifting to make room for her. "It's nice and warm in here."

Down on all fours, a flashlight in one hand, Robin squeezed her way inside. Jeff had constructed the flimsy tent using clothespegs to hold up the blankets and rocks to secure the base. The space was tight, but she managed to maneuver into her sleeping bag.

"Isn't this great?" Jeff asked. He stuck his head out of the front opening and gazed at the dark sky and the spattering of stars that winked back at them. On second thought, Robin decided they were laughing at her, those stars. And with good reason. There probably wasn't another thirty-year-old woman in the entire state of California who would've agreed to this craziness.

It was the first night in their new house and Robin was exhausted. They'd started moving out of the apartment before five that morning and she'd just finished unpacking the last box. The beds were assembled, but Jeff wouldn't hear of doing anything as mundane as sleeping on a real mattress. After waiting years to camp out in his own backyard, her son wasn't about to delay the adventure by even one night.

Robin couldn't let him sleep outside alone and, since he hadn't met any neighbors yet, there was only one option left. Surely there'd be a Mother of the Year award in this for her.

"You want to hear a joke?" Jeff asked, rolling on to his back and nudging her.

"Sure." She swallowed a yawn, hoping she could stay awake long enough to laugh at the appropriate time. She needn't have worried.

For the next half hour, Robin was entertained with a series of riddles, nonsense rhymes and off-key renditions of Jeff's favourite songs from summer camp.

"Knock knock," she said when it appeared her son had run through his repertoire.

"Who's there?"

"Wanda."

"Wanda who?"

"Wanda who thinks up these silly jokes?"

Jeff laughed as though she'd come up with the funniest line ever devised. Her son's enthusiasm couldn't help but rub off on Robin and some of her weariness eased. Camping was fun—sort of. But it'd been years since she'd slept on the ground and, frankly, she couldn't remember it being quite this hard.

"Do you think we'll be warm enough?" she teased. Jeff had used every blanket they owned, first to construct the tent and then to pad it. To be on the safe side, two or three more were piled on top of their sleeping bags on the off-chance an arctic frost descended upon them. It was spring, but a San Francisco spring could be chilly.

"Sure," he answered, missing the kidding note in her voice. "But if you get cold, you can have one of mine."

"I'm fine," she assured him.

"You hungry?"

Now that she thought about it, she was. "Sure. Whatcha got?"

Jeff disappeared into his sleeping bag and returned a moment later with a limp package of licorice, a small plastic bag full of squashed marshmallows and a flattened box of raisins. Robin declined the snack.

"When are we going to buy me my dog?" Jeff asked, chewing loudly on the raisins.

Robin listened to the sound and said nothing.

"Mom…the dog?" he repeated after a few minutes.

Robin had been dreading that question most of the day. She'd managed to forestall Jeff for the past month by telling him they'd discuss getting a dog after they were settled in their house.

"I thought we'd start looking for ads in the paper first thing tomorrow," Jeff said, still munching.

"I'm not sure when we'll start the search for the right dog." She was a coward, Robin freely admitted it, but she hated to disappoint Jeff. He had his heart set on a dog. How like his father he was, in his love for animals.

"I want a big one, you know. None of those fancy little poodles or anything."

"A golden retriever would be nice, don't you think?"

"Or a German shepherd," Jeff said.

"Your father loved dogs," she whispered, although she'd told Jeff that countless times. Lenny had been gone for so many years, she had trouble remembering what their life together had been like. They'd been crazy in love with each other and married shortly after their high-school graduation. A year later, Robin became pregnant. Jeff had been barely six months old when Lenny was killed in a freak car accident on his way home from work. In the span of mere moments, Robin's comfortable world had been sent into a tailspin, and ten years later it was still whirling.

With her family's help, she'd gone back to school and obtained her degree. She was now a certified public accountant working for a large San Francisco insurance firm. Over the years she'd dated a number of men, but none she'd seriously consider marrying. Her life was far more complicated now than it had been as a young bride. The thought of falling in love again terrified her.

"What kind of dog did Dad have when he was a kid?" Jeff asked.

"I don't think Rover was any particular breed," Robin answered, then paused to recall exactly what Lenny's childhood dog had looked like. "I think he was mostly... Labrador."

"Was he black?"

"And brown."

"Did Dad have any other animals?"

Robin smiled at her warm memories of her late husband. She enjoyed the way Jeff loved hearing stories about his father—no matter how many times he'd already heard them. "He collected three more pets the first year we were married. It seemed he was always bringing home a stray cat or lost dog. We couldn't keep them, of course, because we weren't allowed pets in the apartment complex. We went to great lengths to hide them for a few days until we could locate their owners or find them a good home. For our first wedding anniversary, he bought me a goldfish. Your father really loved animals."

Jeff beamed and planted his chin on his folded arms.

"We dreamed of buying a small farm someday and raising chickens and goats and maybe a cow or two. Your father wanted to buy you a pony, too." Hard as she tried, she couldn't quite hide the pain in her voice. Even after all these years, the memory of Lenny's sudden death still hurt. Looking at her son, so eager for a dog of his own, Robin missed her husband more than ever.

"You and Dad were going to buy a farm?" Jeff cried, his voice ebullient. "You never told me that before." He paused. "A pony for me? Really? Do you think we'll ever be able to afford one? Look how long it took to save for the house."

Robin smiled. "I think we'll have to give up on the idea of you and me owning a farm, at least in the near future."

When they were first married, Robin and Lenny had talked for hours about their dreams. They'd charted their lives, confident that nothing would ever separate them. Their love had been too strong. It was true that she'd never told Jeff about buying a farm, nor had she told him how they'd planned to name it Paradise. Paradise, because that was what the farm would be to them. In retrospect, not telling Jeff was a way of protecting him. He'd lost so much— not only the guidance and love of his father but all the things they could have had as a family. She'd never mentioned the pony before, or the fact that Lenny had always longed for a horse....

Jeff yawned loudly and Robin marvelled at his endurance. He'd carried in as many boxes as the movers had, racing up and down the stairs with an energy Robin envied. He'd unpacked the upstairs bathroom, as well as his own bedroom and had helped her organize the kitchen.

"I can hardly wait to get my dog," Jeff said, his voice fading. Within minutes he was sound asleep.

"A dog," Robin said softly as her eyes closed. She didn't

know how she was going to break the bad news to Jeff. They couldn't get a dog—at least not right away. She was unwilling to leave a large dog locked indoors all day while she went off to work and Jeff was in school. Tying one up in the backyard was equally unfair, and she couldn't afford to build a fence. Not this year, anyway. Then there was the cost of feeding a dog and paying the vet's bills. With this new home, Robin's budget was already stretched to the limit.

Robin awoke feeling chilled and warm at the same time. In the gray dawn, she glanced at her watch. Six-thirty. At some point during the night, the old sleeping bag that dated back to her high-school days had come unzipped and the cool morning air had chilled her arms and legs. Yet her back was warm and cozy. Jeff had probably snuggled up to her during the night. She sighed, determined to sleep for another half hour or so. With that idea in mind, she reached for a blanket to wrap around her shoulders and met with some resistance. She tugged and pulled, to no avail. It was then that she felt something wet and warm close to her neck. Her eyes shot open. Very slowly, she turned her head until she came eyeball to eyeball with a big black dog.

Robin gasped loudly and struggled into a sitting position, which was difficult with the sleeping bag and several blankets wrapped around her legs, imprisoning her.

"Where did you come from?" she demanded, edging away from the dog. The Labrador had eased himself between her and Jeff and made himself right at home. His head rested on his paws and he looked perfectly content, if a bit disgruntled about having his nap interrupted. He didn't seem at all interested in vacating the premises.

Jeff rolled over and opened his eyes. Immediately he

bolted upright. "Mom," he cried excitedly. "You got me a dog!"

"No—he isn't ours. I don't know who he belongs to."

"Me!" Jeff's voice was triumphant. "He belongs to me." His thin arms hugged the animal's neck. "You really got me a dog! It was supposed to be a surprise, wasn't it?"

"Jeff," she said firmly. "I don't know where this animal came from, but he isn't ours."

"He isn't?" His voice sagged in disappointment. "But who owns him, then? And how did he get inside the tent with us?"

"Heavens, I don't know." Robin rubbed the sleep from her eyes while she attempted to put her garbled thoughts in order. "He looks too well fed and groomed to be a stray. He must belong to someone in the neighborhood. Maybe he—"

"Blackie!" As if in response, she was interrupted by a crisp male voice. "Blackie. Here, boy."

The Labrador lifted his head, but stayed where he was. Robin didn't blame him. Jeff was stroking his back with one hand and rubbing his ears with the other, all the while crooning to him softly.

With some effort, Robin managed to divest herself of the sleeping bag. She reached for her tennis shoes and crawled out of the tent. No sooner was she on her feet than she turned to find a lanky man standing a few yards from her, just on the other side of the three-foot hedge that separated the two properties. Obviously he was her neighbor. Robin smiled, but the friendly gesture was not returned. In fact, the man looked downright *un*friendly.

Her neighbor was also an imposing man, at least six feet tall. Since Robin was only five-three, he towered head and shoulders above her. Instinctively, she stiffened her back, meeting his dark eyes. "Good morning," she said coolly.

He barely glanced in her direction, and when he did, he dismissed her with little more than a nod. After a night on the ground, with her son and a dog for bedmates, Robin realized she wasn't looking her best, but she resented the way his eyes flicked disinterestedly over her.

Robin usually gave people the benefit of the doubt, but toward this man, she felt an immediate antipathy. His face was completely emotionless, which lent him an intimidating air. He was clearly aware of that and used it to his advantage.

"Good morning," she said again, clasping her hands tightly. She drew herself to her full height and raised her chin. "I believe your dog is in the tent with my son."

Her news appeared to surprise him; his expression softened. Robin was struck by the change. When his face relaxed, he was actually a very attractive man. For the most part, Robin hardly noticed how good-looking a man was or wasn't, but this time...she noticed. Perhaps because of the contrast with his forbidding demeanor of a moment before.

"Blackie knows better than to leave the yard. Here, boy!" He shouted for the Labrador again, this time including a sharp whistle loud enough to pierce Robin's eardrums. The dog emerged from the tent and approached the hedge, slowly wagging his tail.

"Is that your dog?" Jeff asked, dashing out behind Blackie. "He's great. How long have you had him?"

"I'll make sure he doesn't bother you again," the man said, ignoring Jeff's question. Robin supposed his words were meant to be an apology. "He's well trained—he's never left my yard before. I'll make sure it doesn't happen again."

"Blackie wasn't any bother," Jeff hurried to explain, racing forward. "He crawled into the tent with us and made himself at home, which was all right with us, wasn't it, Mom?"

"Sure," Robin answered, flipping her shoulder-length auburn hair away from her face. She'd had it tied back when she'd gone to bed, but it had pulled free during the night. Robin could well imagine how it looked now. Most mornings it tended to resemble foam on a newly poured mug of beer.

"We're friends, aren't we, Blackie?" Jeff knelt, and without hesitation the dog came to him, eagerly licking his face.

The man's eyes revealed astonishment, however fleeting, and his dark brows drew together over his high-bridged nose. "Blackie," he snapped. "Come."

The Labrador squeezed between two overgrown laurel bushes and returned to his master, who didn't look any too pleased at his dog's affection for Jeff.

"My son has a way with animals," Robin said.

"Do you live here?" Jeff asked next. He seemed completely unaware of their new neighbor's unfriendliness.

"Next door."

"Oh, good." Jeff grinned widely and placed his right hand on his chest. "I'm Jeff Masterson and this is my mom, Robin. We moved in yesterday."

"I'm Cole Camden. Welcome to the neighborhood."

Although his words were cordial, his tone wasn't. Robin felt about as welcome as a punk-rock band at a retirees' picnic.

"I'm getting a dog myself," Jeff went on affably. "That's why we moved out of the apartment building—I couldn't have a pet there except for my goldfish."

Cole nodded without comment.

Oh, great, Robin thought. After years of scrimping and saving to buy a house, they were going to be stuck with an ill-tempered next-door neighbor. His house was older than the others on the block. Much bigger, too. Robin guessed that his home, a sprawling three-story structure, had been built in the early thirties. She knew that at one time this neighborhood had been filled with large opulent homes like Cole Camden's. Gradually, over the years, the older places had been torn down and a series of two-story houses and trendy ramblers built in their place. Her neighbor's house was the last vestige of an era long past.

"Have you got any kids?" Jeff could hardly keep the eagerness out of his voice. In the apartment complex there'd always been plenty of playmates, and he was eager to make new friends, especially before he started classes in an unfamiliar school on Monday morning.

Cole's face hardened and Robin could have sworn the question had angered him. An uncomfortable moment passed before he answered. "No, I don't have any kids." His voice held a rough undertone, and for a split second Robin was sure she saw a flash of pain in his eyes.

"Would it be okay if I played with Blackie sometimes? Just until I get my own dog?"

"No." Cole's response was sharp, but, when Jeff flinched at his vehemence, Cole appeared to regret his harsh tone. "I don't mean to be rude, but it'd probably be best if you stayed in your own yard."

"That's all right," Jeff said. "You can send Blackie over here to visit anytime you want. I like dogs."

"I can see that." A hint of a smile lifted the corners of his mouth. Then his cool gaze moved from Jeff to Robin, his face again expressionless, but she sensed that he'd made up his mind about them, categorized them and come to his own conclusions.

If Cole Camden thought he could intimidate her, Robin

had news for him. He'd broadcast his message loud and clear. He didn't want to be bothered by her or her son, and in exchange he'd stay out of her way. That was fine with her. Terrific, in fact. She didn't have time for humoring grouches.

Without another word, Cole turned and strode toward his house with Blackie at his heels.

"Goodbye, Mr. Camden," Jeff called, raising his hand.

Robin wasn't surprised when their neighbor didn't give them the courtesy of a reply.

In an effort to distract Jeff from Cole Camden's unfriendliness, she said brightly, "Hey, I'm starving. How about you?"

Jeff didn't answer right away. "Do you think he'll let me play with Blackie?"

Robin sighed, considering the dilemma that faced her. She didn't want Cole to hurt Jeff's feelings, but it wasn't likely their neighbor would appreciate her son's affinity with his Labrador. By the same token, a neighbor's dog, even one that belonged to a grouch, would ease her guilt over not being able to provide Jeff with the dog she'd promised him.

"What do you think, Mom?" Jeff prompted. "He'll probably let me play with Blackie sometimes, don't you think?"

"I don't know, honey," she whispered. "I just don't know."

Later the same day, after buying groceries to stock their bare kitchen shelves and picking up other necessities, Robin counted the change at the bottom of her purse. She needed to be sure she had money for the subway on Monday morning. Luckily she had enough spare change for BART—Bay Area Rapid Transit—to last the week, but it was packed lunches for her and Jeff until her next payday, which was in two weeks.

Her finances would've been in better shape if she'd waited another year to move out of the apartment. But interest rates were at a two-year low and she'd decided soon after the first of the year that if they were ever going to move out of the apartment this was the time.

"Mom!" Jeff crashed through the back door, breathless. "We're in trouble."

"Oh?" Robin glanced up from the salad she was mixing. A completely disgusted look on his face, her son flung himself into a chair and propped his elbows on the table. Then he let out a forceful sigh.

"What's wrong, Jeff?"

"I'm afraid we made a bad mistake."

"How's that?"

"There's nothing but girls in this neighborhood." He made it sound as though they'd unexpectedly landed in enemy territory. "I rode my bike up and down the street and all I saw were *girls*." He wrinkled his nose.

"Don't worry, you'll be meeting lots of boys in school on Monday."

"You aren't taking this seriously!" Jeff cried. "I don't think you understand what this means. There are seven houses on this block. Six of them have kids and only one has a boy, and that's me. I'm surrounded by women!"

"How'd you find all this out?"

"I asked, of course." He sighed again. "What are you going to do about it, Mom?"

"Me?" Robin asked. "Are you suggesting we move back to the apartment?"

Jeff considered this for only a moment. "I'd think we

should if it wasn't for two things. We can't have a dog there. And I found a fort."

"A fort?"

"Yes," he said solemnly. "It's hidden way back in Mr. Camden's yard and covered by a bunch of brush. It's real neat there. I don't think he knows about it, because the word on the street is he doesn't like kids. Someone must've built it and I'm going to find out who. If there's a club going, I want in. I've got the right—I live closer to Mr. Camden than anyone else does."

"Agreed." Robin munched on a slice of green pepper and handed one to Jeff. "So you think it'd be all right if we stayed?"

"I guess so," Jeff conceded, "at least until I find out more about the fort."

Robin was about to say something else when the doorbell chimed.

Jeff's blue eyes met hers. "I bet it's one of those pesky girls," he said in disgust.

"Do you want me to get rid of her?"

Jeff nodded emphatically.

Robin was smiling when she answered the front door. Jeff was right; it was a girl, one who seemed to be a couple of years younger than her son. She hadn't come alone, though. Standing with the youngster was an adult.

"Hi," the woman said cheerfully, flashing Robin a warm smile. "I know you've hardly had a chance to get settled, but I wanted to introduce myself. I'm Heather Lawrence and this is my daughter, Kelly. We live next door, and we'd like to welcome you to the neighborhood."

Robin introduced herself as she opened the door and invited them in. Heather was cute and perky. Her hair was cut in a short bob that bounced when she spoke. Robin knew right away that she was going to like these neighbors. Heather's warm reception was a pleasant change from the way Cole Camden had greeted her.

"Would you like some coffee?" Robin asked.

"If you're sure I'm not interrupting anything."

"I'm sure." Robin led her into the kitchen, where Jeff sat waiting. He cast her a look that suggested she should be shot for treason, then muttered something about forgetting that mothers were really *girls* in disguise. Then he headed out the front door.

Robin reached for two matching ceramic mugs and poured coffee for herself and her new friend. She offered Kelly a glass of juice, then slid into a chair across the table from the girl and her mother. "I'm sorry about Jeff." She felt obliged to apologize. "He's at the age where he thinks girls are a plague to society."

"Don't worry about it," Heather said, smiling. "Kelly isn't keen on boys herself."

"They're creeps. I'd rather ride my bicycle than play with a boy," the girl announced. "But Mom wanted me to come over with her so she didn't look like a busybody. Right, Mom?"

Heather blushed and threw her daughter a murderous glance.

Robin laughed. "I thought it would take several weeks to get to know my neighbors and I've met two in one day."

"Someone else has already been over?"

"Cole Camden introduced himself this morning," she explained, keeping her eyes averted to hide the resentment she felt toward her unfriendly neighbor. Even now, hours later, she couldn't help thinking about the way he'd reacted to her and Jeff.

"Cole Camden introduced himself?" Heather repeated,

sounding shocked. She frowned, staring into space as though digesting the fact.

"To be honest, I think he would've preferred to avoid me, but his dog wanted to make friends with Jeff."

Heather's mouth opened and closed twice. "Blackie did?"

"Is there something strange about that?"

"Frankly, yes. To say Cole keeps to himself is an understatement. I don't think he's said more than a handful of words to me in the entire two years since Kelly and I moved here. I don't know why he stays in the neighborhood." She paused to respond to her daughter, who was asking permission to go home. "Thank Robin for the juice, honey. Anyway," she went on, turning back to Robin when her daughter had skipped out the door, "he's all alone in that huge house and it's ridiculous, really. Can you imagine what his heating bills must be? Although, personally, I don't think money is much of a problem for him. But I've never heard any details."

It didn't surprise Robin to learn Cole lived alone. She'd barely met the man, but guessed that life held little joy for him. It was as though love, warmth and friendship had all been found lacking and had therefore been systematically dismissed.

"Apparently, he was married once, but he was divorced long before I came here."

Robin had dealt with unfriendly men before, but something about Cole struck her hard and deep, and she wasn't sure what it was or why he evoked such a strong feeling within her.

"He and his dog are inseparable," Heather added.

Robin nodded, hardly listening. He'd intimidated her at first, but when she'd pulled herself together and faced him squarely he'd loosened up a bit and, later, even seemed amused. But then Jeff had asked him about children, and Robin had seen the pain in his eyes.

As if by magic, her son's face appeared around the door. When he saw that Kelly was gone, he walked into the room, hands in his back pockets.

"Do you have a dog?" he asked Heather.

"Unfortunately, no. Kelly's allergic."

Jeff nodded as though to say that was exactly the kind of thing he expected from a girl. "We're getting a German shepherd soon, aren't we, Mom?"

"Soon," Robin responded, feeling wretched. After Heather left, she was going to tell Jeff the truth. She fully intended to let him have his dog, but he'd have to wait a while. She'd been practicing what to say. She'd even come up with a compromise. They could get a cat. Cats didn't seem to mind being left on their own, and they didn't need to be walked. Although she wasn't happy about keeping a litter box in the house, Robin was willing to put up with that inconvenience. Then, when she could afford to have a fence built, they'd get a dog. She planned to be positive and direct with Jeff. He'd understand. At least she hoped he would.

Heather stayed only a few more minutes. The visit had been a fruitful one. Robin had learned that Heather was divorced, worked mornings in an office and provided after-school day care in an effort to spend more time with Kelly. This information was good news to Robin, and the two women agreed that Jeff would go to the Lawrence house before and after school, instead of the community center several blocks away. The arrangement suited them both; even Jeff shrugged in agreement.

Robin would've liked to ask her new friend more about

Cole, but his name didn't come up again, and she didn't want to seem too curious about him.

After Heather left, Robin braced herself for the talk with Jeff about getting a dog. Unfortunately, it didn't go well. It seemed that after waiting nearly ten years, a few more months was completely unacceptable.

"You promised!" he shouted. "You said I could have a dog when we moved into the house!"

"You can, sweetheart, but not right away."

Unusual for Jeff, tears gathered in his eyes, and he struggled to hold them back. Soon Robin felt moisture filling her own eyes. She hated disappointing Jeff more than anything. His heart was set on getting a dog right away, and he considered the offer of a cat a poor substitute.

He left the house soon afterward. In an effort to soothe his hurt feelings, Robin cooked her son's favorite meal— macaroni and cheese with sliced sausage and lots of ketchup.

She didn't see him on the pavement or the street when she went to check half an hour later. She stood on the porch, wondering where he'd gone. His bike was inside the garage, and he'd already aired his views about playing with any of the girls in the neighborhood.

It would be just like him to storm into his room in a fit of indignation and promptly fall asleep. Robin hurried upstairs to his bedroom, which was across the hall from her own.

His bed was made and his clothes hung neatly in the closet. Robin decided that in another day or two, everything would be back to normal.

It wasn't until she turned to leave that she saw the note on his desk. Picking it up, Robin read the first line and felt a swirling sense of panic.

Dear Mom,
You broke your promise. You said I could have a dog
and now you say I have to wait. If I can't have a dog,
then I don't want to live with you anymore. This is
goodbye forever.
Love, Jeff

Two

For a moment, Robin was too stunned to react. Her heart was pounding so hard it echoed in her ears like thunder, so loud it seemed to knock her off balance.

Rushing down the stairs, she stood on the porch, cupped her hands over her mouth and screamed frantically. "Jeff! Jeffy!"

Cole Camden was standing on his front porch, too. He released a shrill whistle and stood waiting expectantly. When nothing happened, he called, "Blackie!"

"Jeff!" Robin tried again.

"Blackie!"

Robin called for Jeff once more, but her voice cracked as the panic engulfed her. She paused, placed her hand over her mouth and closed her eyes, trying to regain her composure.

"Blackie!" Cole yelled. He looked furious about his dog's disappearance.

It took Robin only a moment to put two and two together. "Cole," she cried, running across the lawn toward him. "I think Jeff and Blackie might have run away together."

Cole looked at her as if she was deranged, and Robin

couldn't blame him. "Jeff left me a note. He wants a dog so badly and we can't get one right now because...well, because we can't, and I had to tell him, and he was terribly disappointed and he decided to run away."

Cole's mouth thinned. "The whole idea is ridiculous. Even if Jeff did run away, Blackie would never go with him."

"Do you honestly think I'd make this up?" she shrieked. "The last time I saw Jeff was around four-thirty, and I'd bet cold cash that's about the same time Blackie disappeared."

Cole's gaze narrowed. "Then where are they?"

"If I knew that, do you think I'd be standing around here arguing with you?"

"Listen, lady, I don't know your son, but I know my dog and—"

"My name's not lady," Robin flared, clenching her hands at her sides. He was looking at her as though she were a madwoman on the loose—which she was where her son was concerned. "I'm sorry to have troubled you. When I find Jeff, I'll make sure your dog gets home."

Cole's eyes shot sparks in her direction, but she ignored them. Turning abruptly, she ran back to her own house. Halfway there, she stopped dead and whirled around to face Cole again. "The fort."

"What fort?" Cole demanded.

"The one that's in the back of your yard. It's covered with brush.... Jeff found it earlier today. He wouldn't know anywhere else to go and that would be the perfect hiding place."

"No one's been there in years," Cole said, discounting her suggestion.

"The least we can do is look."

Cole's nod was reluctant. He led the way to his backyard, which was much larger than hers. There was a small grove of oak trees at the rear of the property and beyond that a high fence. Apparently the fort was situated between the trees and the fence. A few minutes later, in the most remote corner of the yard, nestled between two trees, Robin saw the small wooden structure. It blended into the terrain, and if she hadn't been looking for the hideaway, she would never have seen it.

It was obvious when they neared the space that someone had taken up residence. Cole lowered himself down to all fours, peered inside, then looked back at Robin with a nod. He breathed in sharply, apparently irritated by this turn of events, and crawled through the narrow entrance.

Not about to be left standing by herself, Robin got down on her knees and followed him in.

Just as she'd suspected, Jeff and Blackie were huddled together in a corner. Jeff was fast asleep and Blackie was curled up by his side, guarding him. When Cole and Robin entered, the Labrador lifted his head and wagged his tail in greeting.

The fort wasn't much bigger than the tent Jeff had constructed the night before, and Robin was forced to pull her knees close and loop her arms around them. Cole's larger body seemed to fill every available bit of space.

Jeff must have sensed that his newfound home had been invaded because his eyes fluttered open and he gazed at Robin, then turned his head to stare at Cole.

"Hi, Mom," he said sheepishly. "I bet I'm in trouble, aren't I?"

Robin was so grateful to find him that all she could do was nod. If she'd tried to speak, her voice would've been shaking with emotion, which would only have embarrassed them both.

"So, Jeff," Cole said sternly. "You were going to run away from home. I see you brought everything you needed." He pushed the frying pan and atlas into the middle of their cramped quarters. "What I want to know is how you convinced Blackie to join you."

"He came on his own," Jeff murmured, but his eyes avoided Cole's. "I wouldn't have taken him on purpose—he's your dog."

"I'm glad you didn't...coerce him."

"All you took was a frying pan and an atlas!" Robin cried, staring at the cast-iron skillet and the atlas with its dog-eared pages.

Cole and Jeff both ignored her outburst.

"I take it you don't like living here?" Cole asked.

Jeff stiffened, then shook his head vigorously. "Mom told me that when we moved I could have a dog and now I can't. And...and she dragged me into a neighborhood filled with girls. That might've been okay if I had a dog, but then she broke her promise. A promise is a promise and it's sacred. A guy would never do that."

"So you can't have a dog until later?"

"All because of a stupid fence."

Cole nodded. "Fences are important, you know. And you know what else? Your mom was worried about you."

Jeff looked at Robin, who was blinking furiously to keep the tears from dripping down her face. The upheaval and stress of the move had drained her emotionally and she was an unmitigated mess. Normally, she was a calm, controlled person, but this whole drama with Jeff was her undoing. That and the fact she'd hardly slept the night before in his makeshift tent.

"Mom," Jeff said, studying her anxiously, "are you all right?"

She covered her face with both hands. "I slept with a dog and you ran away and all you took was a frying pan and an atlas." That made no sense whatsoever, but she couldn't help it, and once the tears started they wouldn't stop.

"I'm sorry, Mom," Jeff said softly. "I didn't mean to make you cry."

"I know," she whimpered. "I want you to have a dog, I really do, but we can't keep one locked up in the house all day and we don't have a fence and…and the way you just looked at me, I swear it was Lenny all over again."

"Who's Lenny?" Cole cocked his head toward Jeff, speaking in a whisper.

"Lenny was my dad. He died when I was real little. I don't even remember him."

Cole shared a knowing look with her son. "It might be a good idea if we got your mother back inside the house."

"You think I'm getting hysterical, don't you?" Robin burst out. "I want you both to know I'm in perfect control. A woman can cry every now and then if she wants. Venting your emotions is healthy—all the books say so."

"Right, Mom." Jeff gently patted her shoulder, then crawled out of the fort. He waited for Robin, who emerged after him, and offered her a hand. Cole and Blackie followed.

Jeff took Robin's arm, holding her elbow as he led her to the back door of their house, as if he suspected she couldn't find her way without his guidance.

Once inside, Robin grabbed a tissue and loudly blew her nose. Her composure was shaky, but when she turned to Cole, she intended to be as reasonable as a judge. As polite as a preacher.

"Have you got any aspirin?" Cole asked Jeff.

Jeff nodded, and dashed up the stairs to the bathroom,

returning in thirty seconds flat with the bottle. Cole filled a glass with water and delivered both to Robin. How he knew she had a fierce headache she could only guess.

"Why don't you lie down for a few minutes? I'm sure you'll feel better."

"I feel just fine, thank you," she snapped, more angry with herself for overreacting than with him for taking charge.

"Do you have family close by?" Again Cole directed the question to Jeff, which served to further infuriate Robin. Jeff was ten years old! She, on the other hand, was an adult. If this man had questions they should be directed to her, not her son.

"Not anymore," Jeff answered in an anxious whisper. "Grandma and Grandpa moved to Arizona last year, and my uncle lives in LA."

"I don't need to lie down," Robin said forcefully. "I'm perfectly fine."

"Mom," Jeff countered, his voice troubled, "you don't look so good."

"You were talking about frying pans and sleeping with dogs in the same breath," Cole elaborated, his eyebrows raised.

"I think Mr. Camden's right," Jeff said. "You need rest— lots of rest."

Her own son had turned traitor on her. Robin was shocked. Jeff took her hand and led her into the family room, which was off the kitchen. He patted the quilted pillow on the sofa, wordlessly suggesting she place her head there. When she resisted, he pulled the afghan from the chair and draped it around her, tucking the ends behind her shoulders.

Robin couldn't believe she was allowing herself to be

led around like a…like a puppy. As if reading her thoughts, Blackie wandered over to her side and lowered his bulk onto the carpet beside the sofa.

"That's a neat fort you've got there," Jeff told Cole once he'd finished tucking in the blanket. Robin watched him hurry back to the kitchen, grab a plate, then load it with macaroni and cheese and hand it to Cole, apparently wanting to share his favorite meal with their neighbor.

Cole set the plate on the counter. "Thanks anyway, Jeff, but I've got to get back to the house. In the future, if you're thinking about running away—don't."

"Yeah, I guess you're right," Jeff said with a mildly guilty look. "My mom turned into a basket case."

Cole smiled—at least, it was as close to a smile as Robin had seen. "You're both going to be fine. She intends to get you that dog, you know. Just hang on. It'll be sooner than you think."

Jeff walked to the sliding glass door with Cole. "Mr. Camden, can I ask you something important?"

"Sure."

"Is anyone using the fort?"

"Not that I know of."

Jeff's expression was hopeful. "It didn't look like anyone had been inside for a long time."

"Six years," Cole murmured absently.

"That long? How come?" Jeff asked. "It's a *great* fort. If it's all right with you I'd like to go over there sometimes. I promise not to walk in any flowerbeds or anything, and I won't leave a mess. I'll take real good care of everything."

Cole hesitated for a moment. He looked at Jeff, and Robin held her breath. Then he shook his head. "Maybe sometime in the future, but not now."

Jeff's deep blue eyes brightened; apparently the refusal

didn't trouble him. "Okay. When I can use the fort, would it be all right if I took Blackie with me? He followed me today, you know. I didn't have to do anything to get him to tag along." Jeff paused and lowered his eyes. "Well, hardly anything."

"I thought as much. As your mom said, you have a way with animals."

"My dad did, too. If he hadn't died he would've gotten me a pony and everything."

There was such pride in Jeff's voice that Robin bit her bottom lip to keep from crying all over again. Jeff and Lenny were so much alike. What she'd told her son earlier was true. More and more, Jeff was starting to take on his father's looks and personality.

Cole gazed down at Jeff, and an emotion flashed in his eyes, so transient Robin couldn't recognize it. He laid his hand on Jeff's shoulder. "Since your mother explained there's going to be a delay in getting you a dog, it'd be okay with me if you borrowed Blackie every now and then. You have to stay in your own yard, though. I don't want him running in the neighborhood unless he's on a leash."

"Do you mean it? Thanks, Mr. Camden! I'll do everything you ask."

Robin had the feeling Jeff would've agreed to just about any terms as long as he could see Blackie. It wasn't a dog of his own, but it was as close as he was going to get for the next few months.

Once Cole had left, Jeff joined her on the sofa, his hands folded on his lap. "I'm sorry, Mom," he muttered, his chin buried in his chest. "I promise I'll never run away again."

"I should hope not," she said. Wrapping her arms around him, she hugged him close, kissing his cheek.

"Gee whiz," Jeff grumbled, rubbing his face. "I'd never have apologized if I'd known you were going to kiss me."

A week passed. Jeff liked his new school and, as Robin had predicted, found his class contained an equal number of boys and girls. With his outgoing personality, he quickly collected new friends.

On Sunday afternoon, Robin was in the family room reading the paper when Jeff ambled in and sat down across from her. He took the baseball cap from his head and studied it for a moment.

"Something bothering you?" she asked, lowering the paper to get a better view of her son.

He shrugged. "Did you know Mr. Camden used to be married?"

"That's what I heard," Robin said absently. But other than Heather's remarks the previous week, she hadn't heard anything else. In fact, she'd spoken to her neighbor only when she'd gone to pick up Jeff every afternoon. The child-care arrangement with Heather was working beautifully, but there'd been little opportunity to chat.

As for Cole, Robin hadn't seen him at all. Since he'd been so kind and helpful in the situation with Jeff, Robin had revised her opinion of him. He liked his privacy and that was fine by her; she had no intention of interrupting his serene existence. The memory of their first meeting still rankled, but she was willing to overlook that shaky beginning.

"Mr. Camden had a son who died."

Robin's heart constricted. It made sense: the pain she'd seen when Jeff had asked him about children, the word on the street that Cole didn't like kids, the abandoned fort. "I... How did you find that out?"

"Jimmy Wallach. He lives two streets over and has an older brother who used to play with Bobby Camden. Jimmy told me about him."

"I didn't know," Robin murmured, saddened by the information. She couldn't imagine her life without Jeff—the mere thought of losing him was enough to tear her apart.

"Mrs. Wallach heard Jimmy talking about Bobby Camden, and she said Mr. Camden got divorced and it was real bad, and then a year later Bobby died. She said Mr. Camden's never been the same since."

Robin ached for Cole, and she regretted all the uncharitable thoughts she'd had that first morning.

"I feel sad," Jeff whispered, frowning. His face was as intent as she'd ever seen it.

"I do, too," Robin returned softly.

"Mrs. Wallach seemed real surprised when I told her Mr. Camden said I could play in Bobby's fort someday. Ever since his son died, he hasn't let any kids in the yard or anything. She said he hardly talks to anyone in the neighborhood anymore."

Heather Lawrence had said basically the same thing, but hadn't explained the reason for it. Probably because she didn't know.

"Are you still going to barbecue hamburgers for dinner tonight?"

Robin nodded, surprised by the abrupt way Jeff had changed the subject. "If you want." Next to macaroni and cheese, grilled burgers were Jeff's all-time favorite food.

"Can I invite Mr. Camden over to eat with us?"

Robin hated to refuse her son, but she wasn't sure a dinner invitation was a good idea. She didn't know Cole very well, but she'd already learned he wasn't one to socialize with the neighbors. In addition, Jeff might blurt out questions about Cole's dead son that would be terribly painful for him.

"Mom," Jeff pleaded, "I bet no one ever invites him to dinner and he's all alone."

"Sweetheart, I don't know if that would be the right thing to do."

"But we *owe* him, Mom," Jeff implored. "He let me throw sticks for Blackie twice this week."

"I don't think Mr. Camden's home," Robin said, picking up the newspaper while she weighed the pros and cons of Jeff's suggestion. Since last Sunday, Robin hadn't spoken to Cole once, and she wasn't eager to initiate a conversation. He might read something into it.

"I'll go and see if he's home." Before she could react, Jeff was out the front door, letting the screen door slam in his wake.

He returned a couple of minutes later breathless and excited. "Mr. Camden's home and he said he appreciates the invitation, but he has other plans for tonight."

"That's too bad," Robin said, hoping she sounded sincere.

"I told him we were having strawberry shortcake for dessert and he said that's his favorite."

Robin didn't want to admit it, but she was relieved Cole wouldn't be showing up for dinner. The man made her feel nervous and uncertain. She didn't know why that should be, only that it was a new and unfamiliar sensation.

"Thanks, Mom."

Robin jerked her head up from the paper. "Thanks for what?" She hadn't read a word in five minutes. Her thoughts had been on her neighbor.

Jeff rolled his eyes. "For letting me take a piece of strawberry shortcake over to Mr. Camden."

"I said you could do that?"

"Just now." He walked over to her and playfully tested her forehead with the back of his hand. "You don't feel hot, but then, with brain fever you never know."

Robin swatted playfully at her son's backside.

Laughing, Jeff raced outdoors, where his bicycle was waiting. A half hour later, he was back in the house. "Mom! Mom!" he cried, racing into the kitchen. "Did you know Mr. Camden owns a black Porsche?"

"I can't say I did." She was more interested in peeling potatoes for the salad than discussing fancy cars. She didn't know enough about sports cars to get excited about them.

Jeff jerked open the bottom drawer and rooted through the rag bag until he found what he was looking for. He pulled out a large square that had once been part of his flannel pyjamas, then started back outside. "He has another car, too, an SUV."

"Just where are you going, young man?" Robin demanded.

"Mr. Camden's waxing his car and I'm gonna help him."

"Did he ask for your help?"

"No," Jeff said impatiently.

"He may not want you to."

"Mom!" Jeff rolled his eyes as if to suggest she was overdoing this mothering thing. "Can I go now?"

"Ah…I suppose," she agreed, but her heart was in her throat. She moved into the living room and watched as Jeff strolled across the lawn to the driveway next door, where Cole was busy rubbing liquid wax on the gleaming surface of his Porsche. Without a word, Jeff started polishing the dried wax with his rag. Cole straightened and stopped smearing on the wax, obviously surprised to see Jeff. Robin bit her lip, not knowing how her neighbor would react to

Jeff's willingness to help. Apparently he said something, because Jeff nodded, then walked over and sat cross-legged on the lawn. They didn't seem to be carrying on a conversation and Robin wondered what Cole had said to her son.

Robin returned to the kitchen, grateful that Cole's rejection had been gentle. At least he hadn't sent Jeff away. She peeled another potato, then walked back to the living room and glanced out the window again. This time she saw Jeff standing beside Cole, who was, it seemed, demonstrating the correct way to polish a car. He made wide circular motions with his arms, after which he stepped aside to let Jeff tackle the Porsche again. Cole smiled, then patted him on the head before walking around to the other side of the car.

Once the salad was ready, Robin ventured outside.

Jeff waved enthusiastically when he caught sight of her on the porch. "Isn't she a beaut?" he yelled.

It looked like an ordinary car to Robin, but she nodded enthusiastically. "Wonderful," she answered. "Afternoon, Cole."

"Robin." He returned her greeting absently.

He wore a sleeveless gray sweatshirt and she was surprised by how muscular and tanned his arms were. From a recent conversation with Heather Lawrence, Robin had learned Cole was a prominent attorney. And he seemed to fit the lawyer image to a T. Not anymore. The lawyer was gone and the *man* was there, bold as could be. Her awareness of him as an attractive virile male was shockingly intense.

The problem, she decided, lay in the fact that she hadn't expected Cole to look so...fit. The sight of all that lean muscle came as a pleasant surprise. Cole's aggressive, unfriendly expression had been softened as he bantered with Jeff.

Blackie ambled to her side and Robin leaned over to

scratch the dog's ears while she continued to study his master. Cole's hair was dark and grew away from his brow, but a single lock flopped stubbornly over his forehead and he had to toss it back from his face every once in a while. It was funny how she'd never noticed that about him until now.

Jeff must've made some humorous remark because Cole threw back his head and chuckled loudly. It was the first time she'd ever heard him laugh. She suspected he didn't often give in to the impulse. A smile crowded Robin's face as Jeff started laughing, too.

In that moment the oddest thing happened. Robin felt something catch in her heart. The tug was almost physical, and she experienced a completely unfamiliar feeling of vulnerability....

"Do you need me to roll out the barbecue for you?" Jeff shouted when he saw that she was still on the porch. He'd turned his baseball cap around so the bill faced backward. While he spoke, his arm continued to work feverishly as he buffed the passenger door with his rag.

"Not...yet."

"Good, 'cause Mr. Camden needs me to finish up this side for him. We're on a tight schedule here, and I don't have time. Cole's got a dinner date at five-thirty."

"I see." Standing on the porch, dressed in her old faded jeans, with a mustard-spotted terrycloth hand towel tucked in the waistband, Robin felt as appealing as Ma Kettle. "Any time you're finished is fine."

So Cole Camden's got a date, Robin mused. *Of course he's got a date,* she told herself. Why should she care? And if watching Jeff and Cole together was going to affect her like this, it would be best to go back inside the house now.

Over dinner, all Jeff could talk about was Cole Camden. Every other sentence was Cole this and Cole that, until

Robin was ready to slam her fist on the table and demand Jeff never mention their neighbor's name again.

"And the best part is, he *paid* me for helping him wax his car," Jeff continued, then stuffed the hamburger into his mouth, chewing rapidly in his enthusiasm.

"That was generous of him."

Jeff nodded happily. "Be sure and save some shortcake for him. He said not to bring it over 'cause he didn't know exactly when he'd get home. He'll stop by, he said."

"I will." But Robin doubted her neighbor would. Jeff seemed to be under the impression that Cole would show up at any time; Robin knew better. If Cole had a dinner date, he wasn't going to rush back just to taste her dessert, although she did make an excellent shortcake.

As she suspected, Cole didn't come over. Jeff grumbled about it the next morning. He was convinced Cole would've dropped by if Robin hadn't insisted Jeff go to bed at his regular time.

"I'll make shortcake again soon," Robin promised, hurrying to pack their lunches. "And when I do, you can take a piece over to him."

"All right," Jeff muttered.

That evening, when Robin returned home from work, she found Jeff playing with Blackie in Cole's backyard.

"Jeff," she cried, alarmed that Cole might discover her son on his property. He'd made it clear Jeff wasn't to go into his yard. "What are you doing at Mr. Camden's? And why aren't you at Heather's?" She walked over to the hedge and placed her hands on her hips in frustration.

"Blackie's chain got all tangled up," Jeff said, looking sheepish. "He needed my help. I told Heather it would be okay with you and..." His voice trailed off.

"He's untangled now," Robin pointed out.

"I know, but since I was here it seemed like a good time for the two of us to—"

"Play," Robin completed for him.

"Yeah," her son said, nodding eagerly. Jeff was well aware he'd done something wrong, but had difficulty admitting it.

"Mr. Camden doesn't want you in his yard, and we both know it." Standing next to the laurel hedge, Robin watched with dismay as Cole opened his back door and stepped outside. Blackie barked in greeting, and his tail swung with enough force to knock Jeff off balance.

When Cole saw Jeff in his yard, he frowned and cast an accusing glare in Robin's direction.

"Jeff said Blackie's chain was tangled," she rushed to explain.

"How'd you get over here?" Cole asked her son, and although he didn't raise his voice it was clear he was displeased. "The gate's locked and the hedge is too high for him to jump over."

Jeff stared down at the lawn. "I came through the gap in the hedge—the same one Blackie uses. I crawled through it."

"Was his chain really tangled?"

"No, sir," Jeff said in a voice so low Robin had to strain to hear him. "At least not much... I just thought, you know, that maybe he'd like company."

"I see."

"He was all alone and so was I." Jeff lifted his eyes defiantly to his mother's, as if to suggest the fault was entirely hers. "I go to Mrs. Lawrence's after school, but it's all girls there."

"Don't you remember what I said about coming into my yard?" Cole asked him.

Jeff's nod was sluggish. "Yeah. You said maybe I could sometime, but not now. I thought…I hoped that since you let me help you wax your car, you wouldn't mind."

"I mind," Cole said flatly.

"He won't do it again," Robin promised. "Will you, Jeff?"

"No," he murmured. "I'm sorry, Mr. Camden."

For a whole week Jeff kept his word. The following Monday, however, when Robin came home from the BART station, Heather told her Jeff had mysteriously disappeared about a half hour earlier. She assumed he'd gone home; he'd said something about expecting a call.

Unfortunately, Robin knew exactly where to look for him, and it wasn't at home. Even more unfortunate was the fact that Cole's car pulled into the driveway just as she was opening her door. Throwing aside her briefcase and purse, she rushed through the house, jerked open the sliding glass door at the back and raced across her yard.

Her son was nowhere to be seen, but she immediately realized he'd been with Blackie. The dog wasn't in evidence, either, and she could see Jeff's favorite baseball cap on the lawn.

"Jeff," she called, afraid to raise her voice. She sounded as though she was suffering from a bad case of laryngitis.

Neither boy nor dog appeared.

She tried again, taking the risk of shouting for Jeff in a normal tone, praying it wouldn't attract Cole's attention. No response. Since Jeff and Blackie didn't seem to be within earshot, she guessed they were in the fort. There was no help for it; she'd have to go after him herself. Her only hope was that she could hurry over to the fort, get Jeff and return to her own yard, all without being detected by Cole.

Finding the hole in the laurel proved difficult enough.

The space was little more than a narrow gap between two thick plants, and for a distressing moment, Robin doubted she was slim enough to squeeze through. Finally, she lowered herself to the ground, hunched her shoulders and managed to push her way between the shrubs. Her head had just emerged when she noticed a pair of polished men's shoes on the other side. Slowly, reluctantly, she glanced up to find Cole towering above her, eyes narrowed with suspicion.

"Oh, hi," she said, striving to sound as though it was perfectly normal for her to be crawling into his yard on her hands and knees. "I suppose you're wondering what I'm doing here...."

"The question did cross my mind."

Three

"It was the most embarrassing moment of my entire life," Robin repeated for the third time. She was sitting at the kitchen table, resisting the urge to hide her face in her hands and weep.

"You've already said that," Jeff grumbled.

"What possessed you to even *think* about going into Mr. Camden's yard again? Honestly, Jeff, you've been warned at least half a dozen times. What do I have to do? String barbed wire between our yards?"

Although he'd thoroughly disgraced himself, Jeff casually rotated the rim of his baseball cap between his fingers. "I said I was sorry."

A mere apology didn't begin to compensate for the humiliation Robin had suffered when Cole found her on all fours, crawling through his laurel hedge. If she lived to be an old woman, she'd never forget the look on his face.

"You put me on TV, computer and phone restriction already," her son reminded her.

That punishment could be another mistake to add to her growing list. At times like this, she wished Lenny were there to advise her. She needed him, and even after all these years, still missed him. Often, when there was no one else around, Robin found herself talking to Lenny. She wondered if she'd made the right decision, wondered what her husband would have done. Without television, computer or phone, the most attractive form of entertainment left open to her son was playing with Blackie, which was exactly what had gotten him into trouble in the first place.

"Blackie belongs to Mr. Camden," Robin felt obliged to tell him. Again.

"I know," Jeff said, "but he likes me. When I come home from school, he goes crazy. He's real glad to see me, Mom, and since there aren't very many boys in this neighborhood—" he paused as if she was to blame for that "—Blackie and I have an understanding. We're buds."

"That's all fine and dandy, but you seem to be forgetting that Blackie doesn't belong to you." Robin stood and opened the refrigerator, taking out a package of chicken breasts.

"I wish he was my dog," Jeff grumbled. In an apparent effort to make peace, he walked over to the cupboard, removed two plates and proceeded to set the table.

After dinner, while Robin was dealing with the dishes, the doorbell chimed. Jeff raced down the hallway to answer it, returning a moment later with Cole Camden at his side.

Her neighbor was the last person Robin had expected to see—and the last person she *wanted* to see.

"Mom," Jeff said, nodding toward Cole, "it's Mr. Camden."

"Hello, again," she managed, striving for a light tone, and realizing even as she spoke that she'd failed. "Would you like a cup of coffee?"

"No, thanks. I'd like to talk to both of you about—"

Not giving him the opportunity to continue, Robin nodded so hard she nearly dislocated her neck. "I really am sorry about what happened. I've had a good long talk with Jeff and, frankly, I understand why you're upset and I don't blame you. You've been very kind about this whole episode and I want you to know there won't be a repeat performance."

"From either of you?"

"Absolutely," she said, knowing her cheeks were as red as her nail polish. Did he have to remind her of the humiliating position he'd found her in earlier?

"Mom put me on TV, computer and phone restriction for an entire week," Jeff explained earnestly. "I promise not to go into your fort again, Mr. Camden. And I promise not to go in my backyard after school, either, because Blackie sees me and gets all happy and excited—and I guess I get all happy and excited, too—and that's when I do stuff I'm not supposed to."

"I see." Cole smiled down at Jeff. Robin thought it was a rather unusual smile. It didn't come from his lips as much as his eyes. Once more she witnessed a flash of pain, and another emotion she could only describe as longing. Slowly his gaze drifted to Robin. When his dark eyes met hers, she suddenly found herself short of breath.

"Actually I didn't come here to talk to you about what happened this afternoon," Cole said. "I'm going to be out of town for the next couple of days, and since Jeff and Blackie seem to get along so well I thought Jeff might be willing to look after him. That way I won't have to put him in the kennel. Naturally I'm prepared to pay your son for his time. If he agrees, I'll let him play in the fort while I'm away, as well."

Jeff's eyes grew rounder than Robin had ever seen them. "You want me to watch Blackie?" he asked, his voice incredulous. "And you're going to *pay* me? Can Blackie spend the night here? Please?"

"I guess that answers your question," Robin said, smiling.

"Blackie can stay here if it's okay with your mom," Cole told Jeff. Then he turned to her. "Would that create a problem for you?"

Once more his eyes held hers, and once more she experienced that odd breathless sensation.

"I... No problem whatsoever."

Cole smiled then, and this time it was a smile so potent, so compelling, that it sailed straight through Robin's heart.

"Mom," Jeff hollered as he burst through the front door late Thursday afternoon. "Kelly and Blackie and I are going to the fort."

"Kelly? Surely this isn't the *girl* named Kelly, is it? Not the one who lives next door?" Robin couldn't resist teasing her son. Apparently Jeff was willing to have a "pesky" girl for a friend, after all.

Jeff shrugged as he opened the cookie jar and groped inside. He frowned, not finding any cookies and removed his hand, his fingertips covered with crumbs that he promptly licked off. "I decided Kelly isn't so bad."

"Have you got Blackie's leash?"

"We aren't going to need it. We're playing Sam Houston and Daniel Boone, and the Mexican army is attacking. I'm going to smuggle Blackie out and go for help. I can't use a leash for that."

"All right. Just don't go any farther than the Alamo and be back by dinnertime."

"But that's less than an hour!" Jeff protested.

Robin gave him one of her don't-argue-with-me looks.

"But I'm not hungry and——"

"Jeff," Robin said softly, widening her eyes just a bit, increasing the intensity of her look.

"You know, Mom," Jeff said with a cry of undisguised disgust, "you don't fight fair." He hurried out the front door with Blackie trotting faithfully behind.

Smiling to herself, Robin placed the meat loaf in the oven and carried her coffee into the backyard. The early evening air was filled with the scent of spring flowers. A gentle breeze wafted over the budding trees. How peaceful it seemed. How serene. All the years of pinching pennies to save for a house of their own seemed worth it now.

Her gaze wandered toward Cole Camden's yard. Jeff, Kelly and Blackie were inside the fort, and she could hear their raised voices every once in a while.

Cole had been on her mind a great deal during the past couple of days; she'd spent far too much time dwelling on her neighbor, thinking about his reputation in the neighborhood and the son he'd lost.

The tranquillity of the moment was shattered by the insistent ringing of the phone. Robin walked briskly to the kitchen, set her coffee on the counter and picked up the receiver.

"Hello."

"Robin, it's Angela. I'm not catching you at a bad time, am I?"

"No," Robin assured her. Angela worked in the same department as Robin, and over the years they'd become good friends. "What can I do for you?" she asked, as if she didn't already know.

"I'm calling to invite you to dinner——"

"On Saturday so I can meet your cousin Frank," Robin finished, rolling her eyes. Years before, Angela had taken on the task of finding Robin a husband. Never mind that Robin wasn't interested in meeting strangers! Angela couldn't seem to bear the thought of anyone spending her life alone and had appointed herself Robin's personal matchmaker.

"Frank's a really nice guy," Angela insisted. "I wouldn't steer you wrong, you know I wouldn't."

Robin restrained herself from reminding her friend of the disastrous date she'd arranged several weeks earlier.

"I've known Frank all my life," Angela said. "He's decent and nice."

Decent and *nice* were two words Robin had come to hate. Every man she'd ever met in this kind of arrangement was either decent or nice. Or both. Robin had come to think the two words were synonymous with dull, unattractive and emotionally manipulative. Generally these were recently divorced men who'd willingly placed themselves in the hands of family and friends to get them back into circulation.

"Didn't you tell me that Frank just got divorced?" Robin asked.

"Yes, about six months ago."

"Not interested."

"What do you mean you're not interested?" Angela demanded.

"I don't want to meet him. Angela, I know you mean well, and I apologize if I sound like a spoilsport, but I can't tell you the number of times I've had to nurse the fragile egos of recently divorced men. Most of the time they're emotional wrecks."

"But Frank's divorce was final months ago."

"If you still want me to meet him in a year, I'll be more than happy to have you arrange a dinner date."

Angela released a ragged sigh. "You're sure?"

"Positive."

There was a short disappointed silence. "Fine," Angela said in obvious frustration. "I'll see you in the morning."

"Right." Because she felt guilty, Robin added, "I'll bring the coffee."

"Okay."

Robin lingered in the kitchen, frowning. She hated it when her friends put her on the spot like this. It was difficult enough to say no, but knowing that Angela's intentions were genuine made it even worse. Just as she was struggling with another attack of guilt, the phone rang again. Angela! Her friend must have suspected that Robin's offer to buy the coffee was a sign that she was weakening.

Gathering her fortitude, Robin seized the receiver and said firmly, "I'm not interested in dating Frank. I don't want to be rude, but that's final!"

Her abrupt words were followed by a brief shocked silence, and then, "Robin, hello, this is Cole Camden."

"Cole," she gasped, closing her eyes. "Uh, I'm sorry, I thought you were someone else. A friend." She slumped against the wall and covered her face with one hand. "I have this friend who's always trying to arrange dates for me, and she doesn't take no for an answer," Robin quickly explained. "I suppose you have friends wanting to arrange dates for you, too."

"Actually, I don't."

Of course he didn't. No doubt there were women all over San Francisco who longed to go out with Cole. He didn't require a personal matchmaker. All someone like him had to do was look interested and women would flock to his side.

Her hand tightened around the receiver and a sick weightless feeling attacked the pit of her stomach. "I apologize. I didn't mean to shout in your ear."

"You didn't."

"I suppose you called to talk to Jeff," she said. "He's with Blackie and Kelly—Kelly Lawrence, the little girl who lives on the other side of us."

"I see."

"He'll be back in a few minutes, if you'd like to call then. Or if you prefer, I could run and get him, but he said something about sneaking out and going for help and—"

"I beg your pardon? What's Jeff doing?"

"Oh, they're playing in the fort, pretending they're Houston and Daniel Boone. The fort is now the Alamo."

He chuckled. "I see. No, don't worry about chasing after him. I'd hate to see you waylaid by the Mexican army."

"I don't think I'd care for that myself."

"How's everything going?"

"Fine," she assured him.

She must have sounded rushed because he said, "You're sure this isn't a bad time? If you have company…"

"No, I'm here alone."

Another short silence, which was broken by Cole. "So everything's okay with Blackie? He isn't causing you any problems, is he?"

"Oh, no, everything's great. Jeff lavishes him with attention. The two of them are together practically every minute. Blackie even sleeps beside his bed."

"As you said, Jeff has a way with animals," Cole murmured.

His laugh, so tender and warm, was enough to jolt her. She had to pinch herself to remember that Cole was a prominent attorney, wealthy and respected. She was an accountant. A junior accountant at that.

The only thing they had in common was the fact that they lived next door to each other and her son was crazy about his dog.

The silence returned, only this time it had a relaxed, almost comfortable quality, as though neither wanted the conversation to end.

"Since Jeff isn't around," Cole said reluctantly, "I'll let you go."

"I'll tell him you phoned."

"It wasn't anything important," Cole said. "Just wanted to let you know when I'll be back—late Friday afternoon. Will you be home?"

"Of course."

"You never know, your friend might talk you into going out with Fred after all."

"It's Frank, and there isn't a snowball's chance in hell."

"Famous last words!"

"See you Friday," she said with a short laugh.

"Right. Goodbye, Robin."

"Goodbye, Cole."

Long after the call had ended, Robin stood with her hand on the receiver, a smile touching her eyes and her heart.

"Mom, I need my lunch money," Jeff yelled from the bottom of the stairs.

"I'll be down in a minute," she said. Mornings were hectic. In order to get to the Glen Park BART station on time, Robin had to leave the house half an hour before Jeff left for school.

"What did you have for breakfast?" she hollered as she put the finishing touches on her makeup.

"Frozen waffles," Jeff shouted back. "And don't worry,

I didn't drown them in syrup and I rinsed off the plate before I put it in the dishwasher."

"Rinsed it off or let Blackie lick it for you?" she asked, as she hurried down the stairs. Her son was busy at the sink and didn't turn around to look at her.

"Blackie, honestly, is that maple syrup on your nose?"

At the sound of his name, the Labrador trotted over to her. Robin took a moment to stroke his thick fur before fumbling for her wallet to give Jeff his lunch money.

"Hey, Mom, you look nice."

"Don't act so surprised," she grumbled. "I'm leaving now."

"Okay," Jeff said without the slightest bit of concern. "You won't be late tonight, will you? Remember Mr. Camden's coming back."

"I remember, and no, I won't be late." She grabbed her purse and her packed lunch, putting it in her briefcase, and headed for the front door.

Even before Robin arrived at the subway station, she knew the day would drag. Fridays always did.

She was right. At six, when the subway pulled into the station, Robin felt as though she'd been away forty hours instead of the usual nine. She found herself hurrying and didn't fully understand why. Cole was scheduled to return, but that didn't have anything to do with her, did it? His homecoming wasn't anything to feel nervous about, nor any reason to be pleased. He was her neighbor, and more Jeff's friend than hers.

The first thing Robin noticed when she arrived on Orchard Street was Cole's Porsche parked in the driveway of his house.

"Hi, Mom," Jeff called as he raced across the lawn between the two houses. "Mr. Camden's back!"

"So I see." She removed her keys from her purse and opened the front door.

Jeff followed her inside. "He said he'd square up with me later. I wanted to invite him to dinner, but I didn't think I should without asking you first."

"That was smart," she said, depositing her jacket in the closet on her way to the kitchen. She opened the refrigerator and took out the thawed hamburger and salad makings.

"How was your day?" she asked.

Jeff sat down at the table and propped his elbows on it. "All right, I guess. What are you making for dinner?"

"Taco salad."

"How about just tacos? I don't get why you want to ruin a perfectly good dinner by putting green stuff in it."

Robin paused. "I thought you liked my taco salad."

Jeff shrugged. "It's all right, but I'd rather have just tacos." Once that was made clear, he cupped his chin in his hands. "Can we rent a movie tonight?"

"I suppose," Robin returned absently as she added the meat to the onions browning in the skillet.

"But I get to choose this time," Jeff insisted. "Last week you picked a musical." He wrinkled his nose as if to suggest that being forced to watch men and women sing and dance was the most disgusting thing he'd ever had to endure.

"Perhaps we can find a compromise," she said.

Jeff nodded. "As long as it doesn't have a silly love story in it."

"Okay," Robin said, doing her best not to betray her amusement. Their difference in taste when it came to movies was legendary. Jeff's favorite was an older kids' film, *Scooby Doo,* that he watched over and over, which Robin found boring, to say the least. Unfortunately, her son was equally put off by the sight of men and women staring longingly into each other's eyes.

The meat was simmering in the skillet when Robin glanced up and noted that her son was looking surprisingly thoughtful. "Is something troubling you?" she asked, and popped a thin tomato slice into her mouth.

"Have you ever noticed that Mr. Camden never mentions he had a son?"

Robin set the paring knife on the cutting board. "It's probably painful for him to talk about."

Jeff nodded, and, with the innocent wisdom of youth, he whispered, "That man needs someone."

The meal was finished, and Robin was standing in front of the sink rinsing off the dinner plates when the doorbell rang. Robin knew it had to be Cole.

"I'll get it," Jeff cried as he raced past her at breakneck speed. He threw open the door. "Hi, Mr. Camden!" he said eagerly.

By this time Robin had smoothed her peach-colored sweater over her hips and placed a friendly—but not too friendly—smile on her face. At the last second, she ran her fingers through her hair, striving for the casual I-didn't-go-to-any-trouble look, then wondered at her irrational behavior. Cole wasn't coming over to see *her*.

Robin could hear Jeff chatting away at ninety miles an hour, telling Cole they were renting a movie and how Robin insisted that every show he saw had to have the proper rating, which he claimed was totally ridiculous. He went on to explain that she considered choosing the film a mother's job and apparently a mere kid didn't have rights. When there was a pause in the conversation, she could envision Jeff rolling his eyes dramatically.

Taking a deep breath, she stepped into the entryway and smiled. "Hello, Cole."

"Robin."

Their eyes met instantly. Robin's first coherent thought was that a woman could get lost in eyes that dark and not even care. She swallowed and lowered her gaze.

"Would you like a cup of coffee?" she asked, having difficulty dragging the words out of her mouth.

"If it isn't too much trouble."

"It isn't." Or it wouldn't be if she could stop her heart from pounding so furiously.

"Where's Blackie?" Jeff asked, opening the screen door and glancing outside.

"I didn't bring him over. I thought you'd be tired of him by now."

"Tired of Blackie?" Jeff cried. "You've got to be kidding!"

"I guess I should've known better," Cole teased.

Robin returned to the kitchen and took mugs from the cupboard, using these few minutes to compose herself.

The screen door slammed, and a moment later Cole appeared in her kitchen. "Jeff went to my house to get Blackie."

She smiled and nodded. "Do you take cream or sugar?" she asked over her shoulder.

"Just black, thanks."

Robin normally drank hers the same way. But for some reason she couldn't begin to fathom, she added a generous teaspoonful of sugar to her own, stirring briskly as though she feared it wouldn't dissolve.

"I hope your trip went well," she said, carrying both mugs into the family room, where Cole had chosen to sit.

"Very well."

"Good." She sat a safe distance from him, across the room in a wooden rocker, and balanced her mug on her knee. "Everything around here went without a hitch, but I'm afraid Jeff may have spoiled Blackie a bit."

"From what he said, they did everything but attend school together."

"Having the dog has been wonderful for him. I appreciate your giving Jeff this opportunity. Not only does it satisfy his need for a dog, but it's taught him about responsibility."

The front door opened and the canine subject of their conversation shot into the room, followed by Jeff, who was grinning from ear to ear. "Mom, could Mr. Camden stay and watch the movie with us?"

"Ah…" Caught off guard, Robin didn't know what to say. After being away from home for several days, watching a movie with his neighbors probably held a low position on Cole's list of priorities.

To Robin's astonishment, Cole's eyes searched hers as though seeking her approval.

"You'd be welcome…I mean, you can stay if you'd like, unless…unless there's something else you'd rather do," she stammered. "I mean, I'd…we'd like it if you did, but…" She let whatever else she might have said fade away. She was making a mess of this, and every time she tried to smooth it over, she only stuck her foot further down her throat.

"What movie did you rent?"

"We haven't yet," Jeff explained. "Mom and me had to come to an understanding first. She likes mushy stuff and gets all bent out of shape if there's an explosion or anything. You wouldn't believe the love story she made me watch last Friday night." His voice dripped with renewed disgust.

"How about if you and I go rent the movie while your mother and Blackie make the popcorn?"

Jeff's blue eyes brightened immediately. "That'd be great, wouldn't it, Mom?"

"Sure," she agreed, and was rewarded by Jeff's smile.

Jeff and Cole left a few minutes later. It was on the tip of her tongue to give Cole instructions on the type of movie appropriate for a ten-year-old boy, but she swallowed her concerns, willing to trust his judgment. Standing on the porch, she watched as they climbed inside Cole's expensive sports car. She pressed her hand to her throat, grateful when Cole leaned over the front seat and snapped Jeff's seat belt snugly in place. Suddenly Cole looked at her; she raised her hand in farewell, and he did the same. It was a simple gesture, yet Robin felt as if they'd communicated so much more.

"Come on, Blackie," Robin said, "let's go start the popcorn." The Lab trailed behind her as she returned to the kitchen. She placed a packet of popcorn in the microwave. It was while she was waiting for the kernels to start popping that the words slipped from her mouth.

"Well, Lenny, what do you think?" Talking to her dead husband came without conscious thought. It certainly wasn't that she expected him to answer. Whenever she spoke to him, the words came spontaneously from the deep well of love they'd once shared. She supposed she should feel foolish doing it, but so many times over the long years since his death she'd felt his presence. Robin assumed that the reason she talked to him came from her need to discuss things with the one other person who'd loved her son as much as she did. In the beginning she was sure she needed to visit a psychiatrist or arrange for grief counseling, but later she convinced herself that every widow went through this in one form or another.

"He's grown so much in the past year, hasn't he?" she asked, and smiled. "Meeting Cole has been good for Jeff. He lost a child, you know, and I suppose having Jeff move in next door answers a need for him, too."

About ten minutes later, she'd transferred the popcorn to a bowl and set out drinks. Jeff and Cole came back with a movie that turned out to be an excellent compromise—a teen comedy that was surprisingly witty and entertaining.

Jeff sprawled on the carpet munching popcorn with Blackie by his side. Cole sat on the sofa and Robin chose the rocking chair. She removed her shoes and tucked her feet beneath her. She was enjoying the movie; in fact, several times she found herself laughing out loud.

Cole and Jeff laughed, too. The sounds were contrasting—one deep and masculine, the other young and pleasantly boyish—yet they harmonized, blending with perfect naturalness.

Soon Robin found herself watching Jeff and Cole more than the movie. The two...no, the three of them had grown comfortable together. Robin didn't try to read any significance into that. Doing so could prove emotionally dangerous, but the thought flew into her mind and refused to leave.

The credits were rolling when Cole pointed to Jeff, whose head was resting on his arms, his eyes closed.

"He's asleep," Cole said softly.

Robin smiled and nodded. She got up to bring the empty popcorn bowl into the kitchen. Cole stood, too, taking their glasses to the sink, then returned to the family room to remove the DVD.

"Do you want me to carry him upstairs for you?" he asked, glancing down at the slumbering Jeff.

"No," she whispered. "When he wakes up in the morning, he'll think you treated him like a little kid. Egos are fragile at ten."

"I suppose you're right."

The silence seemed to resound. Without Jeff, awake and chattering, as a buffer between them, Robin felt clumsy and self-conscious around Cole.

"It was nice of you to stay," she said, more to fill the silence than because she had anything important to communicate. "It meant a lot to Jeff."

Jeff had told her Cole had an active social life. Heather Lawrence had confirmed it by casually letting it drop that Cole was often away on weekends. Robin wasn't entirely sure what to think about it all. But if there was a woman in his life, that was his business, not hers.

"It meant a lot to me, too," he said, returning the DVD to its case.

The kitchen and family room, actually quite spacious, felt close and intimate with Cole standing only a few feet away.

Robin's fingers were shaking as she placed the bowls and soda glasses in the dishwasher. She tried to come up with some bright and witty comment, but her mind was blank.

"I should be going."

Was that reluctance she heard in his voice? Somehow Robin doubted it; probably wishful thinking on her part. Half of her wanted to push him out the door and the other half didn't want him to leave at all. But there really wasn't any reason for him to stay. "I'll walk you to the door."

"Blackie." Cole called for his dog. "It's time to go."

The Lab didn't look pleased. He took his own sweet time lumbering to his feet and stretching before trotting to Cole's side.

Robin was about to open the door when she realized she hadn't thanked Cole for getting the movie. She turned, and his dark eyes delved into hers. Whatever thoughts had been taking shape fled like leaves scattering in the wind. She tried to smile, however weakly, but it was difficult when he was looking at her so intently. His gaze slipped to her mouth, and in a nervous movement, she moistened her lips. Before she was fully aware of how it had happened, Cole's fingers were in her hair and he was urging her mouth to meet his.

His eyes held hers, as if he expected her to stop him, then they slowly closed and their lips touched. Robin's eyes drifted shut, but that was the only response she made.

He kissed her again, even more gently than the first time. Robin moaned softly, not in protest, but in wonder and surprise. It had been so long since a man had kissed her like this. So long that she'd forgotten the wealth of sensations a mere kiss could evoke. Her hands crept to his chest, and her fingers curled into the soft wool of his sweater. Hesitantly, timidly, her lips trembled beneath his. Cole sighed and took full possession of her mouth.

Robin sighed, too. The tears that welled in her eyes were a shock. She was at a loss to explain them. They slipped down her face, and it wasn't until then that she realized she was crying.

Cole must have felt her tears at the same moment, because he abruptly broke off the kiss and raised his head. His eyes searched hers as his thumb brushed the moisture from her cheek.

"Did I hurt you?" The question was whispered.

She shook her head vehemently.

"Then why...?"

"I don't know." She couldn't explain something she

didn't understand herself. Rubbing her eyes, she attempted to wipe away the evidence. She forced a smile. "I'm nothing if not novel," she said with brittle cheerfulness. "I don't imagine many women break into tears when you kiss them."

Cole looked as confused as Robin felt.

"Don't worry about it. I'm fine." She wanted to reassure him, but was having too much trouble analyzing her own reactions.

"Let's sit down and talk about this."

"No," she said quietly. Adamantly. That was the last thing she wanted. "I'm sorry, Cole. I really am. This has never happened before and I don't understand it either."

"But…"

"The best thing we can do is chalk it up to a long workweek."

"It's not that simple."

"Probably, but I'd prefer to just forget it. Please?"

"Are you all right?"

"Emotionally or physically?" She tried to joke, but didn't succeed.

"Both."

He was so serious, so concerned, that it was all Robin could do not to dissolve into fresh tears. She'd made a world-class fool of herself with this man, not once but twice.

This man, who had suffered such a tremendous loss himself, was so gentle with her, and instead of helping, that only made matters worse. "I'm sorry, really I am," she said raggedly, "but perhaps you should go home now."

Four

"You know what I'm in the mood for?" Angela Lansky said as she sat on the edge of Robin's desk early Monday afternoon.

"I certainly hope you're going to say food," Robin teased. They had shared the same lunch hour and were celebrating a cost-of-living raise by eating out.

"A shrimp salad," Angela elaborated. "Heaped six inches high with big fresh shrimp."

"I was thinking Chinese food myself," Robin said, "but, now that you mention it, shrimp salad sounds good." She opened her bottom drawer and took out her purse.

Angela was short and enviably thin with thick brown hair that fell in natural waves over her shoulders. She used clips to hold the abundant curls away from her face and looked closer to twenty than the thirty-five Robin knew her to be.

"I know just the place," Angela was saying. "The Blue Crab. It's on the wharf and worth the trouble of getting there."

"I'm game," Robin said.

They stopped at the bank, then headed for the restaurant. They decided to catch the Market Street cable car to Fisherman's Wharf and joined the quickly growing line.

"So how's the kid doing?" Angela asked. She and her salesman husband didn't plan to have children themselves, but Angela enjoyed hearing about Jeff.

"He signed up for baseball through the park program and starts practice this week. I think it'll be good for him. He was lonely this weekend now that Blackie's back with Cole."

"But isn't Blackie over at your place as much as before?" Angela asked.

Robin shook her head. "Cole left early Saturday morning and took the dog with him. Jeff moped around for most of the weekend."

"Where'd your handsome neighbor go?"

"How am I supposed to know?" Robin asked with a soft laugh, hiding her disappointment at his disappearance. "Cole doesn't clear his schedule with me."

The way he'd left—without a word of farewell or explanation—still hurt. It was the kind of hurt that came from realizing what a complete fool she'd made of herself with this worldly, sophisticated man. He'd kissed her and she'd started crying. Good grief, he was probably doing backflips in order to avoid seeing her again.

"Do you think Cole was with a woman?"

"That's none of my business!"

"But I thought your neighbor said Cole spent his weekends with a woman."

Robin didn't remember mentioning that to Angela, but she obviously had, along with practically everything else. Robin had tried to convince herself that confiding in Angela about Cole was a clever way of thwarting her friend's matchmaking efforts. Unfortunately, the whole thing had backfired in her face. In the end, the last person she wanted to talk about was Cole, but of course Angela persisted in questioning her.

"Well?" Angela demanded. "Did he spend his weekend with a woman or not?"

"What he does with his time is his business, not mine," Robin reiterated. She pretended not to care. But she did. Too much. She'd promised herself she wasn't going to put any stock in the kiss or the powerful attraction she felt for Cole. Within the space of one evening, she'd wiped out every pledge she'd made to herself. She hadn't said anything to Jeff—how could she?—but she was just as disappointed as he was that Cole had left for the weekend.

"I was hoping something might develop between the two of you," Angela murmured. "Since you're obviously not interested in meeting Frank, it would be great if you got something going with your neighbor."

Robin cast her a plaintive look that suggested otherwise. "Cole Camden lives in the fanciest house in the neighborhood. He's a partner in the law firm of Blackwell, Burns and Dailey, which we both know is one of the most prestigious in San Francisco. And he drives a car with a name I can barely pronounce. Now, what would someone like that see in me?"

"Lots of things," Angela said.

Robin snickered. "I hate to disillusion you, my friend, but the only thing Cole Camden and I have in common is the fact that my small yard borders his massive one."

"Maybe," Angela agreed, raising her eyebrows. "But I could tell you were intrigued by him the very first time you mentioned his name."

"That's ridiculous!"

"It isn't," Angela insisted. "I've watched you with other

men over the past few years. A guy will show some interest, and at first everything looks peachy-keen. You'll go out with him a couple of times, maybe even more, but before anything serious can develop you've broken off the relationship without really giving it a chance."

Robin didn't have much of an argument, since that was true, but she made a token protest just the same. "I can't help it if I have high standards."

"High standards!" Angela choked back a laugh. "That's got to be the understatement of the century. You'd find fault with Prince Charming."

Robin rolled her eyes, but couldn't hold back a smile. Angela was right, although that certainly hadn't slowed her matchmaking efforts.

"From the time you started talking about your neighbor," Angela went on, "I noticed something different about you, and frankly I'm thrilled. In all the years we've known each other, this is the first time I can remember you giving a man this much attention. Until now, it's always been the other way around."

"I'm not interested in Cole," she mumbled. "Oh, honestly, Angela, I can't imagine where you come up with these ideas. I think you've been reading too many romance novels."

Angela waved her index finger under Robin's nose. "Listen, I'm on to you. You're not going to divert me with humor, or weasel your way out of admitting it. You can't fool me—you're attracted to this guy and it's scaring you to death. Right?"

The two women gazed solemnly at each other, both too stubborn to admit defeat. Under the force of her friend's unyielding determination, Robin was the one who finally gave in.

"All right!" she cried, causing the other people waiting for the cable car to turn and stare. "All right," she repeated in a whisper. "I like Cole, but I don't understand it."

Angela's winged brows arched speculatively. "He's attractive and wealthy, crazy about your son, generous and kind, and you haven't figured it out yet?"

"He's also way out of my league."

"I wish you'd quit categorizing yourself. You make it sound as though you aren't good enough for him, and that's not true."

Robin just sighed.

The cable car appeared then, its bell clanging as it drew to a stop. Robin and Angela boarded and held on tight.

Jeff loved hearing about the history of the cable cars, and Robin loved telling him the story. Andrew Hallidie had designed them because of his deep love for horses. Day after day, Hallidie had watched them struggling up and down the treacherous hills of the city, dragging heavy burdens. Prompted by his concern for the animals, he'd invented the cable cars that are pulled by a continuously moving underground cable. To Jeff and to many others, Andrew Hallidie was a hero.

Robin and Angela were immediately caught up in the festive atmosphere of Fisherman's Wharf. The rows of fishing boats along the dock bobbed gently with the tide, and although Robin had never been to the Mediterranean the view reminded her of pictures she'd seen of French and Italian harbors.

The day was beautiful, the sky blue and cloudless, the ocean sparkling the way it did on a summer day. This spring had been exceptionally warm. It wasn't uncommon for Robin to wear a winter coat in the middle of July, especially in the mornings, when there was often a heavy fog accompanied by a cool mist from the Bay. But this spring, they'd experienced some lovely weather, including today's.

"Let's eat outside," Angela suggested, pointing at a free table on the patio.

"Sure," Robin agreed cheerfully. The Blue Crab was a popular restaurant and one of several that lined the wharf. More elegant dining took place inside, but the pavement was crowded with diners interested in a less formal meal.

Once they were seated, Robin and Angela were waited on quickly and ordered their shrimp salads.

"So," Angela said, spreading out her napkin while closely studying Robin. "Tell me more about your neighbor."

Robin froze. "I thought we were finished with this subject. In case you hadn't noticed, I'd prefer not to discuss Cole."

"I noticed, but unfortunately I was just getting started. It's unusual for you to be so keen on a man, and I know hardly anything about him. It's time, Robin Masterson, to tell all."

"There's nothing to tell. I already told you everything I care to," Robin said crossly. She briefly wondered if Angela had guessed that Cole had kissed her. At the rate things were going, she'd probably end up admitting it before lunch was over. Robin wished she could think of some surefire way to change the subject.

Tall glasses of iced tea arrived and Robin was reaching for a packet of sugar when she heard a masculine chuckle that reminded her instantly of Cole. She paused, savoring the husky sound. Without really meaning to, she found herself scanning the tables, certain Cole was seated a short distance away.

"He's here," she whispered before she could guard her tongue.

"Who?"

"Cole. I just heard him laugh."

Pushing back her chair in order to get a fuller view of the inside dining area, Robin searched through a sea of faces, but didn't find her neighbor's.

"What's he look like?" Angela whispered.

Ten different ways to describe him shot through her mind. To say he had brown hair, neatly trimmed, coffee-colored eyes and was about six foot two seemed inadequate. To add that he was strikingly attractive further complicated the problem.

"Tell me what to look for," Angela insisted. "Come on, Robin, this is a golden opportunity. I want to check this guy out. I'm not letting a chance like this slip through my fingers. I'll bet he's gorgeous."

Reluctantly, Robin continued to scan the diners, but she didn't see anyone who remotely resembled Cole. Even if she did see him, she wasn't sure she'd point him out to Angela, although she hated to lie. Perhaps she wouldn't have to. Perhaps she'd imagined the whole thing. It would've been easy enough to do. Angela's questions had brought Cole to the forefront of her mind; they'd just been discussing him and it was only natural for her to—

Her heart pounded against her rib cage as Cole walked out of the restaurant foyer. He wasn't alone. A tall, slender woman with legs that seemed to go all the way up to her neck and a figure as shapely and athletic as a dancer's was walking beside him. She was blond and, in a word, gorgeous. Robin felt as appealing as milkweed in comparison. The woman's arm was delicately tucked in Cole's, and she was smiling up at him with eyes big and blue enough to turn heads.

Robin's stomach tightened into a hard knot.

"Robin," Angela said anxiously, leaning toward her, "what is it?"

Cole was strolling past them, and in an effort not to be seen, Robin stuck her head under the table pretending to search for her purse.

"Robin," Angela muttered, lowering her own head and peeking under the linen tablecloth, "what's the matter with you?"

"Nothing." Other than the fact that she was going to be ill. Other than the fact that she'd never been more outclassed in her life. "I'm fine, really." A smile trembled on her pale lips.

"Then what are you doing with your head under the table?"

"I don't suppose you'd believe my napkin fell off my lap?"

"No."

A pair of shiny black shoes appeared. Slowly, Robin twisted her head and glanced upward, squinting at the flash of sunlight that nearly blinded her. It was their waiter. Heaving a giant sigh of relief, Robin straightened. The first thing she noticed was that Cole had left.

The huge shrimp salads were all but forgotten as Angela, eyes narrowed and elbows braced on the table, confronted her. "You saw him, didn't you?"

There was no point in pretending otherwise, so Robin nodded.

"He was with someone?"

"Not just someone! The most beautiful woman in the world was draped all over his arm."

"That doesn't mean anything," Angela said. "Don't you think you're jumping to conclusions? Honestly, she could've been anyone."

"Uh-huh." Any fight left in Robin had long since evaporated. There was nothing like seeing Cole with another woman to bring her firmly back to earth—which was right where she belonged.

"She could've been a client."

"She probably was," Robin concurred, reaching for her fork. She didn't know how she was going to manage one shrimp, let alone a whole plate of them. Heaving another huge sigh, she plowed her fork into the heap of plump pink darlings. It was then that she happened to glance across the street. Cole and Ms. Gorgeous were walking along the sidewalk, engrossed in their conversation. For some reason, known only to the fates, Cole looked across the street at that very moment. His gaze instantly narrowed on her. He stopped midstride as though shocked to have seen her.

Doing her best to pretend she hadn't seen *him,* Robin took another bite of her salad and chewed vigorously. When she glanced up again, Cole was gone.

"Mom, I need someone to practice with," Jeff pleaded. He stood forlornly in front of her, a baseball mitt in one hand, a ball in the other.

"I thought Jimmy was practicing with you."

"He had to go home and then Kelly threw me a few pitches, but she had to go home, too. Besides, she's a girl."

"And what am I?" Robin muttered.

"You're a mom," Jeff answered, clearly not understanding her question. "Don't you see? I've got a chance of making pitcher for our team if I can get someone to practice with me."

"All right," Robin agreed, grumbling a bit. She set aside her knitting and followed her son into the backyard. He handed her his old catcher's mitt, which barely fit her hand, and positioned her with her back to Cole's yard.

Robin hadn't been able to completely avoid her neighbor in the past week, but she'd succeeded in keeping her distance. For that matter, he didn't seem all that eager to run into her, either. Just as well, she supposed.

He stayed on his side of the hedge. She stayed on hers.

If he passed her on his way to work, he gave an absent wave. She returned the gesture.

If they happened to be outside at the same time, they exchanged smiles and a polite greeting, but nothing more. It seemed, although Robin couldn't be sure, that Cole spent less time outside than usual. So did she.

"Okay," Jeff called, running to the end of their yard. "Squat down."

"I beg your pardon?" Robin shouted indignantly. "I agreed to play catch with you. You didn't say anything about having to squat!"

"Mom," Jeff said impatiently, "think about it. If I'm going to be the pitcher, you've got to be the catcher, and catchers have to be low to the ground."

Complaining under her breath, Robin sank to her knees, worried the grass would stain her jeans.

Jeff tossed his arms into the air in frustration. "Not like that!" He said something else that Robin couldn't quite make out—something about why couldn't moms be guys.

Reluctantly, Robin assumed the posture he wanted, but she didn't know how long her knees would hold out. Jeff wound up his arm and let loose with a fastball. Robin closed her eyes, stuck out the mitt and was so shocked when she caught the ball that she toppled backward into the wet grass.

"You all right?" Jeff yelled, racing toward her.

"I'm fine, I'm fine," she shouted back, discounting his concern as she brushed the dampness from the seat of her jeans. She righted herself, assumed the position and waited for the second ball.

Jeff ran back to his mock pitcher's mound, gripped both hands behind his back and stepped forward. Robin closed her eyes again. Nothing happened. She opened her eyes cautiously, puzzled about the delay. Then she recalled the hand movements she'd seen pitchers make and flexed her fingers a few times.

Jeff straightened, placed his hand on his hip and stared at her. "What was that for?"

"It's a signal...I think. I've seen catchers do it on TV."

"Mom, leave that kind of stuff to the real ballplayers. All I want you to do is catch my pitches and throw them back. It might help if you kept your eyes open, too."

"I'll try."

"Thank you."

Robin suspected she heard a tinge of sarcasm in her son's voice. She didn't know what he was getting so riled up about; she was doing her best. It was at times like these that she most longed for Lenny. When her parents had still lived in the area, her dad had stepped in whenever her son needed a father's guiding hand, but they'd moved to Arizona a couple of years ago. Lenny's family had been in Texas since before his death. Robin hadn't seen them since the funeral, although Lenny's mother faithfully sent Jeff birthday and Christmas gifts.

"You ready?" Jeff asked.

"Ready." Squinting, Robin stuck out the mitt, prepared to do her best to catch the stupid ball, since it seemed so important to her son. Once more he swung his arms be-

hind him and stepped forward. Then he stood there, poised
to throw, for what seemed an eternity. Her knees were beginning to ache.

"Are you going to throw the ball, or are you going to
stare at me all night?" she asked after a long moment had
passed.

"That does it!" Jeff tossed his mitt to the ground. "You
just broke my concentration."

"Well, for crying out loud, what's there to concentrate
on?" Robin grimaced, rising awkwardly to her feet. Her
legs had started to lose feeling.

"This isn't working," Jeff cried, stalking toward her.
"Kelly's only in third grade and she does a better job than
you do."

Robin decided to ignore that comment. She pressed her
hand to the small of her back, hoping to ease the ache she'd
begun to feel.

"Hello, Robin. Jeff."

Cole's voice came at her like a hangman's noose. She
straightened abruptly and winced at the sharp pain shooting through her back.

"Hi, Mr. Camden!" Jeff shouted as though Cole was a
conquering hero returned from the war. He dashed across
the yard, past Robin and straight to the hedge. "Where have
you been all week?"

"I've been busy." He might've been talking to Jeff, but
his eyes were holding Robin's. She tried to look away—
but she couldn't.

His eyes told her she was avoiding him.

Hers answered that he'd been avoiding *her*.

"I guess you *have* been busy," Jeff was saying. "I haven't
seen you in days and days and days." Blackie squeezed

through the hedge and Jeff fell to his knees, his arms circling the dog's neck.

"So how's the baseball going?" Cole asked.

Jeff sent his mother a disgusted look, then shrugged. "All right, I guess."

"What position are you playing?"

"Probably outfield. I had a chance to make pitcher, but I can't seem to get anyone who knows how to catch a ball to practice with me. Kelly tries, but she's a girl and I hate to say it, but my mother's worthless."

"I did my best," Robin protested.

"She catches with her eyes closed," Jeff said.

"How about if you toss a few balls at me?" Cole offered.

Jeff blinked as if he thought he'd misunderstood. "You want me to throw you a few pitches? You're sure?"

"Positive."

The look on her son's face defied description as Cole jumped over the hedge. Jeff's smile stretched from one side of his face to the other as he tore to the opposite end of the yard, unwilling to question Cole's generosity a second time.

For an awkward moment, Robin stayed where she was, not knowing what to say. She looked up at Cole, her emotions soaring—and tangling like kites in a brisk wind. She was deeply grateful for his offer, but also confused. Thrilled by his presence, but also frightened.

"Mom?" Jeff muttered. "In case you hadn't noticed, you're in the way."

"Are you going to make coffee and invite me in for a chat later?" Cole asked quietly.

Her heart sank. "I have some things that need to be done, and…and…"

"Mom?" Jeff shouted.

"I think it's time you and I talked," Cole said, staring straight into her eyes.

"Mom, are you moving or not?"

Robin looked frantically over her shoulder. "Oh…oh, sorry," she whispered, blushing. She hurried away, then stood on the patio watching as the ball flew across the yard.

After catching a dozen of Jeff's pitches, Cole got up and walked over to her son. They spoke for several minutes. Reluctantly, Robin decided it was time to go back in.

She busied herself wiping kitchen counters that were already perfectly clean and tried to stop thinking about the beautiful woman she'd seen with Cole on the Wharf.

Jeff stormed into the house. "Mom, would it be okay if Mr. Camden strings up an old tire from the apple tree?"

"I suppose. Why?"

"He said I can use it to practice pitching, and I wouldn't have to bother you or Kelly."

"I don't think I have an old tire."

"Don't worry, Mr. Camden has one." He ran outside again before she could comment.

Jeff was back in the yard with Cole a few minutes later, far too soon to suit Robin. She forced a weak smile. That other woman was a perfect damsel to his knight in shining armor, she thought wryly. Robin, on the other hand, considered herself more of a court jester.

Her musings were abruptly halted when Cole walked into the kitchen, trailed by her son.

"Isn't it time for your bath, Jeff?" Cole asked pointedly.

It looked for a minute as though the boy was going to argue. For the first time in recent memory, Robin would've welcomed some resistance from him.

"I guess," he said. Bathing was about as popular as homework.

"I didn't make any coffee," Robin said in a small voice. She simply couldn't look at Cole and not see the beautiful blonde on his arm.

"That's fine. I'm more interested in talking, anyway," he said. He walked purposefully to the table and pulled out a chair, then gestured for her to sit down.

Robin didn't. Instead, she frowned at her watch. "My goodness, will you look at the time?"

"No." Cole headed toward her, and Robin backed slowly into the counter.

"We're going talk about that kiss," Cole warned her.

"Please don't," she whispered. "It meant nothing! We'd both had a hectic week. We were tired.... I wasn't myself."

Cole's eyes burned into hers. "Then why did you cry?"

"I...don't know. Believe me, if I knew I'd tell you, but I don't. Can't we just forget it ever happened?"

His shoulders rose in a sigh as he threaded his long fingers through his hair. "That's exactly what I've tried to do all week. Unfortunately it didn't work."

Five

"I've put it completely out of my mind," Robin said, resuming her string of untruths. "I wish you'd do the same."

"I can't. Trust me, I've tried," Cole told her softly. He smiled and his sensuous mouth widened as his eyes continued to hold hers. The messages were back. Less than subtle messages. *You can't fool me,* they said, and *I didn't want to admit it either.*

"I…"

The sense of expectancy was written across his face. For the life of her, Robin couldn't tear her eyes from him.

She didn't remember stepping into his arms, but suddenly she was there, encompassed by his warmth, feeling more sheltered and protected than she had since her husband's death. This comforting sensation spun itself around her as he wove his fingers into her hair, cradling her head. He hadn't kissed her yet, but Robin felt the promise of it in every part of her.

Deny it though she might, she knew in her heart how badly she wanted Cole to hold her, to kiss her. He must have read the longing in her eyes, because he lowered his mouth to hers, stopping a fraction of an inch from her parted lips.

She could feel warm moist breath, could feel a desire so powerful that she wanted to drown in his kiss.

From a reservoir of strength she didn't know she possessed, Robin managed to shake her head.

"Please," he whispered just before his mouth settled firmly over hers.

His kiss was the same as it had been before, only more intense. More potent. Robin felt rocked to the very core of her being. Against her will, she felt herself surrendering to him. She felt herself forgetting to breathe. She felt herself weakening.

His mouth moved to her jaw, dropping small, soft kisses there. She sighed. She couldn't help it. Cole's touch was magic. Unable to stop herself, she turned her head, yearning for him to trace a row of kisses on the other side, as well. He complied.

Robin sighed again, her mind filled with dangerous, sensuous thoughts. It felt so good in his arms, so warm and safe...but she knew the feeling was deceptive. She'd seen him with another woman, one far more suited to him than she could ever be. For days she'd been tormented by the realization that the woman in the restaurant was probably the one he spent his weekends with.

She pulled away, but even to her, the action held little conviction.

In response, Cole brought a long slow series of featherlight kisses to her lips. Robin trembled, breathless.

"Why are you fighting this?" he whispered. His hands framed her face, his thumbs stroking her cheeks. They were damp and she hadn't even known she was crying.

Suddenly she heard footsteps bounding down the stairs. At the thought of Jeff finding her in Cole's arms, she abruptly broke away and turned to stare out the darkened window, hoping for a moment to compose herself.

Jeff burst into the room. "Did you kiss her yet?" he demanded. Not waiting for an answer, Jeff ran toward Robin and grabbed her by the hand. "Well, Mom, what do you think?"

"About...what?"

"Mr. Camden kissing you. He did, didn't he?"

It was on the tip of her tongue to deny the whole thing, but she decided to brazen it out. "You want me to rate him? Like on a scale of one to ten?"

Jeff blinked, uncertain. His questioning glance flew to Cole.

"She was a ten," Cole said, grinning.

"A...high seven," Robin returned.

"A high seven!" Jeff cried, casting her a disparaging look. He shook his head and walked over to Cole. "She's out of practice," he said confidingly. "Doesn't know how to rate guys. Give her a little time and she'll come around."

"Jeff," Robin gasped, astounded to be having this kind of discussion with her son, let alone Cole, who was looking all too smug.

"She hardly goes out at all," Jeff added. "My mom's got this friend who arranges dates for her, and you wouldn't believe some of the guys she's been stuck with. One of them came to the door—"

"Jeff," Robin said sharply, "that's enough!"

"But one of us needs to tell him!"

"Mr. Camden was just leaving," Robin said, glaring at her neighbor, daring him to contradict her.

"I was? Oh, yeah. Your mom was about to walk me to the door, isn't that right, Robin?"

She gaped at Cole as he reached for her hand and gently

led her in the direction of the front door. Meekly she submitted, but not before she saw Jeff give Cole a thumbs-up.

"Now," Cole said, standing in the entryway, his hands heavy on her shoulders. "I want to know what's wrong."

"Wrong? Nothing's wrong."

"It's because of Victoria, isn't it?"

"Victoria?" she asked, already knowing that had to be the woman with him the day she'd seen him at the restaurant.

"Yes. Victoria. I saw you practically hiding under your table, pretending you didn't notice me."

"I… Why should I care?" She hated the way her voice shook.

"Yes, why should you?"

She didn't answer him. Couldn't answer him. She told herself it didn't matter that he was with another woman. Then again, it mattered more than she dared admit.

"Tell me," he insisted.

Robin lowered her gaze. If only he'd stop holding her, stop touching her. Then she might be able to think clearly. "You looked right together. She was a perfect complement to you. She's tall and blond and—"

"Cold as an iceberg. Victoria's a business associate—we had lunch together. Nothing more. I find her as appealing as…as dirty laundry."

"Please, don't explain. It's none of my business who you have lunch with or who you date or where you go every weekend or who you're with. Really. I shouldn't have said anything. I don't know why I did. It was wrong of me—very wrong. I can't believe we're even talking about this."

Jeff poked his head out from the kitchen. "How are things going in here?"

"Good," Robin said. "I was just telling Cole how much we both appreciated his help with your pitching."

"I was having real problems until Cole came along," Jeff confirmed. "Girls are okay for some things, but serious baseball isn't one of them."

Robin opened the front door. "Thanks," she whispered, her eyes avoiding Cole's, "for everything."

"Everything?"

She blushed, remembering the kisses they'd shared. But before she could think of a witty reply, Cole brushed his lips across hers.

"Hey, Cole," Jeff said, hurrying to the front door. "I've got a baseball game Thursday night. Can you come?"

"I'd love to," Cole answered, his eyes holding Robin's. Then he turned abruptly and strode out the door.

"Jeff, we're going to be late for the game if we don't leave now."

"But Cole isn't home yet," Jeff protested. "He said he'd be here."

"There's probably a very good explanation," Robin said calmly, although she was as disappointed as Jeff. "He could be tied up in traffic, or delayed at the office, or any one of a thousand other things. He wouldn't purposely not come."

"Do you think he forgot?"

"I'm sure he didn't. Come on, sweetheart, let's get a move on. You've got a game to pitch." The emphasis came on the last word. The first game of the season and Jeff had won the coveted position of first-string pitcher. Whether it was true or not, Jeff believed Cole's tutoring had given him an advantage over the competition. Jeff hadn't told him the news yet, keeping it a surprise for today.

"When you do see Cole, don't say anything, all right?"

Jeff pleaded as they headed toward the car. "I want to be the one who tells him."

"My lips are sealed," she said, holding up her hand. For good measure, she pantomimed zipping her mouth closed. She slid into the car and started the engine, but glanced in the rearview mirror several times, hoping Cole would somehow miraculously appear.

He didn't.

The game was scheduled for the baseball diamond in Balboa Park, less than two miles from Robin's house. A set of bleachers had been arranged around the diamonds, and Robin climbed to the top. It gave her an excellent view of the field—and of the parking area.

Cole knew the game was at Balboa Park, but he didn't know which diamond and there were several. Depending on how late he was, he could waste valuable time looking for the proper field.

The second inning had just begun when Heather Lawrence joined Robin. Robin smiled at her.

"Hi," Heather said. "What's the score?"

"Nothing nothing. It's the top of the second inning."

"How's the neighborhood Randy Johnson doing?"

"Jeff's doing great. He managed to keep his cool when the first batter got a hit off his second pitch. I think I took it worse than Jeff did."

Heather grinned and nodded. "It's the same with me. Kelly played goalie for her soccer team last year, and every time the opposing team scored on her I took it like a bullet to the chest."

"Where's Kelly now?"

Heather motioned toward the other side of the field. The eight-year-old was leaning casually against a tall fir tree. "She didn't want Jeff to know she'd come to watch him.

Her game was over a few minutes ago. They lost, but this is her first year and just about everyone else's, too. The game was more a comedy of errors than anything."

Robin laughed. It was thoughtful of Heather to stop by and see how Jeff's team was doing.

Heather laced her fingers over her knees. "Jeff's been talking quite a bit about Cole Camden." She made the statement sound more like a question and kept her gaze focused on the playing field.

"Oh?" Robin wasn't sure how to answer. "Cole was kind enough to give Jeff a few pointers about pitching techniques."

"Speaking of pitching techniques, you two certainly seem to be hitting it off."

Heather was beginning to sound a lot like Angela, who drilled her daily about her relationship with Cole, offering advice and unsolicited suggestions.

"I can't tell you how surprised I am at the changes I've seen in Cole since you two moved in. Kelly's been wanting to play in that fort from the moment she heard about it, but it's only since Jeff came here that she was even allowed in Cole's yard."

"He's been good for Jeff," Robin said, training her eyes on the game. Cole's relationship with her son forced Robin to examine his motives. He'd lost a son, and there was bound to be a gaping hole in his heart. At first he hadn't allowed Jeff in his yard or approved of Blackie and Jeff's becoming friends. But without anything ever being said, all that had fallen to the wayside. Jeff played in Cole's yard almost every day, and with their neighbor's blessing. Jeff now had free access to the fort and often brought other neighborhood kids along. Apparently Cole had given permission. Did he consider Jeff a sort of substitute son? Robin shook off the thought.

"Jeff talks about Cole constantly," Heather said. "In fact, he told me this morning that Cole was coming to see him pitch. What happened? Did he get hung up at the office?"

"I don't know. He must've been delayed, but—"

"There he is! Over there." Heather broke in excitedly. "You know, in the two years we've lived on Orchard Street, I can only recall talking to Cole a few times. He was always so standoffish. Except when we were both doing yard work, I never saw him, and if we did happen to meet we said hello and that was about it. The other day we bumped into each other at the grocery store and he actually smiled at me. I was stunned. I swear that's the first time I've seen that man smile. I honestly think you and Jeff are responsible for the change in him."

"And I think you're crediting me with more than my due," Robin said, craning her head to look for Cole.

"No, I'm not," Heather argued. "You can't see the difference in him because you're new to the neighborhood, but everyone who's known him for any length of time will tell you he's like a different person."

Jeff was sitting on the bench while his team was up at bat. Suddenly he leapt to his feet and waved energetically, as though he was flagging down a rescue vehicle. His face broke into a wide, eager smile. His coach must have said something to him because Jeff nodded and took off running toward the parking area.

Robin's gaze followed her son. Cole had indeed arrived. The tension eased out of her in a single breath. She hadn't realized how edgy she'd been. In her heart she knew Cole would never purposely disappoint Jeff, but her son's anxiety had been as acute as her own.

"Listen," Heather said, standing, "I'll talk to you later."

"Thanks for stopping by."

"Glad to." Heather climbed down the bleachers. She paused when she got to the ground and wiggled her eyebrows expressively, then laughed merrily at Robin's frown.

Heather must have passed Cole on her way out, but Robin lost sight of them as Jeff raced on to the pitcher's mound for the bottom of the second inning. Even from this distance Robin could see that his eyes were full of happy excitement. He discreetly shot her a look and Robin made a V-for-victory sign, smiling broadly.

Cole vaulted up the bleachers and sat down beside her. "Sorry I'm late. I was trapped in a meeting, and by the time I could get out to phone you I knew you'd already left for the field. I would've called your cell," he added, "but I didn't have the number."

"Jeff and I figured it had to be something like that."

"So he's pitching!" Cole's voice rang with pride.

"He claims it's all thanks to you."

"I'll let him believe that," Cole said, grinning, "but he's a natural athlete. All I did was teach him a little discipline and give him a means of practicing on his own."

"Well, according to Jeff you taught him everything he knows."

He shook his head. "I'm glad I didn't miss the whole game."

"There'll be others," she said, but she was grateful he'd come when he had. From the time they'd left the house, Robin had been tense and guarded. Cole could stand *her* up for any date, but disappointing Jeff was more than she could bear. Rarely had she felt this emotionally unsettled. And all because Cole had been late for a Balboa Park Baseball League game. It frightened her to realize how much

Jeff was beginning to depend on him. And not just Jeff, either....

"This is important to Jeff," Cole said as if reading her mind, "and I couldn't disappoint him. If it had been anyone else it wouldn't have been as important. But Jeff matters—" his eyes locked with hers "—and so do you."

Robin felt giddy with relief. For the first time since Lenny's tragic death, she understood how carefully, how completely, she'd anesthetized her life, refusing to let in anyone or anything that might cause her or Jeff more pain. For years she'd been drifting in a haze of denial and grief, refusing to acknowledge or deal with either. What Angela had said was true. Robin had dated infrequently and haphazardly, and kept any suitors at a safe distance.

For some reason, she hadn't been able to do that with Cole. Robin couldn't understand what was different or why; all she knew was that she was in serious danger of falling for this man, and falling hard. It terrified her....

"Have you and Jeff had dinner?" Cole asked.

Robin turned to face him, but it was a long moment before she grasped that he'd asked her a question. He repeated it and she shook her head. "Jeff was too excited to eat."

"Good. There's an excellent Chinese restaurant close by. The three of us can celebrate after the game."

"That'd be nice," she whispered, thinking she should make some excuse to avoid this, and accepting almost immediately that she didn't want to avoid it at all.

"Can I have some more pork-fried rice?" Jeff asked.

Cole passed him the dish and Robin watched as her son heaped his plate high with a third helping.

"You won," she said wistfully.

"Mom, I wish you'd stop saying that. It's the fourth time

you've said it. I *know* we won," Jeff muttered, glancing at Cole as if to beg forgiveness for his mother, who was obviously suffering from an overdose of maternal pride.

"But Jeff, you were fantastic," she couldn't resist telling him.

"The whole team was fantastic." Jeff reached for what was left of the egg rolls and added a dollop of plum sauce to his plate.

"I had no idea you were such a good hitter," Robin said, still impressed with her son's athletic ability. "I knew you could pitch—but two home runs! Oh, Jeff, I'm so proud of you—and everyone else." It was difficult to remember that Jeff was only one member of a team, and that his success was part of a larger effort.

"I wanted to make sure I played well, especially 'cause you were there, Cole." Jeff stretched his arm across the table again, this time reaching for the nearly empty platter of almond chicken.

As for herself, Robin couldn't down another bite. Cole had said the food at the Golden Wok was good, and he hadn't exaggerated. It was probably the best Chinese meal she'd ever tasted. Jeff apparently thought so, too. The boy couldn't seem to stop eating.

It was while they were laughing over their fortune cookies that Robin heard bits and pieces of the conversation from the booth behind them.

"I bet they're celebrating something special," an elderly gentleman remarked.

"I think their little boy must have done well at the baseball game," his wife said.

Their little boy, Robin mused. The older couple dining directly behind them thought Cole and Jeff were father and son.

Robin's eyes flew to Cole, but if he had heard the comment he didn't give any sign.

"His mother and father are certainly proud of him."

"It's such a delight to see these young people so happy. A family should spend time together."

A family. The three of them looked like a family.

Once more Robin turned to Cole, but once more he seemed not to hear the comments. Or if he had, he ignored them.

But Cole must have sensed her scrutiny because his gaze found hers just then. Their eyes lingered without a hint of the awkwardness Robin had felt so often before.

Jeff chatted constantly on the ride home with Robin. Since she and Cole had both brought their cars, they drove home separately. They exchanged good-nights in the driveway and entered their own houses.

Jeff had some homework to finish and Robin ran a load of clothes through the washing machine. An hour later, after a little television and quick baths, they were both ready for bed. Robin tucked the blankets around Jeff's shoulders, although he protested that he was much too old for her to do that. But he didn't complain too loudly or too long.

"Night, Jeff."

"Night, Mom. Don't let the bedbugs bite."

"Don't go all sentimental on me, okay?" she teased as she turned off his light. He seemed to fall asleep the instant she left the room. She went downstairs to secure the house for the night, then headed up to her own bedroom. Once upstairs, she paused in her son's doorway and smiled gently. They'd both had quite a day.

At about ten o'clock, she was sitting up in bed reading a mystery when the phone rang. She answered quickly, always anxious about late calls. "Hello."

"You're still awake." It was Cole, and his voice affected her like a surge of electricity.

"I...was reading," she said.

"It suddenly occurred to me that we never had the chance to finish our conversation the other night."

"What conversation?" Robin asked.

"The one at the front door...that Jeff interrupted. Remind me to give that boy lessons in timing, by the way."

"I don't even remember what we were talking about." She settled back against the pillows, savoring the sound of his voice, enjoying the small intimacy of lying in bed, listening to him. Her eyes drifted shut.

"As I recall, you'd just said something about how it isn't any of your business who I lunch with or spend my weekends with. I assume you think I'm with a woman."

Robin's eyes shot open. "I can assure you, I don't think anything of the sort."

"I guess I should explain about the weekends."

"No. I mean, Cole, it really isn't my business. It doesn't matter. Really."

"I have some property north of here, about forty acres," he said gently, despite her protests. "The land once belonged to my grandfather, and he willed it to me when he passed away a couple of years back. This house was part of the estate, as well. My father was born and raised here. I've been spending a lot of my free time remodeling the old farmhouse. Sometime in the future I might move out there."

"I see." She didn't want to think about Cole leaving the neighborhood, ever.

"The place still needs a lot of work, and I've enjoyed doing it on my own. It's coming along well."

She nodded and a second later realized he couldn't see her action. "It sounds lovely."

"Are there any other questions you'd like to ask me?" His voice was low and teasing.

"Of course not," she denied immediately.

"Then would you be willing to admit you enjoy it when I kiss you? A high seven? Really? I think Jeff's right—we need more practice."

"Uh…" Robin didn't know how to answer that.

"I'm willing," he said, and she could almost hear him smile.

Robin lifted the hair from her forehead with one hand. "I can't believe we're having this discussion."

"Would it help if I told you how much I enjoy kissing you?"

"Please…don't," she whispered. She didn't want him to tell her that. Every time he kissed her, it confused her more. Despite the sheltered feeling she experienced in his arms, something deep and fundamental inside her was afraid of loving again. No, terrified. She was terrified of falling in love with Cole. Terrified of what the future might hold.

"The first time shook me more than I care to admit," he said. "Remember that Friday night we rented the movie?"

"I remember."

"I tried to stay away from you afterward. For an entire week I avoided you."

Robin didn't answer. She couldn't. Lying back against the pillows, she stared at the ceiling as a sense of warmth enveloped her. A feeling of comfort…of happiness.

There was a short silence, and in an effort to bring their discussion back to a less intimate—less risky—level, she said, "Thank you for dinner. Jeff had the time of his life." She had, too, but she couldn't find the courage to acknowledge it.

"You're welcome."

"Are you going away this weekend to work on the property?"

She had no right to ask him that, and was shocked at how easily the question emerged.

"I don't think so." After another brief pause, he murmured, "When's the last time you went on a picnic and flew a kite?"

"I don't recall."

"Would you consider going with me on Saturday afternoon? You and Jeff. The three of us together."

"Yes…Jeff would love it."

"How about you? Would you love it?"

"Yes," she whispered.

There didn't seem to be anything more to say, and Robin ended the conversation. "I'll tell Jeff in the morning. He'll be thrilled. Thank you."

"I'll talk to you tomorrow, then."

"Yes. Tomorrow."

"Good night, Robin."

She smiled softly. He said her name the way she'd always dreamed a man would, softly, with a mixture of excitement and need. "Good night, Cole."

For a long time after they'd hung up Robin lay staring at her bedroom walls. When she did flick off her light, she fell asleep as quickly as Jeff seemed to have. She woke about midnight, surprised to find the sheets all twisted as if she'd tossed and turned frantically. The bedspread had slipped onto the floor, and the top sheet was wound around her legs, trapping her.

Sitting up, she untangled her legs and brushed the curls from her face, wondering what had caused her restlessness. She didn't usually wake abruptly like this.

She slid off the bed, found her slippers and went downstairs for a glass of milk.

It was while she was sitting at the table that it came to her. Her hand stilled. Her heartbeat accelerated. The couple in the Chinese restaurant. Robin had overheard them and she was certain Cole had, too.

Their little boy. A family.

Cole had lost a son. From the little Robin had learned, Cole's son had been about the same age Jeff was now when he'd died. First divorce, and then death.

Suddenly it all made sense. A painful kind of sense. A panicky kind of sense. The common ground between them wasn't their backyards, but the fact that they were both victims.

Cole was trying to replace the family that had been so cruelly taken from him.

Robin was just as guilty. She'd been so caught up in the tide of emotion and attraction that she'd refused to recognize what was staring her in the face. She'd ignored her own suspicions and fears, shoving them aside.

She and Cole were both hurting, needy people.

But once the hurt was assuaged, once the need had been satisfied, Cole would discover what Robin had known from the beginning. They were completely different people with little, if anything, in common.

Six

"What do you mean you want to meet my cousin?" Angela demanded, glancing up from her desk, a shocked look on her face.

"You've been after me for weeks to go out with Fred."

"Frank. Yes, I have, but that was B.C."

"B.C.?"

"Before Cole. What happened with you two?"

"Nothing!"

"And pigs have wings," Angela said with more than a trace of sarcasm. She stood up and walked around to the front of her desk, leaning against one corner while she folded her arms and stared unblinkingly at Robin.

Robin knew it would do little good to try to disguise her feelings. She'd had a restless night and was convinced it showed. No doubt her eyes were glazed; they ached. Her bones ached. But mostly her heart ached. Arranging a date with Angela's cousin was a sure indication of her distress.

"The last thing I heard, Cole was supposed to attend Jeff's baseball game with you."

"He did." Robin walked to her own desk and reached for

the cup of coffee she'd brought upstairs with her. Peeling off the plastic lid, she cautiously took a sip.

"And?"

"Jeff pitched and he played a fabulous game," Robin said, hoping her friend wouldn't question her further.

Angela continued to stare at Robin. Good grief, Robin thought, the woman had eyes that could cut through solid rock.

"What?" Robin snapped when she couldn't stand her friend's scrutiny any longer. She took another sip of her coffee and nearly scalded her lips. If the rest of her day followed the pattern set that morning, she might as well go home now. The temptation to climb back into bed and hide her head under the pillow was growing stronger every minute.

"Tell me what happened with Cole," Angela said again.

"Nothing. I already told you he was at Jeff's baseball game. What more do you want?"

"The least you can do is tell me what went on last night," Angela said slowly, carefully enunciating each word as though speaking to someone who was hard of hearing.

"Before or after Jeff's game?" Robin pulled out her chair and sat down.

"Both."

Robin gave up. Gesturing weakly with her hands, she shrugged, took a deep breath and poured out the whole story in one huge rush. "Cole was held up at the office in a meeting, so we didn't meet at the house the way we'd planned. Naturally Jeff was disappointed, but we decided that whatever was keeping Cole wasn't his fault, and we left for Balboa Park without him. Cole arrived at the bottom of the second inning, just as Jeff was ready to pitch. Jeff only allowed three hits the entire game, and scored two home runs himself. Afterward Cole took us all out for Chinese food at a fabulous restaurant I've never heard of but one you and I will have to try sometime. Our next raise, okay? Later Cole phoned and asked to take Jeff and me on a picnic Saturday. I think we're going to Golden Gate Park because he also talked about flying kites." She paused, dragged in a fresh gulp of air and gave Angela a look that said "make something out of that if you can!"

"I see," Angela said after a lengthy pause.

"Good."

Robin wasn't up to explaining things, so if Angela really *didn't* understand, that was just too bad. She only knew that she was dangerously close to letting her emotions take charge of her life. She was becoming increasingly attracted to a man who could well be trying to replace the son he'd lost. Robin needed to find a way to keep from following her heart, which was moving at breakneck speed straight into Cole's arms.

"Will you introduce me to Frank or not?" she asked a second time, strengthening her voice and her conviction.

Angela was still watching her with those diamond-cutting eyes. "I'm not sure yet."

"You're not sure!" Robin echoed, dismayed. "For weeks you've been spouting his virtues. According to you, this cousin is as close to a god as a human being can get. He works hard, buys municipal bonds, goes to church regularly and flosses his teeth."

"I said all that?"

"Just about," Robin muttered. "I made up the part about flossing his teeth. Yet when I ask to meet this paragon of limitless virtue, you say you're not sure you want to introduce me. I would've thought you'd be pleased."

"I am pleased," Angela said, frowning, "but I'm also concerned."

"It's not your job to be concerned. All you have to do is call Fred and let him know I'm available Saturday evening for drinks or dinner or a movie or whatever. I'll let him decide what he's most comfortable with."

"It's Frank, and I thought you said you were going on a picnic with Cole on Saturday."

Robin turned on her computer, prepared to check several columns of figures. If she looked busy and suitably nonchalant, it might prompt Angela to agree. "Jeff and I will be with Cole earlier in the day. I'll simply make sure we're back before late afternoon, so there's no reason to worry."

Robin's forehead puckered. "I *am* worried. I can't help being worried. Honestly, Robin, I've never seen you like this. You're so...so determined."

"I've always been determined," Robin countered, glancing up from the computer.

"Oh, I agree one hundred percent," Angela said with a heavy sigh, "but not when it comes to anything that has to do with men. My thirteen-year-old niece has more savvy with the opposite sex than you do!"

"Mom, look how high my kite is," Jeff hollered as his box kite soared toward the heavens.

"It's touching the sky!" Robin shouted, and laughed with her son as he tugged and twisted the string. Despite all her misgivings about her relationship with Cole, she was thoroughly enjoying the afternoon. At first, she'd been positive the day would turn into a disaster. She was sure Cole would take one look at her and know she was going out with another man that evening. She was equally sure she'd blurt it out if he didn't immediately guess.

Cole had been as excited as Jeff about the picnic and kite-flying expedition. The two of them had been fussing with the kites for hours—buying, building and now flying them. For her part, Robin was content to soak up the sunshine.

The weather couldn't have been more cooperative. The sky was a brilliant blue and the wind was perfect. Sailboats scudding on the choppy green waters added dashes of bright color.

In contrast to all the beauty surrounding her, Robin's heart was troubled. Watching Cole, so patient and gentle with her son, filled her with contradictory emotions. Part of her wanted to thank him. Thank him for the smile that lit up Jeff's face. Thank him for throwing open the shades and easing her toward the light. And part of her wanted to shut her eyes and run for cover.

"Mom, look!" Jeff cried as the kite whipped and kicked in the wind. Blackie raced at his side as the sleek red-and-blue kite sliced through the sky, then dipped sharply and crashed toward the ground at heart-stopping speed, only to be caught at the last second and lifted higher and higher.

"I'm looking, I'm looking!" Robin shouted back. She'd never seen Jeff happier. Pride and joy shone from his face, and Robin was moved almost to tears.

Cole stood behind Jeff, watching the kite. One hand rested on the boy's shoulder, the other shaded his eyes as he gazed up at the sky. They laughed, and once more Robin was struck by the mingling of their voices. One mature and measured, the other young and excited. Both happy.

A few minutes later, Cole jogged over to Robin's blanket and sat down beside her. He did nothing more than smile at her, but she felt an actual jolt.

Cole stretched out and leaned back on his elbows, grinning at the sun. "I can't remember the last time I laughed so much."

"You two seem to be enjoying this," Robin said.

If Cole noticed anything awry, he didn't comment. She'd managed not to tell him about the date with Angela's cousin; she certainly didn't want him to think she was trying to make him jealous. That wasn't the evening's purpose at all. Actually she wasn't sure *what* she hoped to accomplish by dating Fred…Frank. She mentally shouted the name five times. Why did she keep calling him Fred? She didn't know that any more than she knew why she was going out with him. On the morning she'd talked Angela into making the arrangements for her, it had seemed a matter of life and death. Now she only felt confused and regretful.

"Jeff says you've got a date this evening."

So much for her worry that she might blurt it out herself, Robin thought. She glanced at Cole. He might've been referring to the weather for all the emotion revealed in his voice.

"A cousin of a good friend. She's been after me for months to meet Frank—we're having dinner."

"Could this be the Frank you weren't going out with and that was final?"

Robin stared at him blankly.

"You answered the phone with that when I called to inquire about Blackie. Remember?"

"Oh, yes…" Suddenly she felt an intense need to justify her actions. "It's just that Angela's been talking about him for so long and it seemed like the right thing to do. He's apparently very nice and Angela's been telling me he's a lot of fun and I didn't think it would hurt to meet him…." Once she got started, Robin couldn't seem to stop explaining.

"Robin," Cole said, his eyes tender. "You don't owe me any explanations."

She instantly grew silent. He was right, she knew that,

yet she couldn't help feeling guilty. She was making a terrible mess of this.

"I'm not the jealous type," Cole informed her matter-of-factly.

"I'm not trying to make you jealous," she returned stiffly.

"Good," Cole said and shrugged. His gaze moved from her to Jeff, who was jogging across the grass. Blackie was beside him, barking excitedly.

He hadn't asked, but she felt obliged to explain who'd be looking after her son while she was out. "Jeff's going to the movies with Heather and Kelly Lawrence while I'm out."

Cole didn't say anything. All he did was smile. It was the same smile he'd flashed at her earlier. The same devastating, wickedly charming smile.

He seemed to be telling her she could dine with a thousand different men and it wouldn't disturb him in the least. As he'd said, he wasn't the jealous type. Great. This was exactly the way she'd wanted him to respond, wasn't it? She could date a thousand different men, because Cole didn't care about her. He cared about her son.

"Let me know when you want to leave," he said with infuriating self-assurance. "I wouldn't want you to be late."

On that cue, Robin checked her watch and was surprised to note that it was well past four. They'd been having so much fun, the day had simply slipped away. When she looked up, she found Cole studying her expectantly. "It's... I'm not meeting Frank until later," she said, answering his unspoken question evasively while she gathered up the remains of their picnic.

An hour later, they decided to leave Golden Gate Park. Jeff and Cole loaded up the kites, as well as the picnic cooler, in the back of Cole's car. It took them another hour to get back to Glen Park because of the traffic, which made Robin's schedule even tighter. But that was hardly Cole's fault—it wasn't as if he'd *arranged* for an accident on the freeway.

Cole and Jeff chatted easily for most of the ride home. When they finally arrived at the house, both Robin and Jeff helped Cole unload the car. Blackie's barking only added to the confusion.

"I suppose I'd better get inside," Robin said, her eyes briefly meeting Cole's. She felt awkward all of a sudden, wishing Jeff was standing there as a barrier, instead of busily carrying things onto Cole's porch.

"We had a great time," she added self-consciously. She couldn't really blame her nervousness on Cole; he'd been the perfect companion all day. "Thank you for the picnic."

Jeff joined them, his eyes narrowing as he looked at Cole. "Are you gonna let her do it?"

"Do what?" Robin asked.

"Go out with that other man," Jeff said righteously, inviting Cole to leap into the argument. "I can't believe you're letting her get away with this."

"Jeff. This isn't something we should be discussing with Mr. Camden."

"All right," he murmured with a sigh. "But I think you're making a mistake." He cast a speculative glance in Cole's direction. "Both of you," he mumbled under his breath and headed for the house.

"Thanks for the wonderful afternoon, Cole," Robin said again.

"No problem," he responded, hands in his pockets, his stance relaxed. "Have a good time with Frank."

"Thanks, I will," she said, squinting at him suspiciously just before she turned toward the house. Darn it, she actually felt guilty! There wasn't a single solitary reason she should feel guilty for agreeing to this dinner date with Angela's cousin, yet she did. Cole must've known it, too, otherwise he wouldn't have made that remark about having a good time. Oh, he knew all right.

As Robin was running the bath, Jeff raced up the stairs. "Mom, I need money for the movie." He thrust her purse into her hands. "How much are you giving me for goodies?"

"Goodies?"

"You know, popcorn, pop, a couple of candy bars. I'm starving."

"Jeff, you haven't stopped eating all day. What about the two hot dogs I just fixed you?"

"I ate them, but that was fifteen minutes ago. I'm hungry again."

Robin handed him fifteen dollars, prepared for an argument. That amount should be enough to pay his way into the movie and supply him with popcorn and a soda. Anything beyond that he could do without.

Jeff took the money from her and slowly shook his head. "That's it, kid," she said in a firm voice.

"Did I complain?" Bright blue eyes gazed innocently back at her.

"You didn't have to. I could see it in your face."

Jeff was ready to leave a few minutes later, just as Robin was getting dressed. He stood outside her bedroom door and shouted that Kelly and her mom were there to pick him up.

"Have fun. I won't be any later than ten-thirty," she assured him.

"Can't I wait for you over at Cole's after the movie?"

"Absolutely not!" Robin's heart skidded to a dead stop

at the suggestion. The last person she wanted to face at the end of this evening was Cole Camden. "You didn't ask him, did you?"

"No…but I'm not all that excited about going to Kelly's. I'm there every day, you know."

"Sweetie, I'm sorry. I promise I won't be late."

"You're sure I can't go over to Cole's?"

"Jeffrey Leonard Masterson, don't you *dare* bother Cole. Do you understand me?"

He blinked. She rarely used that tone with him, but she didn't have the time or energy to argue about this.

"I guess," he said with an exaggerated sigh. "But could you make it home by ten?"

"Why ten?"

"Because I don't want to do anything stupid like fall asleep in front of Kelly," he whispered heatedly.

"I'll be back as soon as I can," Robin said.

Glancing at her clock radio, she gasped at the time. She was running late. From the moment she'd made the arrangements to meet Frank, she hadn't given the reality of this evening much thought. Just forcing herself to go through with it had depleted her of energy.

Robin had always hated situations like this. Always. She was going to a strange restaurant, meeting a strange man, and for what? She didn't know.

Tucking her feet into her pumps, Robin hurried to the bathroom to spray on a little perfume. Not much, just enough to give herself some confidence. She rushed down the stairs and reached for her purse.

Her hand was on the doorknob when the phone rang. For a moment, Robin intended to ignore it. It was probably for Jeff. But what if the call was from her parents? Or Frank—calling to cancel? Ridiculous though it was, each ring sounded more urgent than the last. She'd have to answer or she'd spend all evening wondering who it was. Muttering under her breath, she dashed into the kitchen.

"Hello," she said impatiently.

At first there was no response. "Robin, it's Cole." He sounded nothing like himself. "I lied." With that the line was abruptly disconnected.

Robin held the receiver away from her ear and stared at it for several seconds. He'd lied? About what? Good heavens, why had he even phoned? To tell her he'd lied.

There wasn't time to phone him back and ask what he'd meant.

"Would you care for something to drink?" Frank Eberle asked, glancing over the wine list.

"Nothing, thanks," Robin said. Frank had turned out to be a congenial sort, which was a pleasant surprise. He was quite attractive, with light blue eyes and a thick head of distinguished-looking salt-and-pepper hair. Angela had once mentioned he was "a little bit" shy, which had panicked Robin since she was a whole lot shy, at least around men. The way she'd figured it, they'd stare at each other most of the night, with no idea what to say. However, they did have Angela in common. Whereas with Cole, all she shared was—

Her thoughts came to an abrupt halt. She refused to think about her neighbor or his last-minute phone call. She balked at the idea of dining with one man while wistfully longing for another—which was exactly what she was doing.

Robin studied the menu, pretending to decide between the prime-rib special and the fresh halibut. But the entire time she stared at the menu, she was racking her brain for a topic of conversation.

Frank saved her the trouble. "For once," he said, "Angela didn't exaggerate. You're a delightful surprise."

"I am?" It was amusing to hear him echo her own reaction.

Frank nodded, his smile reserved. "When Angie phoned earlier in the week, I wasn't sure what to expect. She keeps wanting me to date her friends. And to hear her talk, she's close friends with dozens of gorgeous women all interested in meeting me."

Robin grinned. "She should run a dating service. I can't tell you the number of times she's matched me up with someone, or tried to, anyway."

"But you're a comfortable person to be around. I could sense that right away."

"Thank you. I...wasn't sure what to expect, either. Angela's raved about you for weeks, wanting to get the two of us together." Robin glanced from the menu to her companion, then back again. She felt the same misgivings every time she agreed to one of these arranged dates.

"I've been divorced six months now," Frank volunteered, "but after fourteen years of married life, I don't think I'll ever get accustomed to dating again."

Robin found herself agreeing. "I know what you mean. It all seems so awkward, doesn't it? When Lenny and I were dating, I was in high school, and there was so little to worry about. We knew what we wanted and knew what we had to do to get there."

Frank sent her a smile. "Now that we're older and—" he paused "—I hesitate to use the word *wiser*...."

"More sophisticated?"

"Right, more sophisticated," Frank repeated. His hand closed around the water glass. "Life seems so complicated now. I've been out of the swing of things for so long...."

The waitress came for their order then, and from that point on the evening went smoothly. The feeling of kinship she felt with Frank astonished Robin. He was obviously at ease with her, too. Before she knew it, Robin found herself telling him about Cole.

"He sounds like the kind of guy most women would leap off a bridge to meet."

Robin nodded. "He's wonderful to Jeff, too."

"Then what's the problem?"

"His wife and son."

Frank's mouth sagged open. "He's married?"

"Was," she rushed to explain. "From what I understand, his wife left him and sometime later his son died."

"That's tough," Frank said, picking up his coffee. "But that was years ago, wasn't it?"

"I...don't know. Cole's never told me these things himself. In fact, he's never mentioned either his wife or his son."

"He's *never* mentioned them?"

"Never," she confirmed. "I heard it from a neighbor."

"That's what's bothering you, isn't it?"

The question was sobering. Subconsciously, from the moment Robin had learned of Cole's loss, she'd been waiting for him to tell her. Waiting for him to trust her enough.

Frank and Robin lingered over coffee, chatting about politics and the economy and a number of other stimulating topics. But the question about Cole refused to fade from her mind.

They parted outside the restaurant and Frank kissed her cheek, but they were both well aware they wouldn't be seeing each other again. Their time together had been a brief respite. It had helped Frank deal with his loneliness and helped Robin understand what was troubling her about Cole.

The first thing Robin noticed when she pulled into her driveway was that Cole's house was dark. Dark and silent. Lonely. So much of her life had been like that—before she'd met him.

She needed to talk to him. She wanted to ask about his phone call. She wanted to ask about his wife and the son he'd lost. But the timing was all wrong.

For a long moment Robin sat alone in her car, feeling both sad and disappointed.

Heather greeted her with a smile and a finger pressed to her lips. "Both kids were exhausted. They fell asleep in the living room almost as soon as we got back."

After Jeff's busy day, she could hardly believe he'd lasted through the movie. "I hope he wasn't cranky."

"Not in the least," Heather assured her.

Robin yawned, completely exhausted. She wanted nothing more than to escape to her room and sleep until noon the following day.

"Would you like a cup of coffee before you go?" Heather asked.

"No, thanks." Robin had been blessed with good neighbors. Heather on her right and Cole on her left....

Together Robin and Heather woke Jeff, who grumbled about his mother being late. He was too drowsy to realize it was only nine-thirty or that she'd returned ahead of schedule.

After telling Heather a little about her evening, Robin guided her son across the yard and into the house. She walked upstairs with him and answered the slurred questions he struggled to ask between wide, mouth-stretching yawns.

Tugging back his quilt, Robin urged him into his bed. Jeff kicked off his shoes and reached for the quilt. It wasn't the first time he'd slept in his clothes and it probably wouldn't be the last.

Smiling to herself, Robin moved quietly down the stairs.

On impulse, she paused in the kitchen and picked up the phone. When Cole answered on the first ring, she swallowed a gasp of surprise.

"Hello," he said a second time.

"What did you lie about?" she asked softly.

"Where are you?"

"Home."

"I'll be right there." Without a further word, he hung up.

A minute later, Cole was standing at her front door, hands in his back pockets. He stared at her as if it had been months since they'd seen each other.

"You win," he said, edging his way in.

"Win what? The door prize?" she asked, controlling her amusement with difficulty.

Not bothering to answer her, Cole stalked to the kitchen, where he sank down in one of the pine chairs. "Did you have a good time?"

She sat down across from him. "I really did. Frank's a very pleasant, very caring man. We met at the Higher Ground—that's a cute little restaurant close to the BART station and—"

"I know where it is."

"About your phone call earlier. You said—"

"What's he like?"

"Who? Frank?"

Cole gave her a look that suggested she have her intelligence tested.

"Like I said, he's very pleasant. Divorced and lonely."

"What's he do for a living?"

"He works for the city, I think. We didn't get around to

Debbie Macomber

talking about our careers." No doubt Cole would be shocked if he knew she'd spent the greater part of the evening discussing her relationship with *him!*

"What did you talk about, then?"

"Cole, honestly, I don't think we should discuss my evening with Frank. Would you like some coffee? I'll make decaf."

"Are you going to see him again?"

Robin ignored the question. Instead she left the table and began to make coffee. She was concentrating so carefully on her task that she didn't notice Cole was directly behind her. She turned—and found herself gazing into the darkest, most confused and frustrated pair of eyes she'd ever seen.

"Oh," she said, startled. "I didn't realize you were so close."

His hands gripped her shoulders. "Why did you go out with him?"

Surely that wasn't distress she heard in Cole's voice? Not after all that casual indifference this afternoon. She frowned, bewildered by the pain she saw in his eyes. And she finally understood. Contrary to everything he'd claimed, Cole was jealous. Really and truly jealous.

"Did he kiss you?" he asked with an urgency, an intensity, she'd never heard in his voice before.

Robin stared, frozen by the stark need she read in him.

Cole's finger rested on her mouth. "Did Frank kiss you?" he repeated.

She shook her head and the motion brushed his finger across her bottom lip.

"He wanted to, though, didn't he?" Cole asked with a brooding frown.

"He didn't kiss me." She was finally able to say the words. She couldn't kiss Frank or anyone else. The only man she wanted to kiss and be kissed by was the man looking down at her now. The man whose lips were descending on hers....

Seven

"So, did you like this guy you had dinner with last night?" Jeff asked, keeping his eyes on his bowl of cold cereal.

"He was nice," Robin answered, pouring herself a cup of coffee and joining him at the table. They'd slept late and were spending a lazy Sunday morning enjoying their breakfast before going to the eleven o'clock service at church.

Jeff hesitated, his spoon poised in front of him. "Is he nicer than Cole?"

"Cole's...nicer," Robin admitted reluctantly. *Nice* and *nicer* weren't terms she would've used to describe the differences between Frank and Cole, but in her son's ten-year-old mind they made perfect sense.

A smile quivered at the edges of Jeff's mouth. "I saw you two smooching last night," he said, grinning broadly.

"When?" Robin demanded—a ridiculous question. It could only have happened when Cole had come over to talk to her. He'd confessed how jealous he'd been of Frank and how he'd struggled with the emotion and felt like a fool. Robin had been convinced she was the one who'd behaved like an idiot. Before either of them could prevent it, they were in each other's arms, seeking and granting reassurance.

"You thought I was asleep, but I heard Cole talking and I wanted to ask him what he was gonna do about you and this other guy, so I came downstairs and saw you two with your faces stuck together."

The boy certainly had a way with words.

"You didn't look like you minded, either. Cole and me talked about girls once, and he said they aren't much when they're ten, but they get a whole lot more interesting later on. He said girls are like green apples. At first they're all sour and make your lips pucker, but a little while later they're real good."

"I see," Robin muttered, not at all sure she liked being compared to an apple.

"But when I got downstairs I didn't say anything," Jeff said, "because, well, you know."

Robin nodded and sipped her coffee in an effort to hide her discomfort.

Jeff picked up his cereal bowl and drank the remainder of the milk in loud gulps. He wiped the back of his hand across his lips. "I suppose this means you're going to have a baby now."

Robin was too horrified to speak. The swallow of coffee got stuck in her throat and she started choking. Trying to help her breathe, Jeff pounded her back with his fist, which only added to her misery.

By the time she caught her breath, tears were streaking down her face.

"You all right, Mom?" Jeff asked, his eyes wide with concern. He rushed into the bathroom and returned with a wad of tissue.

"Thanks," she whispered, wiping her face. It took her a

moment or two to regain her composure. This was a talk she'd planned on having with him soon—but not quite yet. "Jeff, listen…kissing doesn't make babies."

"It doesn't? But I thought… I hoped… You mean you won't be having a baby?"

"I… Not from kissing," she whispered, taking in deep breaths to stabilize her pulse.

"I suppose the next thing you're gonna tell me is we'll have to save up for a baby the way we did for the house and now the fence before we get me a dog."

This conversation was getting too complicated. "No, we wouldn't have to save for a baby."

"Then what's the holdup?" her son demanded. "I like the idea of being a big brother. I didn't think much about it until we moved here. Then when we were having dinner at the Chinese restaurant I heard this grandma and grandpa in the booth next to us talking, and they were saying neat things about us being a family. That's when I started thinking about babies and stuff."

"Jeff," Robin said, rubbing her hands together as she collected her thoughts. "There's more to it than that. Before there's a baby, there should be a husband."

"Well, of course," Jeff returned, looking at her as if she'd insulted his intelligence. "You'd have to marry Cole first, but that'd be all right with me. You like him, don't you? You must like him or you wouldn't be kissing him that way."

Robin sighed. Of course she *liked* Cole, but it wasn't that simple. Unfortunately she wasn't sure she could explain it in terms a ten-year-old could understand. "I—"

"I can't remember ever seeing you kiss a guy like that. You looked real serious. And when I was sneaking back up the stairs, I heard him ask you to have dinner alone with him tonight and that seemed like a real good sign."

The next time Cole kissed her, Robin thought wryly, they'd have to scurry into a closet. The things that child came up with...

"You *are* going to dinner with him, aren't you?"

"Yes, but—"

"Then what's the problem? I'll ask him to marry you if you want."

"Jeff!" she cried, leaping to her feet. "Absolutely not! That's between Cole and me, and neither of us would appreciate any assistance from you. Is that clearly understood?"

"All right," he sighed, but he didn't look too pleased. He reached for a piece of toast, shredding it into thirds. "But you're going to marry him, aren't you?"

"I don't know."

"Why not? Cole's the best thing that's ever happened to us."

Her son was staring at her intently, his baseball cap twisted around to the back of his head. Now that she had his full attention, Robin couldn't find the words to explain. "It's more complicated than you realize, sweetie." She made a show of glancing at the clock. "Anyway, it's time to change and get ready for church."

Jeff nodded and rushed up the stairs. Robin followed at a much slower pace, grateful to put an end to this difficult and embarrassing subject.

The minute they were home from the service, Jeff grabbed his baseball mitt. "Jimmy Wallach and I are going to the school yard to practice hitting balls. Okay?"

"Okay," Robin said absently. "How long will you be gone?"

"An hour."

"I'm going grocery shopping, so if I'm not home when you get back you know what to do?"

"Of course," he muttered.

* * *

"You're Robin Masterson, aren't you?" a tall middle-aged woman asked as she maneuvered her grocery cart alongside Robin's.

"Yes," Robin said. The other woman's eyes were warm and her smile friendly.

"I thought you must be—I've seen you from a distance. I'm Joyce Wallach. Jimmy and Jeff have become good friends. In fact, they're at the school yard now."

"Of course," Robin said, pleased to make the other woman's acquaintance. They'd talked on the phone several times, and she'd met Joyce's husband once, when Jimmy had spent the night. The boys had wanted to play on the same baseball team and were disappointed when they'd been assigned to different teams. It had been Jimmy who'd told Jeff about the death of Cole's son.

"I've been meaning to invite you to the house for coffee," Joyce went on to say, "but I started working part-time and I can't seem to get myself organized."

"I know what you mean." Working full-time, keeping up with Jeff and her home was about all Robin could manage herself. She didn't know how other mothers were able to accomplish so much.

"There's a place to sit down here," Joyce said, and her eyes brightened at the idea. "Do you have time to chat now?"

Robin nodded. "Sure. I've been wanting to meet you, too." The Wallachs lived two streets over, and Robin fully approved of Jimmy as a friend for Jeff. He and Kelly had become friends, too, but her ten-year-old son wasn't as eager to admit being buddies with a girl. Kelly was still a green apple in Jeff's eye, but the time would come when he'd appreciate having her next door.

"I understand Jeff's quite the baseball player," Joyce said at the self-service counter.

Robin smiled. She poured herself a plastic cup of iced tea and paid for it. "Jeff really loves baseball. He was disappointed he couldn't play with Jimmy."

"They separate the teams according to the kid's year of birth. Jimmy's birthday is in January so he's with another group." She frowned. "That doesn't really make much sense, does it?" She chuckled, and Robin couldn't help responding to the soft infectious sound of Joyce's laughter. She found herself laughing, too.

They pulled out chairs at one of the small tables in the supermarket's deli section.

"I feel like throwing my arms around you," Joyce said with a grin. "I saw Cole Camden at Balboa Park the other day and I couldn't believe my eyes. It was like seeing him ten years ago, the way he used to be." She glanced at Robin. "Jeff was with him."

"Cole came to his first game."

"Ah." She nodded slowly, as if that explained it. "I don't know if anyone's told you, but there's been a marked difference in Cole lately. I can't tell you how happy I am to see it. Cole's gone through so much heartache."

"Cole's been wonderful for Jeff," Robin said, then swallowed hard. She felt a renewed stab of fear that Cole was more interested in the idea of having a son than he was in a relationship with her.

"I have the feeling you've *both* been wonderful for him," Joyce added.

Robin's smile was losing its conviction. She lowered her eyes and studied the lemon slice floating in her tea.

"My husband and I knew Cole quite well before the divorce," Joyce went on to say. "Larry, that's my husband,

and Cole played golf every Saturday afternoon. Then Jennifer decided she wanted out of the marriage, left him and took Bobby. Cole really tried to save that marriage, but the relationship had been in trouble for a long time. Cole doted on his son, though—he would've done anything to spare Bobby the trauma of a divorce. Jennifer, however—" Joyce halted abruptly, apparently realizing how much she'd said. "I didn't mean to launch into all of this—it's ancient history. I just wanted you to know how pleased I am to meet you."

Since Cole had told her shockingly little of his past, Robin had to bite her tongue not to plead with Joyce to continue. Instead, she bowed her head and said, "I'm pleased to meet you, too."

Then she looked up with a smile as Joyce said, "Jimmy's finally got the friend he's always wanted. There are so few boys his age around here. I swear my son was ready to set off fireworks the day Jeff registered at the school and he learned you lived only two blocks away."

"Jeff claimed he couldn't live in a house that's surrounded by girls." Robin shook her head with a mock grimace. "If he hadn't met Jimmy, I might've had a mutiny on my hands."

Joyce's face relaxed into another warm smile. She was energetic and animated, gesturing freely with her hands as she spoke. Robin felt as if she'd known and liked Jimmy's mother for years.

"There hasn't been much turnover in this neighborhood. We're a close-knit group, as I'm sure you've discovered. Heather Lawrence is a real sweetie. I wish I had more time to get to know her. And Cole, well… I realize that huge house has been in his family forever, but I half expected him to move out after Jennifer and Bobby were killed."

The silence that followed was punctuated by Robin's soft, involuntary gasp. "What did you just say?"

"That I couldn't understand why Cole's still living in the house on Orchard Street. Is that what you mean?"

"No, after that—about Jennifer and Bobby." It was difficult for Robin to speak. Each word felt as if it had been scraped from the roof of her mouth.

"I assumed you knew they'd both been killed," Joyce said, her eyes full of concern. "I mean, I thought for sure that Cole had told you."

"I knew about Bobby. Jimmy said something to Jeff, who told me, but I didn't have any idea that Jennifer had died, too. Heather Lawrence told me about the divorce, but she didn't say anything about Cole's wife dying...."

"I don't think Heather knows. She moved into the neighborhood long after the divorce, and Cole's pretty close-mouthed about it."

"When did all this happen?"

"Five or six years ago now. It was terribly tragic," Joyce said. "Just thinking about it makes my heart ache all over again. I don't mean to be telling tales, but if there's any blame to be placed I'm afraid it would fall on Jennifer. She wasn't the kind of woman who's easy to know or like. I shouldn't speak ill of the dead, and I don't mean to be catty, but Jen did Cole a favor when she left him. Naturally, he didn't see it that way—he was in love with his wife and crazy about his son. Frankly, I think Cole turned a blind eye to his wife's faults because of Bobby."

"What happened?" Perhaps having a neighbor fill in the details of Cole's life was the wrong thing to do; Robin no longer knew. Cole had never said a word to her about Jennifer or Bobby, and she didn't know if he ever would.

"Jen was never satisfied with Cole's position as a city attorney," Joyce explained. "We'd have coffee together every now and then, and all she'd do was complain how Cole was wasting his talents and that he could be making big money and wasn't. She had grander plans for him. But Cole loved his job and felt an obligation to follow through with his commitments. Jennifer never understood that. She didn't even try to sympathize with Cole's point of view. She constantly wanted more, better, newer things. She didn't work herself, so it was all up to Cole." Joyce shrugged sadly.

"Jen was never happy, never satisfied," she went on. "She hated the house and the neighborhood, but figured out that all the whining and manipulating in the world wasn't going to do one bit of good. Cole intended to finish out his responsibilities to the city, so she played her ace. She left him, taking Bobby with her."

"But didn't Cole try to gain custody of Bobby?"

"Of course. He knew, and so did everyone else, that Jennifer was using their son as a pawn. She was never the motherly type, if you know what I mean. If you want the truth, she was an alcoholic. There were several times I dropped Bobby off at the house and suspected Jen had been drinking heavily. I was willing to testify on Cole's behalf, and I told him so. He was grateful, but then the accident happened and it was too late."

"The accident?" A heaviness settled in her chest. Each breath pained her and brought with it the memories she longed to forget, memories of another accident—the one that had taken her husband.

"It was Jennifer's fault—the accident, I mean. She'd been drinking and should never have been behind the wheel. The day before, Cole had been to see his attorneys, pleading with them to move quickly because he was afraid Jennifer was becoming more and more irresponsible. But it wasn't until after she'd moved out that Cole realized how sick she'd become, how dependent she was on alcohol to make it through the day."

"Oh, no," Robin whispered. "Cole must've felt so guilty."

"It was terrible," Joyce returned, her voice quavering. "I didn't know if Cole would survive that first year. He hid inside the house and severed relationships with everyone in the neighborhood. He was consumed by his grief. Later he seemed to come out of it a little, but he's never been the same.

"The irony of all this is that eventually Jen would've gotten exactly what she wanted if she'd been more patient. A couple of years ago, Cole accepted a partnership in one of the most important law firms in the city. He's made a real name for himself, but money and position don't seem to mean much to him—they never have. I wouldn't be surprised if he walked away from the whole thing someday."

"I think you're right. Cole told me not long ago that he has some property north of here that he inherited from his grandfather. He's restoring the house, and he said something about moving there. It's where he spends most of his weekends."

"I wondered if that was it," Joyce said, nodding. "There were rumors floating around the neighborhood that he spent his weekends with a woman. Anyone who knew Cole would realize what a crock that is. Cole isn't the type to have a secret affair."

Robin felt ashamed, remembering how she'd been tempted to believe the rumor herself.

"For a long time," Joyce murmured, "I wondered if Cole was ever going to recover from Jennifer's and Bobby's deaths, but now I believe he has. I can't help thinking you and Jeff had a lot to do with that."

"I...think he would gradually have come out of his shell."

"Perhaps, but the changes in him lately have been the most encouraging things so far. I don't know how you feel about Cole or if there's anything between you, but you couldn't find a better man."

"I...I'm falling in love with him," Robin whispered, voicing her feelings for the first time. The words hung there, and it was too late to take them back.

"I think that's absolutely wonderful, I really do!" Joyce said enthusiastically.

"I don't." Now that the shock had worn off, Robin was forced to confront her anger. Cole had told her none of this. Not a single word. That hurt. Hurt more than she would've expected. But the ache she felt was nothing compared to the grief Cole must face each morning, the pain that weighed down his life.

"Oh, dear," Joyce said. "I've really done it now, haven't I? I knew I should've kept my mouth shut. You're upset and it's my fault."

"Nonsense," Robin whispered, making an effort to bring a smile to her dry lips and not succeeding. "I'm grateful we met, and more than grateful you told me about Jennifer, and about Cole's son." The knowledge produced a dull ache in Robin's heart. She felt grief for Cole and a less worthy emotion, too—a sense of being slighted by his lack of trust in her.

She was so distressed on the short drive home that she missed the turn and had to take a side street and double back to Orchard Street.

As she neared the house, she saw that Cole was outside watering his lawn. He waved, but she pretended not to see him and pulled into her driveway. Desperate for some time alone before facing Cole, Robin did her best to ignore him as she climbed out of the car. She needed a few more minutes to gather her thoughts and control her emotions.

She was almost safe, almost at the house, when Cole stopped her.

"Robin," he called, jogging toward her. "Hold on a minute, would you?"

She managed to compose herself, squaring her shoulders and drawing on her dignity.

His wonderful eyes were smiling as he hurried over. Obviously he hadn't noticed there was anything wrong. "Did Jeff happen to say anything about seeing us kiss last night?" he asked.

Her mouth was still so dry she had to swallow a couple of times before she could utter a single syllable. "Yes, but don't worry, I think I've got him squared away."

"Drat!" he teased, snapping his fingers. "I suppose this means I don't have to go through with the shotgun wedding?"

She nodded, keeping her eyes lowered, fearing he'd be able to read all the emotion churning inside her.

"You have nothing to fear but fear itself," she said, forcing a lightness into her tone.

"Robin?" He made her name a question and a caress. "Is something wrong?"

She shook her head, shifting the bag of groceries from one arm to the other. "Of course not," she said with the same feigned cheerfulness.

Cole took the bag from her arms. Robin knew she should have resisted, but she couldn't; she felt drained of strength. She headed for the house, knowing Cole would follow her inside.

"What's wrong?" he asked a second time, setting the groceries on the kitchen counter.

It was difficult to speak and even more difficult, more exhausting, to find the words that would explain what she'd learned.

"Nothing. It's just that I've got a lot to do if we're going out for dinner tonight."

"Wear something fancy. I'm taking you to a four-star restaurant."

"Something fancy?" Mentally she reviewed the contents of her closet, which was rather lacking in anything fancy.

"I'm not about to be outclassed by Frank," Cole said with a laugh. "I'm going to wine and dine you and turn your head with sweet nothings."

He didn't need to do any of those things to turn her head. She was already dangerously close to being in love with him, so close that she'd blurted it out to a woman she'd known for a total of twelve minutes.

Abruptly switching her attention to the bag of groceries, Robin set several packages on the counter. When Cole's hands clasped her shoulders, her eyes drifted shut. "It isn't necessary," she whispered.

Cole turned her around to face him. "What isn't?"

"The dinner, the wine, the…sweet nothings."

Their eyes held. As if choreographed, they moved into each other's arms. With a groan that came from deep in his throat, Cole kissed her. His hands tangled in the auburn thickness of her hair. His lips settled on hers with fierce protectiveness.

Robin curled her arms tightly around his neck as her own world started to dip and spin and whirl. She was standing on tiptoe, her heart in her throat, when she heard the front door open.

Moaning, she dragged her mouth from Cole's and broke away just as her son strolled into the kitchen.

Jeff stopped, his brow furrowed, when he saw the two of them in what surely looked like suspicious circumstances.

"Hi, Mom. Hi, Cole." He went casually to the refrigerator and yanked open the door. "Anything decent to drink around this place?"

"Water?" Robin suggested.

Jeff rolled his eyes. "Funny, Mom."

"There are a few more sacks of groceries in the car. Would you get them for me?" He threw her a disgruntled look, until Robin added, "You'll find a six-pack of soda in there."

"Okay." He raced out of the house and returned a minute later, carrying one sack and sorting through its contents as he walked into the kitchen.

"I'll help you," Cole said, placing his hand on Jeff's shoulder. He glanced at Robin and his eyes told her they'd continue their discussion at a more opportune moment.

Robin started emptying the sacks, hardly paying attention as Jeff and Cole brought in the last couple of bags. Cole told her he'd pick her up at six, then left.

"Can I play with Blackie for a while?" Jeff asked her, a can of cold soda clenched in his hand.

"Sure," Robin answered, grateful to have a few minutes alone.

Robin cleared the counters and made Jeff a sandwich for his lunch. He must've become involved in his game with Cole's dog because he didn't rush in announcing he was hungry.

She went outside to stand on her small front porch and smiled as she watched Jeff and Blackie. Her son really had a way with animals—like his father. Every time Robin saw him play with Cole's Labrador, she marveled at how attuned they were to each other.

She smiled when she realized Cole was outside, too; he'd just finished watering his lawn.

"Jeff, I made a sandwich for you," she called.

"In a minute. Hey, Mom, watch," he yelled as he tossed a ball across the lawn. Blackie chased after it, skidding to a stop as he caught the bright red ball.

"Come on, Blackie," Jeff urged. "Throw me the ball."

"He can't do that," Robin said in astonishment.

"Sure, he can. Watch."

And just as Jeff had claimed, Blackie leapt into the air, tossed his head and sent the ball shooting into the street.

"I'll get it," Jeff hollered.

It was Cole's reaction that Robin noticed first. A horrified look came over his face and he threw down the hose. He was shouting even as he ran.

Like her son, Robin had been so caught up in Blackie's antics that she hadn't seen the car barreling down the street, directly in Jeff's path.

Eight

"Jeff!" Robin screamed, fear and panic choking her. Her hands flew to her mouth in relief as Cole grabbed Jeff around the waist and swept him out of the path of the speeding car. Together they fell backward onto the wet grass. Robin ran over to them.

"Jeff, how many times have I told you to look before you run into the street? How many times?" Her voice was high and hysterical.

"I saw the car," Jeff protested loudly. "I did! I was going to wait for it. Honest." He struggled to his feet, looking insulted at what he obviously considered an overreaction.

"Get into the house," Robin demanded, pointing furiously. She was trembling so badly she could barely speak.

Jeff brushed the grass from his jeans and raised his head to a dignified angle, then walked toward the house. Not understanding, Blackie followed him, the ball in his mouth, wanting to resume their play.

"I can't, boy," Jeff mumbled just loudly enough for her to hear. "My mother had some kind of anxiety attack that I'm gonna get punished for."

Cole's recovery was slower than Jeff's. He sat up and

rubbed a hand across his eyes. His face was ashen, his expression stark with terror.

"Everything's all right. Jeff isn't hurt," Robin assured him. She slipped to her knees in front of him.

Cole nodded without looking at her. His eyes went blank and he shook his head, as if to clear his mind.

"Cole," Robin said softly, "are you okay?"

"I...I don't know." He gave her a faint smile, but his eyes remained glazed and distant. He placed one hand over his heart and shook his head again. "For a minute there I thought Jeff hadn't seen that car and...I don't know... If that boy had been hurt..."

"Thank you for acting so quickly," Robin whispered, gratitude filling her heart. She ran her hands down the sides of his face, needing to touch him, seeking a way to comfort him, although her heart ached at his words. So many times over the past few weeks, she'd suspected—and feared—that Cole's feelings had more to do with replacing the family he'd lost than love for her and Jeff.

With a shudder, Cole locked his arms around her waist and pulled her close, burying his face in the curve of her neck as he dragged deep gulps of air into his lungs.

"Come inside and I'll get us some coffee," Robin suggested.

Cole murmured agreement, but he didn't seem in any hurry to release her. Nor she him. Her hands were in his hair and she rested her cheek against his, savoring these moments of closeness now that the panic was gone.

"I lost my son," Cole whispered and the words seemed to be wrenched from the deepest part of his soul. His voice held an agony only those who had suffered such a loss could understand. "In a car accident six years ago."

Robin kissed the crown of his head. "I know."

Cole broke away from her, slowly raising his eyes to meet hers. Mingled with profound grief was confusion. "Who told you?"

"Joyce Wallach."

Cole closed his eyes. "I could use that coffee."

They both stood, and when Cole wrapped his arm around her waist Robin couldn't be sure if it was to lend support or to offer it.

Inside the house, Jeff was sitting at the bottom of the stairs, his knees under his chin. Ever loyal, Blackie lay beside him.

Jeff looked up when Robin opened the front door. "I saw the car," he repeated. "You're getting upset over nothing. I hope you realize that. Hey, what's wrong with Cole?" he asked abruptly. He glanced from Robin to their neighbor and then back to his mother. "He looks like he's seen a ghost."

In some way, Robin supposed, he had.

"You all right, sport?" Cole asked. "I didn't hurt you when we fell, did I?"

"Nah." He bit his lip, eyes lowered.

Cole frowned. "You don't sound all that certain. Are you sure you're okay?"

Jeff nodded reluctantly. "I will be once I find out what my mother plans to do to me. I really was gonna stop at the curb. Honest."

The kid would make an excellent attorney, Robin thought wryly.

"I think I might've overreacted," Cole said. He held open his arms and Jeff flew into them without a second's hesitation. Briefly Cole closed his eyes, as though in silent thanksgiving for Jeff's safety.

"I didn't mean to scare you," Jeff murmured. "I would've stopped."

"I know."

"I promise to be more careful."

"I certainly hope so," Robin said.

Cole released Jeff and sighed deeply, then looked at Robin. "You said something about coffee?"

She smiled and nodded. "I'll get it in a minute. Jeff, you can go outside, but from now on if you're playing ball with Blackie, do it in the backyard. Understand?"

"Sure, Mom," her son said eagerly. "But—" he paused "—you mean that's it? You aren't going to ground me or anything? I mean, of course you're not because I did everything I was supposed to—well, almost everything. Thanks, Mom." He tossed the red ball in the air and caught it deftly with one hand. "Come on, Blackie, we just got a pardon from the governor."

Robin followed the pair into the kitchen and watched as Jeff opened the sliding glass door and raced into the backyard with Blackie in hot pursuit. Reassured, she poured two mugs of coffee while Cole pulled out one of the kitchen chairs. She carried the mugs to the table, then sat down across from him.

Cole reached for her hand, lacing her fingers with his own. He focused his concentration on their linked hands. "Bobby was my son. He died when he was ten."

"Jeff's age," Robin said as a chill surrounded her heart.

"Bobby was so full of life and laughter I couldn't be around him and not smile."

Talking about Bobby was clearly difficult for Cole, and Robin longed to do or say something that would help. But she could think of nothing to ease the agony etched so deeply on his face.

"He was the kind of boy every father dreams of having. Inquisitive, sensitive, full of mischief. Gifted with a vivid imagination."

"A lot like Jeff," she said, and her hands tightened around the mug.

Cole nodded. "Bobby used to tell me I shouldn't worry about Jennifer—she was my ex-wife—because *he,* my ten-year-old son, was taking care of her."

Robin held her breath as she watched the fierce pain in his eyes. "You don't need to tell me this." Not if it was going to rip open wounds that weren't properly healed.

"I should've told you before this," he said, frowning slightly. "It's just that even now, after all this time, it's difficult to talk about my son. For a good many years, I felt as though part of me had died with Bobby. The very best part of me. I don't believe that anymore."

"Jeff reminds you a lot of Bobby, doesn't he?" Robin doubted Cole fully grasped that he was transferring his love from one boy to the other.

A smile tugged at the corners of his mouth. "Bobby had a huskier build and was taller than Jeff. His sport was basketball, but he was more of a spectator than a participant. His real love was computers. Had he lived, I think Bobby would have gone into that field. Jen never understood that. She wanted him to be more athletic, and he tried to please her." Cole's gaze dropped to his hands. "Jennifer and I were divorced before the accident. She died with him. If there's anything to be grateful for in their deaths, it's the knowledge that they both went instantly. I couldn't have stood knowing they'd suffered." He paused long enough to take a sip of the coffee, and grimaced once. "You added sugar?"

"I thought you might need it."

He chuckled. "I have so much to thank you for."

"Me?"

"Do you remember the afternoon Jeff ran away?"

She wasn't likely to forget it. With Jeff around, Robin always figured she didn't need exercise to keep her heart in shape. Her son managed to do it with his antics.

"I left on a business trip to Seattle soon afterward," he reminded her.

She nodded. That was when Jeff had looked after Blackie for him.

"Late one afternoon, when the meeting was over and dinner wasn't scheduled for another couple of hours, I went for a stroll," Cole said. "It was still light and I found myself on the waterfront. The sky was a vivid blue and the waters green and clear. It's funny I'd remember that, but it's all so distinct in my memory. I stood alone on the pier and watched as a ferry headed for one of the islands, cutting a path through the waves. Something brought Bobby to my mind, although he's never far from my thoughts, even now. The most amazing thing happened that afternoon. It's difficult to find the words to explain." He hesitated, as though searching for a way to make Robin understand. Then apparently he gave up the effort and shook his head.

"Tell me about it," Robin said in a quiet voice.

"Well, standing there at the end of the pier…I don't know. For the first time since I lost my son, I felt his presence more than I did his absence. It was as if he was there at my side, pointing out the Olympic Mountains and asking questions. Bobby was always full of questions. My heart felt lighter than it had in years—as though the burden of pain and grief had been lifted from my shoulders. For no reason whatsoever, I started to smile. I think I've been smiling ever since. And laughing. And feeling.

"When I got back to the hotel, I had the sudden urge to

hear your voice. I didn't have any excuse to call you, so I phoned on the pretense of talking to Jeff and checking up on Blackie. But it was your voice I wanted to hear."

Robin smiled through the unexpected rush of tears, wondering if Cole realized what he was saying. It might've been her voice he *thought* he wanted to hear, but it was Jeff he'd called.

"I discovered a new freedom on that Seattle pier. It was as if, in that moment, I was released from the past. I can't say exactly what changed. Meeting you and Jeff played a big role in it, I recognize that much, but it was more than that. It was as if something deep inside me was willing to admit that it was finally time to let go."

"I'm glad for you," Robin whispered.

"The problem is, I never allowed myself to grieve properly or deal with the anger I felt toward Jennifer. She was driving at the time and the accident was her fault. Yet deep in my heart I know she'd never purposely have done anything to hurt Bobby. She loved him as much as I did. He was her son, too.

"It wasn't until I met you that I knew I had to forgive her. I was never the kind of husband she needed and I'm afraid I was a disappointment to her. Only in the last few years of our marriage was I willing to accept that she suffered from a serious emotional and mental illness. Her addiction to alcohol was as much a disease as cancer. I didn't understand her illness, and because of that we all suffered."

"You're being too hard on yourself," Robin said, but she doubted Cole even heard her.

"After the accident, the anger and the grief were a constant gnawing pain. I refused to acknowledge or deal with either emotion. Over the years, instead of healing, I let the agony of my loss grow more intense. I closed myself off from friends and colleagues and threw myself into work, spending far more time in the office than I did at home. Blackie was virtually my only companion. And then a few years ago I started working on my place in the country. But the pleasure that gave me came from hard physical work, the kind that leaves you too tired to think." His features softened and he smiled at her. "I'd forgotten what it was like to fly a kite or laze in the sunshine."

"That's why you suggested the picnic with Jeff and me?"

He grinned and his dark eyes seemed almost boyish. "The last time I was in Golden Gate Park was with Bobby, shortly before the accident. Deciding to have a picnic there was a giant step for me. I half expected to feel pangs of grief, if not a full-blown assault. Instead I experienced joy—and appreciation for the renewal I felt. Laughter is a gift I'd forgotten. You and Jeff helped me see that, as well."

Everything Cole was saying confirmed her worst fears.

"Mom!" Jeff roared into the kitchen with Blackie at his heels. "Is there anything to eat? Are you guys still going out to dinner? I don't suppose you'd bring me, would you?"

Cole chuckled, then leapt to his feet to playfully muss Jeff's hair. "Not this time, sport. Tonight's for your mother and me."

Two hours later, as Robin stood in front of the bathroom mirror, she had her reservations about this dinner date. She was falling in love with a man who hadn't fully dealt with the pain of losing his wife and his son. Perhaps she recognized it in Cole because she saw the same thing in herself. She loved Lenny and always would. He'd died years ago, and she still found herself talking to him, refusing to involve herself in another relationship. A part of her continued to grieve and she suspected it always would.

Examining herself in the mirror, Robin surveyed her calf-length skirt of soft blue velvet and white silk blouse with a pearl necklace.

She was fussing with her hair, pinning one side back with combs and studying the effect, when Jeff wandered in. He leaned casually against the doorway, a bag of potato chips in his hand.

"Hey, you look nice."

"Don't sound so surprised." She decided she'd spent enough time on her hair and fastened her pearl earrings. Jeff was disappointed about not joining them, but he'd been a good sport—especially after Cole promised him lunch at a fish-and-chip place on the Wharf the following Saturday.

"You're wearing your pearls," Jeff mumbled, his mouth full.

"Yes," Robin said, turning to face him. "Do they look all right?"

Jeff's halfhearted shrug didn't do a lot to boost Robin's confidence. "I suppose. I don't know about stuff like that. Mrs. Lawrence could probably tell you." He popped another potato chip in his mouth and crunched loudly. "My dad gave you those earrings, didn't he? And the necklace?"

"For our first wedding anniversary."

Jeff nodded. "I thought so." His look grew reflective. "When I grow up and get married, will I do mushy stuff like that?"

"Probably," Robin said, not bothering to disguise her amusement. "And lots of other things, too. Like taking your wife out to dinner and telling her how beautiful she is and how much you love her."

"Yuck!" Jeff wrinkled his nose. "You really know how to ruin a guy's appetite." With that he turned to march down the stairs, taking his potato chips with him.

Robin stood at the top of the staircase. "Cole will be here any minute, so you can go over to Kelly's now," she called down.

"Okay. I put my plate in the dishwasher. Is there anything you want me to tell Kelly's mom?"

"Just that I won't be too late."

"You're sure I can't come with you?" Jeff tried one more time.

Robin didn't give him an answer, knowing he didn't really expect one. After a moment, Jeff grumbled, more for show than anything, then went out the front door to their neighbor's.

Robin returned to the bathroom and smiled into the mirror, picturing Jeff several years into the future and seeing Lenny's handsome face smiling back at her. She was warmed by the image, certain that her son would grow into as fine a young man as his father had been.

"You don't mind that I'm wearing the pearls for Cole, do you?" she asked her dead husband, although she knew he wouldn't have objected. She ran the tips of her fingers over the earrings, feeling reassured.

The doorbell chimed just as Robin was dabbing perfume on her wrists. She drew in a calming breath, glanced quickly at her reflection one last time, then walked down the stairs to answer the door.

Cole was dressed in a black pin-striped suit and looked so handsome that her breath caught. He smiled as she let him in, but for the life of her she couldn't think of a thing to say.

His eyes held hers as he reached for her hands. Slowly he lowered his gaze, taking in the way she'd styled her hair, the pearl necklace and the outfit she'd chosen with such care.

"You are so beautiful," he said.

"I was just thinking the same about you," she confessed.

His mouth tilted in a grin. "If I kiss you, will it ruin your lipstick?"

"Probably."

"I'm going to kiss you, anyway," he said in a husky murmur. Tenderly he fit his mouth to hers, slipping his fingers through her hair. The kiss was gentle and thorough and slow. A single kiss, and she was like clay ready to be molded. The realization struck her hard—when Cole touched her, Robin felt alive all the way to the soles of her feet. *Alive.* Healthy. A red-blooded woman. He released her, and she was shocked to find she was trembling. From the inside out.

"I've mussed your hair," he apologized. His hands slid under the soft cloud of hair to her nape.

"And you've got lipstick on your mouth," she said with a quaver, reaching up to wipe it away. "There. It'll only take me a moment to fix my hair," she said, picking up her purse and moving to the hallway mirror.

He stood behind her, hands on her shoulders as she brushed her hair, then carefully tucked the loose curls back into place with the tortoiseshell combs.

"Are you ready?" he asked when she'd finished.

Robin nodded, unable to speak.

Cole led her outside to his car and held the passenger door. He dropped a quick kiss on her unsuspecting lips, then hurried around the car, his movements lighthearted, and got into the driver's seat.

"You didn't tell me where we're having dinner."

"I told Heather Lawrence in case she needs to get hold of you, but otherwise it's a surprise."

Robin wasn't sure what to think. A number of San Francisco's restaurants were internationally famous, but her knowledge of fancy dining places was limited. She assumed this one was somewhere in the heart of the city, until he exited from the freeway heading south along Highway 101 toward the ocean.

"Cole?" she asked hesitantly.

"Don't worry," he said, casting her a swift glance that didn't conceal the mischievous twinkle in his eyes. "I promise you dinner will be worth the drive."

The restaurant sat high on a cliff, with a stunning view of the surf battering the jagged rocks below.

Cole parked the Porsche, then came around to help her out, taking the opportunity to steal another kiss. It was with obvious reluctance that he let her go. His arm around her waist, he directed her toward the doors leading into the elegant restaurant. The maître d' escorted them to a table that overlooked the water and with a flourish presented them with elaborate menus.

Robin scanned the entrées, impressed with the interesting variations on basic themes. She was less impressed with the prices—a single dinner cost as much as an entire week's worth of lunches. For her *and* Jeff.

"When you said fancy you weren't joking, were you?" she whispered, biting her lip.

Cole lowered his menu and sent her a vibrant smile. "Tonight is special," he said simply.

"You're telling me. If I wasn't having dinner with you, I'd probably have eaten a toasted cheese sandwich and a bowl of tomato soup with Jeff."

Their waiter appeared and they ordered wine—a bottle of sauvignon blanc. Then they each chose the restaurant's specialty—a scallop and shrimp sauté—which proved as succulent and spicy as the menu had promised.

They talked through dinner and afterward, over steaming cups of Irish coffee. It astonished Robin that they had so much to say to each other, although they hadn't touched on the issue closest to her heart. But she hesitated to broach the subject of Cole's relationship with Jeff. She didn't want to risk the delightful camaraderie they were sharing tonight. Their conversation could have gone on for hours and in fact did. They talked about books they'd read, recent movies they'd seen, music they liked. It came as a pleasant surprise to discover that their tastes were similar.

All evening they laughed, they argued, they talked, as if they'd been friends most of their lives. Cole grinned so often, it was hard for Robin to remember that at one time she'd actually wondered if the man ever smiled.

Robin told Cole about her job and how much she enjoyed accounting. She voiced her fears about not being the kind of mother she wanted to be for Jeff. "There are so many things I want to share with him that I don't have time for. There just aren't enough hours in a day."

Cole talked about his career goals and his dreams. He spoke of the forty acres willed to him by his grandfather and how he'd once hoped to close himself off from the world by moving there.

"But you aren't going to now?" Robin asked.

"No. I no longer have any reason to hide. The house is nearly finished and I may still move there, but I'll maintain my work schedule." He stared down into his coffee. "I was approached last week about running for the state senate."

Robin's heart swelled with pride. "Are you going to do it?"

"No. I'm not the right man for politics. I'll support some-one else, but a political career doesn't interest me. It never has, although I'll admit I'm flattered."

A band started playing then, and several couples took to the dance floor.

"Shall we?" Cole asked, nodding in that direction.

"Oh, Cole, I don't know. The last time I danced was at my cousin's wedding ten years ago. I'm afraid I'll step all over your feet."

"I'm game if you are."

She was reluctant but agreed to try. They stood, and she moved naturally into his embrace, as if they'd been partners for years. Robin's eyes slowly closed when Cole folded her in his arms, and in that moment she experienced a surge of joy that startled her with its intensity.

The dance ended, but they didn't leave the floor.

"Have I told you how lovely you are?" Cole asked, his mouth close to her ear.

Grinning, Robin nodded. "Twice. Once when you picked me up at the house and once during the meal. I know you're exaggerating, but..." She shrugged, then added, "When I'm with you, I feel beautiful."

"I don't think a woman's ever paid me a higher compliment."

She raised her eyes and was shocked by the powerful emotions in his.

"Do you mind if we leave now?" he asked suddenly.

"No, of course not, if that's what you want."

He frowned. "If it was up to me I'd spend the rest of the night here with you in my arms, but I have this sudden need to kiss you, and if I do it here and do it properly we're going to attract a lot of attention."

Cole quickly paid the bill and he hurried Robin to the car. The minute they were settled inside, he reached for her. He did as he'd promised, kissing her until she was breathless. Her arms clung to him as his mouth sought hers once more.

"At least I'm not making you cry this time," he said softly.

"That still embarrasses me," she told him. "It's never happened before. I still don't understand it. I don't know if I ever will."

"I don't think I'll ever forget it."

"Please do."

"No," he said, shaking his head. "It touched me in a way I can't explain. It helped me realize I was going to love you. After Jennifer and Bobby, I doubted there was any love left in me. You taught me otherwise. Jeff taught me otherwise. My heart is full and has been almost from the time we met." He took her hand and pressed her palm to his heart. "Do you feel it?"

Robin nodded. "It's beating so hard," she whispered.

"That's because I'm nervous."

"Nervous? About what?"

Cole slid a hand into his pocket and brought out a small black velvet box.

Robin's heart started to pound in double time. "Cole?" she said anxiously, not sure what she should think or how she should act.

"I love you, Robin." His voice was hoarse. "I knew it the moment I heard your voice when I called from Seattle. And every moment since has convinced me how right this is." He opened the box and revealed the largest diamond Robin had ever seen. Slowly he raised his eyes to hers. "I'm asking you to be my wife."

Nine

"You mean this whole evening...you arranged this whole evening because you intended to ask me to marry you?" Robin asked, pressing the tips of her fingers to her trembling lips. Despite her fears a gentle gladness suffused her heart.

"Surely it isn't that much of a surprise?" he said. "I've never made an effort to hide how I feel about you or how much I enjoy Jeff."

Contrary to what Cole might think, his proposal *did* come as a surprise. "I...I don't know what to say."

"A simple yes would suit me," Cole urged warmly.

"But... Oh, Cole, it would be so easy to marry you, so easy to join my life and Jeff's to yours and never look back. But I don't know if it would be right for us or for you. There's so much to consider, so many factors to weigh, in a decision this important. I'd like nothing better than to just say yes, but I can't."

"Are you asking for time?" Cole's eyes seemed to penetrate hers, even in the dark.

"Please." For now, that seemed the simplest thing to say, although her hesitation was based on something much deeper. Cole had rediscovered a peace within himself since meeting her and Jeff; he'd told her so that very afternoon. She was tempted to say yes, to turn away from her doubts and agree to marry him. Cole had been so good for Jeff, so wonderful to her.

"I hate to disappoint you," she murmured sadly.

"I know exactly what you're thinking, exactly how you're feeling."

"You do?" Somehow she doubted it. But knowing she couldn't delay it any longer, she jumped in with both feet. "I was...just thinking about what you told me this afternoon. How you'd recently dealt with the loss of Jennifer and Bobby. While you were talking, I couldn't help feeling your exhilaration. You've obviously found a newborn sense of freedom. I think the question you need to ask yourself is if this rebirth you've experienced is what prompted the idea of marrying again."

"No," he said flatly. "Falling in love with you did."

"Oh, Cole," she whispered. "It must seem like fate to have Jeff and me move in next door, and it gets more complicated with Jeff being the same age as Bobby...."

"Maybe it does all appear too convenient, but if I was just looking for a woman and a child, then Heather Lawrence would've filled the bill. It's you I fell in love with."

"But how can you be so sure?" she countered quickly. "We barely know each other."

Cole smiled at her doubts. "The first time we kissed was enough to convince me I was going to love you. It was the Friday night after I returned from Seattle, remember?"

Robin nodded, wincing a little.

"I was so stunned by the effect that kiss had on me, I avoided you for an entire week afterward. If you want the truth, I was terrified. You'll have to remember, up until that time I was convinced I was incapable of ever falling in love again. One kiss, and I felt jolted to the core. You hit me hard, Robin, and I needed time to step back and analyze what was happening. That's the reason I don't have any qualms about giving you however long you need to sort out what you're feeling. I want you to be very sure."

Robin released a pent-up sigh. Cole folded her in his arms and his chin brushed against her hair while his hands roved in wide circles across her back. The action was soothing and gentle. She was beginning to feel more confident in his love, but she had to be careful. She *wanted* him to love her, because she was so much in love with him.

Cole tucked a finger under her chin and lifted her face to his. As their eyes met, he slanted his mouth over hers in a wildly possessive kiss, a kiss filled with undisguised need.

When he broke away, Robin was trembling. She buried her face in his neck and drew several deep breaths.

"If you're going to take some time to think about things," Cole whispered against her hair, "then I wanted to give you something else to think about."

"Have you had a chance to check those figures on—" Angela began, then stopped abruptly, waving her hand in front of Robin's face.

"A chance to check what figures?" Robin asked, making a determined effort to focus. She knew she'd been acting like a sleepwalker most of the morning, but she couldn't stop thinking about Cole's proposal.

"What's with you today?" Angela demanded. "Every time I look over here, I find you staring into space with this perplexed expression on your face."

"I was…just thinking," Robin muttered.

"About what?"

"Nothing."

"Come on, girl, you know better than that. You can't fool me." Angela leaned against the edge of Robin's desk and crossed her arms, taking her usual aggressive stance. "I've known you far too long. From everything you *haven't* said, I'd guess your handsome neighbor's involved. What's he done now?"

"Cole? What makes you ask anything so ridiculous?"

Angela frowned, shaking her head. Then she stretched out her hands and made a come-hither motion. "Tell Mama everything," she intoned. "You might as well get it over with and tell me now, because you know that sooner or later I'm going to drag it out of you. What kind of friend would I be if I didn't extract your deepest darkest secrets?"

"He took me to dinner," Robin admitted, knowing that Angela was right. Sooner or later, she'd wheedle it out of her.

"Where'd he take you?"

She shrugged, wanting to keep that to herself. "It was outside the city."

"*Where* outside the city?" Angela pressed.

"Heavens, I don't know. Somewhere along the coast on Highway 101."

Angela uncrossed her arms and started pacing. "It wasn't the Cliffhouse, was it?"

"I...I think it might have been," Robin murmured, concentrating on the task in front of her. The one she should've finished hours earlier. The one she couldn't seem to focus on, even now.

"Aha!" Angela cried, pointing her index finger at the ceiling, like a detective in a comic spoof.

"What?" Robin cried.

"If Cole took you to the Cliffhouse, he did it for a reason."

"Of course he did. The food was fabulous. By the way, you were right about Frank, he's exceptionally nice," Robin said in an effort to interrupt her friend's line of thought.

"You already told me what you think of Frank, remember?" Angela said. "Cole took you to dinner at the Cliffhouse," she repeated slowly, as though reviewing a vital clue in a murder mystery.

"To be honest, I think his choice of restaurant had something to do with Frank," Robin inserted, tossing her sleuth friend a red herring.

"So Cole was jealous?"

"Not exactly," Robin said, leaning back in her chair. "Well, maybe a little," she amended, knowing Angela would never believe her if she denied it completely. "I mean, Cole did invite me to dinner as soon as he learned I was dining with Frank, so I guess you could say he was a *little* jealous. But not much. Cole's not the jealous type—he told me that himself."

"I see." Angela was frowning as she walked back to her desk. Her look remained thoughtful for the rest of the morning, although she didn't question Robin again. But when they left for lunch, she showed a renewed interest in the subject of Cole.

"How's Jeff?" she began as they stood in line in the employees' cafeteria.

"Fine," Robin said as she reached for a plastic tray.

"That's all you're going to say?"

"What more do you want to know?"

"I ask about Jeff once a week or so, then sit back and listen for the next fifteen minutes while you tell me about the latest craziness," Angela said heatedly. "It never fails.

You've told me about him running away with a frying pan and an atlas. You've bragged about what a fabulous pitcher he's turning out to be, and you've given me a multitude of details about every game he's played. After you tell me all about his athletic ability, you generally mention how good he is with animals and all the tricks he's taught Blackie in the past week."

Robin tried to respond but Angela ignored her and kept talking. "Today I innocently ask how Jeff is, and what do I get? *Fine.* All right, Robin, tell me what happened with Cole Camden before I go crazy trying to figure it out."

"It's something I need to figure out myself," Robin said. She paused to study the salads before selecting a mound of cottage cheese and setting it on her tray.

"What are you doing now?" Angela cried, throwing her arms in the air. "You hate cottage cheese. You never eat it unless you're upset and looking for ways to punish yourself." She took the small bowl from Robin's tray and replaced it with a fresh fruit salad, shaking her head the entire time.

The problem with Angela was that she knew Robin all too well.

They progressed a little farther down the line. Robin stood in front of the entrées, but before she chose one, she glanced at her friend. "You want to pick one of these for me, too?" she asked dryly.

"Yes, I do, before you end up requesting liver and onions."

Angela picked the lasagne, thick with melted cheese and spicy tomato sauce. "If you're looking for ways to punish yourself, girl, there are tastier methods."

Despite her thoughtful mood, Robin smiled.

Once they'd paid for their lunches, Angela led her to

a window table that offered a certain amount of privacy. Robin busied herself arranging her dishes and set the tray aside.

Angela sat directly across from her, elbows braced on either side of her lunch. "Are you sure there isn't anything else you'd care to tell me?"

"About what?"

"About you and Cole, of course. I can't remember the last time I saw you like this. It's as if...as if you're trapped in some kind of maze and can't find your way out."

The description was so apt that Robin felt a tingling sensation along her spine. She did feel hopelessly lost. Her mind was cluttered, her emotions confused. She had one foot in the present, one in the past, and didn't know which way to turn.

"I talked to Frank on Sunday afternoon," Angela continued, dipping her fork into a crisp green salad. "He said he enjoyed the evening you spent with him, but doubted you'd be seeing each other·again because it's obvious to him that you're in love with Cole Camden. In fact, Frank said you talked about little else the entire evening."

"He said all that?"

Angela nodded. "He's right, isn't he? You are in love with Cole, aren't you?"

"I...I don't know."

"What do you mean you don't know?" Angela persisted. "It's written all over you. You've got that glazed look and you walk around in a trance, practically bumping into walls."

"You make it sound like I need an ambulance."

"Or a doctor," Angela whispered, leaning across the table. "Or maybe a lawyer... That's it!" she said loudly enough to attract the attention of several people at nearby tables. "Cole took you to bed, and now you're so confused you don't know what to do. I told you I'd stumble on the answer sooner or later." Her eyes flashed triumphantly.

"That's not it," Robin declared, half rising from the table. She could feel the color crowding into her cheeks as she glanced around the cafeteria. When she sat back down, she covered her face with both hands. "If you must know, Cole asked me to marry him."

A moment of shocked silence followed before Angela shrieked with pure delight. "That's fabulous! Wonderful! Good grief, what's wrong with you? You should be in seventh heaven. It isn't every day a handsome, wealthy, wonderful man proposes to you. I hope you leapt at the chance." She hesitated, suddenly still. "Robin? You *did* tell him you'd marry him, didn't you?"

Robin swallowed and shook her head. "No. I asked him for some time to think about things."

"Think about things?" Angela squealed. "What's there to think about? He's rich. He's handsome. He's in love with you and crazy about Jeff. What more could you possibly want?"

Tears brimmed in Robin's eyes as she looked up to meet her friend's avid gaze. "I'm afraid he's more in love with the idea of having a family than he is with me."

"Is Cole coming?" Jeff asked, working the stiffness out of his baseball mitt by slamming his fist into the middle of it several times.

"I don't know," Robin said, glancing at their neighbor's house as they walked to the car. "I haven't talked to him in the last few days."

"You're not mad at him, are you?"

"Of course not," Robin said, sliding into the driver's seat of her compact. "We've both been busy."

Jeff fingered the bill of his baseball cap, then set the cap on his head. "I saw him yesterday and told him about the game, and he said he might come. I hope he does."

Secretly Robin hoped Cole would be there, too. Over the past five days, she'd missed talking to him. She hadn't come to any decision, but he hadn't pressed her to make one, willing to offer her all the time she needed. Robin hadn't realized how accustomed she'd grown to his presence. How much she needed to see him and talk to him. Exchange smiles and glances. Touch him...

When she was married to Lenny, they were two people very much in love, two people who'd linked their lives to form one whole. But Lenny had been taken from her, and for a long time afterward Robin had felt only half alive.

All week she'd swayed back and forth over Cole's proposal, wondering if she should ignore her doubts. Wondering if she *could* ignore them. Sleepless nights hadn't yielded the answer. Neither had long solitary walks in Balboa Park while Jeff practiced with his baseball team.

"Cole said—" Jeff started to say, then stopped abruptly as his hands flew to his head. A panicky look broke out on his face and he stared at Robin.

"What's wrong? Did you forget something?"

"My lucky hat!" Jeff cried. "It's on my dresser. We have to go back."

"For a baseball cap?" Robin didn't disguise how silly she considered that idea. "You're wearing a baseball cap. What's wrong with that one?"

"It won't work. You have to understand, Mom, it's my *lucky* hat. I've been wearing it ever since we played our first game. I had that very same hat on when I hit my first two home runs. I can't play without it," he explained frantically. "We have to go back. Hurry, or we'll be late for the game. Turn here," he insisted, pointing at the closest intersection.

"Jeff," she said, trying to reason with her son. "It isn't the hat that makes you play well."

"I knew you were going to say something like that," he muttered, "and even if it's true, I want to be on the safe side, just in case. We've got to go back and get that hat!"

Knowing it would only waste valuable time to argue, Robin did as he requested. After all, his whole career as a major-league pitcher hung in the balance!

She was smiling as she entered her driveway. Sitting in the car while Jeff ran inside for his lucky cap, Robin glanced over at Cole's place. His car was gone. It'd been gone since early that morning, and she suspected he was at the property, working on his house. Jeff would be disappointed about Cole missing his game, but he'd understand.

Jeff came barreling out of the house, slamming the front door. He leapt into the car and fastened his seat belt. "Come on, Mom," he said anxiously, "let's get this show on the road." As if *she'd* caused the delay, Robin thought to herself, amused by her son's sudden impatience.

By the time they arrived at Balboa Park, the car park was filled to overflowing. Robin was fortunate enough to find a space on the street, a minor miracle in itself. Perhaps there was something to this magic-cap business after all.

Jeff ran across the grass, hurrying toward his teammates, leaving Robin to fend for herself, which was fine. He had his precious cap and was content.

The bleachers were crowded with parents. Robin found a seat close to the top and had just settled in place when she saw Cole making his way toward her. Her heart did an immediate flip-flop and it wasn't until he sat next to her that she was able to speak.

"I thought you were working up on the property this weekend."

"And miss seeing Jeff pitch? Wild horses couldn't have kept me away." He was smiling at her with that cocky heart-stopping smile of his.

"How have you been?" she asked. She couldn't keep her eyes off him. He looked too good to be true, and his dark gaze was filled with warmth and tenderness. How could she help getting lost in eyes that generous? It seemed impossible to resist him any longer.

"I've missed you like crazy," he whispered, and the humor seemed to drain out of him as his eyes searched hers. "I didn't think it was possible to feel this alone. Not anymore."

"I've missed you, too."

He seemed to relax once she'd said that. "Thank you," he said quietly. "Have you been thinking about what I said last weekend?"

She bowed her head. "I haven't thought of anything else."

"Then you've made up your mind?"

"No." She kept her face lowered, not wanting him to see her confusion.

He tilted her chin with one finger, forcing her to meet his eyes. "I promised myself I wouldn't ask you and then I couldn't seem to stop myself. I won't again."

She offered him a weak smile, and Cole looked around him, clearly wanting to kiss her, but not in front of such a large gathering. The funny part was, Robin didn't care about being seen. She was so hungry for the reassurance of his touch, it didn't matter to her that they were in the middle of a crowded park.

"I see Jeff's wearing his lucky hat," Cole said, clasping her hand and giving her fingers a comforting squeeze.

"You know about that?"

"Of course. Jeff tells me everything."

"He panicked when he realized he was wearing the wrong one, and I had to make a U-turn in the middle of the street because he'd left the guaranteed-to-pitch-well baseball cap on his dresser."

"You can't blame him. The luck has lasted through five games now."

"I wonder if it'll last until he reaches the pros," Robin said, sharing a smile with him.

"You're doing all right?" Cole asked unexpectedly.

She nodded, although it wasn't entirely true. Now that she was with Cole, every doubt she'd struggled with all week vanished like fog under an afternoon sun. Only when they were apart was she confronted by her fears.

"After Jeff's finished here, let's do something together," Cole suggested. "The three of us."

She nodded, unable to refuse him anything.

"Come to think of it, didn't I promise Jeff lunch? I seem to recall making a rash pledge to buy him fish and chips because we were leaving him with Heather and Kelly when we went to dinner last week."

Robin grinned. "It seems to me you're remembering that correctly," she said.

They went to a cheerful little fish-and-chip restaurant down by the Wharf. The weather had been chilly all morning, but the sun was out in full force by early afternoon. Jeff was excited about his team's latest win and attributed it to the luck brought to them by his cap.

After a leisurely lunch, the three of them strolled along the busy waterfront. Robin bought a loaf of fresh sourdough bread and a small bouquet of spring flowers. Jeff found a plastic snake he couldn't live without and paid for it with his allowance.

"Just wait till Jimmy Wallach sees this!" he crowed.

"I'm more curious to see how Kelly Lawrence reacts," Robin said.

"Oh, Kelly likes snakes," Jeff told them cheerfully. "Jimmy was over one day and I thought I'd scare Kelly with a live garden snake, but Jimmy was the one who started screaming. Kelly said snakes were just another of God's creatures and there was nothing to be afraid of. Isn't it just like a girl to get religious about a snake?"

Jeff raced down the sidewalk while Cole and Robin stood at the end of the pier, the bread and flowers at their feet.

"You look tired," Cole said, as his fingers gently touched her forehead.

"I'm fine," she insisted, gazing out at the cool green waters of San Francisco Bay. But Cole was right; she hadn't been sleeping well.

"I see so much of myself in you," Cole said softly.

His words surprised her. "How's that?"

"The pain mostly. How many years has Lenny been dead?"

"Ten. In some ways I'm still grieving him." She couldn't be less than honest with Cole.

"You're not sure if you can love another man, are you? At least not with the same intensity that you loved Jeff's father."

"That's not it at all. I...I just don't know if I can stop loving him."

Cole went very still. "I never intended to take Lenny

away from you or Jeff. He's part of your past, an important part. Being married to Lenny, giving birth to Jeff, contributed to making you what you are." He paused, and they both remained silent.

"Bobby had been buried for six years before I had the courage to face the future. I hung on to my grief, carried it with me everywhere I went, dragging it like a heavy piece of luggage I couldn't travel without."

"I'm not that way about Lenny," she said, ready to argue, not heatedly or vehemently, but logically, because what he was saying simply wasn't true. She mourned her dead husband, felt his absence, but she hadn't allowed this sense of loss to destroy her life.

"Perhaps you aren't grieving as deeply as you once were," Cole amended. "But I wonder if you've really laid your husband to rest."

"Of course I have," she answered with a nod of her head, not wanting to talk about Lenny.

"I don't mean to sound unsympathetic," Cole said, his tone compassionate. "I understand, believe me I do. Emotional pain is familiar territory for us both. It seems to me that those of us who sustain this kind of grief are afraid of what lies beyond."

"You're exaggerating, Cole."

"Maybe," he agreed. "You're a lovely woman, Robin. Witty. Intelligent. Outgoing. I'm sure one of the first questions anyone asks you is how long it's been since your husband died. And I'll bet when you tell them, they seem surprised."

That was true, and Robin wondered how Cole had guessed.

"Most young widows remarry."

"Are you suggesting that because I didn't immediately

fling myself back into matrimonial bliss I'm a candidate for therapy? Come on, Cole, even you must realize how ridiculous that is."

"Even me?" he asked, chuckling.

Jeff came loping toward them, his face flushed with excitement. "They're filming a movie," he cried, pointing toward a congested area farther down the pier. "There's cameras and actors and everything. Can I go watch some more?"

Robin nodded. "Just don't get in anyone's way."

"I won't. Promise. Here, Mom, hold my snake." He entrusted her with his precious package before racing back down the pier.

"He's a fine boy, Robin."

"He loves you already. You and Blackie."

"And how does his mother feel?"

The knot in her throat thickened. "She loves you, too."

Cole grinned. "She just isn't sure if she can let go of her dead husband to take on a live one. Am I right?"

His words hit their mark. "I don't know," she admitted. "Maybe it's because I'm afraid you want to marry me because Jeff reminds you of Bobby. Or because you've created a fantasy wife and think I'll fit the role."

Her words seemed to shock him. "No. You've got that all wrong. Jeff is a wonderful plus in this relationship, but it's *you* I fell in love with. It's you I want to grow old with. You, and you alone, not some ideal. If you want to know the truth, I think you're stirring up all this turmoil because you're afraid of ever marrying again. The little world you've made is tidy and safe. But is this what Lenny would've wanted for you?" He gripped her firmly by the shoulders. "If Lenny were standing beside you right now and you could ask him about marrying me, what would he say?"

"I…don't understand."

"If you could seek Lenny's advice, what would he tell you? Would he say, 'Robin, look at this guy. He's in love with you. He thinks the world of Jeff, and he's ready to embark on a new life. This is an opportunity too good to pass up. Don't be a fool. Marry him.'?"

"That sounds like something my friend Angela would say."

"I'm going to like this friend of yours—just as long as she doesn't try to set you up with any more of her divorced cousins," Cole said, laughing. His eyes grew warm as he gazed at her, and she suspected he was longing to take her in his arms and kiss her doubts away. But he didn't. Instead, he looked over his shoulder and sighed. "I think I'll go see what Jeff's up to. I'll leave you to yourself for a few minutes. I don't mean to pressure you, but I do want you to think about what I said."

"You aren't pressuring me," she whispered, staring out over the water.

Cole left her then, and her hands clutched the steel railing as she raised her eyes to the sky. "Oh, Lenny," she whispered. "What should I do?"

Ten

"Cole wants me to ask your advice." Robin continued to look up at the cloudless blue sky. "Oh, Lenny, I honestly don't know what's right for Jeff and me anymore. I love Cole. I love you. But at the same time I can't help wondering about Cole's motives...."

Robin paused, waiting. Not that she expected an answer. Lenny couldn't give her one. He never did; he never would. But unlike the other times she'd spoken to him, she needed a response, even though expecting one was totally illogical.

With every breath she took, Robin knew that, but the futility of it hit her, anyway. Her frustration was so hard and unexpectedly powerful that it felt like a body blow. Robin closed her eyes, hoping the heat of the sun would take away this bitter ache, this dreadful loneliness.

She felt so empty. Hollow all the way through.

Her fists were clenched at her sides as tears fell from her eyes. Embarrassed, she glanced around, grateful that the film crew had attracted most of the sightseers. No one was around to witness her distress.

Anger, which for so many years had lain dormant inside her, gushed forth in an avalanche of grief and pain. The tears continued to spill down her cheeks. Her lips quivered. Her shoulders shook. Her hands trembled. It was as if the emotion was pounding against her chest and she was powerless to do anything but stand there and bear it.

Anger consumed her now. Consumed her because she hadn't allowed it to when Lenny was killed. It had been more important to put on a brave front. More important to hold herself together for Jeff and for Lenny's parents. More important to deal with the present than the past.

Lenny had died and Robin was furious with him for leaving her alone with a child to raise. Leaving her alone to deal with filing taxes and taking out the garbage and repairing leaking pipes. All these years she'd managed on her own. And she'd bottled the anger up inside, afraid of ever letting it go.

"Robin."

Cole's voice, soft and urgent, reached out from behind her. At the sound, she turned and walked into his arms, sobbing, needing his comfort and his love in equal measure. Needing him as she'd never needed anyone before.

She didn't know how long he held her. He was whispering soothing words to her. Gentle words. But she heard none of them over the sound of her own suffering.

Once she started crying, Robin couldn't seem to stop. It was as if a dam had burst inside her and the anguish, stored for too many years, came pouring out.

Cole's arms were securely wrapped around her, shielding her. She longed to control this outburst, longed to explain, but every time she tried to speak her sobbing only grew worse.

"Let it out," he whispered. "You don't have to say anything. I understand."

"He doesn't answer," she sobbed. "I asked him… Lenny never answers me…because he can't. He left me…"

"He didn't want to die," Cole told her.

"But he did…he did."

Cole didn't argue with her. He simply held her, stroking the back of her head as though reassuring a small child.

It took several minutes for Robin to compose herself enough to go on. "Part of me realizes that Lenny didn't want to leave me, didn't want to die. But he did and I'm so angry at him."

"That anger is what makes us human," Cole said. He continued to comfort her and, gradually, bit by bit, Robin felt her composure slip back into place.

She sensed Jeff's presence even before he spoke.

"What wrong with my mom?" he asked Cole.

"She's dealing with some emotional pain," Cole explained, speaking as one adult to another.

"Is she going to be all right?"

Robin hadn't wanted her son to see her crying and made a concerted effort to break away from Cole, to reassure Jeff herself. Cole loosened his hold, but kept his arm around her shoulders.

"I'm fine, Jeff. Really."

"She doesn't look so good."

Her son had developed the irritating habit of talking to Cole and not to her when she was upset. They'd done it that day her son had run away to the fort. Jeff and Cole had carried on an entire conversation about her while she was in their midst then, too.

Cole led her to a bench and they all sat down.

Jeff plopped down next to her and reached for her hand, patting it several times. Leaning toward Cole, he said earnestly, "Chocolate might help. One time Mom told me there wasn't anything in this world chocolate couldn't cure."

She'd actually said that? Robin started to smile. Wrapping her arms around her son, she hugged him close, loving him so much her heart seemed about to burst.

Jeff wasn't all that keen on being cuddled, especially in public, but although he squirmed he put up with his mother's sudden need to hold him.

When she'd finished, Jeff rolled his eyes and once more directed his comments to Cole. "She gets weird like this every once in a while. Remember what happened that day I ran away?"

"I remember," Cole said, and Robin smiled at the trace of amusement she heard in his voice.

"Will you stop excluding me from this conversation? I'm going to be all right. I just had this…urge to cry, but don't worry, it's passed."

"See what I mean?" Jeff muttered to Cole.

"But Jeff's right," Robin said, ignoring her son's comment. "Something chocolaty would definitely help."

"You'll be okay by yourself for a couple of minutes?" Cole asked.

"I'll be fine. I…don't know exactly what came over me, but I'm going to be just fine."

"I know you are." He kissed her, his lips gentle against her cheek.

The two of them left and once more Robin was alone. She didn't really understand why the pain and anger had hit her so hard now, after all this time. Except that it had something to do with Cole. But the last place she would ever have expected to give in to her grief was on Fisherman's Wharf with half of San Francisco looking on.

Jeff returned less than a minute later, running to her side

with a double-decker chocolate ice cream cone. "Cole's bringing two more for him and me," he explained. "I told the guy it was an emergency and he gave me this one right away."

"That was nice of you," Robin said, wondering what the vendor must have thought. Smiling, she ran her tongue over the ice cream, savoring the cold chocolate. As profoundly as she'd wept, she felt almost giddy with relief now, repressing the impulse to throw back her head and laugh.

Cole arrived, and with Jeff on her left and Cole on her right she sat on the concrete bench and ate her ice cream cone.

"I told you this would work," Jeff told Cole smugly.

"And to think I scoffed at your lucky baseball cap," she teased, feeling much better.

When they finished the cones, Cole gathered up their packages and led them back to where he'd parked his car.

Blackie was there to greet them the instant they returned to Orchard Street. Jeff ran into the backyard to play with the dog, and Cole walked Robin to her door. He accepted her offer of coffee.

"I'm probably going to be leaving soon for my property," he said, watching her closely. He sat down at the table, his hands cupping the mug as though to warm them. "Will you be all right?"

Robin nodded. She walked over and stood beside him and pressed a hand to his strong jaw. "I realize you delayed going up there today because of Jeff and his baseball game. We're both grateful."

Cole placed his hand over hers and harshly expelled his breath. "I feel responsible for what you went through there on the pier. I should never have said what I did. I'm sorry, Robin, it wasn't any of my business."

"You only said what I needed to hear."

He smiled. "If I did, it was because of what happened to me in Seattle. It's quite a coincidence that both of us would come to grips with our pain while standing on a pier—me in Seattle, you here in San Francisco. I went home with this incredible sense of release. For the first time since Bobby and Jennifer's deaths, I surrendered my grief. In a way it was as though I reached up and God reached down and together we came to an understanding."

That so completely described what Robin had been feeling that for a long moment she couldn't say anything. What Cole had said earlier about carrying the pain, dragging it everywhere, was right on the mark, too. He understood; he'd done the same thing himself. A surge of love swelled within her.

"I know you don't want to hear this," he was saying. "I honestly don't mean to pressure you. But once I returned from Seattle and realized I was falling in love with you I started thinking about having another baby." He hesitated and took a gulp of his coffee. Then he stood up abruptly, nearly knocking the chair backward. "I'd better go before I say or do something else I shouldn't."

Robin followed him into the entryway, not wanting him to leave, but not quite ready to give him what he needed.

He paused at the screen door and his eyes immediately found hers. He couldn't seem to keep himself from touching her, brushing an auburn curl from her cheek. His knuckles grazed her skin lightly, and Robin's eyes closed of their own accord at the sensation that shot through her. Her heart was full, and she seemed to have all the answers now— except to the one question that was the most important in her life. And Jeff's.

"I'll see you sometime next week," Cole said roughly,

pulling his hand away. Without another word, he walked out the door, pausing at the top of the porch steps.

He called for his dog and in response both Blackie and Jeff came running.

"You're not leaving, are you?" Jeff asked breathlessly.

"I'm taking Blackie for the rest of the weekend. You think you can get along without him till Monday, sport?"

Jeff shrugged and stuck his fingers in the hip pockets of his blue jeans. "I suppose. Where are you taking him?"

"To my property." Cole didn't turn toward Robin. It was as if he had to ignore her in order to walk away from her.

"Oh, yeah!" Jeff said enthusiastically. "I remember you said something about it once. You're building a house, aren't you?"

"Remodelling one. My grandfather lived there as a boy and he left it to me, only it's been a lot of years since anyone's cared for that old house properly and there's plenty of work that needs to be done."

"I'll work for you," Jeff piped up eagerly. He made a fist and flexed his arm, revealing the meager muscles. "I know it doesn't look like much, but I'm strong. Ask anyone."

Cole tested Jeff's muscles, pretending to be impressed. "Yes, I can tell you're strong, and I'm sure I couldn't ask for a harder worker." Jeff beamed until Cole added regretfully, "I'll take you up there another time, sport."

Jeff's face fell.

Before she even realized what she was doing, Robin moved onto the porch. "Cole."

He turned to face her, but the movement seemed reluctant.

Perhaps it was because she didn't want to be separated from him any more than he wanted to be away from her. Perhaps it was the thought of Jeff's disappointment when he'd already had so many other disappointments in his life. Perhaps it was this newborn sense of freedom she was just beginning to experience.

She stepped toward Cole. "Could Jeff and I go up to the property with you?"

Jeff didn't wait for Cole to answer before leaping excitedly into the air. "Hey, Mom, that's a great idea! Really great. Can we, Cole? Blackie and I can help you, and Mom can... Well, she can do things..."

"I'll have you both know I pound a mean hammer," Robin felt obliged to inform them. If she was going to Cole's farm, she fully intended to do her share.

Cole looked perplexed for a moment, as if he wasn't sure he'd heard her correctly. "I'd love to have you come—if you're sure that's what you want."

Robin just nodded. All she knew was that she couldn't bear to be separated from him any longer.

"Be warned—the house is only half done. The plumbing isn't in yet."

"We'll manage, won't we, Jeff?"

"Yeah," Jeff said eagerly. "Anyway, boys got it easy."

Cole laughed. "How long will it take you to pack?"

"We're ready now, aren't we, Blackie?" Jeff almost jitterbugged across the front lawn in his enthusiasm.

"Give me a few minutes to throw some things together," Robin said, grinning. Jeff was smiling, too, from ear to ear, as he dashed past her into the house and up the stairs.

Cole's eyes held Robin's in silent communication—until Jeff came bursting out of the house, dragging his sheets and quilt with him, straight from his bed.

"Jeff," she cried, aghast, "what are you doing?"

"I took everything off my bed. I can go without plumbing, but I need my sleep." He piled the bedding at their feet. "You two can go back to looking at each other. I'll get everything else we need."

"Jeff," Robin groaned, casting Cole an apologetic glance. "I'll pack my own things, thank you."

"You want me to get your sheets, too?" he called from inside the house.

"No." She scooped up the bedding and hurried into the house, taking the stairs two at a time. She discovered Jeff sitting on the edge of her bed, his expression pensive.

"What's wrong?"

"Are you ever going to marry Cole?" her son asked.

At the unexpectedness of the question, Robin's heart flew to her throat, then slid back into place. Briefly she wondered if Cole had brought up the subject with her son, but instinctively knew he hadn't. "Wh-what makes you ask that?"

He shrugged. "Lots of things. Every time I turn around you two are staring at each other. Either that or kissing. I try to pretend I don't notice, but it's getting as bad as some of those movies you like. And when you were crying on the pier, I saw something. Cole had his arms around you and he was looking real sad. Like...like he wished he could do the crying for you. It's the same look Grandpa sometimes gives Grandma when he figures out that she's upset, and she doesn't even have to talk. Do you know what I mean?"

"I think so," Robin said, casually walking over to her dresser drawer and taking out a couple of old sweatshirts. "And what would you think if I said I was considering marrying Cole?"

Robin expected shouts of glee and wild shrieks, but instead her son crossed his arms over his chest and moved his mouth in odd ways, stretching it to one side and then the other. "You're serious, aren't you?"

"Yes." She folded and refolded one of the sweatshirts, her heart pounding in anticipation. "It would mean a lot of changes for all of us."

"How many other people are involved in this?"

Robin hesitated, not understanding Jeff's concern. "What do you mean?"

"Will I get an extra set of grandparents in this deal?"

"Uh…probably. I haven't talked to Cole about that yet, but I assume so."

"That means extra gifts on my birthday and at Christmas. I say we should go for it."

"Jeffrey Leonard Masterson, you shock me!"

He shrugged. "That's how a kid thinks."

Robin shook her head in dismay at her son's suddenly materialistic attitude toward her possible marriage. She was still frowning as she stepped outside.

Cole was in his garage, loading up the trunk of his SUV when Robin joined him. She handed him one small suitcase and a bag of groceries she'd packed at the last minute.

Cole stowed them away, carefully avoiding her eyes. "I guess you said something to Jeff about us?" She could hear amusement in his voice.

"Yes. How'd you know?"

"He brought down a paper bag full of clothes and asked what kind of presents he could expect from my parents at Christmas. He also asked if there were any aunts or uncles in the deal." Robin's embarrassment must have showed, because Cole started chuckling.

"That boy's got a mercenary streak in him I knew nothing about," she muttered.

Cole was still grinning. "You ready?"

She nodded, drawing an unsteady breath, eager for this adventure to begin. Jeff and Blackie were already in the backseat when Robin slipped into the front to wait for Cole.

"Are we going to sing camp songs?" Jeff asked, leaning forward. He didn't wait for a response, but immediately launched into the timeless ditty about bottles of beer on the wall. He sang ninety-nine verses of that, then performed a series of other songs until they left the freeway and wound up on a narrow country road with almost no traffic.

Jeff had tired of singing by then. "Knock knock," he called out.

"Who's there?" Robin said, falling in with his game.

"Eisenhower."

"Eisenhower who?"

Jeff snickered. "Eisenhower late, how about you?" With that, the ten-year-old broke into belly-gripping guffaws, as if he should be receiving awards for his ability to tell jokes.

Cole's mouth was twitching and Robin had to admit she was amused, too.

"The turnoff for the ranch is about a mile up the road," Cole explained. "Now remember, this is going to be a lot like camping. It's still pretty primitive."

"You don't need to worry," Robin said, smiling at him.

A couple of minutes later, Cole slowed, about to turn down the long driveway. It was then that Robin saw the sign. Her heart jumped into her throat and her hands started to shake.

"Stop!" she screamed. "Stop!"

Cole slammed on the brakes, catapulting them forward. "Robin, what is it?"

Robin threw open the front door and leapt out of the car,

running to the middle of the road. She stared at the one word on the sign even as the tears filled her eyes.

Cole's farm was named *Paradise*.

Eleven

"Robin, I don't understand," Cole said for the third time, his dark eyes worried.

"I bet my allowance she's crying again," Jeff muttered, poking his head out the side window. "Something weird's going on with my mother. She's been acting goofy all day. Why do you think it is?"

"I'm not really sure," Cole said as he continued to study Robin.

For her part, Robin couldn't take her eyes off the sign. Jeff was right about her crying; the tears streamed unrestrained down her face. But these were tears of joy. Tears of gratitude. Tears of acknowledgment. It was exactly as Cole had described. She'd reached up and God had reached down and together they'd come to an understanding. She'd finally resolved her dilemma.

Unable to stop herself, Robin hurled her arms around Cole's neck. Her hands roamed his face. His wonderful, wonderful face.

Because her eyes were blurred with emotion, she couldn't accurately read Cole's expression, but it didn't matter. Her heart spilled over with love for him.

"Robin..."

She didn't let him finish, but began spreading a long series of kisses across his face, starting with his eyelids. "I love you, I love you," she repeated between kisses, moving from his cheek to his nose and downward.

Cole put his arms around her waist and pulled her closer. Robin was half-aware of the car door slamming and Jeff marching up the road to join them.

"Are you two getting all mushy on me again?"

Robin barely heard her son. Her mouth had unerringly found Cole's.

The unexpected sharp sound of a hand clap brought her out of her dream world. The kiss ended, and her eyes immediately went to Jeff, who was looking very much like a pint-size adult. His face and eyes were stern.

"Do the two of you know where you're standing?" Jeff demanded as though he'd recently been hired by the state police to make sure this type of thing didn't happen. "There are proper places to kiss, but the middle of the road isn't one of them."

"He's right," Cole said, his eyes devouring Robin. He clearly didn't want to release her and did so with a reluctance that tugged at her heart.

"Come with me," Jeff said, taking his mother by the hand and leading her back to the car. He paused in front of the door and frowned. "Maybe she has a fever."

"Robin," Cole said, grasping her hand, "can you explain now?"

She nodded. "It's the sign—Paradise. Tell me about it. Tell me why your grandfather named his place Paradise."

"I'm not sure," Cole said, puzzled. "He lived here his whole life and always said this land was all he'd ever needed. From what I remember, he once told me he thought of this place as the Garden of Eden. I can only assume that's why he named it Paradise."

Robin nodded, unsurprised by his explanation. "When Lenny and I were first married, we talked...we dreamed about someday buying some land and raising animals. Enough land for Jeff to have a pony and for me to have a huge garden. We decided this land would be our own piece of heaven on earth and...from that we came up with the idea of naming it Paradise."

Cole shook his head slowly, and she could tell he didn't completely understand.

"This afternoon, when I was standing on Fisherman's Wharf, you suggested I talk over my feelings about our getting married with Lenny."

"What I suggested," Cole reminded her, "was that you *imagine* what he'd say to advise you. I certainly didn't expect you to really communicate with him."

"I know this won't make any sense to you, but I've talked to Lenny lots of times over the years. This afternoon, what hit me so hard was the fact that Lenny would never answer me. That realization was what finally forced me to deal with the pain. To forgive Lenny for dying."

Jeff was looking at her in confusion, his mouth open and eyes wide.

"Here you were wanting to marry me and I didn't know what to do. I had trouble believing your proposal was prompted by anything more than the desire to replace the family you'd lost. I do love you, and I desperately wanted to believe you loved me—and Jeff. But I wasn't sure...."

"And you're sure now?"

She nodded enthusiastically. "Yes. With all my heart, I'm confident that marrying you would be the right thing for all of us."

"Of course we're going to marry Cole!" Jeff cried. "Good grief, all you had to do was ask me and I would've told you. We belong together."

"Yes, we do, don't we?" Robin whispered. "Cole," she said, taking both his hands with her own. "I'd consider it a very great honor to become your wife."

"Jeff?" Cole said, tearing his eyes away from Robin.

The boy's face shone and his eyes sparkled. "I'd consider it a very great honor to become your son."

Cole brushed his lips across Robin's and then reached for Jeff, hauling him into his arms and squeezing him tight. Blackie started barking then, wanting out of the car. Robin quickly moved to open the passenger door, and the black Lab leapt out. She crouched down and wrapped her arms around his thick neck, hugging him. "You're going to have a whole family now, Blackie," she said happily.

Two hours later, just at dusk, Robin was standing in the middle of the yard. She'd loved everything about Paradise, just as she'd known she would. The house and property were nothing like the place she and Lenny had dreamed about, but she hadn't expected them to be. The four-bedroom house was much larger than anything they'd ever hoped to own. The land was covered with Ponderosa pine, and the rocky ground was more suitable to grazing a few sheep or cattle than planting crops.

Cole was showing Jeff the barn, and Robin had intended to join them, but the evening was redolent with a sweet-smelling breeze and she'd stopped to breathe in the fresh cool air. She folded her arms and stood there, smiling into the clear sky. A multitude of twinkling stars were just beginning to reveal themselves.

Cole walked quietly up behind her, and slipped his arms

around her waist, pulling her against him. "Have I told you how much I love you?"

"In the last fifteen minutes? No, you haven't."

"Then allow me to correct that situation." He nibbled the back of her neck gently. "I love you to distraction."

"I love you, too."

He sighed then and whispered hoarsely, "It was a difficult decision to marry me, wasn't it?"

Robin agreed with a nod.

"Had I given you so many reasons to doubt me?"

"No," she said quickly, turning in his arms. She pressed her palms against his jaw. "I had to be sure in my heart that you weren't trying to replace the son you'd lost with Jeff. And I had to be equally certain you loved me for myself and not because I was Jeff's mother and we came as a package deal."

He shook his head decisively. "Jeff's a great kid, don't get me wrong, but there's never been any question in my mind about how I felt. The first time we met, you hit me square between the eyes. I didn't mean to fall in love again. I didn't even want to."

"I don't think I did, either," Robin confessed.

"Past experience taught us both that loving someone only causes pain. I loved Jennifer, but I could never make her happy. When we divorced I accepted my role in the breakup."

"But she had a drinking problem, Cole. You can't blame yourself."

"I don't, not entirely, but I accept a portion of the blame for what went wrong. It tore me apart to see Bobby caught in the middle, and in an effort to minimize the pain I didn't fight for custody. He was an innocent victim of the divorce, and I didn't want him to suffer any further distress. I was willing to do anything I could to spare him. Later, when I realized how serious Jennifer's problem with alcohol had become, I tried to obtain custody, but before I could get the courts to move on it, the accident happened. Afterward, I was left facing the guilt of having waited too long.

"The thought of ever marrying again, having children again, terrified me. I couldn't imagine making myself vulnerable a second time." He paused, and a slow, gentle smile spread across his face, smoothing away the tension. "All of that changed when I met you. It was as if life was offering me another chance. And I knew I had to grab hold of it with both hands or live with regret forever."

"Oh, brother," Jeff said as he dashed into the yard. "Are you two at it again?"

"We're talking," Robin explained.

"Your mouths are too close together for talking." He strolled past them, Blackie trotting at his side. "I don't suppose you thought about making me anything to eat, did you, Mom?"

"I made sandwiches."

"Great. Are there enough for Blackie to have one?"

"I think so. There's juice and some corn chips in the kitchen, too."

"Great," Jeff repeated, hurrying into the house.

"Are you hungry?" Robin asked Cole.

"Yes," he stated emphatically, "but my appetite doesn't seem to be for food. How long will you keep me waiting to make you my wife?"

"I'll have to call my parents and my brother so we can arrange everything. It's important to me that we have a church wedding. It doesn't have to be fancy, but I'd like to invite a handful of good friends and—"

"How long?"

"To make the arrangements? I'm not sure. Three, possibly four months to do it properly."

"One month," Cole said.

"What do you mean, one month?"

"I'm giving you exactly thirty days to arrange whatever you want, but that's as long as I'm willing to wait."

"Cole—"

He swept her into his arms then and his mouth claimed hers in a fury of desire. Robin found herself trembling and she clutched his shirt, her fingers bunching the material as she strove to regain her equilibrium.

"Cole..." She felt chilled and feverish at the same time. Needy, yet wealthy beyond her wildest dreams.

"One month?" he repeated.

"One month," she agreed, pressing her face against his broad warm chest. They'd both loved, profoundly, and lost what they'd valued most. For years, in their own ways, they'd sealed themselves off from others, because no one else could understand their pain. Then they'd discovered each other, and nothing would ever be the same again. Their love was the mature love that came when one had suffered and lost and been left to rebuild a shattered life. A love that was stronger than either could have hoped for.

"Do you see what I was telling you?" Jeff muttered to Blackie, sitting on the back porch steps. "I suppose we're going to have to put up with this for a while."

Blackie munched on a corn chip, apparently more interested in sharing Jeff's meal than listening to his comments.

"I can deal with it, if you can," Jeff continued. "I suspect I'll be getting at least one brother out of this deal, and if we're lucky maybe two. A sister would be all right, too, I guess—" he sighed deeply "—but I'll have to think about that. Girls can be a real headache, if you know what I mean."

The dog wagged his tail as Jeff slipped him another corn chip. "And you know what, Blackie? It's gonna be Father's Day soon. My very first. And I've already got a card picked out. It's got a picture of a father, a mother and a boy with a baseball cap. And there's a dog on it that looks just like you!"

* * * * *

SAME TIME, NEXT YEAR

Prologue

New Year's Eve—Las Vegas, Nevada

James had been warned. Ryan Kilpatrick, a longtime friend and fellow attorney, had advised him to stay clear of the downtown area tonight. The crowd that gathered on Fremont Street between Main and Las Vegas Boulevard was said to be close to twenty thousand.

But James couldn't resist. Although he had a perfectly good view of the festivities from his hotel room window, he found the enthusiasm of the crowd contagious. For reasons he didn't care to examine, he wanted to be part of all this craziness.

The noise on the street was earsplitting. Everyone seemed to be shouting at once. The fireworks display wasn't scheduled to begin for another thirty minutes, and James couldn't see how there was room for a single other person.

A large number of law-enforcement officers roamed the area, confiscating beer bottles and handing out paper cups. A series of discordant blasts from two-foot-long horns made James cringe. Many of the participants wore decorative hats handed out by the casinos and blew paper noisemakers that uncurled with each whistle.

James remained on the outskirts of the throng, silently enjoying himself despite the noise and confusion. If he were younger, he might have joined in the festivities.

Thirty-six wasn't old, he reminded himself, but he looked and felt closer to forty. Partners in prestigious law firms didn't wear dunce caps and blow noisemakers. He was too conservative—some might say stodgy—for such nonsense, but it was New Year's Eve and staying in his room alone held little appeal.

Impatient for the fireworks display, the crowd started chanting. James couldn't make out the words, but the message was easy enough to understand. It amused him that the New Year's celebration would be taking place three hours early in order to coordinate with the one in New York's Times Square. Apparently no one seemed to care about the time difference.

As if in response to the demand, a rocket shot into the air from the roof of the Plaza Hotel. The night sky brightened as a starburst exploded. The crowd cheered wildly.

Although he'd intended to stand on the sidelines, James found himself unwillingly thrust deeper and deeper into the crowd. Luckily he wasn't prone to claustrophobia. People crushed him from all sides. At another time, in another place, he might have objected, but the joy of the celebration overrode any real complaint.

It was then that he saw her.

She was struggling to move away from the crowd, with little success. James wasn't sure what had originally attracted his attention, but once he noticed her, he couldn't stop watching. Joyous shouts and cheers rose in the tightly packed crowd, but the young woman didn't share the excitement. She looked as if she'd rather be anywhere else in the world.

She was fragile, petite and delicate in build. He saw that she fought against the crowd but was trapped despite her best efforts.

James soon found himself gravitating in her direction. Within minutes she was pressed up against him, chin tucked into her neck as she tried to avoid eye contact.

"Excuse me," he said.

She glanced up at him and attempted a smile. "I was the one who bumped into you."

He was struck by how beautiful she was. Her soft brown hair curved gently at her shoulders, and he was sure he'd never seen eyes more dark or soulful. He was mesmerized by her eyes—and by the pain he read in their depths.

"Are you all right?" he felt obliged to ask.

She nodded and bit her lip. He realized how pale she was and wondered if she was about to faint.

"Let me help." He wasn't some knight who rescued damsels in distress. Life was filled with enough difficulties without taking on another person's troubles. Yet he couldn't resist helping her.

She answered him with a quick nod of her head.

"Let's get out of here," he suggested.

"I've been trying to do exactly that for the last twenty minutes." Her voice was tight.

James wasn't sure he could do any better, but he planned to try. Taking her by the hand, he slipped around a couple kissing passionately, then past a group of teens with dueling horns, the discordant sound piercing the night. Others appeared more concerned with catching the ashes raining down from the fireworks display than with where they stood.

Perhaps it was his age or the fact that he sounded authoritative, but James managed to maneuver them through the crush. Once they were off Fremont Street, the crowd thinned considerably.

James led her to a small park with a gazebo that afforded them some privacy. She sank onto the bench as if her legs had suddenly given out from under her. He saw that she was trembling and sat next to her, hoping his presence would offer her some solace.

The fireworks burst to life overhead.

"Thank you," she whispered. She stood, teetered, then abruptly sat back down.

"You want to talk about it?" he asked.

"Not really." Having said that, she promptly burst into tears. Covering her face with both hands, she gently rocked back and forth.

Not knowing what to do, James put his arms around her and held her against him. She felt warm and soft in his embrace.

"I feel like such a fool," she said between sobs. "How could I have been so stupid?"

"We're often blind to what we don't want to see."

"Yes, but… Oh, I should've known. I should've guessed there was someone else. Everything makes sense now… I couldn't have been any blinder."

He shrugged, murmuring something noncommittal.

She straightened, and James gave her his pressed handkerchief. She unfolded it, wiped away the tears and then clutched it in both hands.

"I'm sorry," she choked out.

"Talking might help," he said.

She took several moments to mull this over. "I found him with another woman," she finally said. "He wanted me to come to Vegas with him after Christmas, and I couldn't get time off from work. So I said he should go and have fun with his friends. Then...then I was able to leave early this afternoon. I wanted to surprise him on New Year's Eve and I drove straight here. I surprised him, all right."

And got the shock of her life, too, James mused.

"They were in bed together." Her words were barely audible, as if the pain was so intense she found it difficult to speak. "I ran away and he came after me and...and tried to explain. He's been seeing her for some time.... He didn't mean to fall in love with her, or so he claims." She laughed and hiccuped simultaneously.

"You were engaged?" he asked, noting the diamond on her left hand.

She nodded, and her gaze fell to her left hand. She suddenly jerked off the diamond ring and shoved it into her purse. "Brett seemed distant in the last few months, but we've both been busy with the holidays. I noticed he didn't seem too disappointed when I couldn't get time off from work. Now I know why."

It was preferable to learn about her fiancé's roving eye before she married him, but James didn't offer platitudes. He hadn't wanted to hear them himself.

"The problem is, I really love him." She shook almost uncontrollably. "I want to claw his eyes out, and yet I know I'll always love him."

"Are you hoping to patch things up?"

She raised her head. "No. It's over. I told him that and I meant it. I could never trust him again, but you know what?" She hesitated and drew in a deep breath. "I think he was grateful when I broke the engagement. He doesn't want me back—he wants *her*." She stiffened, as if bracing herself against an attack.

"It hurts right now, but it'll get better in time," James said, squeezing her hand.

"No, it won't," she whispered. "It'll never get better. I know it won't."

James partially agreed with her. Part of him would always belong to Christy Manning. Even now, he had trouble remembering her married name. She wasn't Christy Manning anymore, but Christy Franklin, and her husband was the sheriff of Custer County, Montana.

"Yes, it will, but it'll take a year," James said briskly.

"Not with me. I'll never get over Brett."

"You believe that right now, because the pain's so bad you can't imagine it'll ever go away, but it does, I promise you."

Slowly she turned to study him. "You know? It sounds as if you're talking from experience."

He nodded. "Five years ago the woman I loved broke off our engagement." He laughed derisively. "You see, there was a small problem. She married someone else while she was engaged to me."

"That's terrible," she said with a sigh of righteous indignation. "What kind of woman would do that?"

"It's not as bad as it sounds. You see, her parents are good friends of mine, and I realize now they pressured Christy into accepting my engagement ring. She was fond of me and agreed because she wanted to make her family happy. I don't think she ever realized how much I loved her."

"Do you still love her?"

It might have been a kindness to lie, but James found he couldn't. "Yes, but not in the same way."

"Despite what I know, I can't picture myself not loving Brett." She straightened and wiped the tears from her cheeks. "I suppose I should introduce myself since I've cried all over your shoulder. I'm Summer Lawton. From Anaheim."

"James Wilkens. Seattle."

They exchanged brief handshakes. Summer lowered her gaze. "I wish I could believe you."

"Believe me?"

"That it'll take a year to get over Brett. It doesn't seem possible. We've been dating for nearly five years and got engaged six months ago. My whole life revolved around him."

At one time James's life had revolved around Christy.

"We were apart for less than a week," Summer continued, "and I was so lonely, I practically went through contortions to get to Vegas just so we could be together tonight."

"The first three months are the most difficult," he told her, remembering the weeks after the breakup with Christy. "Keep busy. The worst thing to do is stay at home and mope, although that's exactly what you'll want to do."

"You don't understand," she insisted. "I really love Brett."

"I really love Christy."

"It's different for a man," she said.

"Is it really?" he countered. "A year," he reiterated. "It'll take a year, but by then you'll have worked through the pain."

Her look revealed her doubt.

"You don't believe me?"

"I just don't think it's possible. Not for me. You see, I'm not the type who falls in love at the drop of a hat. I gave everything I had to Brett. It's like my whole world caved in and there's nothing left to live for."

"Shall we test my theory?" he asked.

"How?"

"Meet me back here on New Year's Eve, one year from tonight."

"Here? In this gazebo?"

"That's right," he said. "Right here."

"Same time, same place, next year."

"Same time, same place, next year," he echoed.

One

Summer picked up the mail on the way into her apartment and shuffled through the usual bills and sales flyers. The envelope was there, just as it had been on the first of the month for the past eleven months. A letter from James.

He couldn't possibly have any idea how much she looked forward to hearing from him. The first letter had come shortly after they'd met on New Year's Eve and had been little more than a polite inquiry. She hadn't written him back mainly because she was embarrassed about spilling her heart out to a complete stranger.

His second letter had arrived February first. He told her about the weeks immediately after his breakup with Christy, how the pain had intensified when he'd expected it to lessen. His honesty and generosity touched her heart. It seemed uncanny that her anguish mirrored his so completely. She wrote back then, just a short note to tell him how she was doing, to thank him for writing.

That was how it had started. James would write at the beginning of every month and she'd answer. Gradually their letters grew in length, but were never any more frequent. She liked the formality of exchanging letters, preferring that to the quick and casual convenience of e-mail.

In the year since Summer had met James Wilkens, she'd been tempted to phone him only once. That was the day Brett got married. Ironically, his wife wasn't the girl he'd brought to Las Vegas, but someone he'd met recently. Summer had felt wretched and holed herself up in her apartment with a quart of gourmet ice cream and three rented movies. She'd made it through the day with a little fudge swirl and a lot of grit.

Holding James's letter in her hand, Summer tore open the envelope and started reading on her way into the apartment.

"That's from your lawyer friend, isn't it?" Julie, her roommate, asked. Wearing shorts and a halter top, Julie wandered barefoot through the apartment, munching on a carrot.

Summer nodded, kicked off her shoes and lowered herself onto a padded wicker chair. Her eyes never wavered from the page.

"He wants to remind me of our agreement," Summer said, pleased he hadn't forgotten.

"Agreement?"

"To meet him in Vegas on New Year's Eve."

"Are you going?"

Summer had always planned to follow through on her promise, although she probably should've thought twice about meeting a stranger. But he wasn't *really* a stranger. She felt she knew James, was comfortable with him. He was a friend, that was all, someone who'd been there when she needed him.

"Are you going?" Julie repeated.

Summer looked up and nodded.

"What's James like?" Julie asked, sitting across from her. The two of them had been close ever since high school and both of them were in the production at Disneyland. Summer had been especially grateful for Julie's unwavering friendship in the past year.

"He's older," Summer said, chewing the corner of her mouth as she tried to recall everything she could about him. "I'd guess he's at least forty. Kind of a stuffed shirt, to tell you the truth. He's about six feet tall and he must work out or something because I remember being surprised by how strong he was."

"Is he handsome?"

Summer had to smile. "You know, I don't actually remember."

"You don't *remember?*" Julie was incredulous. "I realize you were upset, but surely you noticed."

"He has very nice brown eyes and brown hair with some gray in it." She raised her hand to her own hair and wove a strand around her finger. "I'd say he's more distinguished-looking than handsome."

"Is there something romantic going on between the two of you?"

Summer did care for James, but not in the romantic sense. He'd helped her through the most difficult night of her life. Not only had she clung to him and cried on his shoulder, but he'd stayed with her until the early hours of the morning, listening to her pain, comforting and reassuring her.

"We have a lot in common," was all she'd say to Julie's question about a romance.

"I have a feeling about you and the mysterious James," Julie said, her forehead creased in a frown. "I think you're falling in love."

Love? Not Summer. She'd decided last New Year's Eve that she was finished with love. It sounded melodramatic and a bit ridiculous to be so confident that she'd never love again, but she'd come to that conclusion the minute she found Brett with his girlfriend. Her feelings hadn't changed in the past eleven months.

Although he'd never said as much, she was sure James felt the same way after losing Christy. It'd been six years, and from what she knew about him, there wasn't a woman in his life even now. There wouldn't be a man in hers, either.

This didn't mean that Summer never intended to date again. She'd started going out with other men almost immediately. Pride had prompted her actions in the beginning. Later, she wanted to be able to write James and tell him she was back in the swing of things. He'd applauded her efforts and recounted his own endeavors in that area after Christy had broken off the engagement. As she read his account of various disastrous dates, she'd laughed, truly laughed, for the first time in months.

"You're going to meet James on New Year's Eve, and everything will change," Julie said with a knowing smile.

"What do you mean, everything will change?"

"You won't see him as just a friend anymore," Julie predicted. "You might be surprised to discover there's more to him than you suspect."

"Julie, I told you he's got to be forty years old."

"You're sure of this?"

"No," she said reluctantly. "But... I don't know. I picture James sitting in front of a fireplace, smoking a pipe, with his faithful dog sprawled at his side."

"A basset hound, no doubt."

"No doubt," Summer agreed with a laugh. James was wonderful—no argument about that—but she could never see herself falling for him. Nor would he be interested in someone like her. The man was a distinguished attorney, while she starred in a musical version of *Beauty and the Beast* at Disneyland. Working in the theater wasn't an easy way to make a living, but Summer loved the challenge and the excitement.

"You might be surprised," Julie said again. The tone of her voice suggested that great things were going to happen for her friend this New Year's Eve.

New Year's Eve

Summer freely admitted she was nervous about the rendezvous with James. She got to the gazebo nearly fifteen minutes early and was astonished to find him already there. He was sitting on the bench, the one they'd shared a year earlier. In that moment Summer had a chance to study him with fresh eyes.

The first thing that struck her was that Julie was right. He was nothing like she remembered. Dignified and proper to the very back of his teeth, but there was something compelling about him. She recalled how Julie had wanted to know if James was handsome. If Summer were to answer that question now, she'd give an unequivocal *yes*. But he wasn't handsome in a Hollywood sense. He certainly wasn't boyishly good-looking like Brett, with his sun-streaked blond hair. But James Wilkens was appealing in a way that spoke directly to her heart. She knew from his letters that this was a man of conscience, a man of integrity, a man of honor. All at once Summer felt as if the oxygen had flown from her lungs.

He saw her then and slowly stood. "Summer?" He sounded equally surprised. His eyes widened briefly.

"Hello, James. I'm early," she said, feeling guilty at being caught staring so blatantly. "I'm always early…it's a family trait."

"I am, too." He grinned. "Usually early, I mean."

Summer had been looking forward to this evening for weeks. There was so much she wanted to say, so much she had to tell him. All at once she couldn't think of a single thing. "The streets are crazy," she said in a hurried effort to make conversation. "I didn't want to risk being late."

"Me, neither," he said. "I hope you don't mind, but I made dinner reservations."

"Thank you." She stepped into the gazebo and sat down next to him.

"So," he said, as if he wasn't sure where to start. "How are you?"

Summer laughed lightly. "A lot better than I was last year at this time. I told you Brett got married, didn't I?"

"You wrote about it."

Summer rarely felt shy, but she did now. She owed James more than she could possibly repay. "Your letters were a godsend," she said, "especially during the first few months. I don't know what I would've done without you."

"You would've done just fine." How confident he sounded, as if there was never a doubt that she'd get over her fiancé's betrayal.

"The first of every month, I'd run to the mailbox. Your letters were regular as clockwork and I counted on them." It had become a ritual for her, an important part of her recovery.

"I enjoyed your letters, too," he said. Fireworks splashed across the night sky, momentarily diverting their attention. "Do you want to join in the festivities?" he asked.

Summer shook her head. "Do you mind?"

He smiled. "Actually I'm just as glad. The crowd got to be a bit much last year."

"I'm so glad you were there," Summer said fervently. "You were like a guardian angel. You helped me so much that night."

"You helped me, too."

"Me? How?" Summer could hardly believe that.

"It's true," James assured her. "Seeing your pain reminded me how far I'd come in the years since losing Christy."

"Was it worse knowing she'd married that sheriff?" Summer asked tentatively. For her, learning about Brett's wedding hurt the most. Friends, under the guise of being kind, were more than happy to relate the details and what they knew about his bride. Every piece of information had cut like a knife.

"Yes."

"Weren't you angry?" she asked. How anyone could treat James in such a shabby manner was beyond her. To be engaged to a man as wonderful as James and then to secretly marry someone else was the most underhanded thing Summer had ever heard of.

"I wasn't angry at first, so much as depressed," he said thoughtfully. "Anger came later. It's the reason I took up squash. I worked out my aggression on the court. It helped."

Summer figured that was a sport an attorney would enjoy.

"It must've been hard finding out Brett was married."

She lowered her gaze and nodded. "Other than the first few weeks after he broke our engagement, the day of his wedding was the worst. It seemed so completely unfair that he should be happy while I was hurting so terribly. If it was ever in me to hate him, it would've been then."

"And now?"

"Now," she repeated. "I certainly don't hate Brett, but I don't love him like I did a year ago. He was a big part of my life, and for a long time my world felt empty without him."

"Does it feel empty now?"

"Not in the least. I'm happy, James, and I didn't believe that would ever be possible."

"Then I was right. It took you a year."

She laughed. "I'm over him and happy to be with you tonight."

"There isn't anyone I'd rather be with on New Year's Eve." He glanced at his watch and stood. "I hope you haven't eaten."

"I didn't. I only arrived a little over an hour ago, and I'm starved." She'd been anxious about their meeting, so her appetite had been nil all day. Her stomach wanted to make up for lost time now.

James led her into the Four Queens Hotel, weaving through the crowds gathered around slot machines and gaming tables. With several thousand people milling around outside, she'd assumed the casinos would be less crowded, but she was wrong.

James took her hand then, gripping it firmly in his own. Summer was surprised by how good that felt. By the time they walked down the stairs to Hugo's Cellar, an elegant, romantically lit restaurant, Summer felt as if she'd survived a riot. So much for all the effort she'd taken with her appearance. She thought she was fortunate to be in one piece.

After a five-minute wait, they were escorted to a booth and presented with elaborate menus. Candles flickered gently, casting dancing shadows on the walls. The noise and bustle upstairs and on the street outside the casino were blessedly absent.

They dined in leisure, shared a bottle of white wine and a calorie-rich dessert. They had so much to talk about—books, movies, world events, their families and more. James asked about her job at Disneyland and seemed genuinely interested in her budding career as an actress.

When she learned he'd recently been appointed a superior court judge to the King County bench, she insisted on ordering champagne to celebrate.

"You should've told me sooner," she said. "It's such wonderful news—so well-deserved."

"It's just temporary," James explained, looking uncomfortable. "I've been appointed to serve out the term of Judge Killmar, who had to retire for medical reasons."

Summer wasn't sure he would've told her if she hadn't asked him about his own hopes and dreams. Only then did he mention it was one of his lifetime goals to serve as a superior court judge.

"You intend on running for the position yourself, don't you?"

"Yes," he said. "But the primary isn't until September, and the election's in November. There're no guarantees."

"You'll win," Summer told him with supreme confidence. Wagging her finger at him, she added, "And don't give me that look. I can't imagine anyone *not* voting for you."

James's eyes met hers. "You're good for my ego," he said. She thought she heard him mutter "too good" under his breath but decided to ignore that.

By the time they'd finished dinner, it was close to twelve. As they made their way out of the casino, someone handed Summer a foil crown and a noisemaker. She donned the hat and handed James the whistle.

The New Year was fast approaching, which meant that

her night with James was nearly over. She didn't want it to be.

The crowds had thinned out considerably after the fireworks display. They were standing on the sidewalk outside the Golden Nugget casino when a cheer rose from inside.

"It must be midnight," James commented and ceremoniously blew the noisemaker. "Happy New Year, Summer," he said in a voice so low it was almost a whisper.

"Happy New Year, James."

They stood facing each other, and then, as if this were the moment they'd anticipated all evening, slowly moved toward each other. Summer saw how James's eyes darkened as her own fluttered closed. She wanted this. Needed it.

She sighed audibly as his mouth settled over hers.

Two

Summer was no novice when it came to kissing, but James left her breathless and clinging to him for support. She hadn't expected anything like this. She'd expected them to lightly brush lips and then laugh and wish each other a happy New Year.

It hadn't happened like that.

The instant James's mouth was on hers, she'd gone languid. She was immobile, her arms locked around his neck and her body pressed intimately to his, her lips seeking more.

Summer would've liked James to kiss her again. And again. She didn't want it to end. But she didn't know how to ask him to continue.

Slowly, with what she thought might be reluctance, he released her. She stood there looking at him, arms dangling stiffly at her sides while her face reddened with embarrassment. She considered telling him she wasn't usually this blatant.

"Happy New Year," James said. He didn't sound like himself at all. He cleared his throat and swallowed visibly.

"Happy New Year," she whispered, and stepped away from him.

James reached for her hand and held it in his own. Summer was grateful for his touch. They started walking, with no destination in mind, or none that Summer was aware of. She looked at James, wondering if he felt as confused and uncertain as she did. Apparently he did, because he grew quiet and introspective.

"I believe I'll call it a night," he announced unexpectedly. He checked his watch and frowned. Summer suspected it had been a year since he'd last stayed up past midnight. He was so proper, so serious and sober. Yet she'd enjoyed every minute of her evening with him. They'd talked and laughed, or at least she'd laughed. James had smiled, and she had the impression he didn't do that often, either. Every time he'd grinned, Summer had felt rewarded.

Now she'd ruined everything. She couldn't bear to know what he thought of her. An apology, words of explanation, stumbled over themselves, but she couldn't make herself say them—because she *wasn't* sorry about their kiss. She'd savored it, relished it, and hoped he had, as well.

"I'll call it a night, too," Summer said. She waited, hoping he'd suggest they meet the following day. He didn't.

By the time they returned to the Four Queens, where they were both booked for the week, Summer was miserable.

"James," she said as they walked across the lobby. Either she apologized now or regretted saying nothing. "I'm sorry. I...don't know what came over me. I don't generally... I can only guess what you must think of me and..."

"You?" He hesitated in front of the elevator. "I was wondering what you thought of *me*. I can only beg your indulgence."

The security guard asked to see their room keys before calling for the elevator. James easily produced his while Summer sifted through the contents of her oversize purse before finding hers.

The elevator arrived, and they both entered. There was no one else inside. Still, James didn't ask to see her again, and Summer's heart grew heavier as they ascended. Her room was on the tenth floor, and his was on the fifteenth.

The silence closed in on them. When the elevator stopped at her floor, the doors slid open, and James moved aside.

Summer glanced at him expectantly. Okay, so he didn't intend to see her again. It made sense, she supposed. A superior court judge wouldn't be interested in dating an actress.

"Good night," she said brightly as she walked out of the elevator.

"Good night, Summer," James said softly.

She hesitated, hoping he'd ask her at the last minute, but he didn't. Discouraged, Summer trudged to her room, unlocked the door and went in. She sat on the edge of her bed, trying to sort out her muddled thoughts.

When Summer had requested a week's vacation, she hadn't planned to spend every available second with James. She knew he'd taken the same length of time, and he'd probably been thinking the same thing.

She slipped off her shoes and wiggled her toes in the thick carpet. If it wasn't so late, she'd call Julie and tell her friend she was right. One evening with James, and she saw him in a completely different light. The moment she'd seen him in the gazebo that evening, she dismissed the father-figure image she'd had in her mind all these months. More than anything, that kiss convinced her James was more than a friend. What became of their relationship would depend on several factors, the most important of which was James himself.

The phone on the nightstand rang, and Summer groped for it. "Hello?"

"Summer, I'm sorry to bother you."

Her heart gave a sigh of relief. "Hello, James."

"I've got a rental car," he said. "I know it might not be something you'd consider fun, but I thought I'd drive over to Hoover Dam in the morning. Would you care to join me?"

"Why wouldn't I consider that fun?" she asked.

"I'm sure there are friends here your own age you'd prefer to spend time with and—"

"Friends? I thought you were my friend."

"Yes, but I was thinking of friends closer to your own age."

His answer irritated her. "I'm not exactly sure what you're insinuating, but if it is what I think it is, you're wrong, James."

"Listen, Summer, all I want to know is if you'd like to join me in the morning."

That might have been his original question, but she wasn't finished with what she had to say. "I took a week's vacation, and I know you have several days. I don't expect you to entertain me, if that's what you're worried about, because I can find plenty to do on my own."

"I see."

"And yes, there are any number of people my age in Vegas. There would be in any city. If you want my company, fine, but if you'd rather not see me again, I can accept that, too." Not easily, but she'd do it and have a perfectly good week without him.

He was strangely silent.

"James? Are you still there?"

"Yes. Are you always this direct?"

"No, but I didn't want there to be any misunderstanding between us. I value your friendship, and I don't want it ruined because of something silly."

"Nor do I." A short pause followed. "Forgive me for being dense, but I'm not sure I understood your answer. Are you going to Hoover Dam with me or not?"

Summer had waited all evening for this kind of invitation, and now the words were almost anticlimactic. "Would you like me to come?"

"Attorneys do this all the time, you know," he said with a chuckle.

"Do what?"

"Answer a question with one of their own. Yes, Summer, I'd very much enjoy your company."

"Great. When do you want to leave in the morning?"

James told her, and they set a time to meet in the lobby. Summer replaced the receiver and lay back on the bed. She smiled to herself, eager for morning.

James hadn't thought of himself as all that old, since at thirty-seven he was the youngest superior court judge in Washington State. Being with Summer, however, made him feel downright ancient.

She was perfectly named. Being with her was like walking along Green Lake in the middle of August, when the air carried the scent of blooming flowers and sunshine warmed the afternoon. She shone with a summery brightness that made him feel content. More than content. Happy.

James couldn't remember any time he'd smiled more than during their dinner together. She'd told him about playing her role at Disneyland. Her joy and enthusiasm for her job bubbled over like champagne. He could have listened to her all night.

She certainly hadn't done all the talking, however, and to his surprise he'd found himself telling her about the ins and outs of his own position with the court and the upcoming election, which was vital to his career.

His life was very different from hers. While Summer worked in the delightful world of fantasy, he struggled with the often cruel, unjust world of reality.

Naturally he couldn't give her any details about the cases he'd heard, but just talking about his short time on the bench had lifted his spirits considerably. It felt good to share his thoughts with her and he'd enjoyed her opinions and her sometimes unpredictable views.

Then they'd kissed. Talk about sexual chemistry! For the life of him, James couldn't explain what had happened when she'd slipped into his arms. He'd never intended the kiss to become that intense, but once he'd started, nothing could have stopped him.

He'd been afraid his reaction had shocked Summer, but apparently that wasn't the case. Later she'd apologized to him and James hadn't known what to say. She seemed to think she'd done something wrong. She hadn't. The truth was, she'd done everything right.

The next morning James sat down in the lobby to wait for Summer. He was excited about this outing. He'd decided earlier not to invite her, feeling it would be unfair to dominate her time. She was young and beautiful, and he doubted she wanted to spend her vacation with a staid older guy like him.

He'd gone to his hotel room and congratulated himself on not mentioning the trip to Hoover Dam. Ten minutes later he'd talked himself into calling her on the off chance she might be interested.

Well, she'd told him. A smile pulled at the edges of his mouth. Summer had seemed downright angry when he suggested she'd prefer to be with friends her own age.

James liked the idea of being her friend. The operative word being *friend*. He wasn't going to kiss her again—that was for sure.

First, he was afraid of a repeat performance of that kiss in the street. Secondly, he was way too old for her. He enjoyed her company tremendously, but then any man would. He wasn't going to ruin the bond they'd created; becoming romantically involved, if she even wanted to, would do exactly that.

Summer stepped off the elevator, and James watched as every eye in the place seemed to gravitate toward her. She was stunning. It wasn't the clothes she wore, although the pretty pink pants and matching sweater flattered her. It was Summer herself.

She searched the lobby until she saw him, and then she smiled. James felt as though the sun was beaming directly down on him.

He stood and waited for her to join him. "Did you have breakfast?" he asked.

She nodded. "Hours ago."

"Me, too."

"If you're ready, we can be on our way." All he had to do now was stop staring at her....

A few minutes later, the valet took his ticket for his rental car, and they waited for him to drive the luxury sedan to the back of the hotel. When the car arrived, the young man opened the car door and helped Summer inside. James was almost jealous to have been denied the privilege.

They drove out of Las Vegas in companionable silence. James had studied the map so he knew which freeway to take.

"Do you ever think about her?" Summer asked.

James had no idea what she was talking about. "Who?"

She laughed. "That's answer enough. Christy. Your ex-fiancée."

"Ah yes, Christy." James mulled over Summer's question. "Sometimes. Generally when I'm feeling especially lonely or when I see a couple with kids. That's when I wonder what Christy's and my children would have looked like.

"Do you still think about Brett?" he asked.

She lifted one shoulder in a halfhearted shrug. "Sometimes. It's different with me, though."

"Different?"

"From what you told me about Christy, she went to Montana to help her sister and met someone there."

"She would've broken the engagement right away, but it seemed like a heartless thing to do over the phone." Despite everything James felt a need to defend her. "When she did get back, her mother had arranged for a huge engagement party and I was extremely busy with an important lawsuit. I never blamed Christy for not telling me about Cody right away. She had her reasons."

"*I* blame her," Summer said stiffly. "It was a rotten thing to do."

"You blame Brett, too, don't you?" This was what their conversation was really about, James suspected. Something had happened recently that had hurt her all over again.

"Right before I left," she said in a small voice, "a friend called to tell me Brett and his wife are expecting a baby."

"A friend?" James wondered about that. There seemed

to be a certain type of person who delighted in being the first to deliver bad news.

"I'm going to be twenty-eight next month," she told him.

He smiled. "From the way you said that, one would think you're ready to apply for your retirement benefits."

Summer smiled back. "I suppose I sound ridiculous."

"No, you sound hurt. It's only natural, but that pain will fade in time, as well, especially if you meet someone else and get involved in another relationship."

"You didn't."

James couldn't argue. "It wasn't because I'd dedicated myself to loving Christy for the rest of my life. To be fair, I'm not sure why I never got involved again. It's not like I made the decision not to."

"Do you date?"

"Occasionally." A few months ago, two women had let him know that they'd welcome his attentions. James was flattered and he did enjoy a night out now and then, but he could never seem to dredge up much enthusiasm for either woman.

"What about you?" he asked, then mentally kicked himself. The answer was obvious. Someone like Summer had a long line of men waiting to ask her out.

"I don't date all that often," Summer surprised him by saying. "It's funny, when Brett and I first broke up I saw a different man every night. Within a month I was sick of it, sick of pretending I didn't care, sick of telling everyone about all the fun I was having."

"And now?"

"I haven't been out all month. December is crazy, anyway, with Christmas and family obligations and everything else. In November, I went to a dinner party with a member of the cast, but it was as friends, and it was more a favor to Steve than anything."

Silly as it seemed, James was offended that she didn't count their dinner the night before as a date. He certainly had. Their time together had been the highlight of the year for him.

"My parents want me married," she murmured thoughtfully. "They hinted at it over Christmas."

Now, that was something James could identify with. "My father's a longtime widower and I don't have any siblings. He's been hounding me for years to marry, but his real interest lies in grandchildren."

"I'm not willing to marry just anyone," she insisted.

"I feel the same way."

They glanced at each other and then immediately looked away. Silence again filled the car. James didn't know what Summer was thinking, but he knew where his thoughts were taking him and it spelled trouble.

As they neared the outskirts of Boulder City, James mentioned some of the local facts he'd read. "This is the only city in Nevada that doesn't allow gambling."

"Why?"

"It was built for the men who worked on the construction of the dam. I'd guess it has something to do with making sure the workers wouldn't squander their hard-earned cash on the gaming tables. If that happened, their families would see none of it."

"I wonder if it helped," Summer mused aloud.

The next hour and a half was spent driving over Hoover Dam. They didn't take the tour. The day was windy, and James was afraid Summer's sweater wouldn't be enough protection against the cold.

Once they were back on the Nevada side, they stopped long enough for pictures. James felt the wind as he took several scenic photos of the dam with the digital camera he'd bought last year.

Far more of his shots were aimed at Summer. She was a natural ham and struck a variety of poses for him. He wanted a keepsake of his time with her.

James asked another tourist to get a picture of the two of them together. He placed his arm around her shoulder and smiled into the camera.

"Can you send them to me?" she asked, rubbing her arms in an effort to warm herself.

"Of course," James agreed, pleased that she'd asked.

He turned up the heater when they returned to the car. He noticed that Summer's eyes were drooping about ten miles outside Boulder City. He located a classical-music station on the radio, and the soft strains of Mozart lulled her to sleep.

She woke when they were on the Las Vegas freeway. Startled, she sat up and looked around. "Wow, I must be stimulating company," she said, and smiled.

"I'm accustomed to quiet. Don't worry about it."

"James," she began, then yawned, covering her mouth. "What do you think of women who ask men out on dates?"

"What do I think?" He repeated her question, never having given the subject much thought. "Well, it seems fine in theory but I can't really say since it's never happened to me."

"Do you view them as aggressive?"

"Not necessarily. I know women invite men out all the time these days."

She smiled, and her eyes fairly danced with excitement.

"I'm glad to hear you say so, because I bought two tickets to a magic show. It's this evening at one of the other downtown hotels. I'd enjoy it very much if you went with me."

James had walked into that one with his eyes wide-open. "A magic show," he murmured with pleasure. He hadn't even dropped her off at the hotel yet and already he was looking for an excuse to see her again.

"It's the late show, as it happens, which doesn't start until eleven. You'll come with me, won't you?"

"Of course," he said. If he wasn't driving, James would have pumped his fist in the air.

Although she'd spent nearly the entire day with James, including lunch and a light dinner on the road, Summer counted the hours until they met for the magic show. She was dressing when the phone rang.

"Hello," she said, thinking it could only be James. Her heart began to beat faster.

"Summer, it's Julie."

"Julie!" Summer had tried to call her friend earlier that evening, but she hadn't answered either her cell or the apartment phone. "Happy New Year!"

"Same to you. How's it going with the distinguished attorney?"

Summer sank onto the edge of the bed. "Really well. By the way, he's a superior court judge now."

"Wow. That's great. So you're getting along well," her friend echoed in knowing tones. "Do you still see him as a father figure?"

"No way," Summer said, and laughed. "There's less than ten years between us."

"So." Her friend's voice fell. "Tell me what's been happening."

"Well." Summer wasn't sure where to start, then decided to plunge right in. "He kissed me last night, and Julie, it was incredible. I don't ever remember feeling like this in my life."

"So you'd say there's electricity between you?"

That was putting it mildly. Hoover Dam should produce that much electricity. "You could put it that way."

"This is just great!"

"We went to see Hoover Dam this morning, and tonight we're going to a magic show."

"This sounds promising."

That was how it felt to Summer, as well. "James invited me to drive to Red Rock Canyon with him tomorrow to feed the burros."

"Are you?"

"Of course." It had never occurred to Summer to refuse. She didn't care if he asked her to study goat dung; she would gladly have gone along just to be with him.

"Julie…"

"Yeah?"

"Would you laugh at me if I told you I'm falling in love with this guy?"

"Nope. I've seen it coming for months. You pored over his letters, and for days after you got one, it was James this and James that. I'm not the least bit surprised. This guy must really be something."

Summer's heart sank as she confronted the facts. "He's a judge, Julie. A superior court judge. I'm an actress. We're too different. I live in Anaheim and he's in Seattle. Oh, it's fine here in Vegas, but once we leave, everything will go back to the way it was before."

"You don't want that?"

"No," Summer admitted after some hesitation.

"Then you need to ask yourself exactly what it is you *do* want," Julie said.

Her roommate's words rang in her mind all through the magician's performance. Summer sat beside James and was far more aware of him than the talented performer onstage. There was magic in the air, all right. It sizzled and sparked, but it didn't have a thing to do with what was happening onstage.

After the show, James escorted her to his car, which was parked in a lot outside the casino.

"You've been quiet this evening," James commented.

"I talked to my roommate earlier," she told him when he slid into the driver's seat.

"Does it have something to do with Brett?"

"No," she said, shaking her head for emphasis. When James inserted the key to start the car, she placed her hand on his forearm to stop him. "James," she said softly, "I know this is an unusual request, and I'm sorry if it embarrasses you, but would you mind kissing me again?"

He didn't look at her. "I don't think it's a good idea."

"Why not?"

"Considering what happened the first time, it seems unnecessarily risky."

"I see," she murmured, disappointed.

"Summer, listen," he said impatiently. "You're beautiful and very sweet, but I'm too old for you."

"If you're looking for an excuse, James, you're going to

need something better than that." This was the second time he'd brought up their age difference, and it made her mad. "Forget I asked," she said heatedly. "It was a stupid idea."

"That's exactly what I said." He turned the ignition switch, and the engine fired to life.

"You're probably going to tell me you didn't feel anything. Go ahead and lie, but we both know that's exactly what it is—a lie."

James expelled a labored sigh. "I didn't say anything of the sort."

"Then you're afraid."

Summer noticed the way his hands tightened around the steering wheel.

"I prefer to think of myself as cautious."

"Naturally," she mumbled.

What surprised Summer was how much his rejection hurt. No doubt James viewed her as immature and naive. Pushy, as well. She was probably the first woman who'd ever asked him out and the only one who'd sought a kiss.

Shame burned in her cheeks. The sooner they were back at the hotel and she could escape, the better.

The engine revved, but they weren't going anywhere. In fact, James had pulled the car onto the side of the road.

"You might as well know," he muttered, turning off the car. "I've had one hell of a time keeping my hands off you as it is. It doesn't help that you're asking me to kiss you again."

Having said that, he drew her into his arms. His lips were hungry and hard, his kiss long and deep. He broke it off abruptly.

"There," he whispered. "Satisfied now?"

"No," she whispered back, and directed his mouth back to hers.

This time the kiss was slow and sweet. Her mouth nibbled his, and she was completely and utterly amazed by how good it was.

"Summer," he said, "we're going to have to stop."

"Why?" she asked, and her tongue outlined his lips.

James groaned, and she experienced an intense sense of power.

"I don't have a lot of control when it comes to you," he admitted.

"I don't mind."

"I wish you hadn't said that." He kissed her again, deeply, and when the kiss ended, she was clinging to James, mindless of anything but what was happening between them.

James rested his forehead against hers, his breathing uneven. After he'd regained some control, he locked his arms around her and drew her close. For the longest time all he did was hold her.

It felt like heaven to be in James's arms. Summer felt cherished, protected...*loved*.

"I was afraid of something like this," he said quietly.

"Something like what?"

He groaned. "Think about it, would you?"

"I *am* thinking about it. I don't understand the problem. I like it when you kiss me and touch me. I assumed you liked it, too."

"I do," he said. "That's the problem."

"If you say you're too old for me, I won't be held responsible for my actions."

He chuckled at that. "All right," he said, brushing the hair away from her face. "I'm not too old for you in years, but in attitude."

"Well, that's easy enough to change. We'll start first thing in the morning."

"Start what?" he asked, clearly confused.

She kissed him, letting her lips play over his. "You'll see."

Three

James was waiting in the lobby early the following morning. Summer's face broke into a disgruntled look when she saw him. Hands braced on her hips, shaking her head, she walked around him.

"What?" he asked, thinking he might have left part of his shirttail out.

"Where did you say we were going?" she asked.

"Red Rock Canyon."

"Do you always wear a shirt and tie to feed wild burros?"

James wore a shirt and tie to everything. "Yes," he answered.

"That's what I thought. Then I'd like to suggest we stop at a mall first."

"A mall? Whatever for?"

She looked at him as if she questioned his intelligence. "I'm taking you shopping," she announced. "If you have any objections, you'd better voice them now."

"Shopping," James repeated slowly. That was probably his least favorite thing to do. He avoided malls whenever possible. "But why?" he asked innocently. He wasn't giving in without a fight.

"Clothes," she informed him, then added in case he hadn't figured it out, "for you."

He frowned.

"You don't have to do this," Summer said. "I think you look wonderful in a suit and tie, but you'd be far more comfortable in jeans and a T-shirt."

So this was what she meant about altering his attitude. She hadn't mentioned that it involved torturing him by dragging him in and out of stores.

"James?" She gazed up at him with wide eyes. "Are we going to the mall or not?"

It was on the tip of his tongue to tell her he felt perfectly relaxed in what he was wearing. He would've said it, too, if she hadn't blinked just then and her long, silky lashes fanned her cheek. Without much effort this woman was going to wrap him around her little finger. James could see it coming, but he lacked the strength to offer even token resistance.

"How long will it take?" he asked, and glanced at his watch, trying to give the impression that the burros only made their appearance at certain times. They did, but not in the way he was hoping to imply. The minute they suspected visitors had something edible, they appeared.

"We won't be more than an hour," she promised. "Two at most."

He was being fed a line, and he knew it. They'd be lucky to make Red Rock Canyon before nightfall.

"All right," he said with a sigh, wondering how a mature, reasonable male would allow a woman he'd barely met to dictate his wardrobe.

A relationship between them was unrealistic for so many reasons. The age factor, for one. And then she lived and worked in southern California, while his life was in Seattle.

He didn't know much about acting, but it seemed to him that if she was serious about her career, California was the place to be. Long-distance relationships rarely survived.

"You won't regret this," she said with a smile.

She was wrong. James already regretted it.

The only shopping mall he knew of in Vegas was the one located on the Strip between two of the largest casino hotels. He drove there and pulled into the underground parking.

When he turned off the ignition, Summer leaned over and kissed him.

"What was that for?" he asked, although he realized he should be counting his blessings instead of questioning them.

"To thank you for being such a good sport."

Little did she know.

To his surprise, Summer stuck to her word. It took less than two hours for her to locate everything she felt he needed. James followed her around like a dutiful child—and discovered he was actually enjoying himself. He let her choose for him, and she did well, generally picking styles he might have picked himself.

"I feel like I squeak when I walk," he said as he led the way back into the underground garage. Almost everything he had on was new. Right down to the running shoes and socks. He'd changed in a washroom at the mall.

"You look twenty years younger," Summer told him.

"In which case, you could be accused of cradle-robbing."

She laughed and slipped her arm through his. She pressed her head against his shoulder, and James derived a good deal of pleasure from having her so close. He was still trying to figure out how he was going to keep his hands off her.

"Sometimes it feels like I've known you forever," she whispered.

James felt the same way. It was as if she'd been part of his life for a very long time. "I have the feeling I'm going to have a huge long-distance phone bill once I get back to Seattle."

Summer closed her eyes and sighed deeply.

"What was that about?" He unlocked the car door and loaded the shopping bags into the backseat.

"I'm grateful, that's all," Summer told him.

"Grateful?" James asked, joining her inside the car.

She was quiet for a moment. "I don't respond to other men this way—the way I have with you. I can't give you a reason or a logical explanation. In the last year, since we've been writing, I've felt close to you. It's as if you know all there is to know about me. My secrets, my faults, everything.

"That night a year ago, when we met, was probably the most devastating of my life. I don't know what I would've done if it hadn't been for you. Generally I'm the first person to dismiss this sort of thing, but I believe we were destined to meet."

James had wondered about that himself, although he'd always seen himself as a rational man. Of all the people in that massive New Year's crowd, they'd found each other. It had to mean *something*. He didn't doubt that fate, kismet or whatever you wanted to call it, had brought them together.

"I've never experienced the things I do when you kiss me," she confided.

She wasn't alone in that, either. He started the engine and pulled into the traffic that continuously flowed along the Strip. Concentrating on his driving rather than looking at Summer helped him restrain his emotions—and his impulses.

If they'd stayed in the parking garage much longer, James knew they'd have had a repeat performance of the night before.

Kissing her again had been a big mistake. He'd spent half the night fighting off the image of her in bed with him. If he took any more cold showers, the hotel was going to complain about the amount of water he used.

Summer's voice was unsure when she spoke. "I thought that after last evening you wouldn't want to see me again."

James nearly drove the car off the road. "Why would you think that?"

She lowered her gaze to her hands, which were folded primly in her lap. "Well, I behaved so…brazenly."

"You?" She obviously didn't know how close he'd come to losing control. Superior court judges weren't supposed to lose control. James couldn't remember the last time something like this had happened. Probably because it never had…

"It's good to know I'm not in this alone. I don't think I could stand that."

"Trust me, I'm experiencing the same feelings you are," he told her in what had to be the understatement of the century.

"We'll both be going our separate ways in the next few days. Until just now, I didn't know if I'd ever hear from you again."

"We've been in touch all year—why would that end?" He didn't expect anything permanent to develop between them, though; that would be asking too much.

"We can take turns calling each other," she offered. "Maybe exchanging e-mails."

"All right," he agreed.

Summer was silent following that, and he was beginning to recognize quiet moments as a warning. "What's wrong?"

She glanced at him and smiled softly. "I was thinking it would be nice to see each other every once in a while. I hope I don't seem pushy."

Seeing her on a regular basis suited him just fine. They hadn't even gone their separate ways yet, and James was already starting to feel withdrawal symptoms.

"I could fly up and visit you one month, and you could fly down and visit me the next," she suggested, again sounding uncertain.

James's hands tightened around the steering wheel. He suspected that the more often he saw her, the harder it would be to let her go.

"You're not saying anything."

"I was thinking."

"What?"

The complete truth would have embarrassed them both. "I was reviewing my schedule." The primary wasn't until September, but Ralph Southworth, a businessman and long-time friend who'd agreed to head James's campaign, had made it clear long ago: From here on out, James's life wasn't his own. Every place he went, every civic event he attended, would be a campaign opportunity.

"And?"

"February might be difficult for me to get away." His workload had suffered because of this vacation, and another trip, however brief, so soon afterward could cause additional problems.

"That's okay, I can come to you. In fact, I've probably got enough frequent-flyer miles to make the trip free."

"Great. Then I'll try to come to Anaheim in March."

"Wonderful." She lit up like a sparkler on the Fourth of July. Then she hesitated and bit her lower lip. "April might be difficult. Disneyland stays open until midnight during spring break, and we add a second *Beauty and the Beast* show in the evenings. It's hard to get a free weekend then."

"We can work around it." He didn't want to mention that from June onward, his schedule would be impossible. There was no hope of visiting California, and even if she was able to come to Seattle, he couldn't guarantee he'd be able to spend any time with her.

"Yes, we can work around any obstacle," she agreed. But she didn't sound optimistic.

They were outside the city now, driving on a two-lane highway that led to Red Rock Canyon. "I'll be very involved in my campaign this summer." He didn't feel he could be less than honest.

"Summer's the busiest time of year for me, too," she said with an air of defeat. "But we can make this work, James, if we both want it badly enough."

It frightened him how much he wanted Summer, but he was a realist, so he pointed out the obvious. "Long-distance relationships hardly ever work."

"How do you know? You've had several and you speak from experience?"

James resisted the urge to laugh at her prim tone. If memory served him, his first-grade teacher, Mrs. Bondi, had used precisely that voice. Come to think of it, he'd been in love with her, too.

"You'd be shocked by how few relationships I've had," he confessed.

"Do we have a relationship?" Summer asked softly.

James certainly hoped so. "Yes," he answered. And then, because she seemed to need convincing, he pulled onto a dirt road, behind a ten-foot rock. A trail of red dust plumed behind them.

"Why are you stopping?" she asked.

James wore a wide grin and held out his arms. "It appears to me you need a little reminder of how involved we are." James knew he was asking for trouble. Trouble with a capital *T*. His resistance was about as weak as it could get.

"Oh, James."

"A few kisses is all, understand? I don't have much willpower when it comes to you."

"You don't?" The words were whispered. "That's probably the most beautiful thing you've said to me."

"Has anyone ever told you that you talk too much?" James asked as his mouth swooped down on hers. He kissed her the way he'd been wanting to all morning. No, from the moment he'd watched her approach him in the gazebo.

He kissed her again and again, unable to get his fill. He demanded and she gave. Then she demanded and he gave. He moaned and she sighed. Then and there, James decided he'd do whatever he had to—move heaven and earth, take a red-eye flight—to be with her. He doubted once a month would be enough.

He plowed his hands into her hair and sifted the long strands through his fingers. With their mouths still joined, he lowered one hand to her throat. Her pulse beat savagely against his fingertips.

James had never thought of himself as a weak man. But with Summer he felt as hot and out of control as a seventeen-year-old in his dad's car.

Reluctantly he dragged his mouth from hers and trailed moist kisses along the side of her neck.

"James."

"Hmm?" He brought his mouth back to hers, kissing her slow and easy. Talking was the last thing on his mind.

She pulled slightly away. "James."

"Yes?" he asked, distracted.

"We seem—" she whispered breathlessly.

His lips returned to her face, lighting on her forehead, her nose, her chin.

"—to have company."

James went still. When he'd left the road, he'd made sure they were out of sight of other drivers. "Company?" he repeated. He could already imagine the headlines. King County Superior Court Judge Caught in Compromising Position in Las Vegas.

"They look hungry."

James's gaze followed Summer's. Burros, five of them, stood outside the car, studying them intently. They were waiting for a handout.

James grinned. At least the burros didn't carry a camera.

Summer smiled, too.

"I brought along a loaf of bread," he said, and reached into the seat behind him.

"Should we get out of the car?" she asked.

"I don't think that's a good idea." He'd read about the burros, but wasn't sure how tame they were. "Perhaps we should lower the window a bit and feed them that way."

Summer opened her window a couple of inches, far enough to ease a slice of bread out to the eager mouths. Just how eager was something they were to quickly learn.

"Oh!" Summer backed away from the window as a large tongue poked through the small opening.

Soon they were both laughing and handing out the bread as fast as they could. James was going to be sorry when it ran out. Summer certainly seemed to be enjoying herself, and so was he.

When the loaf was finished, they raised the windows. It took the burros a while to realize their food supply had come to an end.

When the burros finally left, James started the engine and pulled back onto the road. They drove for another hour, stopped and toured a visitors' center, taking in the beauty of the countryside.

James felt Summer staring at him as he drove back to the city.

"Now what?" he asked.

"I can't get over the change in you."

"You mean the clothes?"

"Yes. You look like a Jim instead of a James."

James grinned. "There's a difference?"

"Oh, yes, a big one."

"Which do you prefer?" he asked, studying her from the corner of his eye.

His question made her hesitate. "I'm not sure. I like the way Jim dresses, but I like the way James kisses."

"What about how Jim kisses?" The conversation was getting ridiculous.

"Too impatient, I think."

"Really?" He couldn't help feeling a bit miffed. "What's so wonderful about James?"

"His restraint. When James kisses me, it's as if he's holding back part of himself. I have the feeling he's afraid to let go, and it drives me crazy. I want to discover what he's hiding from me. I know this probably sounds a little crazy, but I find James intriguing."

"And Jim?"

She giggled. "Don't tell him, but he's sexy as hell."

"Really?" James was beginning to feel downright cocky.

"He's got that devil-may-care attitude. I have a strong feeling we should be grateful to those burros, because there's no telling what could've happened between us in the canyon."

She was right about that.

"It's those shoes you made me buy," James told her. "The minute I put them on, I had this incredible urge to look for a basketball court and do slam dunks." James loved the sound of Summer's laughter. He'd never been one to tease and joke, but he reveled in her appreciation of his wit.

It was midafternoon when they arrived back at the hotel. After showing the security guard their keys, they stepped into the elevator.

"How about dinner?" he asked, hoping he sounded casual when in reality he felt anything but.

"Sure. What time?"

"Six," he said. Three hours, and he'd be more than ready to see her again. He wanted to suggest they do something until then, but didn't feel he should monopolize her time, although he'd pretty much succeeded in doing that anyway.

"Six o'clock. In the lobby?"

"The lobby," he agreed.

The elevator stopped at her floor, and Summer stared down at her room key. "I'll see you at six."

"Six." They sounded like a couple of parrots.

"Thanks for taking me this morning," she said, easing toward the door. "And for coming to the mall."

"Thank you." He bounced an imaginary basketball and pretended to make a hoop shot.

She smiled, and acting on pure instinct, James lowered his mouth to hers. The kiss was gentle, and when they broke apart, it was all James could do not to follow her to her room.

* * *

Summer sat on the end of her bed, trembling. She closed her eyes and tried to relive those last seconds with James and couldn't. Being in his arms was the only possible way to recapture the sensation she experienced each time she was with him.

Julie, her roommate, had known long before Summer had realized it herself. When James had asked her how often she dated, she'd invented an excuse to explain why her social life was nonexistent of late.

But it was really because of his letters.

Hearing from James had become an important part of her life. On the first day of every month she rushed to the mailbox, knowing there'd be a letter from him, each longer than the one before. She'd fallen in love with the man who'd written her those beautiful letters.

Unfortunately she hadn't realized it until she'd seen James. She was worried that she alone experienced all this feeling, all this awareness. But after he'd kissed her, she knew that couldn't be true. He felt it, too.

She smiled to herself, remembering how flustered he'd looked when she'd said they had an audience.

Summer smiled at the memory.

Lying down on the bed, she stared up at the ceiling and soon found herself giggling. She was in love with James. She didn't feel a second's doubt, not the slightest qualm or uncertainty. To think she'd actually believed she'd never love another man after Brett.

She might have drowned in a pool of self-pity if it hadn't been for James. She owed him so much.

As she considered their plans to continue seeing each other, she knew it would be difficult to maintain the relationship, especially since they lived such separate lives.

It would require effort and commitment on both their parts. Summer was willing. She could tell that James wasn't as convinced as she was that they could make this work, but she didn't harbor a single doubt.

Summer dressed carefully for her dinner date with James. She chose a simple sundress with a lacy shawl and pretty sandals.

He was waiting at the same place in the lobby, but he surprised her by not wearing a suit and tie. He'd worn one of the short-sleeved shirts they'd bought that day and a pair of khaki pants. For a moment she barely recognized him. He looked relaxed, as though he hadn't a care in the world.

"James," she whispered when she joined him.

"Jim," he corrected, and grinned. He placed his hand inside his pant pocket and struck a catalog pose.

Summer laughed delightedly.

"I hope you're hungry," James said. He tucked her hand in the crook of his arm and guided her toward the door.

"I'm starved."

"Great. We're about to indulge ourselves in a feast fit for the gods." When they reached the sidewalk of Glitter Gulch, the lights made it as bright as the noonday sun.

"I thought about the conversation we had this afternoon," he announced out of the blue.

"About keeping in touch?"

He nodded. "I'm not sure what we have, the two of us, but whatever it is, I don't want to lose it."

"I don't, either."

"I've only felt this strongly about one other woman in my life."

"I've only felt this way about one other man."

"If I was going to put a name on this…this thing be-tween us…"

"Yes?" she asked when he hesitated. James was a thoughtful man. She didn't mean to rush him, but she wanted him to say what was already on the tip of *her* tongue. Consequently, she had no qualms about leaping in. "I love you, James Wilkens. I want to throw my arms in the air and sing."

He looked at her as if he were actually afraid she'd do exactly that. "What you feel is just gratitude."

"Gratitude," she repeated scornfully. "*Just* gratitude." She shook her head. "I'm capable of knowing my own mind, thank you kindly, and when I say I love you, I mean it."

"I see," James said, and his voice fell.

"You don't have to worry about telling me how you feel, either," she was quick to assure him. It wasn't necessary; his kiss told her everything she needed to know.

"But…"

She stopped in the middle of the crowded sidewalk and pressed her finger to his lips.

"I'm too old for you," he muttered.

She narrowed her eyes.

"But I'm crazy about you, Summer. Call me the biggest fool that ever lived, but it's true."

"Thank you very much."

James chuckled. "I haven't been doing a very good job of hiding how I feel. Maybe that's because I didn't expect to feel like *this*." He splayed his fingers through his hair. "In retrospect, I wonder what I did expect."

"I assumed we'd have dinner that first night and we'd talk about what we said in our letters, and then we'd more or less go our separate ways, me back to my life in California, you back to yours…"

"Really." He arched his eyebrows.

"I wanted Julie to fly in for the weekend, but she refused and I couldn't get her to give me a reason. I know now. She realized what I hadn't—that I'm in love with you. My feelings developed slowly over the past year, and Julie saw it happening." She inhaled a deep breath. "I don't want to lose you, James. We can make this work if we try."

"It's not going to be easy."

As his words faded an idea struck Summer. "Oh, my goodness."

James stopped abruptly. "What is it?"

"James." She clasped his arm as she stared up at him. With every passing second the idea gained momentum. "I just thought of something...wonderful," she said urgently.

"What is it?" His arm circled her waist.

"Oh, James. Kiss me, please, just kiss me."

"Kiss you *here?*" James asked, appalled.

"Never mind." She laughed and, throwing her arms around his neck, she stood on the tips of her toes and kissed him, a deep, lingering kiss that communicated her feelings to him—and his to her.

He stared down at her dumbstruck when she stepped away.

"James," she said breathlessly, "I think we should get married."

"Married." The word was barely audible.

"It makes sense, don't you agree? I know how I feel about you, and you've admitted your feelings for me. Here we are, both worried about the most ridiculous things, when we already have what's most important. Each other."

Still James didn't say anything. He looked around, and his expression seemed slightly desperate, but that could have been her imagination.

"I can guess what you're thinking," she said with a laugh, "but I've got an answer for every one of your arguments."

"We hardly know each other."

That was a pretty weak argument. "Is that so? You know me better than friends I've had all my life. You've seen me at my worst. You've listened to my pain and my frustrations. There isn't a thing I can't talk about with you."

He frowned, and Summer longed to smooth the lines from his brow and kiss away his doubts.

"Don't look so worried! Honestly, James, anyone would think you were in a state of shock."

"I am." This came through loud and clear.

"But why?" His hesitation took her by surprise. She knew the idea would take some getting used to on James's part. He didn't leap into projects and ideas the way she did. He was methodical and thoughtful and carefully weighed every decision.

"Perhaps I'm assuming something here that I shouldn't," she said slowly. "You don't want to marry me, do you, James?"

Four

Summer was mortified to the very marrow of her bones. Without even trying, she'd managed to make a complete fool of herself. James had never come right out and *said* he was in love with her. But with all their talk about how important they were to each other, she'd naturally assumed he cared as deeply for her as she did for him. She'd assumed he'd want to marry her.

"James, I'm sorry," she said in a weak voice. Past experience had taught her to right wrongs as quickly as possible.

"Summer..."

"Of course you don't want to marry me. I understand. Really, I do," she said and pretended to laugh, but it sounded more like a muffled sob. "Now I've embarrassed us both. I don't know why I say the ridiculous things I do." She tried to make light of it by gesturing with her hands. "I guess I should've warned you that I blurt out the most incredibly awkward stuff. Forget I said anything about marriage, please—otherwise it'll ruin our evening."

James was silent, which made everything ten times worse. She'd rather he ranted and raved than said nothing.

In an effort to fill the terrible silence, she started chattering, talking fast, jumping from one subject to another.

She commented on how busy the casinos were. She talked about the big-name stars performing in town. She mentioned a friend of a friend who'd won the California State lottery, and then brought up air pollution problems in Los Angeles.

"Summer, stop," James finally told her. "It's fine."

She snapped her mouth shut. How she was going to get through the evening without humiliating herself further, she didn't know.

Her stomach was in such a knot that by the time they reached the hotel where the restaurant was located, she felt sure she'd only be able to make a pretense of eating.

The hostess seated them, but Summer got up as soon as the hostess left them.

"If you'll excuse me," she said.

James looked up from his menu.

"I'll be right back." She was hoping that a few minutes alone in the ladies' room would help her regain her composure.

"Summer, wait," James said. "I don't want you to feel bad about this."

She nodded, determined to drop the subject entirely. "Did you notice they had lobster on the menu?" She didn't actually know if this was true or not.

"It's just that most men prefer to do the asking."

"Of course." And it went without saying that the very proper King County Superior Court Judge James Wilkens wouldn't want an empty-headed actress for a wife.

Summer asked a passing waiter directions for the ladies' room. As she walked across the restaurant, weaving around tables, she felt James's eyes following her.

Once inside the restroom, Summer sat on the pink velvet sofa and closed her eyes. After a number of deep, calming breaths, she waited for the acute embarrassment to pass.

It didn't.

Briefly she toyed with the idea of slipping away, but that would've been childish and unfair to James. His only crime had been his silence, and he'd already explained that was simply his way. Just like making a world-class fool of herself seemed to be hers.

Five minutes later she rejoined him.

He looked up, almost as if he was surprised to see her. "I wasn't sure you'd be back."

"I wouldn't be that rude. It isn't your fault I'm an idiot."

"Stop," he said sharply. "Don't say such things about yourself."

"I can't believe I thought you'd marry someone like me," she said, poking fun at herself. "The girl who always speaks before she thinks and leaps before she looks."

"As a matter of fact, I do plan to marry you." He announced this while scanning the menu, which he then set aside. He watched her as if he expected some kind of argument. Summer might have offered him one if her throat hadn't closed up, making talking impossible.

The menu slid from her fingers and fell onto the table. Nervously she groped for it.

"Have you decided?" James asked.

She stared at him blankly.

"What would you like to order for dinner?"

"Oh." She hadn't even glanced at the menu. Frazzled as she was, she chose the first thing she saw. "Chicken Dijon," she said.

"Not lobster? It isn't every day one becomes engaged. I think we should celebrate, don't you?"

Somehow she managed a nod.

The waiter came, and James ordered for them both, requesting lobster and champagne. Their server nodded approvingly and disappeared. A moment later he returned with a champagne bottle for James's inspection.

"We'll need to see about an engagement ring," James said as though they were discussing something as mundane as the weather. "I imagine Las Vegas has quite a few good jewelers."

The waiter opened the champagne bottle with a loud pop and poured a small amount into the fluted glass for James to sample. He tasted it and nodded. Soon both their glasses were filled.

Summer breathed easier once they were alone. "James," she whispered, leaning forward. "Are you sure you want to marry me?"

He leaned toward her, too, and a grin slowly formed. "Yes."

"All at once I'm not convinced I'm the right person for you."

"Shouldn't I be the one to decide that?"

"Yes, but… I'd hate to think we're reacting to circumstances that wouldn't repeat themselves in a hundred years."

"Then we'll have a long engagement. We'll both be positive before we take that final step."

"All right." Summer felt only mildly reassured.

"We'll continue to see each other on a regular basis," James told her.

"Yes…we'll need that." She didn't like the idea of being apart so much, but that couldn't be helped.

"I wouldn't want the engagement to be *too* long," Summer said. "I dated Brett for five years, and we were unofficially and then officially engaged almost that whole time. We both know where that ended up."

"Do you wish you'd married him?"

"No," she answered emphatically. "I don't have a single regret. I know you'd never do the things Brett did."

James's eyes brightened with intensity. "It isn't in me to hurt you."

"And I'd never knowingly hurt you," she promised.

"In light of what happened between Christy and me, I'm not fond of long engagements, either."

"Do you regret not marrying her sooner? That way she would've gone to visit her sister as a married woman."

"I've thought about that," James said. "Christy would never have allowed anything to develop between her and Cody if we'd been married. Getting involved with him behind my back was almost more than she could bear."

"I see." Summer figured she could read the writing on the wall. "You wish you'd married her, don't you?"

"No."

His quick response surprised her. "Why not?"

"Christy Manning didn't love me as much as I loved her. I'm sure she would have done her best to be a good wife, and we probably would have grown close over the years, but she would've married me for the wrong reasons."

"The wrong reasons? What reasons?"

"She was trying to make her parents happy."

"Okay," Summer said slowly, still feeling her way carefully around the subject. "So neither of us wants a long engagement. How long is long? A year?"

"That's too long," James said with feeling.

"Six months?"

He hesitated. "That'll make it June."

"June's a nice month," Summer said without any real enthusiasm. "Will you want me to live with you in Seattle?"

"Yes. Is that going to be possible?"

"Of course." She nodded vigorously.

"What about your career?"

She lifted one shoulder. "To tell you the truth, I was getting a little tired of playing Belle anyway. From what I understand, theater in Seattle is thriving. There wouldn't be any problem with me being your wife and an actress, would there? You being a judge and all."

"None that I can think of."

"Good." Summer picked up her fork and ran her fingers along the smooth tines. "My current contract expires in April."

"April," James said. "Can you arrange a wedding on such short notice?"

"You bet I can," she said, grinning. "Oh, James, I can't believe this is happening."

"To be honest, neither can I," he admitted.

Summer had never seen him smile as brightly.

The waiter brought their dinner, and James looked at the man who was a complete stranger and said, "The young lady and I have just become engaged."

Their server smiled broadly. "Congratulations."

"Thank you."

Summer would have added her thanks, but James had shocked her speechless. He wasn't joking; he really meant to follow through with their wedding and he was excited about it. Excited enough to announce their plans to a stranger.

"This hotel has an excellent wedding chapel," the waiter continued. "I gather that more than one celebrity has been married in our chapel."

"Right here in the hotel?" James asked.

"Many of the larger hotels provide wedding services for their guests."

"Don't arrangements have to be made weeks in advance?"

"Not always," the waiter explained. "A lot of people don't decide which chapel to use until after they arrive. Apparently you can get married with a few hours' notice—if the chapel's available, of course."

"Of course," James murmured.

A look came over him, one she'd seen before. "Our wedding will be in April," she said hastily.

"My very best to both of you." The waiter refilled their flutes with champagne.

"James," Summer said after the server had left their table, "is something wrong?"

"Nothing. What makes you ask?"

"You're wearing an odd look."

"What do you mean?"

"It's a look that says you're not sure you like what you're thinking. Or hearing or seeing. The same one you got when I said we had company in Red Rock Canyon the other day."

"In this case, it's what I'm thinking," he muttered

"You want to call off the wedding?" She should've realized that when James said he wanted to marry her, it was too good to be true. This had to be the shortest engagement in history.

"I don't know where you get the idea that I'm looking for a way out when I'm thinking exactly the opposite. I can only assume impulsive thoughts must be transmitted from one brain to another." He drew in a deep breath and seemed to hold it for a long time. "Would you be willing to marry me now?"

"Now? You mean tomorrow?"

"Yes. Then we'll repeat the ceremony later with family and friends in April."

Speechlessness happened rarely with Summer, and yet James had managed to cause it twice in the same evening. Her mouth dropped open, but no words came out.

"Summer, have I utterly shocked you?"

"Yes," she admitted in a squeaky voice.

James grinned. "I'll admit this is the first impulsive thought I've entertained in years. If you can propose marriage at the drop of a hat, then I should be able to come up with something equally thrilling."

Summer knew she was going to cry now. She could feel the tears welling up in her eyes. She used her linen napkin to dab them away.

"Just remember when we tell the children about this night. You're the one who proposed to me."

"Children." Summer blew her nose. "Oh, James, I'm looking forward to being a mother."

"Then you agree to my plan?"

"Married twice?" Everything was going too fast for her. "I'd want Julie here as my maid of honor."

"Of course. We'll phone her as soon as we're finished dinner. I'll be happy to pay for her airfare."

The tears were back, filling her eyes. These were tears of happiness and relief; she loved him so much. "James, we're doing the right thing, aren't we?"

He didn't hesitate. "Yes. It's what we both want."

"You love me?" He'd never said the words.

His look softened. "Very much."

Her mind whirled with everything they'd need to do. "I'll have to tell my parents. You didn't intend to keep our marriage a secret from our families, did you?"

"No. I'll call my father, as well."

Already Summer could hear her mother's arguments. "They're going to think we're crazy."

James grinned again. "Probably."

"What should we do first?" Summer asked as they left the restaurant after dinner.

"I suppose we should find an available wedding chapel."

"Shouldn't we contact our families before we do that?" This was the part Summer dreaded most, and she wanted it over with as quickly as possible.

"But if we have the chapel booked, we'll be able to tell them the time and place," James said.

"Oh, yes." Trust him to be so logical even when he was acting impulsive.

"The ring." James snapped his fingers. "I almost forgot."

"Don't look so concerned. We can pick something out later. A plain gold band is perfect for now. In April we can exchange those for a diamond if you want."

"I'd like you to have my mother's ring."

"I'd be honored to wear it," she said quietly.

He kissed her, and Summer blinked in surprise. It was the first time he'd ever initiated a kiss in public.

Since the waiter had mentioned the wedding chapel at this particular hotel, they tried there first. Summer hadn't expected it to be so easy, but booking their wedding took only a few minutes. The hotel would see to everything, from obtaining the license to the music and flowers. They'd be getting married at seven the next night.

"If I'd known it was this simple," James said as they walked back to the Four Queens, "I might have suggested it sooner."

Summer pressed her head against his shoulder. They stopped at a crosswalk and waited for the red light.

"I wish you'd kiss me again," she breathed close to his ear.

His gaze found her lips, and he cleared his throat. "I don't think that would be a good idea."

"I suppose you're right," she murmured, but disappointment underscored her words.

"You can call your family from my room."

"Okay," she said, but her mind wasn't on making the dreaded phone call as much as it was on being alone with James.

His thoughts must have been the same because their pace quickened as they hurried across the street and into the hotel.

The elevator ride seemed to take an eternity. As if James couldn't keep himself from touching her in some way, he reached out and brushed a stray curl from her cheek. His knuckle grazed her skin.

"I can't believe you're willing to marry me," he said.

"I feel like the luckiest woman alive."

"You?" He held his hand to his brow. "I want you so much I think I'm running a fever."

"I've got a fever, too. Oh, James, we're going to be so good for each other."

"Don't," he growled.

"Don't?"

"Don't look at me like that, Summer. I'm weak enough where you're concerned. Much more of this, and I'm going to make love to you right in this elevator."

Summer smiled and moved against the back wall. "You're so romantic, James—and I mean that."

"You're doing it again."

"Doing what?"

"Looking at me like you know exactly what I want. Your eyes are telling me you want it as much as I do."

The elevator eased to a stop, and the doors slid open. Summer's heart pounded fast as neither of them made the slightest effort to leave.

"We were going to call our families," she reminded him just as the doors started to close.

James swallowed hard. "Yes, of course."

With precise movements he led the way out of the elevator and down the hallway to his room. She noticed that when he inserted the key his hand trembled slightly, and she loved him all the more for it.

"The phone's over by the—"

"Bed." She completed his sentence, and the word seemed to stick in her throat. She walked across the room and sat on the edge of the mattress, then picked up the phone to dial the familiar number.

It might've helped if she'd taken the time to figure out what to tell her parents. But she was afraid she'd lose her nerve.

She couldn't put into words what she felt for James. She'd never loved anyone this way, this much, and she believed he hadn't, either. They'd each been in love with someone else, and that other person had caused deep pain. This time was different.

She knew, even before they answered the phone, what her mother and father were going to say.

"James," she said, in a panic, banging down the telephone receiver and holding out her arms. "Please, could you kiss me first?"

She glanced over at the man she'd marry in less than twenty-four hours, and his face was a study in raw sexual need. He walked across the room. The bed dipped as his weight joined hers. With loving care he gathered her in his arms and claimed her mouth. The kiss was slow and sensual.

He broke away, and his breath was hard and labored. Eager for the taste of him, the touch and feel of him, she brushed her lips over the curve of his jaw, then brought her mouth back to his.

"Maybe you should call your father first," she whispered when she pulled away.

"All right," he agreed. Reluctantly he sat up and reached for the bedside phone. Summer knelt behind him, wrapping her arms around his waist and pressing her head against his shoulder.

"Dad, it's James," she heard him say.

"Fine...yes, Vegas is just fine." Summer could hear a voice on the other end of the line, but she couldn't make out what was being said.

"I'm calling to let you know I'm getting married."

The voice went silent.

"Dad? Are you still there?"

The faraway voice returned, this time speaking very fast.

"Dad... Dad... Dad." Each time James tried to cut in, he was prevented from saying anything.

In frustration, he held the phone away from his ear. "I think you'd better talk to him."

"Me?" Summer cried. "What do you want *me* to say?"

"Anything."

Summer took the receiver and covered it with her hand. "Just remember this when we talk to my parents."

"I will." He kissed her briefly.

"Mr. Wilkens," Summer said. It sounded as if the line had suddenly gone dead. "My name's Summer Lawton.

James and I have known each other a year. I love him very, very much."

"If you've known my son for a year, how is it we've never met?"

"I live in California."

"California?"

"Anaheim. I'm an actress." She might as well give him all the bad news at once. She didn't dare look at James.

"An actress?"

"That's correct."

"You're sure you've got the right James Wilkens? My son's the superior court judge."

"Yes, I know. James and I are going to be married tomorrow evening at seven but we're planning a larger ceremony in April. We felt it was only right to tell you about our plans." Convinced she'd done a miserable job, Summer handed the telephone back to James.

Father and son talked a few moments more, and the conversation ended with James abruptly replacing the receiver. He looked at Summer, but she had the strangest feeling he wasn't seeing her.

"James?"

"He's decided to fly in for the ceremony."

"That's great. I'll look forward to meeting him."

"He's anxious to meet you, as well. He hasn't set eyes on you and already he thinks you're the best thing that's ever happened to me."

Summer laughed and slipped her arms around James's neck. "He could be right."

James grinned up at her. "I know he is."

"I love you, James."

"I know. I love you, too. Now it's time to make that call."

Summer had been delaying the inevitable and knew it.

She stared at the phone, expelled a heavy sigh and said, "All right, I'll call my parents. Be prepared, James. They're going to have a lot of questions."

"They couldn't be any worse than my father," he muttered.

"Wanna bet?" Summer punched out the number to the family home a second time and waited. It was the decent thing to do, call her family with the news of her marriage, but if they just happened to be away, out of town themselves, no one would blame her and James for going ahead with the ceremony.

Four rings. Summer was about to hang up.

"Hello," her mother answered cheerfully.

"Mom," Summer said. "It's me."

"I thought you were in Vegas this week with Julie."

"Julie couldn't come."

"You went alone?" Summer could hear the disapproval in her mother's voice.

"I met a friend here. That's the reason I'm calling."

"Your friend is the reason? What's the matter? You don't sound right. You're gambling and you've lost everything? Is that it?"

"Mom, it's nothing like that."

"I never did understand why you'd go back to Vegas after what happened there last year."

"Mom, can I explain?"

"All right, all right."

"I'm calling to tell you—"

"Don't beat around the bush. Just say it."

Summer rolled her eyes. She knew where her flair for drama had come from. "I'm getting married."

Her mother screamed, and the next thing Summer heard

was the phone hitting the floor. Her father's voice could be heard in the background, followed by moaning and crying.

"What the hell's going on?" It was her father on the line.

"Hi, Dad," Summer said casually, as if nothing was out of the ordinary. "I called to tell you and Mom that I'm getting married tomorrow evening."

Summer's father said nothing for several seconds. "Do we know this young man?"

"No. But he's wonderful, Dad, really wonderful."

"Like Brett was wonderful?" her mother shouted into the extension.

"Helen, get off the phone. You're too emotional to talk any sense."

"Don't tell me what to do, Hank Lawton. This is our little girl who's marrying some stranger."

"His name's James Wilkens. He's from Seattle and, Daddy, I'm crazy about him."

"He's an actor, isn't he?" her mother demanded. "What did I tell you over and over again? Stay away from actors. But do you listen to me?"

"Mom, James is a judge."

Silence.

"Mom, Dad, did you hear me?"

"What kind of judge? Beauty pageants?" This came from her mother.

Summer almost groaned out loud. "No. Superior court. He was recently appointed to the bench and he'll run for election to his first full term this November."

"A judge, Hank," Helen said softly. "Abby's daughter married that attorney, and we never heard the end of it. Summer's got herself a judge."

"Would you like to talk to James?" Summer offered. It

only seemed fair that he talk to her family, since he'd put her on the phone with his father.

"No," her father surprised her by saying. "When I talk to him, it'll be face-to-face. Pack our bags, Helen. We're headed for Vegas."

Five

"Summer," James said patiently when he saw her distress, "what did you expect your family to do?"

"I didn't think they'd insist on coming here," Summer answered. "I wanted it to be just you and me. We can involve our families later, in April. I felt obliged to let my parents know what we were doing—but I didn't expect anything like *this*."

"You don't want them to come?"

"No," she said quickly.

In some ways James could understand her regret. If truth be known, he would've preferred his father to stay in Seattle. As it was, James's time with Summer was already limited, and he didn't want to share with family the precious few days they had left.

"I'm afraid once you meet my mother, you'll change your mind about marrying me," she moaned.

"Honey, it isn't possible."

"My mother—she sometimes doesn't think before she speaks."

"I see." James felt he was being diplomatic by not mentioning that Summer possessed the same trait.

"My dad's really great… You'll like him, but probably not at first." She gazed at James with large, imploring eyes. "Oh, James, he's going to give you the third degree. I'll bet he's having a background check done on you this very minute."

"I don't have anything to hide."

"See, Dad's been working with the seamy side of life for so many years, he suspects everyone."

"He's a policeman?"

Summer nodded. "I don't think he trusts anyone."

"Summer, if twenty-odd years down the road our daughter phones to tell us she's marrying a man neither of us has ever met before, you can bet I'll have a background check done, too."

"You know what this means, don't you?" she said, biting her lip. "We aren't going to have much of a honeymoon."

James chuckled. "Wanna bet?"

Summer grinned.

If this woman's smile could be bottled, James thought, it would be the most potent aphrodisiac ever made. He couldn't look at Summer and not want to make love to her.

"What about Julie?" James said in an effort to get Summer's mind off her parents' imminent arrival.

"Oh—I nearly forgot my best friend." She reached for the phone and called Julie's cell.

Since there were a number of things to do before the actual ceremony, James walked over to the desk and sat down to write out a list, not wanting to forget anything.

He was only half listening to the conversation between Summer and her roommate when he heard Summer's soft gasp and the mention of Brett, the man she'd once loved. James's ears perked up, and his fingers tightened around the pen.

"What did you tell him?" Summer asked in low tones. This was followed by "Good. Then you're coming? Great. You might want to talk to my parents and see if you can fly in with them. I'm sure they'll be eager to pump you for whatever you can tell them about James." After a few words of farewell, Summer replaced the receiver.

James turned around in his chair, wondering if she'd volunteer the information about Brett.

"Julie's flying in, too. I suggested she catch the same flight as my parents." She seemed self-conscious all at once.

Her eyes avoided his.

"So I heard." James waited, not wanting to approach the subject of her ex-fiancé, hoping she'd save him the trouble.

After an awkward moment, she blurted out, "Julie… Julie said Brett phoned."

James relaxed, grateful she chose not to hide it from him. "Did she find out what he wanted?"

"No. She hung up on him before he got a chance to say."

James had the distinct feeling he was going to like Summer's roommate.

Summer's shoulders moved in an expressive sigh. "I don't think either of us is going to be nearly as happy once our families arrive."

"How bad can it be?" he asked. All he cared about, all that was important, was marrying the woman he loved.

"My mother's going to insist we follow tradition and not see each other all day."

James frowned. He wasn't keen on that idea.

"My dad will keep you occupied with a whole bunch of questions. If you've got the slightest blemish on your record, he'll find it."

"I don't. Trust me, sweetheart, my background's been

scrutinized by the very best. Your father isn't going to find anything."

She laughed softly. "In which case, Dad will probably thank you repeatedly for taking me off his hands."

James laughed, too. "Never mind. By this time tomorrow, we'll be husband and wife."

Summer's parents arrived early the following morning with Julie in tow. By chance Summer met them in the lobby on her way down for breakfast. James had called her room an hour earlier, before she was dressed, to tell her he was headed for the coffee shop. Summer had been too nervous to eat then, but had developed a healthy appetite since. She'd need fortification in order to deal with her parents.

"Mom! Dad! Julie!"

They threw their arms around her as if the separation had been ten years instead of a few days.

"I called Adam and told him his little sister's getting married," were the first words out of her mother's mouth. "He's taking time off work and he and Denise are driving in for the wedding."

"Mom," Summer protested, "James and I are having another ceremony later."

"Fine," Helen Lawton said briskly, "Adam will be there, too. Now stop fussing. It isn't like I held a gun to his head and told him he had to come. Your brother *wants* to be here."

"Daddy." Summer hugged her father. Stepping back, she placed her hands on her hips. "James is squeaky-clean, right?"

"How'd you know I had him checked out?"

"You're my father, aren't you?" She slipped her arm around his waist.

"How'd you ever meet a man like this?" Hank Lawton wanted to know. "He's as good as gold."

"Yes, I know. He's wonderful."

James appeared then, coming from the direction of the coffee shop, a newspaper under his arm.

Summer made the introductions, and while Julie and her family checked in to their rooms, Summer and James reserved a table at the coffee shop. They sat next to each other, holding hands.

"Are you ready for all this?" he asked her.

"I don't know." She sighed. "My brother's taking the day off and driving in for the ceremony. I thought we'd have a small, intimate wedding."

"It is small and intimate."

"My brother and his wife have three little kids, who'll probably cry through the entire ceremony."

"I don't mind if you don't," James said and gently squeezed her hand. "I suspect folks will talk about us the same way when we drag our children to family get-togethers."

"Our children," Summer repeated. She felt weak with pleasure at the thought of having a family with James. "I know I've said it before, but I'm looking forward to being a mother."

"Not nearly as much as I am to making you one," he said in a low voice. The teasing light left his eyes. "If you have no objections, I'd like a large family. Maybe four kids?"

"Four." She nodded. "I'd love to have four children. We're going to have a good life, James. I can feel it in my heart. We're going to be so happy."

"I feel that way, too. Being an only child, I was always drawn to large families. I suspect that's why I've been such good friends with the Mannings over the years."

"Christy's family?"

He nodded. "She's the youngest of five."

Her parents and Julie appeared just then, and ever the gentleman, James stood until the ladies were seated.

"I hope you don't mind if we steal Summer away from you for the day," Helen said even before she looked at the menu. "We have a million and one things to do before the wedding."

"We do?" Summer didn't know why she bothered to protest. She'd realized this would happen the moment her parents announced they were coming.

"First, we need to buy you a dress."

Silly as it seemed, Summer hadn't given much thought to her attire. A nice suit would do, she supposed, something flattering and stylish. The elaborate gown and veil could wait for the April ceremony.

"Then there's the matter of finding a preacher."

"The hotel provides a justice of the peace," James said.

"Do you object to a man of the cloth?" Hank asked sternly.

Summer wanted to leap to her feet and tell James this was a test, but she bit her tongue. Sooner or later her soon-to-be husband would have to sink or swim on his own with her family.

"Not at all. I'd prefer one myself."

Summer had to restrain herself from cheering. James had passed with flying colors.

"I've got the names of several ministers from our pastor in Anaheim." Her father patted his shirt pocket. "We'll leave the women to do their thing, and you and I can find us a proper preacher." His tone implied that his little girl wasn't being married by any justice of the peace.

"What about rings?" Helen asked.

"I thought I'd pick up a couple of plain gold bands for now," James explained. "I'd like Summer to wear my mother's diamond. She can choose the setting at a later date, and it'll be ready before the April ceremony."

Breakfast wasn't the ordeal Summer had expected. Julie sent her curious looks now and then, and Summer knew her friend was waiting for an opportune moment so they could talk.

"We'll meet again at what time?" Helen asked, glancing at her watch.

Summer's father studied his, while Summer and James gazed longingly at each other.

"Six," Helen suggested.

"That late?" Summer protested. They were being cheated out of an entire day. No one seemed to appreciate that her time with James was already limited.

"I'll see to everything," her mother assured everyone. "Hank, all you need to do is get James to the chapel on time."

"Don't worry about my not showing up," James said. "I'm deeply in love with your daughter."

Julie's elbow connected with Summer's ribs. "What did I tell you?" she whispered out of the corner of her mouth.

Julie had more than gloating on her mind, and so did Summer's mother. When they'd finished their coffee, Helen organized a shopping expedition. She made it clear that a suitable wedding dress wasn't the only thing on her list. If her daughter was about to marry a superior court judge, she'd go to him with a complete trousseau.

The minute Summer and Julie were alone in the store, her roommate grabbed Summer's arm. "I heard from Brett again," she whispered.

"Did he phone?"

"No. This time he stopped by the apartment, right before I left for the airport."

"No." Summer closed her eyes, not because she had any regrets or because she harbored any doubts about James.

It was as if Brett possessed some kind of radar that told him when he could cause her the most trouble.

"He's been asking about you. Apparently he talked with a couple of the cast members at Disneyland. Steve and Karen? Do those names sound familiar?"

"Yes." Summer clenched her fists. "I can't tell you how much this irritates me."

"You? The man's been making a pest of himself all week. According to Brett, you're pining away for him." Julie made a melodramatic gesture, bringing the back of one hand to her forehead. "You've been unhappy ever since the two of you split up—he says."

"Oh, puhleese."

"That's what I told him."

"If I was pining for anyone," Summer said, "it was for James."

"Exactly. I told Brett that, too."

"Thanks."

"I explained, with a great deal of satisfaction, that you're involved with someone else now, and he should stay out of your life."

"Good grief, he's married and about to become a father. The man has no principles." The thought of Brett trying to reestablish their relationship while his wife was pregnant with their child made Summer sick to her stomach. "I'm glad to be rid of him."

"You couldn't be getting married at a more opportune time. I'm telling you, Summer, from the way Brett argued with me, your marriage is about the only thing that'll convince him it's over."

"You did tell him I'm getting married, didn't you?"

"Yes, but he wouldn't believe me. He accused me of fabricating the whole thing."

"Girls, girls." Helen returned with a salesclerk.

"I wonder how long it'll be before she considers us women?" Summer asked her friend under her breath.

By evening Summer felt more like a French poodle than a bride. She'd been shampooed, her nails polished, her hair curled, her body massaged and moisturized. She'd been in and out of more clothes than a New York fashion model. And she was exhausted.

The idea of a white suit for the wedding was one of the first ideas to go. Before Summer could argue, she was draped in satin and silk from head to toe.

"You look absolutely stunning," Helen said.

Summer wasn't sure she could trust her mother's assessment. Her eyes went to Julie.

"She's right."

"But what about April?"

"What about it?" Helen's hands flew into the air. "You'll wear the dress twice. Big deal. No one needs to know."

She tried another argument. "It's so much money."

"My baby girl only gets married once."

Well, no. She'd be getting married twice—to the same man, but still, there were going to be two ceremonies.

Julie arranged the veil and the long train for the photographer who was on his way, then handed Summer the intricate gardenia bouquet. "If you're going to throw that, just be sure and aim it my way."

Summer smiled. "You got it."

"Not yet, I haven't," Julie reminded her.

A knock sounded at the door, and Helen answered it. Summer didn't pay any attention, assuming it was the photographer her father had hired.

A few minutes later, Helen introduced the tall, balding man. "Summer, this is James's father, Walter. You should've told me he was a retired superior court judge himself."

Summer would have been happy to, had she known.

"My, oh, my," Walter said as he entered the room. He stood in front of Summer, hands on his hips, and he slowly shook his head. "And where did my son meet such a beauty?"

"Here in Vegas," Summer said. "A year ago."

"I was about to give up hope for that son of mine. It seemed to me he'd settled a little too comfortably into bachelorhood. This comes as a very pleasant surprise."

"I'm so glad you came to meet me and my family, especially on such short notice."

Walter withdrew a thick cigar from the inside of his suit pocket and examined the end of it. "Wouldn't have missed it for the world."

Walter sat down and made himself comfortable. After a moment he returned the cigar to his inside pocket. "I quit smoking five years ago and I still miss it. Every now and then I take one out and look at it, just for the thrill."

Summer could see she was going to like James's father.

"To be frank, I didn't think that boy of mine possessed this much common sense."

"He's a judge," Summer said, eager to defend her husband-to-be.

"When it comes to the law, James is one of the finest men on the bench. He seems to be worried about the November election, but as far as I can see, he won't have a problem. No, what I'm talking about is something else entirely."

Summer felt like sitting down, too. Both her mother and Julie had mysteriously disappeared, and since the photographer had yet to show up, she decided to relax.

"Have you seen James?" she asked, missing him dreadfully.

"Oh, yes."

"How is he?" She folded her hands, wondering what James was thinking and if he was sorry he'd gotten involved in all this. Everything had seemed so uncomplicated when they discussed it the night before.

"He's pacing in his room."

"Pacing," she repeated, certain this was a bad sign.

"It's just as well this wedding's going to happen less than an hour from now. I don't think your father and brother could keep James away from you much longer than that."

Summer smiled in relief.

"Never thought I'd see the day my boy would fall head over heels in love like this."

"But he was engaged before. I know about Christy Manning."

"Ah, yes, Christy. She's a dear girl, and James had strong feelings for her, but deep down I believe what he found so attractive about Christy was her family. There's quite a difference between the love James has for you and what he felt for Christy Manning. As you'll recall, he was content to stay engaged to Christy for a good long while. But you... He's marrying you so fast, my head's spinning. His, too, from the looks of him. You've thrown him for quite a loop."

"I love James, too," Summer said with feeling, "very much."

"Good. I hope the two of you will seriously consider

making me a grandfather soon. I'm hoping for a grand-child or two to spoil."

"We'd like to have four."

"Four." Walter nodded, looking pleased. "But you're worried about something."

"Yes," she said softly, wondering how he knew. "My biggest fear is that I'm not the right kind of wife for James. I'm afraid I might inadvertently harm his career."

"What makes you think that?"

"I have this tendency to speak my mind."

"I find that refreshing."

"You will until I put my foot in my mouth and embarrass James. To give you an example…" She hesitated, not sure she should continue, then realized she couldn't very well stop now. "I'm the one who suggested we get married."

"Really?"

"It just…came out. It seemed like a brilliant idea at the time…you know how good things can sound until you've thought them through. Well, anyway, James stared at me like he'd swallowed his tongue."

Walter burst out laughing. "Forgive me, my dear. Continue, please."

"Naturally I felt like a fool. Mainly because James didn't say anything and didn't say anything and didn't say anything, and I was convinced I'd ruined everything."

"He said nothing, did he?"

"Well, he did mumble something about preferring to do the asking himself."

"And you clammed up."

"Oh, quite the opposite. I started talking at hurricane speed until he told me it was fine and I needn't worry. And then, after I'd fallen all over myself telling him how sorry

I was, he said he thought it was a good idea. James came up with the idea of a ceremony now and then one in April."

"He did?" Clearly this was news to his father.

"Yes." Summer grinned sheepishly. "He said something about impulsive thoughts being contagious."

"There's more to the boy than I assumed."

There was another knock at the door, and the photographer let himself inside.

"I'd better get back to James," Walter said. "It's been a delight meeting you, Summer. I don't have a shred of doubt that you're the best thing to come into my son's life for a very long time. Make him happy, Summer, make him very happy."

"I intend to do my best."

"And while you're at it, teach him how to laugh."

Summer nodded. "I'll try." She had a sneaking suspicion they had plenty to teach one another.

James looked at his watch for the third time that minute. No one seemed to understand that he *needed* to see Summer. Needed to talk to her, find out about her day, tell her about his.

If he'd had even an inkling that their wedding was going to cause such a big commotion, he would never have agreed to contact their families.

James liked Summer's parents, but he'd prefer to spend his time with her. Alone.

"We can go into the chapel now," Hank Lawton said.

James was so grateful he felt like cheering. According to his calculations, the ceremony would take approximately twenty minutes, thirty at most. They'd sign the marriage certificate, and the rest of the night would be theirs. He couldn't tolerate any more of these separations, however brief. The next time Summer left his sight would be at the airport.

He saw her family in the small chapel, her brother's children wide-eyed and excited as the organ music rose triumphantly. He noticed that the wedding chapel was almost full and wondered for just a moment who the other guests were.

James went to stand in front with the minister, Reverend Floyd Wilson. James had rented the tuxedo because it seemed odd for the father of the bride to be wearing one and not the groom. Now, however, the shirt seemed too tight around the collar. He resisted the urge to insert his finger and give himself a little extra breathing space.

It was then that Summer appeared.

James felt as if someone had smashed him in the knees with a bat. Never in all his life had he seen anyone more beautiful. His heart beat so hard he thought it might pound straight through his chest.

Her dress was silk and lace with pearls, as traditional a wedding gown as any he'd seen. One would think Summer was a debutante and this a society wedding.

When she joined him at the altar and placed her arm in his, James felt this was the proudest moment of his life. He knew they'd repeat the ceremony in a few months, but nothing would match the blend of humility and pride he experienced right then.

Her brother, Adam, was kind enough to serve as his best man, while Julie, of course, was the maid of honor.

The ceremony itself was a blur. James's full concentration was on the woman at his side. He knew she was feeling the same emotions he was when she began to repeat her vows.

Summer's voice shook slightly, and she sounded close to tears. His arm tightened around hers as the minister said, "I now pronounce you husband and wife. You may kiss your bride."

James didn't need to hear that twice. Carefully he gathered Summer close, sighing when their lips met in the tenderest, sweetest kiss of his life.

She clung to him. "Oh, James, how soon can we get rid of everyone?"

He'd entertained that very question from the moment Summer's mother had taken her away that morning.

"Soon," he promised. Heaven only knew how they were going to cope with being separated for the next four months. "After dinner."

They were hit with a barrage of birdseed on their way out the door. They laughed and tried to catch it in their outstretched hands.

"Pictures," Helen insisted, and when Summer groaned, she added, "Just a few more. That's all."

"Mother, you'll get plenty of pictures later."

"I want some now," her mother insisted. But "some" turned out to be at least a hundred by James's estimation.

They signed the marriage license, and James took the opportunity to kiss his bride. "I don't ever want to spend another day like this one," he whispered.

"Me, neither," she said, then giggled. "But you're going to get something out of it. Mother bought me this cute little black nightie."

James could feel the hot blood circle his ears and...other places. "Your mother bought you a nightie?"

"She said it's her wedding gift to you."

"I'll thank her later."

"Wait until you see what Julie got us," she whispered.

"I have the feeling it isn't a toaster," he said wryly.

Summer laughed. "No. She picked it out when Mom wasn't looking. You do like tassels, don't you?"

"Tassels?"

"Shh." Summer looked around to be sure no one was listening. "I'll save them for after the honeymoon."

"Why?"

"Because, my darling husband, they cover—" She stopped abruptly.

"Yes?" he coaxed.

"Husband," she said the word as if saying a prayer. "James, you're my *husband*."

"I know. And you're my wife." It hit him then, too. The beauty of it, of belonging to each other, of the word itself.

Their families all seemed to return at once.

"I don't know about anyone else," Helen Lawton was saying, "but I'm starved."

There was a chorus of agreement. They trooped into the hotel's elegant restaurant and ordered dinner and champagne, although Summer could barely eat and had trouble following the conversation.

"We'll say good-night, then," James announced the minute they could leave without being rude. "Thank you all for making this the most incredible day of my life."

"It's still early," Helen protested.

"Helen," Hank snapped. "Think about it."

"Oh, yes, sorry." Helen's face brightened, and she smiled apologetically at James.

"Will we see you in the morning?"

"Helen!" her husband growled.

"I'm just asking, Hank. What harm is there in asking?"

"I don't know, Mom. What time is your flight?"

James didn't listen to the answer, although he supposed he should have. As it was, he had a hard time hiding his impatience. He and his wife—his wife—would only have two more days together. Luckily that was two days and *three* nights. Their flights were leaving within a half hour of each other, and then it would be a whole month before he saw her again.

"All right, then, darling," Helen said, hugging Summer, "we'll see you both in the morning."

The entourage left, and James was alone with Summer at last.

"Are we going to my room or yours?" she asked, smiling up at him.

"Neither. I rented the honeymoon suite here for the rest of our stay. Your mother packed your suitcase and had it sent over."

"You think of everything." She reached up and removed the wedding veil and shook her head, freeing her curls. "I can't tell you how anxious I am to get out of this dress."

James chuckled as he led the way to the elevator. "Not nearly as anxious as I am to get you out of it."

"Who were all those guests?" she asked him when they stepped inside the elevator car.

"I thought they were friends of your family."

"I've never seen them before in my life."

James shrugged. "Me, neither."

"You know what? I'll bet my mother invited them. She couldn't bear to have us married in an empty chapel."

James fingered his room key. "Are you hungry?"

"No."

"Good. Let's go work up an appetite."

Summer smiled and moistened her lips with the tip of her tongue. "I have a feeling you aren't talking about racquetball."

James cleared his throat. He wanted her so much his body trembled with the strength of his need. "You're right about that."

Six

James astonished Summer. She didn't know what to expect from him as a lover, but it wasn't this. They'd made love no less than three times during their wedding night, and Summer woke the following morning to find him standing at the foot of their bed, fresh from the shower.

His nude body glistened in the early-morning light. Droplets of water dripped from his hair and onto the dark curls that covered his chest.

"Good morning, Mrs. Wilkens."

Summer smiled and stretched her arms high above her head, arching her back. The sheet slipped away, exposing her breasts.

"Good morning, James." She saw that he was fully aroused and slowly lifted her gaze to his. Already her body was responding to him, throbbing with readiness and need. James's eyes narrowed as they focused on her.

Wordlessly she knelt on the bed and held out her arms to him. She smiled, thinking someone should've warned her about this man before they were married. At this rate, they'd both be dead within a week.

He walked over to the side of the bed, kissed her once, twice, and then knelt beside it.

All her life Summer had never experienced such power. Or such love. Her breathing grew slow and shallow. She half closed her eyes in pleasure at the simple touch of his hand.

James groaned, and Summer recognized his meaning. He couldn't wait any longer. Neither could she. She threw her arms around his neck and slowly lay back against the bed, bringing him with her.

She smiled contentedly as they began to make love. All of a sudden her eyes flew open. "James, you forgot—"

"It'll be all right," he assured her breathlessly. "Just this one time."

She didn't want him to stop. Not now. "Okay."

James reached his climax soon after she experienced hers. A harsh groan tore from his throat, and his powerful body shuddered.

His shoulders still heaving, he gathered her in his arms and spread soft, delicate kisses over her face. He started to move away from her, but she wouldn't let him.

"Not yet," she pleaded. "I want to be a part of you."

"You are. You always will be. You could travel to Mars, and my heart would be with you." He brushed the damp hair from her forehead. "I can't believe you love me."

"I do, so much my heart feels like it's about to burst wide open. Will it always be like this?" she asked. "Two weeks ago, you were someone whose letters I looked forward to. This week you're the most important person in my life."

James kissed the tip of her nose. "It's only going to get better from here on out."

"Better?" She laughed delightedly. "I can't imagine it."

In one uninterrupted movement James rolled onto his

back, taking her with him so she was sprawled across his chest. Across his heart. "I can't, either. Summer, I love you."

"Good." She pressed her head against his shoulder. "But what about—"

"I'll remember next time," he promised. "The last thing we need now is an unplanned pregnancy."

"I'm pretty sure this is my safe time, so don't worry."

James kissed her neck. "I suppose we should get dressed and meet everyone for breakfast."

"I suppose," she agreed, but neither of them showed any signs of moving.

"It won't be so bad," James whispered.

They'd been married less than twenty-four hours and already Summer could read her husband's thoughts. "Being separated? It's going to be terrible. I don't know how I'll last four months without you."

"Four months." He made it sound like an eternity.

"James, where do you live?"

He gave her a puzzled look. "Seattle. You know my address."

"But is it an apartment? A condo? A town house or what?"

"A house."

Summer liked the idea of that.

A slow grin spread across his face. "I must've known I was going to meet you. This is a big house on Queen Anne Hill with seven bedrooms."

"James!"

"It's a lovely older home. I'm quite proud of the garden. I hope you'll like it."

"I love it already."

"You haven't seen it."

"No, but I saw the look on your face when you talked

about it. The house is going to be perfect for us, just perfect."

His eyes grew dark. "*You're* perfect."

"I hope we'll always love each other as much as we do at this moment." Summer laid her head on his chest and sighed.

Time had never passed more quickly for James. He'd dreaded leaving Summer almost from the moment they'd met again on New Year's Eve. It was as though Seattle was another world, one he wasn't that eager to return to. Not when it meant having to say goodbye to Summer.

His wife of two days was unusually quiet as they packed their suitcases on Saturday morning, the day of their departure. When she found him watching her, she offered him a reassuring smile.

The bellboy carried their luggage to the lobby. While James was checking out of the hotel, he noticed Summer twisting the plain gold band around her finger. His own felt awkward and heavy, and he wondered if she was experiencing any regrets. For his own part, he didn't have a single one.

Having returned the rental car earlier, James ordered a car. He and Summer held hands as they rode silently to the airport.

He wanted to assure her it wouldn't be so bad, but that would've been a blatant lie. Every minute he was away from her was a minute too long. He wanted to be sure she understood how much he loved her, how crucial she was to him. But the backseat of a limo with a driver listening in didn't seem the most appropriate place to tell her those things.

Nothing would ever be the same for either of them, and they both knew it.

The car dropped them off, and since they were flying on different airlines, they separated to check in their luggage and receive their seat assignments.

James finished first and caught sight of Summer hurrying through the crowd toward him. Even from that distance he sensed her sadness. He met her halfway and they went through security together.

"My flight leaves from Concourse B," she said, looking down at her ticket. Her voice was small and tight.

"Mine's Concourse A."

"What time's your flight?"

She already knew, but apparently needed to hear it again. "Ten-thirty," James told her.

"My departure's at ten."

He was perfectly aware of what time her plane left. "I'll walk down to Concourse B with you."

"You can't, James, you might miss your own flight."

Frankly he didn't give a damn. "Then I'll catch the next one."

"I'll worry. James, really, I'm a big girl. I can find my way around the airport."

"I didn't say you couldn't," he snapped, surprising himself.

Summer looked up at him, her eyes brimming with tears. She turned and walked away from him and headed for Concourse B.

James followed and wanted to kick himself. He wouldn't see his wife for weeks and here he was, apparently doing his utmost to start an argument. No doubt there was some psychological reason for his attitude. He'd examine what was happening later, but at the moment he was more concerned about saying goodbye to her properly.

Summer arrived at her gate and walked over to the window. James could see her plane and knew it wouldn't be more than a few moments before the boarding call was announced.

"I'm sorry, sweetheart." He rested his hands on her shoulders and closed his eyes.

"Me, too."

He frowned. She'd done nothing wrong. "For what?"

"Oh, James," she whispered brokenly, slipping her arms around his waist. "I'm going to be so lost without you."

"It's going to be hard." He wasn't willing to pretend otherwise. "I'll phone as often as I can."

"Do you have my work schedule?" she asked.

"Yes. Do you have everything you need?" They'd gone over the details a dozen times.

"No. I need you, James."

His hold on her tightened. He wondered if they were afraid they'd lose the magic. Afraid that once they returned to their respective lives, everything would change.

Her flight number was announced, and James tensed. It wouldn't be long before he saw her, he promised himself. He'd try for a week, two at the most. A few minutes later her row was called.

"That's you," he said reluctantly.

"I know."

But neither of them made a move to break apart.

Summer was the last one to board the plane, and James had to tear through the airport in order to catch his own flight. If anyone had suggested even ten days ago that the dignified James Wilkens would race through an airport so he could spend a few extra minutes with a woman, he would have scoffed. He wasn't scoffing now.

He arrived in the nick of time and collapsed into his seat, his heart racing.

Between dashing through airports and hours spent making love, Summer would be the death of him yet. He smiled as he snapped his seat belt into place. If he was to die that very moment, he'd leave this earth a happy man.

James's house had never seemed so empty. By the time he got home, it was dark and shadowy. His first mistake had been stopping at the office on his way back from the airport. After he arrived in Seattle, he'd spent what remained of the day working through the memos, briefs and case histories. No one else was in, so he was able to accomplish quite a bit, catching up on some of his backlog. He'd do anything he had to so he could arrange time away as soon as possible.

Summer was never far from his thoughts.

Once he reached his house, suitcase in hand, he was exhausted. He switched on the light in the kitchen, put down his bags and set his briefcase on the walnut table in the breakfast nook.

He hadn't eaten since that morning, and a look inside the refrigerator reminded him he'd been away all week. He'd need to order out or microwave something from the freezer.

Deciding against both, he heated a can of soup, ate, then showered. He'd showered that morning, but Summer had been in the stall with him and neither one had seemed particularly concerned about washing.

James stood in front of the mirror in the steamy bathroom and wiped off some of the condensation, then stared at his reflection. He didn't look all that different from the man he'd been a week ago. But he *was* different.

Unable to delay talking to Summer, he dressed quickly and headed for his book-lined den.

Having memorized her apartment and cell phone numbers, James called her at home.

Summer answered on the first ring. "Hello."

"Hello, darling."

"James!"

"I would've called sooner, but I went to the office. I needed to clear off my desk."

"Did you check your calendar?"

"First thing. I can fly down on a Saturday morning in two weeks, but I'll need to be back Sunday afternoon. That doesn't give us much time."

"No," she agreed, "but we'll make the most of it." Her relief was evident. "I was afraid once you looked at your schedule you'd find it impossible to get away."

"I don't care what it takes, I'll be in California in two weeks."

"Wonderful. I traded weekends with a friend so I can come to you in February. My mother's already started to plan the wedding. She's left a message with the secretary at the Moose Hall. It's a very nice building."

"Your mother's enjoying every minute of this, isn't she?"

Summer laughed. "Yes. But the one who surprises me most is my dad. I don't know what you said or did, but my dad thinks you walk on water."

It was his turn to laugh.

Then they were both silent. They'd spent nearly every minute of the previous week together. They'd discussed everything there was to discuss. Yet neither was willing to break the connection.

An hour later they were still on the phone. They hadn't spoken more than a few words between whispered promises and deep sighs. They'd shared a few secrets and memories, some of them very private. Very intimate...

In their next conversation, he'd let Summer know he couldn't handle much more of that.

"I've gotten together with a group of businessmen and spread the word," Ralph Southworth was saying.

James sat in his office, gazing into the distance. As always, his thoughts were fifteen hundred miles to the south with Summer. He barely heard his campaign manager. In eight days he'd be with his wife. The last six had been the purest form of torture.

He lived for the times he could phone her. Because she performed in the last show of the night, he couldn't reach her until after ten, and more often than not they spoke until past midnight.

"There's a dinner party this Friday night at the Morrisons'," Ralph announced.

James didn't comment.

"You're going, aren't you?"

"You mean to the Morrisons'?"

Ralph Southworth looked at him oddly. "Who else do you think I mean?"

James shrugged. Ralph was a good man, a bit abrasive at times, but sincere and hardworking. According to people James trusted, Ralph Southworth was the best man for the job of getting James elected to the superior court.

"What's with you lately, James?" Ralph asked abruptly. He pulled out a chair and sat down across from James's desk.

Ralph was nothing if not direct. "What makes you ask?"

"Something's not right. Ever since you got back from vacation, you haven't been the same."

James considered telling Ralph the truth. Part of him was eager to share the news of his marriage. Marrying

Summer was nothing to be ashamed of—the opposite, in fact—but arrangements for the second ceremony were already being made. If he was willing to face the truth, James would have to admit he wasn't keen on explaining his sudden marriage, especially to the man who'd frowned on his vacation in Vegas. He preferred to leave things as they were and invite Ralph to the wedding in April. So far, he'd told no one about Summer and for the time being even left his wedding band at home.

"Have you ever been in love?" he asked, unable to resist.

Ralph shook his head adamantly. "Never, and proud of it."

James's eyebrows shot to his hairline. "I see."

"Women have ruined more than one good man. Don't be a fool, James. Don't do anything stupid at this point. Unless it's with someone who can help you politically, of course. Now, if you told me you were seeing Mary Horton…"

"Who?"

"Mary Horton—never mind, she's not your type. All I can say is that if you're going to fall for someone now, just make sure it's a woman who can help you politically."

"She can't."

Ralph tossed his hands in the air. "Somehow, I knew you were going to say that. Listen. Keep your head screwed on tight and your pants zipped up. The last thing we need now is a scandal, understand?"

"Of course. Summer's not like—"

"Her name is *Summer?*" Ralph rolled his eyes expressively. "James, listen to me. You've asked me to run your campaign, and I'm glad to do it, but I'm telling you right now, getting involved with a woman named Summer is asking for trouble."

"Don't you think you're being unfair?"

"No. Where'd you meet her?"

"Vegas."

Ralph's mouth thinned. "Don't tell me she's a showgirl," he muttered.

"No—but she's an actress."

A muscle leapt in his friend's jaw. "Don't say anything more. Not a single word. I've got high blood pressure and don't want to know any more than you've already told me."

"Summer has nothing to do with you," James said, finding it difficult to quell his irritation. Ralph made Summer sound like…like a mistake.

"Don't you remember a certain congressman who got involved with a stripper a few years back?"

"Summer isn't a stripper!"

"It ruined him, James. Ruined him. I don't want the same thing to happen to you."

"It won't. Furthermore, I won't have you speaking about her in those terms." In light of Ralph's reaction, James didn't think now was the time to announce they were already married. "If you must know, I intend to marry her."

"Great. Do it after the election."

"We've decided on April."

"April!" Ralph barked. "That's much too soon. Listen, you're paying me big money to run this campaign. You want my advice, you've got it. What difference would a few months make?" He paused, waiting for James's response. "Will you do that one thing?"

"I don't know."

"Are you afraid you'll lose her?"

"No."

"Then put off the wedding until after the election. Is that so much to ask?"

* * *

"I'm not sure which is worse," Julie said, applying bright red polish to her toenails, "this year or last."

"What do you mean?" Summer asked.

"You." She swirled the brush in the red paint and started with the little toe on her left foot. "Last year, after you broke up with Brett, you moped around the apartment for months."

Summer laughed. "This year isn't much better, is it?"

"Not that I can see. Listen, I understand how much you miss James. The guy's hot. No wonder you fell for him. If the situation was reversed, you can bet I'd be just as miserable. The thing is, you won't be apart for long. April's right around the corner."

Summer folded her arms and leaned against the back of the sofa. "I didn't know it was possible to love someone as much as I love James."

"If the number of times he calls you is any indication, I'd say he feels the same about you."

"He works so hard." Summer knew that many of James's late-night calls came from his office. She also knew he was putting in extra-long hours in order to free up time he could spend with her.

"Summer, he'll be here in a few days."

"I know."

"You haven't told him about Brett?" Julie asked.

Summer's nails bit into her palms. "What good would it do? James is fifteen hundred miles away. Brett hasn't got a chance with me. Unfortunately he doesn't seem ready to accept that. But he's going to get the same message whenever he calls."

"By the way, when James visits, I'm out of here."

"Julie, you don't need to leave. We can get a hotel room—really, we don't mind."

"Don't be ridiculous. This is your home. You'd be more relaxed, and both of you have been through enough stress lately."

Summer was so grateful it was all she could do not to weep. It was the stress, she decided, this tendency to be over emotional. "Have I told you how glad I am that you're my friend?"

"Think nothing of it," Julie said airily.

"I mean it, Julie. I don't know what I would've done without you these last weeks. I feel like my whole world's been turned upside down."

"It has been. Who else goes away for a week and comes home married? Did you think James had lost his mind when he suggested it?"

"Yes," she admitted, remembering the most fabulous dinner of her life. "I don't think he's done anything that impulsive his whole life."

Julie grinned. "Until he met you."

"Funny, James made the same comment."

The phone rang just then, and Summer leapt up to answer it on the off chance it was James.

"Hello," she said breathlessly.

"Summer, don't hang up, please, I'm begging you."

"Brett." Her heart sank. "Please," she told him, "just leave me alone."

"Talk to me. That's all I'm asking."

"About what? We have absolutely nothing to say to each other."

"I made a mistake."

Summer closed her eyes, fighting the frustration. "It's

too late. What do I have to say to convince you of that? You're married, I'm married."

"I don't believe it." His voice grew hoarse. "If you're married, then where's your husband?"

"I don't owe you any explanations. Don't phone me again. It's over and has been for more than a year."

"Summer, please...please."

She didn't wait to hear any more. His persistence astonished her. When she'd found him with another woman, he'd seemed almost glad, as though he was relieved to be free of the relationship. In retrospect, Summer realized that Brett had fallen out of love with her long before, but had lacked the courage to say anything. Later, when he'd married, and she learned it wasn't the same woman he'd been with in Vegas, she wondered about this man she thought she knew so well, and discovered she didn't know him at all.

His behavior mystified her. After loving Brett for six years, she expected to feel *something* for him, but all the feeling she could muster was pity. She wanted nothing to do with him. He'd made his choice and she'd made hers.

"Brett? Again?" Julie asked when Summer joined her in the living room.

Summer nodded. "I hope this is the end of it."

"Have you thought about having the phone number changed?"

"That's a good idea. And I'm going to get call display, too."

Julie studied her for a moment. "Are you going to tell James why we've got a new phone number?"

"No. It would only worry him, and there's nothing he can do so far away. Brett doesn't concern me."

"Maybe he should."

* * *

Summer arrived at the Orange County airport forty minutes before James's flight was due, in case it came in early. Every minute of their day and a half together was carefully planned.

The only negative for Summer was the brunch with her parents Sunday morning. Her mother had several questions about the wedding that she needed to discuss with James. Summer begrudged every minute she had to share James; she knew she was being selfish, but she didn't care.

Julie, true to her word, had made a weekend trip to visit a family member, an elderly aunt in Claremont.

By the time James's plane touched down, she was nearly sick to her stomach with anticipation. As soon as he stepped out of the secure area, he paused, searching for her.

Their eyes connected and in the second before he started toward her, her heart seemed to stop. Then it began to race.

When they'd parted in Las Vegas, it felt as if everything had come to an abrupt standstill. Now she could see him, could *feel* him, for the first time since they'd parted two weeks ago.

Dashing between the other passengers, she ran toward him. James caught her in his arms and crushed her against him. His hands were in her hair, and his mouth hungrily sought hers.

His embrace half lifted her from the ground. She clung to him, fighting back a flood of emotion. Unexpectedly tears filled her eyes, but she was too happy to care.

James broke off the kiss, and Summer stared up at him, smiling. It was so good to see him.

"What's this?" he asked, brushing his thumb across the moisture on her cheeks.

"I guess I missed you more than I realized."

"You're beautiful," he said in a low voice.

"I bet you tell all the women that," she joked.

"Nope, only the ones I marry."

Summer slipped her arm around his waist, and together they headed toward the luggage carousel. "I packed light."

"Good." Because it felt so good to be close to him, she stood on the tips of her toes and kissed his cheek. "You'll be glad to hear Julie's gone for the weekend."

"Remind me to thank her."

"She's been wonderful."

"Any more crank calls?"

Summer had almost forgotten that was the excuse she'd given him when she'd had her phone numbers changed. "None." And then, because she was eager to change the subject, she told him, "I've got every minute planned."

"Every minute?"

"Well, almost. Mom and Dad invited us over for brunch in the morning. I couldn't think of any way to get out of it."

"It might be a good idea to see them."

"Why?"

James frowned, and she noticed the dark circles under his eyes. He was working too hard, not sleeping enough, not eating properly. That would all change when she got to Seattle. The first thing she'd do was make sure he had three decent meals a day. As for time in bed, well, she didn't think that would be a problem.

"There might be a problem with the wedding date," he said reluctantly.

Summer halted midstep. "What do you mean?"

"April might not work, after all." He paused. "It doesn't matter, does it? We're already married."

"I know, but…"

"We can talk about it later, with your family. All right?"

She nodded, unwilling to waste even one precious minute arguing over a fancy wedding when she already wore his ring.

Seven

For years James had lived an impassive and sober life. He'd never considered himself a physical man. But three weeks after marrying Summer, making love occupied far more of his thoughts than it had in the previous thirty-odd years combined.

"How far is it to your apartment?" he asked, as they walked to her car.

Summer didn't immediately respond.

"Summer?"

"It seems to me we have a few things to discuss."

"All right," he said, forcing himself to stop staring at her. She had him at a distinct disadvantage. At the moment he would have agreed to just about anything, no matter where the discussion led—as long as they got to her place soon. As long as they could be alone…

"I want to know why there's a problem with the wedding date."

He should've realized. "Sweetheart, it has more to do with your parents than you and me. Let's not worry about it now."

"You want to delay the wedding, don't you?"

"No," he responded vehemently. "Do you honestly think I'm enjoying this separation? I couldn't be more miserable."

"Me, neither."

"Then you have to believe I wouldn't do anything that would keep us apart any longer than necessary." James glanced at her as she drove. He was telling the truth, although not, perhaps, the whole truth. Time enough for that later, he thought. He was worried about Summer. She seemed pale and drawn, as if she weren't sleeping well or eating right. This situation wasn't good for either of them.

After fifteen minutes they arrived at her apartment building. He carried in his suitcase and set it down in her small living room, gazing around.

Summer's personality seemed to mark each area. The apartment was bright and cheerful. The kitchen especially appealed to him; the cabinets had been painted a bold yellow with red knobs. Without asking, he knew this was her special touch.

She led him into her bedroom, and he stopped when he noticed the five-foot wall poster of her as Beauty posing with the Beast. She looked so beautiful he couldn't take his eyes off it. He felt a hint of jealousy of the man who was able to spend time with her every night, even if it was in costume.

His gaze moved from the picture to the bed. A single. He supposed it wouldn't matter. The way he felt just then, they'd spend the whole night making love anyway.

He turned toward his wife. She smiled softly, and in that instant James knew he couldn't wait any longer. His need was so great that his entire body seemed to throb with a need of its own.

He held out his hand, and she walked toward him.

If he had any regrets about their time in Vegas, it was

that he'd been so eager for her, so awkward and clumsy. Tonight would be slow and easy, he'd promised himself. When they made love, it would be leisurely so she'd know how much he appreciated her. They'd savor each other without interruption.

"Summer, I love you." He lifted the shirt over her head and tossed it carelessly aside. His hands were at the snap of her jeans, trembling as he struggled to hold back the urgency of his need.

He kissed her with two weeks' worth of pent-up hunger, and all his accumulated frustration broke free.

He eased the jeans over her slender hips and let them fall to her feet, then released her long enough to remove his own clothes. As he was unbuttoning his shirt, he watched her slip out of her silky underwear. His breath caught in his throat.

When James finished undressing, they collapsed on the narrow bed together. And then he lost all sense of time….

Summer woke to the sound of James humming off-key in the kitchen. The man couldn't carry a tune in a bucket, as her dad liked to say. Smiling, she glanced at her clock radio—almost 6:00 p.m. She reached for her housecoat and entered the kitchen to find him examining the contents of her refrigerator.

"So you're one of those," she teased, tying the sash of her robe.

"One of what?" He reappeared brandishing a chicken leg.

"You get hungry after sex," she whispered.

"I didn't eat on the plane, and yes," he said, grinning shyly at her, "I suspect you're right."

She yawned and sat on the bar stool. "Anything interesting in there?"

"Leftover chicken, cottage cheese three weeks past its expiration date, Swiss cheese and an orange."

"I'll take the orange." She yawned again.

"Have you been getting enough sleep?" He peeled the orange and handed it to her, frowning. It wasn't his imagination; she was pale.

"More than ever. I seem to be exhausted lately. All I do is work and sleep."

"Have you seen a doctor?"

"No. I'm fine," she said, forcing a smile. She didn't want to waste their precious time together discussing her sleeping patterns. She ate a section of the rather dry orange. "I better shower and get dressed."

"For the show?"

She nodded, sad that part of her weekend with James would be spent on the job, but there was no help for it. It was difficult enough to trade schedules in order to fly up to Seattle.

"I'm looking forward to seeing what a talented woman I married."

"I hope I don't disappoint you."

"Not possible." He shook his head solemnly.

"James," she said, staring down at the orange. "Do you ever wonder what's really there between us?"

He tossed the chicken bone into the garbage. "What do you mean?"

"Sometimes I'm afraid all we share is a strong physical attraction. Is there more?"

He swallowed; the question seemed to make him uncomfortable. "What makes you ask that?"

"In case you haven't noticed, we can't keep our hands off each other."

"What's wrong with that?"

"I think about us making love—a lot. Probably more than I should. You're a brilliant man. I'm fairly sure you didn't marry me because I challenge you intellectually."

"I married you because I fell in love with you."

He made it sound so uncomplicated.

"I love the way a room lights up when you walk into it," he said. "When you laugh, I want to laugh, too. I've never heard you sing or seen you perform on stage, but there's music in you, Summer. I sensed it the first night we met.

"Just being with you makes me want to smile. Not that you're telling jokes or doing pratfalls or anything—it's your attitude. When I'm with you, the world's a better place."

Summer felt her throat tighten.

"Like your father, an attorney or a judge can develop a jaded perspective in life. It's difficult to trust when the world's filled with suspicion. It's difficult to love when you deal with the consequences of hate every day. Perhaps that's been my problem all along."

"Not trusting?"

"Yes. You came to me without defenses, devastated, vulnerable, broken. I'd been hurt, too, so I knew how you felt because I'd experienced those same emotions. I'd walk through the fires of hell before I'd allow anyone to do that to you again." He walked over and held out his hand. "It's more than just words when I say I love you, Summer. It's my heart, my whole heart."

She gripped his hand with both of hers.

"If you're afraid our relationship is too much about sex-ual attraction, then maybe we should put a hold on anything physical for the rest of the weekend. Instead, we'll concentrate on getting to know each other better."

"Do you think it's possible?" She gave him a knowing look, then leaned forward. The front of her robe gaped open, and Summer watched as he stared at her breasts, then carefully averted his eyes.

"It's possible," he said in a low voice. "Not easy, but possible."

"I need to take a shower before I leave for work." She slipped off the stool and started to walk away. Then she turned, looked over her shoulder and smiled seductively. "Remember what fun we had in the shower, James?"

James paled. "Summer," he warned through clenched teeth. "If we're going to stay out of the bedroom, I'll need your help."

She turned to face him full on. "The shower isn't in the bedroom."

"Go have your shower," he said stiffly. "I'll wait for you here."

"You're sure?" She released the sash and let the silk robe fall open.

He made a sound that could mean various things—but he didn't make a move. Feeling slightly disappointed, Summer walked slowly into the bathroom and turned on the shower.

She'd just stepped inside and adjusted the water when the shower door was pulled open.

Naked, James joined her there. "You know I can't resist you," he muttered.

"Yes," she said softly. "I can't resist you, either."

Summer and her mother were busy in the kitchen at the Lawton family home. James sat in the living room with his father-in-law, watching a Sunday-morning sports show.

James didn't have the heart to tell Hank that he didn't follow sports all that much. And he sure wasn't going to admit he found them boring.

"Helen's going to be talking to you later," Hank said, relaxing during a spell of uninterrupted beer commercials. "She's having trouble getting a decent hall for the wedding reception in April. The church is no problem, mind you, but finding a hall's become pretty complicated."

"Summer said something about the Moose Hall."

"That fell through. I'll let Helen do the explaining."

"Does Summer know this?"

"Not yet. Couldn't see upsetting her. The girl's been miserable ever since she got back from Vegas. You want my opinion?" He didn't wait for a response. "You should take her to Seattle with you now and be done with it. It's clear to me the two of you belong together."

James wished it was that easy.

"I know, I know," Hank said, scooting forward to the edge of his chair as some football players ran back onto a muddy field. "She has to fulfill her contract. Never understood where the girl got her singing talent."

"She's fabulous." Summer's performance had shocked James. Her singing had moved him deeply and her acting impressed him.

Hank beamed proudly. "She's good, isn't she? I'll never forget the night I first went to see her perform at Disneyland. It was all I could do not to stand up and yell out, 'Hey, that's my little girl up there.'"

"There's such power in her voice."

"Enough to crack crystal, isn't it? You'd never suspect it hearing her speak, but the minute she opens her mouth to sing, watch out. I've never heard anything like it."

James had come away awed by her talent. That she'd

willingly walk away from her career to be his wife, willingly take her chances in a new city, humbled him.

"She could go all the way to the top."

Hank nodded. "I think so, too, if she wanted, but that's the thing. She loves singing, don't get me wrong, but Summer will be just as happy humming lullabies to her babies as she would be performing in some hit Broadway show."

James's heart clutched at the thought of Summer singing to their children.

"Helen's mother used to sing," Hank said, but his eyes didn't leave the television screen. He frowned when the sports highlights moved on to tennis. "Ruth didn't sing professionally, but she was a member of the church choir for years. Talent's a funny business. Summer was singing from the time she was two. Now, Adam, he sounds like a squeaky door."

"Me, too." All James could hope was that their children inherited their mother's singing ability.

"Don't worry about it. She loves you anyway."

James wasn't quite sure how to respond, but fortunately he didn't have to, because Helen poked her head in at that moment.

"Brunch is ready," she said. "Hank, turn off that blasted TV."

"But, Helen—"

"Hank!"

"All right, all right." Reluctantly Hank reached for the TV controller and muted the television. His wife didn't seem to notice, and Hank sent James a conspiratorial wink. "Compromise," he whispered. "She won't even know."

James sat next to Summer at the table. "This looks delicious," he said to Helen. His mother-in-law had obviously gone to a lot of trouble with this brunch. She'd prepared sausages and ham slices and bacon, along with some kind of egg casserole, fresh-baked sweet rolls, coffee and juice.

Helen waited until they'd all filled their plates before she mentioned the April wedding date. "The reason I wanted to talk to the two of you has to do with the wedding date." She paused, apparently unsure how to proceed. "I wasn't too involved with Adam's wedding when he married Denise. I had no idea we'd need to book the reception hall so far in advance."

"But I thought you already *had* the place," Summer wailed.

"Didn't happen, sweetheart," Hank said. "Trust me, your mother's done her best. I can't tell you how many phone calls she's made."

"If we're going to have the wedding you deserve," her mother said pointedly, "it'll need to be later than April. My goodness, it takes time just to get the invitations printed, and we can't order them until we have someplace *nice* for the reception."

"How much later?" was James's question.

Helen and Hank exchanged looks. "June might work, but September would be best."

"September," Summer cried.

"September's out of the question." With the primary in September, James couldn't manage time away for a wedding. "If we're going to wait that long, anyway, then let's do it after the election in November." The minute he made the suggestion, James realized he'd said the wrong thing.

"November." Summer's voice sagged with defeat. "So what am I supposed to do between April and November?"

"Move up to Seattle with James, of course," Hank said without a qualm.

"Absolutely not," Helen protested. "We can't have our daughter living with James before they're married."

"Helen, for the love of heaven, they're already married. Remember?"

"Yes, but no one knows that."

"James?"

Everyone turned to him. "Other than my dad, no one knows I'm married, either."

Summer seemed to wilt. "It sounds like what you're saying is that you don't want me with you."

"No!" James could hear the hurt and disappointment in her voice and wished he knew some way to solve the problem, but he didn't. "You know that isn't true."

"Why is everything suddenly so complicated?" Summer asked despondently. "It seemed so simple when James and I first decided to do things this way. Now I feel as if we're trapped."

James had the same reaction. "We'll talk about it and get back to you," he told his in-laws. Both were content to leave it at that.

After brunch he and Summer took a walk around her old neighborhood. Their pace was leisurely, and she didn't say anything for a couple of blocks. She clasped her hands behind her back as if she didn't want to be close to him just then. He gave her the space she needed, but longed to put his arm around her.

"I know you're disappointed, sweetheart. So am I," he began. "I—"

"This is what you meant about problems with the April date, isn't it? The election."

"Yes, but…"

"I feel like excess baggage in your life."

"Summer, you *are* my life."

"Oh, James, how did everything get so messed up?"

"It's my fault," he muttered, ramming his fingers through his hair. "I was the one who suggested we go ahead with the wedding right away."

"Thank heaven. I'd hate to think how long we'd have to wait if you hadn't."

"I was being purely selfish and only a little practical. I knew I wouldn't be able to keep from making love to you much longer."

"And you're traditional enough—*gentleman* enough—to prefer to marry me first," she suggested softly.

"Something like that." She made him sound nobler than he was. He'd married her because he wanted to. Because he couldn't imagine *not* marrying her.

"As you said, the problem is the election. I had no business marrying you when I did. Not when I knew very well what this year would be like."

"The campaign?"

He nodded. "I've never been a political person, but it's a real factor in this kind of situation."

"I thought judges were nonpartisan."

"They are, but trust me, sweetheart, there's plenty of politics involved. I want to be elected, Summer, but not enough to put you through this."

She was silent again for a long moment. "One question."

"Anything."

She lowered her head and increased her pace. "Why didn't you tell anyone we're married?"

"I told my campaign manager you and I were engaged." James hesitated, selecting his words carefully.

"And?"

"And he asked me to wait until after the election to go through with the wedding. He had a number of reasons, some valid, others not, but he did say one thing that made sense."

"What?"

"He reminded me that I'm paying him good money for his advice."

"I see." She gave a short laugh that revealed little amusement. "I don't even know your campaign manager and already I dislike him."

"Ralph. Ralph Southworth. He isn't so bad."

"What will we do, James?"

"I don't know."

"Do you want me to wait until after the election to move to Seattle?"

"No," he said vehemently.

"But you have to consider Ralph's advice."

"Something like that." They walked past a school yard with a battered chain-link fence. It looked as if every third-grade class for the past twenty years had made it their personal goal to climb that fence.

"I've been thinking about this constantly," James told her. It had weighed down his heart for nearly two weeks, ever since his talk with Ralph. "There are no easy solutions."

"We don't need to decide right now, do we?"

"No." Actually James was relieved. At the moment he was more than willing to say the heck with it and move Summer to Seattle in April.

"Then let's both give it some thought in the next few weeks."

"Good idea." He placed one arm around her shoulders. "I've worked hard for this opportunity to sit on the bench, Summer, but it's not worth losing you."

"Losing me?" She smiled up at him. "You'd have a very

hard time getting rid of me, James Wilkens, and don't you forget it."

James chuckled and kissed her lightly. It was a bittersweet kiss, reminding him that in a matter of hours he'd be leaving her again. Only this time he didn't know exactly when he could be with her again.

Summer rubbed her face against the side of his. "Not so long ago, I had to practically beg you to kiss me in public."

"That was before you had me completely twisted around your little finger." The changes she'd already wrought in his life astonished him. "I don't know what I did to deserve you, but whatever it was I'm grateful."

"Your flight leaves in less than five hours."

"I know."

"I suppose we should go back to the apartment." She looked up at him and raised her delicate eyebrows. "That's plenty of time for what I have in mind."

"Summer..."

"Yes, James?" She batted her eyelashes at him. He grinned. She managed to be sexy and funny simultaneously, and he found that completely endearing.

They made their farewells to her family and were soon on their way back to the apartment. There was time to make love, he decided, shower and pack. Then he'd be gone again.

Summer must have been thinking the same thing because she said, "We always seem to be leaving each other."

James couldn't even tell her it wouldn't be for long. They parked in the lot outside her apartment, but as soon as they were out of the car James knew something wasn't right. Summer tensed, her gaze on the man climbing out of the car next to theirs.

"Summer?" James asked.

"It's Brett," she said in a low voice.

"Brett?" It took James a moment to make the connection. "*The* Brett?"

Her nod was almost imperceptible.

"What's he want?"

"I don't know."

Apparently they were about to find out. He was big—football-player size—and tanned. He wore faded cutoff jeans, a tank top and several gold chains around his neck.

"Hello, Brett," Summer said stiffly.

"Summer." He turned to James. "Who's this? A friend of your father's?"

"This is my husband. Kindly leave. We don't have anything to say to each other."

"Your husband?" Brett laughed mockingly. "You don't expect me to believe *that,* do you?"

"It's true," James answered. "Now I suggest you make yourself scarce like the lady asked."

Brett planted his muscular hands on lean hips. "Says you and what army? No way am I leaving Summer."

"As I recall, you already left her," James said smoothly, placing himself between Summer and the other man. "I also remember that you got married shortly afterward. And didn't I hear, just recently, that you and your wife are expecting a baby?"

"We're separated."

"I'm sorry to hear that. Unfortunately Summer and I are now married and she's not interested in starting anything with you."

"I don't believe that," he muttered stubbornly.

"Oh, honestly, Brett," Summer said, not concealing her impatience. "Are you such an egotist you actually think I'd want you back?"

"You love me."

"Loved," she said. "Past tense."

"Don't give me any bull about you and granddaddy here."

"Granddaddy?" she snapped. "James is ten times the man you'll ever be." She pushed in front of James and glared at her former fiancé. "You know what? Every day of my life I thank God we ended our engagement—otherwise I'd never have met James. He's taught me what loving someone really means. Which is something *you* don't have a clue about."

James had Summer by the shoulders. "It won't do any good to argue with him," he told her. He looked at Brett, who was red-faced and angry. "I think it would be best if you left."

"Stay out of this," Brett growled.

"We're married," James said, trying to add reason to a situation that was fast getting out of hand. "Nothing you say is going to change that."

Brett spit on the ground. "She's nothing but a whore anyway."

James would've walked away for almost anything. But he refused to allow anyone to speak in a derogatory way about Summer. He stepped toward Brett until they were face-to-face. "I suggest you apologize to the lady."

"Gonna make me?"

"Yes," James said. He'd been a schoolboy the last time he was in a fistfight, but he wasn't going to let this jaded, ugly man insult his wife.

Brett's hands went up first. He swung at James, who was quick enough to step aside. The second time James wasn't so fortunate. The punch hit him square in the eye, but he didn't pay attention to the pain since he was more intent on delivering his own.

"James!" Summer repeatedly screamed his name. James could vaguely hear her in the background, pleading with him to stop, that Brett wasn't worth the trouble.

The two men wrestled to the ground, and James was able to level another couple of punches. "You'll apologize," he demanded from between clenched teeth when Brett showed signs of wanting to quit.

Blood drooled from Brett's mouth, and one eye was swollen. He nodded. "Sorry," he muttered.

James released him just as the police arrived.

Eight

Summer wouldn't have believed James was capable of such anger or such violence. Part of her wanted to call him a fool, but another part wanted to tell him how grateful she was for his love and protection.

His left eye was badly swollen, even with the bag of ice she'd given him. James had refused to hold it to his face while he talked to the police.

His black eye wasn't the only damage. His mouth was cut, and an ugly bruise was beginning to form along his jaw. Brett was in much worse shape, with what looked to be a broken nose.

After talking to both Brett and James and a couple of witnesses, the police asked James if he wanted to press charges. James eyed Brett.

"I don't think that'll be necessary. I doubt this...gentleman will bother my wife again. Isn't that right?" he asked, turning to Brett.

Brett wiped the blood from the side of his mouth. "I didn't come here looking for trouble."

"Looks like that's what you got, though," the police officer told him. "I'd count my blessings and stay away." He studied him for a moment, then asked, "Want to go to the hospital?"

"Forget it. I'm out of here," Brett said with disgust. He climbed inside his car and slammed the door, then drove off as if he couldn't get away fast enough.

"He won't be back," Summer said confidently. She knew Brett's ego was fragile and he wouldn't return after being humiliated.

"You're right, he won't," James insisted darkly, "because you're filing a restraining order first thing tomorrow morning."

Summer nodded, wishing she'd thought of doing it earlier.

"This isn't the first time he's pestered you, is it?"

Summer lowered her gaze.

"He's the reason you had your phone number changed, isn't he?"

She gave a small nod.

"Why didn't you tell me?"

"What could you have done from Seattle?"

"You should have told me. I could at least have offered you some advice. For that matter, why didn't you tell your father?"

James was furious and she suspected she was about to receive the lecture of her life. When nothing more came, she raised her eyes to her husband—and wanted to weep.

His face was a mess. His eye was completely swollen now. It might have been better if she could've convinced him to apply the ice pack. Anyone looking at him would know instantly that her husband the judge had been involved in an altercation—and all because of her.

The police left soon afterward.

"Can I get you anything?" Summer asked guiltily as they entered the apartment.

"I'm fine," he said curtly.

But he wasn't fine. His hands were swollen, his knuckles scraped and bleeding. All at once he started to blur, and the room spun. Everything seemed to be closing in on her. Panic-stricken, Summer groped for the kitchen counter and held on until the waves of dizziness passed.

"Summer? What's wrong?"

"Nothing. I got a little light-headed, that's all." She didn't mention how close she'd come to passing out. Even now, she felt the force of her will was the only thing keeping her conscious.

James came to her and placed his arm around her waist, gently guiding her into the living room. They sat on the sofa, and Summer rested her head against his shoulder, wondering what was wrong with her.

"I'm so sorry," she whispered, fighting back tears.

"For what?"

"The fight."

"That wasn't your fault."

"But, James, you have a terrible black eye. What will people say?" She hated to think about the speculation he'd face when he returned to Seattle, and it was all on account of her. Perhaps she should've told him that Brett was bothering her, but she hadn't wanted to burden him with her troubles.

"Everyone will figure I was in a major fistfight," James teased. "It'll probably be the best thing to happen to my reputation in years. People will see me in an entirely new light."

"Everyone will wonder...."

"Of course they will, and I'll tell them they should see the other guy."

Summer made an effort to laugh but found she couldn't. She twisted her head a bit so she could look at him. The bruise on his jaw was a vivid purple. She raised tentative fingers to it and bit her lip when he winced.

"Oh, James." Gently she pressed her lips to the underside of his jaw.

"That helps." He laughed and groaned at the same time.

She kissed him again, easing her mouth toward his. He moaned and before long, they were exchanging deep, hungry kisses.

"I refuse," James said, unbuttoning her blouse but having difficulty with his swollen hands, "to allow Brett to ruin our last few hours together."

She smiled and slid her arms around his shoulders. "Want to have a shower?" she breathed.

"Yes, but do you have a large enough hot-water tank?"

Summer giggled, recalling their last experience in her compact shower stall and how the water had gone cold at precisely the wrong moment.

The sound of the key turning in the lock told Summer her roommate was home. She sat back abruptly and fastened her blouse.

"Hi, everyone." Julie stepped into the living room and set her suitcase on the floor. "I'm not interrupting anything, am I?" Her gaze narrowed. "James? What on earth happened to you?"

James didn't expect his black eye to go unnoticed, but he wasn't prepared for the amount of open curiosity it aroused.

"Morning, Judge Wilkens." Louise Jamison, the assistant he shared with two other judges, greeted him when he entered the office Monday morning. Then she dropped her pencil. "Judge Wilkens!" she said. "My goodness, what happened?"

He mumbled something about meeting the wrong end of a fist and hurried into his office. It was clear he'd need to come up with an explanation that would satisfy the curious.

Brad Williams knocked on his door five minutes later. His fellow judge let himself into James's office and stared. "So it's true?"

"What's true?"

"You tell me. Looks like you've been in a fight."

"It was a minor scuffle, and that's all I'm going to say about it." James stood and reached for his robe, eager to escape a series of prying questions he didn't want to answer. He had the distinct feeling the rest of the day was going to be like this.

And he was right.

By the time he pulled out of the parking garage that evening, he regretted that he hadn't called in sick. He might've done it if a black eye would disappear in a couple of days, but that wasn't likely, so there was no point in not going in. He checked his reflection in the rearview mirror. The eye looked worse than it had the previous day. He pressed his index finger against the swelling and was surprised by the pain it caused. Still, he could live with the discomfort; it was the unsightliness of the bruises and the questions and curious glances he could do without.

Irritated and not knowing exactly whom to blame, James drove to his father's house. He hadn't been to see Walter in a couple of weeks and wanted to discuss something with him.

His father was doing a *New York Times* crossword puzzle when James let himself into the house. He looked up from the folded newspaper and did a double take, but to his credit, Walter didn't mention the black eye. "Hello, James."

"Dad."

James walked over to the decanter of Scotch Walter kept on hand and poured himself a liberal quantity. He wasn't fond of hard liquor and rarely indulged, but he felt he needed something potent. And fast.

"It's been one of those days, has it?"

James's back was to his father. "You might say that." He took his first sip and the Scotch burned its way down his throat. "This stuff could rot a man's stomach."

"So I've heard."

Taking his glass, James sat in the leather chair next to his father. "I suppose you're wondering about the eye."

"I'll admit to being curious."

"You and everyone else I've seen today."

"I can imagine you've been the object of more than one inquisitive stare."

"I was in a fistfight."

"You?"

"Don't sound so surprised. You're the one who told me there'd be times in a man's life when he couldn't walk away from a fight. This happened to be one of those."

"Want to talk about it?" His father set aside the paper.

"Not particularly, but if you must know, it was over Summer."

"Ah, yes, Summer. How is she? I'm telling you, son, I like her. Couldn't have chosen a better mate for you if I'd gone looking myself."

James smiled for the first time that day. "She's doing well. I was with her this weekend." James raised the Scotch to his lips and grimaced. "We had brunch with her parents."

"Helen and Hank. Good people," Walter commented.

"There's a problem with the April wedding date—on their end and mine. Helen suggested we wait until September. I said November, because of the election."

"Do you want that?" Walter asked.

"No. Neither does Summer."

"Then the hell with it. Let her finish out her contract with Disneyland and join you after that. You've already had a wedding. I never could understand why you wanted two ceremonies, but then I'm an old man with little appreciation for fancy weddings. What I *would* appreciate is a couple of grandkids. I'm not getting any younger, you know, and neither are you."

"Do away with the second ceremony?"

"That's what I said," Walter muttered.

James closed his eyes in relief. Of course. It made perfect sense. He'd suggested a second wedding because he thought that was what Summer wanted, but if he asked her, James suspected he'd learn otherwise. The wedding was for her parents' sake.

"How'd you get so smart?" James asked his father.

"Don't know, but I must be very wise," Walter said, and chuckled. "I've got a superior court judge for a son."

James laughed, feeling comfortable for the first time all day.

"Stay for dinner," his father insisted. "It's been a while since we spent any real time together. Afterward you can let me beat you in a game of chess, and I'll go to bed a happy man."

"All right." It was an invitation too good to refuse.

When James got home after ten, the light on his phone was blinking. He was tempted to ignore his messages.

He felt tired but relaxed and not particularly interested

in returning a long list of phone calls. Especially when he suspected most of his callers were trying to learn what they could about his mysterious black eye.

The only person he wanted to talk to was Summer. He reached for the phone, and she answered on the second ring.

"I just got in," he explained. "Dad and I had dinner."

"Did you give him my love?"

"I did better than that—I let him beat me at chess."

She laughed, and James closed his eyes, savouring the melodic sound. It was like a balm after the day he'd endured.

"How's the eye?" she asked next.

"Good." So he lied. "How was the show today?"

"I didn't go in. I seem to have come down with the flu, so my understudy played Belle. I felt crummy all day. When I woke up this morning, I just felt so nauseous. At first I thought it was nerves over what happened with Brett, but it didn't go away, so I had to call in sick."

"Have you been to a doctor?"

"No. Have you?"

She had him there. "No."

"I'll be fine. I just want to be sure I didn't give you my flu bug while you were here."

"There's no sign of it," he assured her.

They must have talked for another fifteen minutes, saying nothing outwardly significant yet sharing the most important details of their lives. Their conversation would have gone on a lot longer, had someone not rung his doorbell.

It was Ralph Southworth. His campaign manager took one look at James and threw his arms dramatically in the air. "What the hell happened to you?"

"Good evening to you, too," James said evenly.

Ralph rammed all ten fingers through his hair. "Don't

you listen to your messages? I've left no fewer than five, and you haven't bothered to return one."

"Sit down," James said calmly. "Do you want a drink?"

Ralph's eyes narrowed as he studied James's face. "Am I going to need it?"

"That depends." James pointed to the recliner by the large brick fireplace. He'd tell Ralph the truth because it was necessary and, knowing his campaign manager's feelings about Summer, he suspected Ralph *would* need a stiff drink. "Make yourself at home."

Instead, Ralph followed him into the kitchen. "I got no less than ten phone calls this afternoon asking about your black eye. You can't show up and then say nothing about it."

"I can't?" This was news to James, since he'd done exactly that. "I thought you were here to discuss business."

"I am." Ralph frowned when James brought an unopened bottle of top-shelf bourbon out of a cabinet. "So I'm going to need that."

"Yes."

"I met with the League of Women Voters and I've arranged for you to speak at their luncheon in July. It's a real coup, James, and I hope you appreciate my efforts."

"Yes," he murmured. "Thanks."

"Now tell me about the eye. And the bruises."

"All right," James said, adding two ice cubes to the glass. He half filled it with bourbon and handed it to his friend. "I got hit in the face with a fist more than once."

"Whose fist?"

"Some beach bum by the name of Brett. I don't remember his last name if I ever heard it."

Ralph swallowed his first sip of liquor. "Does the beach bum have anything to do with the woman you mentioned?"

"Yeah."

The two men stared across the kitchen at each other.

"Were the police called?" Ralph demanded.

It took James a moment to own up to the truth. "Yes."

Ralph slammed his hand against the counter. "I should've known! James, what did I tell you? A woman's nothing but trouble. Mark my words, if you get involved any further with Spring..."

"Summer!"

"Whatever. It doesn't matter, because her name spells just one thing. Trouble. You've worked all your life for this opportunity. This is your one shot at the bench. We both know it. You asked me to manage your campaign and I agreed, but I thought it would be a team effort. The two of us."

"It is." James wanted to hold on to his seat on the bench more than he'd ever wanted anything—other than to marry Summer. He also felt he was the best man for the position. To get this close and lose it all would be agonizing.

"Then why," Ralph asked, palms out, "are you sabotaging your own campaign?"

"I'm not doing it on purpose."

"Stay away from this woman!"

"Ralph, I can't. I won't."

Ralph rubbed his face with both hands, clearly frustrated.

"Summer's in California, but I plan on bringing her to Seattle as soon as I can arrange it. Probably April."

"Tell me you're joking."

"I'm not." James figured he should admit the truth now and be done with it. "We're married."

"What?" Ralph pulled out a chair and sank into it. "When?"

"Over New Year's."

"Why?"

"It was just…one of those things. We fell in love and got married. We were hoping for a more elaborate ceremony later, but I can see that's going to be a problem."

"You want to know what's the real problem, James? It's the marriage. Why didn't you tell me right away?"

"I should have," James said, sorry now that he hadn't. "But when you told me you'd never been in love, I didn't think there was much of a chance you'd understand."

"What you've done is jeopardize your entire campaign."

Somehow he doubted that. "Aren't you overreacting?"

"Time will tell, won't it?" Ralph asked smugly.

James decided to ignore that. "If anything, Summer will be an asset. She's lovely and she's good at connecting with people. Unfortunately her contract with Disney doesn't expire until April."

"That's right," Ralph said sarcastically. "I forgot, she's a showgirl."

"A singer and an actress and a very talented one at that," James boasted.

"An actress, a showgirl, it's all the same."

"Once she's finished with her contract, I want her to move in with me."

"Here in Seattle?" Ralph made it sound like a world-class disaster.

"A wife belongs with her husband."

"What about the beach bum?"

James frowned. "We don't have to worry about him. He's gone for good."

"I certainly hope so. And while we're making out a wish list, let's add a couple of other things. Let's wish that your worthy opponent doesn't find out about this little skirmish between you and Summer's previous lover-boy. And let's make a great big wish that he doesn't learn that the police were called and a report filed."

"He won't," James said confidently, far more confidently than he felt.

"I hope you're right," Ralph said, and downed what was left of his bourbon in one gulp. The glass hit the counter when he put it down. "Now tell me, what kind of damage did you do to the beach bum?"

"You didn't tell him, did you?" Julie said when Summer set the telephone receiver back in place.

"No." She sighed reluctantly. She rested her hand protectively on her stomach.

"A man has the right to know he's going to be a father," Julie said righteously. She bit into an apple as she tucked her feet beneath her on the sofa.

Summer closed her eyes. Even the smell of food or the sound of someone eating made her sick to her stomach. In the past two months she'd seen parts of toilets that weren't meant to be examined at such close range. She hadn't kept down a single breakfast in weeks. The day before, she'd wondered why she even bothered to eat. Dumping it directly into the toilet would save time and trouble.

"How long do you think James is going to fall for this lie about having the flu?"

It had been more than a month since she'd last seen him, and in that time Summer had lost ten pounds. Her clothes hung on her, and she was as pale as death. She seemed to spend more time at the doctor's office than she did at her own apartment. Her biggest fear was that being so ill meant there was something wrong with the baby, although the doctor had attempted to reassure her on that score.

"Why haven't you told him?" Julie wanted to know.

"I just can't do it over the phone." Besides, she remembered James mentioning that a pregnancy now would be a mistake. Well, she hadn't gotten this way by herself!

She knew exactly when it had happened, too. There was only the one time they hadn't used protection.

"When are you going to see him again?"

Summer shook her head. "I don't know."

"You talk on the phone every night. He sends you gifts. I can't think of anyone else who got six dozen red roses for Valentine's Day."

"He's extravagant…."

"Extravagant with everything but his time."

"He's so busy, Julie. I never realized how much there was to being a judge, and he really cares about the people he works with. Not only the people who stand before him, but the attorneys and his staff, too. Then there's the election…."

"So, go to him. He's just as unhappy without you."

"I've got three weeks left on my contract, and—"

"Do you really suppose no one's figured out that you're pregnant? Think about it, Summer. You came back from Vegas all happy and in love, and two weeks later you're heaving your guts out after every meal. No one expects you to perform when you feel this crummy."

"But…"

"Do everyone a favor and—" Julie stopped when there was a knock at the door. "Is anyone coming over tonight?"

"No." Summer laid her head back against the sofa and drew in several deep breaths, hoping that would ease her nausea.

"It's for you," Julie said, looking over her shoulder as soon as she'd opened the door. "It's Walter Wilkens."

Summer threw aside the blanket and scurried off the

sofa, anxious to see her father-in-law. "Walter?" What could he possibly be doing here? "Come inside, please."

The refined, older gentleman stepped into the apartment. "Summer?" He gazed at her, his expression concerned. "James said you'd been ill with the flu, but, my dear..."

"She looks dreadful," Julie finished for him. Her roommate took another noisy bite of her apple. "I'm Julie. We met at the wedding. Summer's roommate and best friend."

Walter bowed slightly. "Hello, Julie. It's nice to see you again."

"Sit down, please," Summer said, motioning toward the only chair in the house without blankets or clean laundry stacked on it.

"Would you like something to drink?" Julie asked.

"No...no, thank you." He cleared his throat. "Summer, my dear." He frowned. "Have you been to a doctor?"

"Yup," Julie answered, chewing on her apple. "Three times this week, right, Summer?"

"Julie," she snapped.

"Are you going to tell him or not?"

Summer tossed the tangled curls over her shoulder and groaned inwardly. "I don't have much choice now, do I?" She met Walter's eyes and realized her lower lip was trembling. She was suddenly afraid she might burst into tears. Her emotions had been like a seesaw, veering from one extreme to another.

"Summer, what is it?" Walter prodded.

"I'm pregnant," she whispered. She smiled happily all the while tears streamed down her cheeks.

Walter bolted out of his chair. "Hot damn!"

"Other than me, you're the first person she's told," Julie felt obliged to inform him. "Not even her own family knows, although her mother would take one look at her and guess."

"James doesn't know?"

"Nope." Again it was Julie who answered.

"And why not?"

"A woman doesn't tell her husband that sort of thing over the phone," Summer insisted. "Or by e-mail." She needed to see his face, to gauge James's reaction so she'd know what he was really thinking.

"She's been sicker than a dog."

"Thank you, Julie, but I can take it from here."

"I can see that," Walter said, ignoring Summer.

"What brings you to California?" Summer asked cordially, looking for a way to change the subject.

"A business trip. I thought James might have mentioned it."

If he had, Summer had missed it. She had a feeling she'd been doing a lot of that lately.

"Well, my dear," Walter said, sitting back in his chair and grinning broadly. "This is a pleasant surprise."

"It was for me, too."

"I can just see James's face when you tell him."

"He probably won't know what to do, laugh or cry."

"He'll probably do a little of both."

Walter himself was laughing, Summer noticed. He hadn't stopped smiling from the moment he'd heard the news.

"Everything's always been so carefully planned in James's life," Walter said, still grinning. "Then he met you and bingo. He's a husband, and now he's about to be a father. This is terrific news, just terrific."

"James might not find it all that wonderful," Summer

said, voicing her fears for the first time. "He's in the middle of an important campaign."

"Don't you worry about a thing."

"I *am* worried. I can't help it."

"Then we're going to have to do something about that."

"We are?" Summer asked. "What?"

"If my son's going to become a father, you should tell him, and the sooner the better. Pack your bags, Summer. It's about time you moved to Seattle with your husband where you belong."

"But…"

"Don't argue with me, young lady. I'm an old man and I'm accustomed to having my own way. If you're worried about his campaign, this is how we fix that. You'll be introduced to the public as his wife and we're going to put an end to any speculation right now."

Nine

Something was wrong with Summer. James had sensed it weeks ago. He would have confronted her and demanded answers if she hadn't sounded so fragile.

There was that business with the flu, but exactly how long was that going to last? When he asked her what the doctor said, she seemed vague.

Part of the problem was the length of time they'd been apart. He hadn't meant it to be so long. Summer had intended to come to Seattle, but that had fallen through, just as his last visit to California had. Neither of them was happy about it, but there was nothing James could have done on his end. He was sure that was the case with her, too.

James paced in his den, worrying. When he had to mull over a problem, that was what he did. Lately he'd practically worn a path in the carpet. He felt helpless and frustrated. Despite Ralph's dire warnings, he wished he'd brought Summer back to Seattle. This separation was hurting them both.

His greatest fear was that she regretted their marriage.

Their telephone conversations weren't the same anymore. He felt as if she was hiding something from him.

They used to talk about everything but he noticed that she steered him away from certain topics now. She didn't want to talk about herself or her job or this flu that had hung on for few weeks. They used to talk for hours; now he had the feeling she was eager to get off the line.

James wondered about Brett, but when he asked, Summer assured him she hadn't seen or heard from him since the fight.

The fight.

His black eye had caused a great deal of speculation among his peers. James had never offered any explanation. Via the grapevine, he'd heard Ralph's version and found it only distantly related to the truth. According to his campaign manager, James had been jumped by gang members and valiantly fought them off until the police arrived.

When James confronted Ralph with the story, the other man smiled and said he couldn't be held accountable for rumors. Right or wrong, James had let it drop. He was eager to put the incident behind him.

James certainly hadn't expected married life to be this lonely. He'd never felt this detached from the mainstream of everyday life, this isolated. Missing Summer was like a constant ache in his stomach. Except that a store-bought tablet wasn't going to cure what ailed him.

His desk was filled with demands. He felt weary. Unsure of his marriage. Unsure of himself.

He went into the kitchen to make a cup of instant coffee when he saw a car turn into his driveway and around to the backyard.

His father.

He wondered why Walter would stop by unannounced on a Sunday afternoon. James wasn't in the mood for company—but then again, maybe a sounding board was exactly what he needed. Other than his father, there was no one with whom he could discuss Summer.

The slam of a car door closing was followed almost immediately by another. James frowned. Dad had brought someone with him. Great. Just great.

He took the hot water out of the microwave, added the coffee granules and stirred briskly. There was a knock at the back door.

"Come in, the door's open," he called, not turning around. He didn't feel like being polite. Not today, when it felt as if the world was closing in around him.

He sipped his coffee and stared out the window. The daffodils were blooming and the—

"Hello, James."

James whirled around. "Summer?" He couldn't believe she was really there. It was impossible. A figment of his imagination. An apparition. Before another second passed, James walked across the kitchen and swept her into his arms.

Laughing and sobbing at once, Summer hugged him close.

Then they were kissing each other. Neither could give or get enough.

Walter stood in the background and cleared his throat. "I'll wait for the two of you in the living room," he said, loudly enough to be sure he was heard.

As far as James was concerned, his father might as well make himself comfortable. Or leave. This could take a while.

Summer in his arms was the closest thing to heaven James had ever found. Not for several minutes did he notice how thin and frail she was. The virus had ravaged her body.

"Sweetheart," he whispered between kisses. He paused and brushed back her hair to get a good look at her.

She was pale. Her once-pink cheeks were colorless, and her eyes appeared sunken. "Are you over the flu?"

She lowered her eyes and stepped away from him. "I... You'd better sit down, James."

"Sit down? Why?"

Her hands closed around the back of a kitchen chair. "I have something important to tell you."

He could see she was nervous and on the verge of tears. The worries that were nipping at his heels earlier returned with reinforcements. Summer had more than a common flu bug.

"Just tell me," he said. A knot was beginning to form in his stomach. Was she ill? Was it something life threatening? The knot twisted and tightened.

"I don't have the flu," she whispered.

Whatever it was, then, must be very bad if his father had brought her to Seattle.

"How serious is it?" he asked. He preferred to confront whatever they were dealing with head-on.

"It's serious, James, very serious." Slowly she raised her eyes to his. "We're going to have a baby."

His relief was so great that he nearly laughed. "A baby? You mean to tell me you're pregnant?"

She nodded. Her fingers had gone white, and she was watching him closely.

James took her in his arms. "I thought you were really sick."

"I have been really sick," she told him crisply. "Morning sickness. Afternoon sickness. Evening sickness. I...I can't seem to keep food down.... I've never been more miserable in my life."

"I suspect part of her problem has been psychological," Walter announced from the doorway. "The poor girl's been terribly worried about how you were going to take the news."

"Me?"

"My feelings exactly," Walter said. "The deed's done, what's there to think about? Besides, you've made me an extremely happy man."

"A baby." James remained awestruck at the thought.

"Now tell him your due date, Summer—he'll get a real kick out of that."

"September twenty-third," Summer announced.

Everyone seemed to be studying him, waiting for a reaction. James didn't know what to think. Then it hit him. "September twenty-third? That's the date of the primary."

"I know. Isn't it great?" Walter asked.

"How long can you stay?" James asked, taking Summer's hands in his own.

Summer looked at Walter.

"Stay?" his father barked. "My dear son, this is your wife. I brought her to Seattle to live with you. This is where she belongs."

"You can live with me?" A man could only take in so much news at one time. First, he'd learned that his wife didn't have some life-threatening disease. Then he discovered he was going to be a father. Even more important, he was going to have the opportunity to prove what kind of husband he could be.

"Yes. I got out of my contract for medical reasons, and Julie's getting a roommate. So…everything's settled."

James pulled out the chair and sat Summer down. Then he knelt in front of her and took her hands in his. "A baby."

"You're sure you don't mind?"

"Of course he doesn't mind," Walter said, "and if he does I'll set up an appointment with a good psychiatrist I know. This is the best news we've had in thirty years."

"When did it happen?" James asked.

Summer laughed at him. "You mean you don't remember?" She leaned toward him and whispered, reminding him of the one episode the morning after their honeymoon night.

"Ah, yes," James said, and chuckled. "As I recall, I was the one who said one time wouldn't matter."

"I don't suppose there's anything to eat in this house?" Walter asked, banging cupboard doors open and shut.

"Why have you been so ill?" James wanted to know. It worried him. "Is it routine?"

"My doctor says some women suffer from severe morning sickness for the first few months. He's been very reassuring. I try to remember that when I'm losing my latest meal."

"Is there anything that can help?"

"She's got what she needs now," Walter said.

Summer laid her head on his shoulder. "I was worried you'd be upset with me."

"Why would I be upset when the most beautiful woman in the world tells me she's having my baby?" He reached for her hand and pressed her palm over his heart. "Notice anything different?" he asked.

She shook her head, giving him a puzzled look.

"My heart's racing because I'm so excited. Because I'm so happy. We're going to have a baby, Summer! I feel like I could conquer the world."

He wanted his words to comfort her. The last thing he expected was that she'd burst into tears.

"But you said a baby would be a mistake right now," she reminded him between sobs.

"I said that?"

"He said that?" Walter glared at James.

"I don't remember saying it," James told him. "I'm sorry, my love. Just knowing we're going to have a baby makes me happier than I have any right to be."

"Damn straight he's happy," Walter tossed in, "or there'd be hell to pay. I should've been a grandfather two or three times over by now. As far as I'm concerned, James owes me."

"I'll try and make it up to you," James promised his father with a grin.

Summer couldn't remember ever being so hungry. She'd been with James a week and had settled so contentedly into her new life it was almost as if she'd always been there.

"Would you like another piece of apple pie?" James asked. "Better yet, why don't we buy the whole thing and take it home with us?"

"Can we do that?" Summer was sure her appetite must be a source of embarrassment to him. They were at a sidewalk restaurant on the Seattle waterfront. Summer couldn't decide between the French onion soup and the Cobb salad, so she'd ordered both. Then she'd topped off the meal with a huge slice of apple pie à la mode.

"I'll ask the waitress," James said as though it was perfectly normal to order a whole pie for later.

"Have I embarrassed you?" she asked, keeping her voice low.

James's mouth quivered. "No, but I will admit I've rarely seen anyone enjoy her food more."

"Oh, James, you have no idea how good it is to be able to

eat and keep everything down. I felt a thousand times better this past week than I did the whole previous two months."

"Then Dad was right," he said.

"About what?"

"The psychological effects of the pregnancy were taking their toll along with the physical. In other words, you were worried and making yourself more so. I could kick myself."

"Why?"

"For not guessing. You have to forgive me, sweetheart, I'm new to this husband business."

"You're forgiven."

"Just promise me one thing. Don't keep any more secrets from me, all right?"

She smiled. "You've got yourself a deal."

"James?" A striking-looking couple approached their table.

"Rich and Jamie Manning." Sounding genuinely pleased, James stood and exchanged handshakes with the man. Then he turned to Summer. "These are good friends of mine, Rich and Jamie Manning. This is my wife, Summer."

"Your wife?" Rich repeated, doing a poor job of hiding his surprise. "When did this happen?"

"Shortly after New Year's," James explained. "Would you care to join us?"

"Unfortunately we can't," Rich said. "The baby-sitter's waiting. But this is great news. I hope there's a good reason I didn't get a wedding invitation."

"A very good one." James grinned. "I've been meaning to let everyone know. But Summer just moved here from California."

"Well, the word's out now," Jamie said, smiling at her. "Once Rich's mother hears about it, she'll want to throw a party in your honor." Jamie and her husband shared a private, happy look.

"I'd better call your parents before I alienate them completely," James said.

"I'll be seeing you soon," Rich said and patted James's shoulder as he passed by. "Bye, Summer."

James was silent for a moment, and Summer wasn't sure if he was glad or not that his friends had stopped to talk. She didn't think he intended to keep their marriage a secret, yet he hadn't made a point of introducing her around, either.

"Is there a problem?" she asked.

"No. It's just that I was hoping to give you some time to regain your strength before you met my friends."

Summer's gaze followed the couple as they made their way toward the front of the restaurant.

"They're happy, aren't they?"

"Rich and Jamie?"

Summer nodded.

"Yes." He relaxed in his chair. "They came to see me a few years back with perhaps the most unusual request of my career." He smiled, and Summer guessed he must've been amused at the time, as well.

"What did they want?"

"They asked me to draw up a paper for a marriage of convenience."

"Really." That seemed odd to Summer. Although she'd just met the couple, it was clear to her that they were in love.

"They'd come up with some harebrained scheme to have a baby together—by artificial insemination. Rich would be the sperm donor."

"Did they have a baby?"

"Yes, but Bethany was conceived the old-fashioned way without a single visit to a fertility clinic."

Summer shook her head. "This doesn't make any sense to me. Why would two healthy people go to such lengths to have a child? Especially when they're perfectly capable of doing things…the usual way?"

"It does sound silly, doesn't it?"

"Frankly, yes."

James leaned forward and placed his elbows on the table. "Jamie and Rich had been friends for years. Since their high school days, if I recall correctly. Jamie couldn't seem to fall in love with the right kind of man and, after a couple of disastrous relationships, she decided she was giving up dating altogether."

"I love the tricks life plays on people," Summer said, licking melted ice cream off her spoon. She looked across the table at the remnants on James's plate. "Are you going to eat that?" she asked.

He pushed the plate toward her.

"Thanks," she said, and blew him a kiss. "Go on," she encouraged, scooping up the last bits of pie and ice cream. "What happened?"

"Apparently Jamie was comfortable with her decision, except that she wanted a child. That's when she approached Rich about being the sperm donor."

"Just between friends, that sort of thing?"

"Exactly. At any rate, Rich didn't think it was such a bad idea himself, the not-marrying part. He'd had his own ups and downs in the relationship department. But the more he thought about her suggestion, the more problems he had with being nothing more than a sperm donor. He suggested they get married so their child could have his name. He also wanted a say in the baby's upbringing."

"And Jamie agreed to all this?"

"She wanted a child."

"So they asked you to draw up a contract or something?"

"Yes, but I have to tell you I had my reservations."

"I can imagine."

"They have two children now."

"Well, this so-called marriage of convenience certainly worked out," Summer told him.

"It sure did."

While she was looking around the table for anything left to eat, she noticed that James was studying her. "How are you feeling?" he asked.

"A thousand times better." She smiled and lowered her voice so he alone could hear. "If what you're really asking is if I'm well enough to make love, the answer is yes."

He swallowed hard.

"Shall we hurry home, James?"

"By all means."

He paid the tab and they were gone. "You're sure?" he asked as he unlocked the car door and helped her inside.

Sitting in the passenger seat, Summer smiled up at her husband. "Am I sure? James, it's been months since we last made love. I'm so hot for you I could burst into flames."

James literally ran around the front of the car. He sped the entire way home, and Summer considered it fortunate that they weren't stopped by a traffic cop.

"Torture...every night for the last week," James mumbled as he pulled into the driveway. "I couldn't trust myself to even touch you."

"I know."

Her time in Seattle hadn't started out well. The first morning, she'd woken and run straight for the bathroom. James helped her off the floor when she'd finished. He'd cradled her in his arms and told her how much he loved her for having their baby.

Her first few dinners hadn't stayed down, either. But each day after her arrival, the nausea and episodes of vomiting had become less and less frequent. Now, one week later, she was almost herself again.

He left the car and came around to her side. When he opened the door, she stepped out and into his embrace—and kissed him.

James groaned and swung her into his arms.

"What are you doing?" she asked.

"Carrying you over the threshold," he announced. "You've been cheated out of just about everything else when it comes to this marriage."

"I haven't been cheated."

"You should've had the big church wedding and—"

"Are we going to argue about that again? Really, James, I'd rather we just made love."

He had a problem getting the door unlocked while holding her, but he managed. The minute they were inside, he started kissing her, doing wonderful, erotic things that excited her to the point of desperation.

Summer kicked off her shoes.

James kissed her and unsnapped the button to her skirt. The zipper slid down. All the while he was silently urging her toward the stairs.

Her jacket went next, followed by her shirt.

She made it to the staircase and held out her hand. James didn't need any more encouragement than that. They raced to the bedroom together.

Summer fell on the bed, laughing. "Oh, James, promise you'll always love me this much."

"I promise." He tried to remove his shirt without taking off his tie, with hilarious results. Arms clutching her stomach, Summer doubled over, laughing even harder. It was out of pure kindness that she climbed off the bed and loosened the tie enough to slip it over his head. Otherwise, she was afraid her normally calm, patient husband would have strangled himself.

"You think this is funny, do you?"

"I think you're the most wonderful man alive. Will you always want me this much?"

"I can't imagine not wanting you." And he proceeded to prove it....

James was half-asleep when he heard the doorbell chime. He would have ignored it, but on the off chance it was someone important, he decided to look outside and see if he recognized the car.

Big mistake.

Ralph Southworth was at his door.

James grabbed his pants, threw on his shirt and kissed Summer on the cheek. Then he hurried down the stairs, taking a second to button his shirt before he opened the door. "Hello, Ralph," he said, standing, shoes and socks in hand.

Ralph frowned. "What the hell have you been—never mind, I already know."

"Summer's here."

"So I gather."

"Give her a few minutes, and she'll be down so you can meet her," James told him. He sat in a chair and put on his shoes and socks. "What can I do for you?"

"A number of things, but mainly I'd…" He hesitated as Summer made her way down the stairs. Her hair was mussed, her eyes soft and glowing.

"Ralph, this is my wife, Summer," James said proudly, joining her. He slipped his arm around her shoulders.

"Hello, Summer," Ralph said stiffly.

"Hello, Ralph."

"When did you get here?"

"Last week. Would you two like some coffee? I'll make a pot. James, take your friend into the den, why don't you, and I'll bring everything in there."

James didn't want his wife waiting on him, but something about the way she spoke told him this wasn't the time to argue. That was when he saw her skirt draped on a chair, and her jacket on the floor.

"This way, Ralph," he said, ushering the other man into the den.

He looked over his shoulder and saw Summer delicately scoop up various items of clothing, then hurry into the kitchen.

"Something amuses you?"

James cleared his throat. "Not really."

"First of all, James, I have to question your judgment. When you told me you married a showgirl—"

"Summer's an actress."

Ralph ignored that. "As I was saying, your judgment appears to be questionable."

This was a serious accusation, considering that James was running for a position on the superior court.

Ralph's lips were pinched. "It worries me that you'd marry some woman you barely know on the spur of the moment."

"Love sometimes happens like that."

"Perhaps," Ralph muttered. "Personally I wouldn't know, but James, how much younger is she?"

"Not as much as you think. Nine years."

"She's unsuitable!"

"For whom? You? Listen, Ralph, I asked you to manage my campaign, not run my life. I married Summer, and she's going to have my child."

"The girl's pregnant, as well?"

"Yes, the baby's due September twenty-third."

Ralph's lips went white with disapproval. "Could she have chosen a more inconvenient date?"

"I don't think it really matters."

"That's the primary!"

"I'm well aware of it."

"Good grief, James." Ralph shook his head. "This won't do. It just won't. Once people learn what you've done, they'll assume you were obligated to marry the girl. The last thing we need now is to have your morals questioned."

"Ralph, you're overreacting."

"I can't believe you brought her here, after everything I said."

James gritted his teeth. "She's my wife."

Ralph paced back and forth for a moment or two. "I don't feel I have any choice," he said with finality.

"Choice about what?"

"I'm resigning as your manager."

Summer appeared just then, carrying a tray. "Coffee, anyone?"

Ten

Summer settled easily into life with James. She adored her husband and treasured each moment that they were together.

Her days quickly began to follow a routine of sorts. She rose early and, because she was feeling better, resumed her regular workout, which included a two-mile run first thing in the morning.

James insisted on running with her, although he made it clear he didn't like traipsing through dark streets at dawn's early light. But he wasn't comfortable with her running alone, so he joined her, protesting every step of the way.

James was naturally athletic, and Summer didn't think anyone was more surprised than he was by how enjoyable he started to find it. After their run, they showered together. Thankfully James's hot-water tank was larger than the meager one back in her Orange County apartment.

This was both good and bad. The negative was when James, a stickler for punctuality, got to court late two mornings in a row.

"You shower first," he told her after their Monday-morning run.

"Not together?" she asked, disappointed.

"I can't be late this morning."

"We'll behave," she promised.

James snickered. "I can't behave with you, Summer. You tempt me too much."

"All right, but you shower first, and I'll get us breakfast."

Ten minutes later, he walked into the kitchen, where Summer was pouring two glasses of orange juice. He wore his dark business suit and carried his briefcase, ready for his workday.

"What are your plans?" he asked, downing the juice as he stood by the table. He sat down to eat his bagel and cream cheese and picked up the paper.

"I'm going to send Julie a long e-mail. Then I thought I'd stop in at the library and volunteer to read during story-time."

"Good idea," he said, scanning the paper.

Summer knew reading the paper was part of his morning ritual, which he didn't have as much time for since her arrival. She drank the last of her juice and kissed his cheek.

"I'm going upstairs for my shower," she told him.

"All right. Have a good day."

"I will. Oh, what time will you be home tonight?" she asked.

"Six or so," he mumbled absently and turned the front page.

Summer hesitated. His schedule had changed. Rarely did he get home before eight the first week after she'd moved in. It seemed that every night there was someone to meet, some campaign supporter to talk to, some plan to outline— all to do with the September primary, even though it was still months away.

In the past week James had come directly home from the

courthouse. Not that she was complaining, but she couldn't help wondering.

"What about your campaign?" she asked.

"Everything's under control," was all he said.

Summer wondered.

All at once James looked up, startled, as if he'd just remembered something. "What day's your ultrasound?"

"Thursday of next week. Don't look so worried. You don't need to be there."

"I *want* to be there," he stated emphatically. "Our baby's first picture. I wouldn't miss it for the world. Besides, I'm curious to find out if we're going to have a son or daughter."

"Don't tell me," she said. "I don't want to know."

"I won't," he said, chuckling. He reached out to stroke her abdomen. "I can't believe how much I love this little one, and he isn't even born yet."

"He?" she asked, hands on her hips in mock offense.

"A daughter would suit me just fine. Actually Dad's hoping for a granddaughter. It's been a long time since there's been a little girl in the family."

Summer pressed her hand over her husband's. She'd never been this happy. It frightened her sometimes. Experience had taught her that happiness almost always came with a price.

Walter joined them for dinner Wednesday evening. From the moment she'd met him, Summer had liked her father-in-law.

"Did you know Summer could cook this well when you married her?" Walter asked when they'd finished eating.

She'd found a recipe for a chicken casserole on the Internet and served it with homemade dinner rolls and fresh asparagus, with a fresh fruit salad made of seedless grapes and strawberries. For dessert she picked up a lemon torte at the local bakery.

"Summer's full of surprises," James told his father. His eyes briefly met hers.

"What he's trying to say is no one knew how fertile I was, either."

"That's the best surprise yet," Walter said. He dabbed the corner of his mouth with his napkin in a blatant effort to hide a smile.

"It certainly is," James put in.

Walter studied her. "How are you feeling these days?"

"Wonderful."

"What's the doctor have to say?"

"That I'm in excellent health. The baby's growing by leaps and bounds. I haven't felt him move yet, but—"

"Him?" James and Walter chimed in simultaneously.

"Or her," she retorted, smiling. She stood and started to clear the table.

"Let me do that," James insisted.

"I'm not helpless, you know," Walter added.

Both men leapt from their chairs.

"Go have your coffee," Summer told them. "It'll only take me a few minutes to deal with the dishes."

Walter shrugged, then looked at his son. "There are a few things I need to discuss with James," he said.

"Then off with you." She shooed them out of the kitchen.

James poured two cups of coffee and took them into the living room. He paused in the doorway and looked over his shoulder. "You're sure?"

"James, honestly! Go talk to your father."

Although she didn't know Walter well, she sensed that something was on his mind. Throughout the meal she'd noticed the way he watched his son. James was acting odd, too.

Walter wanted to discuss the campaign, but every time he'd introduced the subject, James expertly changed it. He did it cleverly, but Walter had noticed, and after a while Summer had, too.

She ran tap water to rinse off the dinner plates before putting them in the dishwasher, and when she turned off the faucet she heard the end of James's comment.

"...Summer doesn't know."

She hesitated. Apparently the two men didn't realize how well their voices carried. She didn't mean to eavesdrop, but it did seem only fair to listen, since she was the topic of conversation.

"What do you plan to do about it?" his father asked.

It took James a long time to answer. "I haven't decided."

"Have you tried reasoning with him?"

"No," James answered bitterly. "The man said he has doubts about my judgment. He's insulted me, insulted my wife. I don't need Southworth if he's got an attitude like that."

"But you will need a campaign manager."

"Yes," James admitted reluctantly.

So *that* was what this was about. Summer leaned against the kitchen counter and closed her eyes. Ralph had resigned, and from the evidence she'd seen, James had, too. Resigned himself to losing, even before the election. It didn't sound like him.

"What's the problem?" Walter asked as if reading Summer's mind.

James lowered his voice substantially, and Summer had to strain to hear him. "He disapproves of Summer."

"What?" Walter had no such compunction about keeping quiet. "The man's crazy!"

"I've made a series of mistakes," James said.

"Mistakes?"

"With Summer."

The world collapsed, like a house falling in on itself. Summer struggled toward a chair and literally fell into it.

"I should never have married her the way I did," James elaborated. "I cheated her out of the wedding she deserved. I don't know if her mother's forgiven me yet. The last I heard, her family's planning a reception in November. By then the baby will be here and, well, it seems a little after the fact."

"You can't blame Summer for that."

"I don't," James remarked tartly. "I blame myself. In retrospect I realize I was afraid of losing her. So I insisted on the marriage before she could change her mind."

"I don't understand what any of this has to do with Ralph," Walter muttered.

"Ralph thinks Summer's too young for me."

"Nonsense."

"He also seems to think I've done myself harm by not letting everyone know immediately that I was married. Bringing Summer here to live with me now, pregnant, and saying we've been married all along, is apparently too convenient to believe."

"It's the truth."

"You and I know that, but there's already speculation."

"So? People will always talk. Let them. But you've got to do something about getting this campaign organized. There are worse things you could be accused of than marrying in secret or getting Summer pregnant before your wedding day. As far as I'm concerned, Southworth's looking for excuses."

"I refuse to subject Summer to that kind of speculation," James said stubbornly.

"Have you talked this over with her?"

"Not yet…"

"You haven't?"

"I know, I know." The defeatist attitude was back in James's voice. "I've put it off longer than I should have."

After that, Summer didn't hear much more of the conversation between father and son. Their marriage had hurt her husband; it might have robbed him of his dreams, cheated him out of his goals.

The phone rang long before she had time to gather her thoughts. "I'll get it," she called out to James, and reached for the extension in the kitchen. Her hand trembled as she lifted the receiver.

"Hello," she said, her voice weak.

"Hello," came the soft feminine reply. "You don't know me. My name's Christy Manning Franklin."

"Christy… Manning?" Summer said, stunned. She hadn't recovered from one shock before she was hit with another. "Just a moment. I'll get James."

"No, please. It's you I want to talk to."

"Me?"

"From your reaction, I'd guess James has mentioned me."

"Yes." Summer slumped down in a chair and closed her eyes. "You and James were engaged at one time."

"That's right. I understand you and James recently got married."

"Three months ago," Summer said, embarrassed by how weak her voice still was. "In Las Vegas," she added a little more loudly.

"I hope you'll forgive me for being so forward. I talked it over with Cody—he's my husband—and he said since I felt so strongly about it I should call you."

"So strongly about what?"

"About you…and James. I'll always regret the way I treated James. He deserved a lot better, but I was younger then. Immature in some ways. At one time I thought I was in love with him. I knew he loved me, and my family thought the world of him. Then I met Cody." She hesitated. "I didn't phone to tell you all this. I'm sure James filled in the details."

"Why did you call?" Summer was sure that under other circumstances she might have liked Christy Franklin.

"I wanted to tell you how happy I am that James found someone to love. I know it's presumptuous of me but I wanted to ask a favor of you."

"A favor?" The woman had a lot of nerve.

"Love him with all your heart, Summer. James is a special, special man and he deserves a woman who'll stand by his side and love him."

"I do," she said softly.

"For quite a while I despaired of James ever getting married. I can't tell you how pleased I was when Mom phoned to tell me Rich and Jamie had met you. Cody and I want to extend our very best wishes to you both."

"Thank you."

"I know it's a lot to ask, but I do hope you'll keep Cody and me in mind when you count your friends. There's a place in my heart for James. He's been a friend to our family for years. He was a tremendous help to Paul when Diane died, and again later when he married Leah. James helped Rich and Jamie, too, and he's been a good friend to Jason and Charlotte, as well. We're all indebted to him one way or another."

"I do love him so much." She was fighting back tears and not even sure what she was crying about. The fact that

Ralph Southworth had resigned as James's campaign manager because of her? Or that James's ex-fiancée still cared for him deeply?

Summer had just replaced the receiver when James stepped into the kitchen. He stood with one hand on the door.

"Who was that on the phone?" he asked.

Summer met his look straight on, waiting to read any emotion. "Christy Franklin."

"Christy?" he repeated. "What did she want?" He looked more surprised than anything.

"She called to give us her and Cody's best wishes. She said it was high time you were married and she can hardly wait to meet me."

"Really?"

"Really."

"And what did you tell her?"

Summer grinned. "I said she's to keep her cotton-pickin' hands off my husband."

James chuckled, obviously delighted by her possessive attitude. "You aren't going to get much of an argument from me."

"Good thing," she said, and slid her arm around his waist. Together they joined his father.

"I don't understand it," Summer muttered. She sucked in her stomach in order to close her skirt. "I can barely zip this up. It fit fine just last week."

"Honey, you're pregnant," James said matter-of-factly.

"Three months. I'm not supposed to show yet."

"You're not?" James's eyes left the mirror, his face covered with shaving cream. He carefully examined her rounded belly.

"Tell me the truth, James. If you were meeting me for the first time, would you guess I was pregnant?"

He frowned. "This isn't one of those trick questions, is it?"

"No."

"All right," he said, then cleared his throat. He seemed to know intuitively that she wasn't going to like the answer. "You do look pregnant to me. But then you *are* pregnant, so I don't understand what the big deal is."

"I'm fat already," she wailed, and felt like breaking into tears.

"*Fat* is not the word I'd use to describe you."

"If I'm showing at three months, can you just imagine what I'll look like at nine?"

His grin revealed pride and love. "I'd say you'll look like the most beautiful woman in the world."

"No wonder I love you so much," she told her husband, turning back to the closet. She sorted through the hangers, dismissing first one outfit and then another.

"Where are you going that you're so worried about how you look?" James asked.

Summer froze. "An appointment." She prayed he wouldn't question her further. She'd arranged a meeting with Ralph Southworth, but she didn't want James to know about it.

"Okay. Don't forget tonight," he reminded her. "We're going to the Mannings' for dinner."

"I won't forget," she promised. "Eric and Elizabeth, right?"

"Right. Knowing Elizabeth, she'll probably spend the whole day cooking. She's called me at least five times in the past week. She's anxious to meet you."

"I'm anxious to meet them, too." But not nearly as anxious as she was about this meeting with Southworth. In setting up the appointment, Summer hoped to achieve several objectives. Mainly she wanted Ralph to agree to manage James's campaign again. And she wanted to prove to James that he didn't need to protect her from gossip and speculation.

James left for court shortly after he'd finished shaving. Summer changed into the outfit she'd finally chosen, a soft gray business suit with a long jacket that—sort of—disguised her pregnancy. She spent the morning doing errands and arrived at Ralph's office at the Seattle Bank ten minutes ahead of their one-o'clock appointment.

She announced her name to the receptionist and was escorted into Southworth's office a few minutes later.

Ralph stood when she entered the room. He didn't seem pleased to see her.

"Hello again," she said brightly, taking the chair across from his desk. She wanted it understood that she wouldn't be easily dissuaded.

"Hello," he responded curtly.

"I hope you don't object to my making an appointment to see you. I'm afraid I may have, uh, misled your secretary into thinking it had to do with a loan."

"I see. Are you in the habit of misleading people?"

"Not at all," she assured him with a cordial smile, "but sometimes a little inventive thinking is worth a dozen frustrating phone calls."

Southworth didn't agree or disagree.

"I'll get to the point of my visit," she said, not wanting to waste time, his or hers.

"Please do."

"I'd like to know why you've resigned as my husband's campaign manager."

Southworth rolled a pencil between his palms, avoiding eye contact. "I believe that's between James and me. It has nothing to do with you."

"That isn't the way I understand it," she said, grateful he'd opened the conversation for her. "I overheard James and his father talking recently, and James said something different."

"So you eavesdrop, as well?"

He was certainly eager to tally her less than sterling characteristics.

"Yes, but in this case, I'm glad I did because I learned that you'd resigned because of me."

Southworth hesitated. "Not exactly. I questioned James's judgment."

"About our marriage?" she pressed.

Once again he seemed inclined to dodge the subject. "I don't really think…"

"I do, Mr. Southworth. This election is extremely important to James. *You're* extremely important to him. When he first mentioned your name to me, he said you were the best man for the job."

"I am the best man for the job." The banker certainly didn't lack confidence in his abilities. "I also know a losing battle when I see it."

"Why's that?"

"Mrs. Wilkens, please."

"Please what, Mr. Southworth? Tell me why you question James's judgment. Until he married me, you were ready to lend him your full support. I can assure you I'll stay right here until I have the answers to these questions." She raised her chin a stubborn half inch and refused to budge.

"If you insist…"

"I do."

"First, you're years younger than James."

"Nine years is hardly that much of a difference. This is a weak excuse and unworthy of you. I do happen to look young for my age, but I can assure you I'm twenty-eight, and James is only thirty-seven."

"There's also the fact that you're a showgirl."

"I'm an actress and singer," she countered. "Since I worked at Disneyland, I hardly think you can fault my morals."

"Morals is another issue entirely."

"Obviously," she said, finding she disliked this man more every time he opened his mouth. It seemed to her that Ralph Southworth was inventing excuses, none of which amounted to anything solid.

"You're pregnant."

"Yes. So?"

"So…it's clear to me, at least, that you and James conveniently decided to marry when you recognized your condition."

Summer laughed. "That's not true, and even if it were, all I need to do is produce our marriage certificate, which I just happen to have with me." Somehow or other she knew it would come down to this. She opened her purse and removed the envelope, then handed it to the man whom her husband had once considered his friend.

Southworth read it over and returned it to her. "I don't understand why the two of you did this. No one meets in Vegas, falls in love and gets married within a few days. Not unless they've got something to hide."

"We're in love." She started to explain that she and James had known each other for a year, but Ralph cut her off.

"Please, Mrs. Wilkens! I've known James for at least a

decade. There had to be a reason other than the one you're giving me."

"He loves me. Isn't that good enough for you?"

Southworth seemed bored with the conversation. "Then there's the fact that he kept the marriage a secret."

Summer had no answer to that. "I don't really know why James didn't tell anyone about the wedding," she admitted. "My guess is that it's because he's a private man and considers his personal life his own."

"How far along is the pregnancy?" he asked, ignoring her answer.

"Three months," she told him.

"Three months? I don't claim to know much about women and babies, but I've had quite a few women work for me at the bank over the years. A number of them have had babies. You look easily five or six months."

"That's ridiculous! I know when I got pregnant."

"Do you, now?"

Summer drew in her breath and held it for a moment in an effort to contain her outrage. She loved James and believed in him, but she refused to be insulted.

"I can see we aren't going to accomplish anything here," she said sadly. "You've already formed your opinion about James and me."

"About you, Mrs. Wilkens. It's unfortunate. James would've made an excellent superior court judge. But there's been far too much speculation about him lately. It started with the black eye. People don't want a man on the bench who can't hold on to his own temper. A judge should be above any hint of moral weakness."

"James is one of the most morally upright men I know," she said heatedly. "I take your comments as a personal insult to my husband."

"I find your loyalty to James touching, but it's too little, too late."

"What do you mean by that?" Summer demanded.

"You want your husband to win the election, don't you?"

"Yes. Of course." The question was ludicrous.

"If I were to tell you that you could make a difference, perhaps even sway the election, would you listen?"

"I'd listen," she said, although anything beyond listening was another matter.

Southworth stood and walked over to the window, which offered a panoramic view of the Seattle skyline. His back was to her and for several minutes he said nothing. He seemed to be weighing his words.

"You've already admitted I'm the best man to run James's campaign."

"Yes," she said reluctantly, not as willing to acknowledge it as she had been when she'd first arrived.

"I can help win him this September's primary and the November election. Don't discount the political sway I have in this community, Mrs. Wilkens."

Summer said nothing.

"When James first told me he'd married you, I suggested he keep you out of the picture until after the election."

"I see."

"I did this for a number of reasons, all of which James disregarded."

"He…he really didn't have much choice," she felt obliged to tell him. "I turned up on his doorstep, suitcase in hand."

Ralph nodded as if he'd suspected this had been the case. "I can turn James's campaign around if you'll agree to one thing."

Her stomach tightened, knowing before the words were out what he was going to say. "Yes?"

"Simply disappear for several months. Stay away from Seattle, and once the November election is over, you can move back into his house. It won't matter then."

She closed her eyes and lowered her head. "I see."

"Will you do it?"

"Summer, I'm sorry I'm late." James kissed her soundly and rushed up the stairs to change clothes.

He was late? She hadn't noticed. Since her meeting with Ralph Southworth, Summer had spent what remained of the afternoon in a stupor. She felt numb and sad. Tears lay just beneath the surface, ready to break free.

This decision should've been far less difficult. She could give her husband the dream he'd always wanted or ruin his life.

Five minutes later James was back. He'd changed out of his suit and tie and wore slacks and a shirt and sweater. "Are you ready?" he asked.

"For what?"

"Dinner tonight with the Mannings. Remember?"

"Of course," she said, forcing a smile. How could she have forgotten that? James was like a schoolboy eager to show off his science project. Only in this case, *she* was the project. She still wore her gray suit, so after quickly brushing her hair and refreshing her makeup, she considered herself ready—in appearance if not in attitude.

He escorted her out the front door and into his car, which he'd parked in front of the house. "You haven't had much campaigning to do lately," she commented.

"I know."

"What does Ralph have to say?" she asked, wanting to see how much James was willing to tell her.

"Not much. Let's not talk about the election tonight, okay?"

"Why not?"

"I don't want to have to think about it. These people are my friends. They're like a second set of parents to me."

"Do they know I'm pregnant?"

"No, but I won't need to tell them, will I?" He gently patted her abdomen.

"James," she whispered. "When we get home this evening, I want to make love."

His gaze briefly left the road and he nodded.

The emptiness inside her could only be filled with his love.

"Are you feeling all right?"

She made herself smile and laid her head against his shoulder. "Of course."

"There's something different about you."

"Is there?" Just that her heart felt as if it had been chopped in half. Just that she'd never felt so cold or alone in her life. Southworth had asked her to turn her back on the man she loved. He'd asked that she leave and do it in such a way that he wouldn't follow. He'd asked that she bear her child alone.

When they got to the Manning home, James parked his car on the street and turned to Summer. He studied her for an intense moment. "I love you."

"I love you," she whispered in return. She felt close to tears.

James helped her out of the car. They walked to the front porch, and he rang the doorbell. When she wasn't looking, he stole a kiss.

A distinguished older gentleman opened the door for them. "James! It's good to see you again."

"Eric, this is my wife, Summer."

"Hello, Summer." Instead of shaking her hand, Eric Manning hugged her.

They stepped inside, and all at once, from behind every conceivable hiding space, people leapt out.

They were greeted with an unanimous chorus of "Surprise!"

Eleven

Summer didn't understand what was happening. A large number of strange people surrounded her. People with happy faces, people who seemed delighted to be meeting her.

"Elizabeth," James protested. "What have you done?"

The middle-aged woman hugged first James and then Summer. "You know how much I love a party," she told him, grinning broadly. "What better excuse than to meet your wife? I'm the mother of this brood," she told Summer proudly, gesturing around the room. There were men, women and children milling about. "You must be Summer."

"I am. You must be Elizabeth."

"Indeed I am."

Before she could protest, Summer was lured away from James's side. The men appeared eager to talk to James by himself. Summer looked longingly at her husband. He met her eyes, then shrugged and followed his friends into the family room.

Soon Summer found herself in the kitchen, which bustled with activity. "I'm Jamie. We met the other day in the restaurant," Rich's wife reminded her.

"I remember," Summer told her, stepping aside as a youngster raced past her at breakneck speed.

"These two women with the curious looks on their faces are my sisters-in-law. The first one here," Jamie said, looping her arm around the woman who was obviously pregnant, "is Charlotte. She's married to Jason. He's the slob of the family."

"But he's improving," Charlotte told her.

"When's your baby due?"

"July," Charlotte said. "This is our second. Doug's asleep. I also have a daughter from my first marriage, but Carrie's working and couldn't be here. I'm sure you'll get a chance to meet her later."

"Our baby's due in September," Summer said, ending speculation.

The women exchanged glances. "You're just three months pregnant?"

Miserable, Summer nodded. "I think something must be wrong. The first couple of months I was really sick. I'm much better now that I'm in Seattle with James. But I'm ballooning. Hardly any of my clothes fit anymore."

"It happens like that sometimes," Elizabeth said with the voice of experience. "I wonder…" Then she shook her head. "I showed far more with Paul, my first, than I did with Christy, my youngest. Don't ask me why nature plays these silly tricks on us. You'd think we have enough to put up with, dealing with men."

A chorus of agreement broke out.

Elizabeth took the hors d'oeuvre platter out of the refrigerator. "The good news is I was blessed with three sons. The bad news is I was blessed with three sons." She laughed. "My daughters are an entirely different story."

"I don't know what to expect with this baby," Summer

told everyone, pressing her hand to her stomach. "We didn't plan to get pregnant so soon."

"I'll bet James is thrilled."

Summer smiled and nodded. "We both are."

"This is Leah," Jamie said, introducing her other sister-in-law, who'd just entered the kitchen. "She's Paul's wife. Paul's the author in the family."

"He's very good," Leah said proudly. "His first book was published last year, and he's sold two more."

"That's great!"

"Let me help," Jamie insisted, removing the platter from Elizabeth's hands. She carried it to the long table, beautifully decorated with paper bells and a lovely ceramic bride-and-groom centerpiece.

"I've been waiting for a long time to use these decorations," Elizabeth said disparagingly. "My children didn't give me the opportunity. It all started with the girls. Neither one of *them* saw fit to have a church wedding. Then Rich married Jamie and Paul married Leah, again without the kind of wedding I always wanted."

"Jason and Charlotte were the only ones to have a big wedding," Leah explained. "I don't think Eric and Elizabeth have ever forgiven the rest of us."

"You're darn right, we haven't," Eric said, joining them.

"They made it up to us with grandchildren, dear," his wife interjected. "Now, don't get started on that. We're very fortunate."

Summer couldn't remember the last time she'd sat down at a dinner table with this many people. A rowdy group of children ate at card tables set up in the kitchen. Twin boys seemed to instigate the chaos, taking delight in teasing their younger cousins. The noise level was considerable, but Summer didn't mind.

More than once, she caught James watching her. She smiled and silently conveyed that she was enjoying herself. Who wouldn't be?

There were gifts to open after the meal and plenty of marital advice. Summer, whose mood had been bleak earlier, found herself laughing so hard her sides ached.

The evening was an unqualified success, and afterward Summer felt as if she'd met a houseful of new friends. Jamie, Leah and Charlotte seemed eager to make her feel welcome. Charlotte was the first to extend an invitation for lunch. Since they were both pregnant, they already had something important in common.

"A week from Friday," Charlotte reminded her as Summer and James prepared to leave. She mentioned the name of the restaurant and wrote her phone number on the back of a business card.

"I'll look forward to it," Summer told her and meant it.

It wasn't until they were home that she remembered her meeting with Southworth. She didn't know if she'd be in Seattle in another week, let alone available for lunch.

Sadness pressed against her heart.

James slipped his arm around her waist. He turned off the downstairs lights, and together they moved toward the stairs. "As I recall," he whispered in her ear, "you made me a promise earlier."

"I did?"

"You asked me to make love to you, remember?"

"Oh, yes…" Shivers of awareness slid up and down her spine.

"I certainly hope you intend to keep that promise."

She yawned loudly, covering her mouth, fighting back waves of tiredness. "I have no intention of changing my mind."

"Good." They reached the top of the stairs, and he nuzzled her neck. "I wonder if it'll always be like this," he murmured, steering her toward their bedroom.

"Like what?"

"My desire for you. I feel like a kid in a candy store."

Summer laughed, then yawned again. "I enjoyed meeting the Mannings. They're wonderful people."

"Are those yawns telling me something?" he asked.

She nodded. "I'm tired, James." But it was more than being physically weary. She felt a mental and emotional exhaustion that left her depleted.

"Come on, love," James urged gently. He led her into the bedroom and between long, deep kisses, he undressed her and placed her on the bed. He tucked her in and kissed her cheek.

The light dimmed, and Summer snuggled into the warmth. It took her a few minutes to realize James hadn't joined her.

"James?" She forced her eyes open.

"Yes, love?"

"Aren't you coming to bed?"

"Soon," he said. "I'm taking a shower first."

A shower, she mused, wondering at his sudden penchant for cleanliness.

Then she heard him mutter, "A nice, long, *cold* shower."

James had been looking forward to the ultrasound appointment for weeks. He'd met Dr. Wise, Summer's obstetrician, earlier and had immediately liked and trusted the man, who was in his late forties. David Wise had been delivering babies for more than twenty years, and his calm reassurance had gone a long way toward relieving James's fears.

The ultrasound clinic was in the same medical building as Dr. Wise's office. He'd said he'd join them there, although James wasn't convinced that was his regular policy. Still, he felt grateful.

Summer sat next to him in the waiting room, her face pale and lifeless. She hadn't been herself in the past few days, and James wondered what was bothering her. He didn't want to pry and hoped she'd soon share whatever it was.

They held hands and waited silently until Summer's name was called.

It was all James could do to sit still as the technician, a young woman named Rachel, explained the procedure.

Summer was instructed to lie flat on her back on the examining table. Her T-shirt was raised to expose the bump that was their child. As James smiled down on her Dr. Wise entered the room.

A gel was spread across Summer's abdomen. It must have been cold because she flinched.

"It's about this time that women start to suggest the male of the species should be responsible for childbearing," Dr. Wise told him.

"No, thanks," James said, "I like my role in all this just fine."

Dr. Wise chuckled. Rachel pressed a stethoscope-like instrument across Summer's stomach, and everyone's attention turned toward the monitor.

James squinted but had trouble making out the details on the screen.

"There's the baby's head," Dr. Wise said, pointing to a curved shape.

James squinted again and he noticed Summer doing the same.

"Well, well. Look at this," the physician continued. "I'm not altogether surprised."

"Look at what?" James studied the screen intently.

"We have a second little head."

"My baby has two heads?" Summer cried in alarm.

"Two heads?" James echoed.

"What I'm saying," Dr. Wise returned calmly, "is that there appear to be two babies."

"Twins?"

"It certainly seems that way." As the ultrasound technician moved the instrument across Summer's abdomen, Dr. Wise pointed to the monitor. "Here's the first head," he said, tracing the barely discernible round curve, "and here's the second."

James squinted for all he was worth just to see one. "Twins," he murmured.

"That explains a lot," Dr. Wise said, patting Summer's arm. "Let's run a copy of this for you both," he said, and Rachel pushed a series of buttons.

Within minutes they had the printout to examine for themselves. While Summer dressed, James studied the picture.

"Twins," he said again, just for the pleasure of hearing himself say it. He turned to Summer and smiled broadly. "Twins," he repeated, grinning from ear to ear.

She smiled, and James thought he saw tears in her eyes.

"It won't be so bad," he said, then immediately regretted his lack of sensitivity. He wasn't the one carrying two babies, nor would he be the one delivering them. "I'll do whatever I can to help," he quickly reassured her.

She gave him a watery smile.

"Say something," he pleaded. "Are you happy?"

"I don't know," she admitted. "I'm still in shock. What about you?"

"Other than the day I married you, I've never been happier." He couldn't seem to stop smiling. "I can hardly wait to tell my father. He's going to be absolutely thrilled."

Summer stared at the ultrasound. "Can you tell? Boys? Girls? One of each?" Strangely, perhaps, it hadn't occurred to her to ask Dr. Wise.

James scratched his head. "I had enough trouble finding the two heads. I decided not to try deciphering anything else."

They left the doctor's office and headed for the parking garage across the street.

"This calls for a celebration. I'll take you to lunch," he said.

"I was thinking more along the lines of a nap."

James grinned and looked his watch. "Is there time?"

"James," she said, laughing softly. "I meant a *real* nap. I'm exhausted."

"Oh." Disappointment shot through him. "You don't want to celebrate with a fancy lunch?"

She shook her head. "Don't be upset with me. I guess I need time to think about everything."

That sounded odd to James. What was there to think about? True, Summer was pregnant with twins, but they had plenty of time to prepare. As for any mental readjustment, well, he'd made that in all of two seconds. The twins were a surprise, yes, but a pleasant one.

"This news has upset you, hasn't it?" he asked.

"No," she was quick to assure him. "It's just that…well, it changes things."

"What things?"

She shook her head again and didn't answer. James

frowned, not knowing how to calm her fears or allay her doubts. She didn't seem to expect him to do either and instead appeared to be withdrawing into herself.

"You don't mind if I tell my dad, do you?" he asked. If he didn't share the news with someone soon, he was afraid he'd be reduced to stopping strangers on the street.

She smiled at him, her eyes alight with love. "No, I don't mind if you tell Walter."

He walked her to where she'd parked and kissed her, then walked the short distance back to the King County Courthouse. His thoughts were so full of Summer that he went a block too far before he realized what he'd done.

In his office, the first thing he did was reach for the phone.

His father answered immediately. "You'll never guess what I'm looking at," he told Walter.

"You're right, I'll never guess."

"Today was Summer's ultrasound," James reminded him. Hiding his excitement was almost impossible.

"Ah, yes, and what did you learn?"

James could hear the eagerness in Walter's voice. "I have the picture in front of me."

"And?"

"I'm staring at your grandchildren right this second."

"Boy or girl?"

James couldn't help it. He laughed. "You didn't listen very well."

"I did, too, and I want to know—what do we have? A boy or a girl?"

"Could be one of each," James informed him calmly.

"Twins!" Walter shouted. "You mean Summer's having twins?"

"That's what I'm telling you."

"Well, I'll be! This is good news. No, it's great news. The best!"

James had never heard Walter this excited—practically as excited as he was himself.

It wasn't every day that a man learned he was having not one baby but two!

Summer didn't go directly home. Instead, she drove around for at least an hour, evaluating the situation between her and James. She loved him so much. The thought of leaving him, even when she knew it was the best thing for his career, brought her to the verge of tears.

What she wanted was to talk with her mother, but her parents were vacationing, touring the south in their motor home. They weren't due back for another month. Summer received postcards every few days with the latest updates and many exhortations to look after herself and their unborn grandchild. Wait till she told them it was grand-*children,* she thought with a brief smile.

This vacation was good for them, but she really needed her mother now.

Without realizing she knew the way, Summer drove to the Manning family home. She parked, wondering whether she was doing the right thing.

It took her a full five minutes to gather up enough nerve to get out of the car, walk up the steps and ring the bell.

Elizabeth Manning answered the door. Her face lit up with warmth. "Summer! What a lovely surprise."

"I hope I haven't come at an inconvenient time."

"Not at all," Elizabeth said, ushering her in. "I was making meatballs. It's Eric's favorite. Today's his bowling day, so he's out just now. Can I get you a cup of tea?"

"No, thank you."

Elizabeth sat down in the living room.

"Would it be all right if we talked in the kitchen?" Summer asked after an awkward moment.

"Of course."

"I…I'm aware that you barely know me, and it's an imposition for me to drop in like this."

"Not at all. I'm delighted to see you again."

"I…my parents have a motor home," Summer said, wishing now she'd thought this through more carefully before she approached James's friends. "They're traveling across the south."

"Eric and I do quite a bit of traveling in our own motor home. We visit Christy and her sister, Taylor, at least once a year. Montana's become like a second home to us." She dug her hands into the bowl of hamburger and removed a glob of meat. Expertly she formed it into a perfect round shape.

"I really just wanted to thank you for everything you did the other night," Summer said. "The party for James and me…"

She suddenly decided she couldn't burden this woman with her troubles. She would've welcomed advice, but felt uncomfortable discussing her problems with someone who was little more than a stranger to her.

"When you know me better," Elizabeth was saying, "you'll learn that I love throwing parties. James has always been a special friend to our family, and we were so happy to find out about his marriage. Naturally we wanted to celebrate."

Summer nodded. "I didn't think it was possible to love anyone so much," she confessed, and then because tears began to drip from her eyes, she stood abruptly. "Listen, I should go, but thank you. I'll see myself to the door."

"Summer," Elizabeth called after her. "Summer, is everything all right?"

Summer was in her car by the time Elizabeth appeared in the doorway. She hurriedly started the engine and drove off, sure that she'd done more harm than good with her impromptu visit.

Wiping away tears, Summer went home. She walked into the house and up the stairs, then lay down on the bed and closed her eyes.

She had to leave, but she didn't know where to go. If she didn't do it soon, she'd never find the courage. Only minutes earlier, she'd declared to James's family friend how deeply she loved her husband. That was the truth, so doing what was best for him shouldn't be this difficult.

But it was.

Sobbing and miserable, Summer got up from the bed and pulled a big suitcase from the closet. She packed what she thought she'd need and carried it down to the car.

At the last minute she decided she couldn't leave without writing James. She sat at his desk for several minutes, trying to compose a letter that would explain what she was doing and why. But it was all so complicated, and in the end she simply said he was better off without her and signed her name. She read it twice before tucking it in an envelope.

Tears streamed down her cheeks. It wouldn't be so bad, or so she attempted to convince herself. The babies would be less than two months old when the election was over, and then she'd be free to return.

If James wanted her back.

James had seldom been in a better mood. He sat in the courtroom, convinced he must be grinning like a fool.

His assistant didn't know what to think. During a brief

recess, he waltzed back to his office to phone Summer, whistling as he went.

His wife might not have wanted to celebrate with lunch, but their news deserved some kind of festivity. Dinner at the Space Needle. A night on the town.

While he was in his office, he ordered flowers for Summer with a card that said she'd made him the happiest man alive. Twice. He wondered what the florist would make of *that*.

The phone rang four times before voice mail kicked in. James hung up rather than leave a message. He'd try again later. Summer was probably resting; he hoped the phone hadn't disturbed her.

"Judge Wilkens?" Mrs. Jamison, his assistant, stopped him as he was leaving his office.

"Yes?"

"Your father phoned earlier. He wanted me to let you know he's been to the toy store and purchased two giant teddy bears. He also asked me to tell you he'll be dropping them off around six this evening. And he said he made dinner reservations in case you hadn't thought of it."

"Great." James laughed and discovered his assistant staring at him blankly.

"See this," James said, taking the ultrasound picture from inside his suit pocket. "My wife and I just learned we're having twins."

"Your wife? Twins for you and Summer. Why, Your Honor…" Her mouth opened, then shut, but she recovered quickly. "Congratulations!"

"Thank you," James said. Then, checking his watch, he returned to the courtroom.

The afternoon was hectic. James was hearing the sad case of a man who, crazed with drugs and alcohol, had gone on a shooting rampage. He'd killed three people and injured seventeen more. The case was just getting underway but was sure to attract a lot of media attention. James knew the defense was hinging its case on a plea of temporary insanity.

A door opened at the rear of the courtroom. James didn't look up, but out of the corner of his eye, he saw a lone figure slip into the back row. Whoever it was apparently didn't want to be recognized. She wore a scarf and large sunglasses.

Twice more James found his gaze returning to the figure in the back of the courtroom. If he didn't know better, he'd think it was Summer.

Whoever it was stayed for quite a long time. An hour or more. He wasn't sure when the woman left, but James couldn't help being curious.

His best guess was that the woman was a reporter.

When he was finished for the afternoon, James returned to his office and removed his robe. His secretary brought in a stack of phone messages. The one that seemed most peculiar was from Elizabeth Manning. She'd never called him at court.

Leaning back in his chair, he reached for the phone. "Hello, Elizabeth," he said cheerfully. It was on the tip of his tongue to tell her his and Summer's good news, but she cut him off.

"You'd better tell me what's wrong. I've been worried sick all afternoon."

"Worried? About what?"

"You and Summer."

Sometimes she baffled him. "I don't have a clue what you're talking about. I will tell you that Summer and I were at the doctor's this morning and found out she's pregnant with twins."

"Congratulations." But Elizabeth seemed distracted. "That can't be it," she mulled aloud. "She was here, you know."

"Who?"

"Summer."

"When?"

"This afternoon. Listen to me, James, there's something wrong. I knew it the minute I saw that girl. She was upset and close to tears. At first I thought you two might've had an argument."

"No…" James frowned. "What did she say?"

"She talked about her parents traveling in their motor home. I suppose I should've realized she wanted to discuss something with me, but I started chattering, hoping she'd relax enough to speak her mind."

"Tell me everything that happened."

"After the part about her parents' vacation, she said she'd come to thank me for the party, which we both knew was an excuse. Then she apparently changed her mind about talking with me and started to cry. Before I could stop her, she was gone."

"Gone? What do you mean gone?"

"The girl literally ran out of the house. I tried to catch up with her, but with my bad leg, that was impossible."

"She drove off without another word?"

"That's right." Elizabeth sounded flustered. "What could be wrong, James?"

"I don't know. I just don't know. She was fine this morning." Or was she? James had no idea anymore. "I'll give you a call this evening," he assured Elizabeth. "I'm sure everything's okay."

"I hope so. Summer was very upset, James. Oh. That's odd…."

"What is?"

"I remember something else she said, and it was after this that she started to cry."

"What was it?" James asked anxiously.

"She told me how much she loved you."

A few minutes later, when he'd finished speaking to Elizabeth, James was more confused than ever. He tried calling Summer again—but again there was no answer. He left the office abruptly, without a word to his staff.

When he got to the house he burst through the front door. "Summer!" he shouted, his heart racing.

He was greeted with silence.

He raced up the stairs, taking them two at a time. He searched every room but couldn't find her.

What confused him further was that her clothes still hung in her closet, but one suitcase was missing. Surely if she was planning to leave him, she'd have taken more things. The only items that seemed to be missing were her toothbrush, slippers and a book about pregnancy and birth.

Baffled, he wandered back downstairs. He scouted out the kitchen and the other rooms. The last place he looked was in his den. There he found an envelope propped against the base of the lamp.

James tore open the letter. It was brief and it made no sense. All he understood was that she'd left him. He had no idea why, other than that she seemed to think she was doing what was best for him.

He immediately called her cell. No answer.

A sick feeling attacked his stomach. He sat numbly at his desk for what could've been minutes or hours; he'd lost track of time. The next thing he knew, the doorbell chimed.

He didn't get up to answer. A moment later the door opened on its own and his father came into the house.

"You might've let me in," he grumbled, setting one huge teddy bear in the chair across from James. "I'll be right back." He returned a couple of minutes later with the second bear.

"How'd you get in?" James asked, his voice devoid of emotion.

"You gave me a key, remember?"

He didn't.

"What's going on around here?" Walter asked. "Where's my daughter-in-law who's giving me twin grandkids?"

"Apparently Summer has decided to leave me. She's gone."

Twelve

"Gone?" Walter protested. "What do you mean, gone?"

"Gone, Dad," James said bitterly, "as in packed-a-suitcase-and-walked-out-the-door gone."

His father quickly sat down. "But...why?"

James couldn't answer that; silently he handed Walter the brief letter Summer had left him.

Walter read it, then raised questioning eyes to James. "What's this supposed to mean?"

"Your guess is as good as mine."

"You must've said something," Walter insisted. "Think, boy, think."

"I've done nothing *but* think, and none of this makes sense. I thought at first that she was upset about the twins. I realize now that whatever it is has been worrying her for some time."

"What could it be?"

"I don't know. I'd hoped she'd tell me."

"You mean to say you didn't ask?"

"No."

Walter glared at him in disbelief. "That's the first thing I learned after I married your mother. She never told me a thing that I didn't have to pry out of her with a crowbar. It's a man's duty, a husband's lot in life. When you didn't ask, Summer must've assumed you didn't care. She probably figures you don't love her."

In spite of his heavy heart, James smiled. "Trust me, Dad, Summer has no fear of speaking her mind, and as for my loving her, she couldn't have doubted that for an instant."

"She loves you." Walter's words were more statement than question.

"Yes," James said. He felt secure in her love. Or he had until now.

"Where would she go?"

This was the same question he'd been debating from the moment he discovered her letter. He shrugged. "No idea."

"Have you tried her cell?"

"Of course," he snapped. "She turned it off."

"Did you contact her parents?"

He would have, but it wouldn't help. James rubbed his face, tired to the very marrow of his bones. "They're traveling across the Southwest in their motor home. Half the time they don't have cell phone coverage."

"What about friends she's made since the move?"

"They're more acquaintances than friends. She's planning to volunteer at the library, but she's only mentioned the children's librarian in passing."

"I see." Walter frowned. "What about the Mannings?"

"She went over to talk to Elizabeth earlier this afternoon. Elizabeth phoned me and said Summer started to cry and then left in a hurry."

Walter's look was thoughtful. "Sounds as if she was trying to reach out for help."

"The only other person I can think of is her former roommate, Julie. I'll call her now."

"Julie, of course," his father said as if he should've thought of her himself.

James looked up the number and spoke to Julie's new roommate for several minutes.

"Julie's contract with Disney was up at the same time as Summer's," he said as he hung up. "Now that I think about it, Summer did say something about Julie being on tour with a musical group."

"So she'd be staying in hotels. Unlikely Summer would go to her."

James closed his eyes. His wife had walked out on him into a cold, friendless world.

"What about her brother?"

After another quick call, James shook his head. "Adam and Denise haven't heard from her. All I did was scare them," he said grimly.

"Did you check the airlines?"

"Where would she go?" James asked, losing his patience.

"I don't know," Walter admitted reluctantly. He began pacing.

His movements soon irritated James. "For heaven's sake, will you kindly sit down?"

"I can't sit here and do nothing."

"Yes, you can and you will," James insisted, making a decision. "I'll take the car and drive around, see if I can find her. You stay here by the phone in case she calls or we hear something."

"Okay. Check in with me every half hour."

James nodded. As he climbed into the car, he felt as if he was setting out on a journey without a map. Essentially he was, he thought as he drove through the narrow neighborhood streets. Try as he might, he couldn't figure out where she'd go. He tried to put himself in her shoes. Alone in a strange city with few friends.

The only thing he could do was ask God to guide him.

The wind blew off Puget Sound and buffeted Summer as she stood at the end of the pier. The waterfront was one of her favorite places in all of Seattle. Not knowing where else to instruct the taxi to take her, she'd had the driver bring her here.

She loved to shop at the Pike Place Market. Every Saturday morning James came down to the waterfront with her, and they bought fresh fruit and vegetables for the week. He'd been wonderfully patient while she browsed in the tourist shops that stretched along the waterfront. Some of their happiest moments in Seattle had been spent on this very pier.

How she hated to leave this city. It was as if everything in her was fighting to keep her in Seattle. Her husband was here, her home, her very life.

The instant she'd walked into James's large house, she'd experienced a powerful sense of homecoming. She'd never said anything to her husband—he might think her reaction was silly—but Summer felt that his house had always been meant for them together.

She'd like to think that somewhere in James's subconscious he'd known he was going to fall in love and marry. The house had been his preparation for her entry into his life.

Tears blinded her eyes. She didn't want to focus on her unhappiness, so she turned her attention to the water. The pull of the tide fascinated her. The dark, murky waters of

Elliott Bay glistened in the lights overhead. A green-and-white ferry chugged into the terminal.

Summer closed her eyes, willing herself to walk away. Except that she didn't know where she'd go. One thing was certain; she couldn't spend the night standing at the end of the pier. She'd need to find herself a hotel. In the morning her head would be clearer and she could make some decisions.

She was about to reach for her suitcase when she sensed someone approaching. Not wanting company, even the non-intrusive sort, Summer turned away from the railing. She kept her eyes lowered, but that didn't prevent her from recognizing James.

He sauntered to the railing several feet from where she stood. Wordlessly he stared into the distance.

Summer wasn't sure what she should do. She couldn't very well walk away from him now. It had been difficult enough the first time. She didn't have the strength to do it again.

"How'd…how'd you find me?" she asked.

He continued to stare into the distance. "Lucky guess," he finally said in cool tones.

Summer doubted that James felt lucky being married to her just then. He was furious with her. More furious than she'd ever seen him.

She wanted to explain that she was a detriment to his career, but couldn't force the words through her parched throat.

The tears that had flowed most of the day returned. She brushed them away with her fingertips.

"Was I such a bad husband?" he demanded in the same chilling tone.

"No," she whispered.

"Did I do something so terrible you can't forgive me for?"

Sobbing, she shook her head.

"You've fallen out of love with me," he suggested next.

"Don't be ridiculous," she cried. If she'd loved him any more than she already did, her heart couldn't have stood it.

"Then tell me why you walked out on me."

"My letter…"

"…explained nothing."

"I…I…" She was trembling so much she couldn't speak.

James walked over to her and reached for her suitcase. "We're going back to the house and we're going to talk about this. Then, if you're still set on leaving, I'll drive you to the airport myself. Understand?"

All she could manage was a weak nod.

Thankfully, he'd parked the car close by. Summer felt disoriented. Maybe she shouldn't be this happy that James had found her, but she was. Even if he was angry with her, she was grateful he was taking her home.

James opened the car door for her and set her suitcase in the backseat. He didn't speak so much as a single word on the drive home.

When they pulled into the driveway, Summer saw Walter's car.

"Your father's here?"

James didn't answer her. Nor did he need to. Walter was already out the door.

"Where'd you find her?" he asked, bolting toward them.

"The waterfront."

"Sit down, sit down," her father-in-law murmured, guiding Summer inside and into a chair. She felt she was about to collapse and must have looked it, too.

"Now what the hell is this all about?" James said roughly.

"You can't talk to her like that," Walter chastised. "Can't you see the poor girl's had the worst day of her life?" He turned to Summer, smiling gently. "Now what the hell is this all about?"

Summer looked from one man to the other. "Would it be all right if I spoke to James alone?" she asked her father-in-law. She couldn't deal with both of them at the same time.

It looked for a moment as if Walter wasn't going to leave. "I suppose," he agreed with reluctance. "I'll be in the other room."

"Walter," Summer said, stopping him on his way out the door. "I take it the two teddy bears are your doing."

He nodded sheepishly. "The car's loaded with goodies. I'm afraid I got a little carried away."

"These babies are going to love their grandpa."

Walter grinned, then walked out, closing the door.

James stood by the fireplace, his back to her. Summer suspected he was preparing a list of questions. She wasn't even sure she had all the answers; she wasn't sure she wanted him to ask them. She decided to preempt his interrogation.

"I...I went to see Ralph Southworth," she said in a quavering voice.

James whirled around. "You did *what?*"

"I...I overheard you and your father talking not long ago and I learned that Southworth resigned as your campaign manager."

"So he's what this is all about," James said thoughtfully. His eyes hardened. "What happened between the two of us had nothing to do with you."

"James, please, I know otherwise. I...I knew from the start that Ralph disapproved of me. I'm not sure why, but it doesn't matter."

"No, it doesn't. Because Southworth doesn't matter."

Summer didn't believe that. "Afterward, it seemed like you'd given up on the election. In the last two weeks you haven't made a single public appearance. When I ask, you don't want to talk about it and—"

"There are things you don't know."

"Things you wouldn't tell me."

James sat across from her and leaned forward, elbows on his knees. He didn't say anything for several minutes.

"What was I supposed to think?" she cried when he didn't explain. "Being a judge is the most important thing in the world to you. You were born for this.... I couldn't take it away from you. Don't you understand?"

"You're wrong about something. Being a superior court judge means nothing if you're not with me. I guarantee you, my career's not worth losing my wife and family over."

"I was going to come back," she whispered, her eyes lowered. "After the election..."

"Do you mean to say you were going to deliver our babies on your own? Do you honestly think I wouldn't have turned this city upside down looking for you?"

"I...didn't know what to think. Ralph said—"

"Don't even tell me." A muscle leapt in his jaw. "I can well imagine what he said. The man's a world-class idiot. He saw you as a liability when you're my greatest asset."

"If you truly believe that, then why did you throw in the towel?"

"I haven't," he told her. "I took a few days to think about it and decide who I'll ask to manage the rest of my campaign. It seems there are several people who want the job."

"But Southworth said he could sway the election for you.... He claims to have political clout."

"He seems to think he does," James said tightly.

"We made a deal," she whispered, lowering her gaze.

"What kind of deal?"

"Southworth agreed to manage your campaign if I left Seattle until after the election."

James snickered. "It's unfortunate you didn't check with me first."

"Why?"

"I don't want Southworth anywhere near my campaign."

Summer bristled. "You might've said that earlier."

"True," James admitted slowly. "But I wanted everything squared away before I announced that I'd changed campaign managers."

"So, who did you choose? Who's your new manager?"

"Eric Manning. He's not only an old friend, he was a successful businessman and he's very well connected." He shook his head. "I should've asked him in the first place."

"James, that's wonderful! I like him so much better than Ralph."

James reached for her hands and held them in his own. "What you don't understand is that I wouldn't have taken Southworth back under any circumstances. First of all, I won't allow any man to talk about my wife the way he did. It's true I made some mistakes when we first got married. I blame myself for not publishing our wedding announcement immediately. Frankly, I didn't think of it."

"I didn't, either. And remember, we were talking about an April ceremony back then." Summer wasn't willing to have him accept all the blame.

"You're my wife, and I couldn't be prouder that someone as beautiful and talented as you would choose to marry me. Ralph made it sound as if we should keep you under wraps until after the election, which is utterly ridiculous. I'm angry with myself for not taking a stand sooner."

"What about the election?" She didn't care to hear any more about Southworth.

"I'll get to that in a minute. When Southworth said he questioned my judgment, I realized what a fool I'd been to listen to the man for even a minute."

"But—"

"Let me finish, sweetheart. The best thing I ever did in my life was marry you."

"It was impulsive and—"

"Smart," he said, cutting her off. "I don't need Southworth to win this campaign for me. He had me convinced I did, but I know otherwise now."

"What about his political friends?"

"That's a laugh. A man as narrow-minded and self-righteous as Ralph Southworth can't afford the luxury of friends. He has none, but he doesn't seem to know it. If he hadn't decided to leave my campaign, I would've asked him to resign."

It was a good thing Summer was sitting down. "You mean to say I went through all that grief and left you for *nothing?*"

"Exactly."

"Oh."

James gathered her in his arms. "Summer, whatever I am, whatever I may become, I'm nothing without you."

Summer sobbed into his shoulder.

"Winning the election would be an empty victory if you weren't standing at my side. I want you to share that moment with me. I love you, Summer, and I love our babies, too."

"Oh, James, I've been so unhappy. I didn't know what to do."

"Don't ever leave me again. It was like I'd lost my mind,

my heart—everything—until I saw you standing at the end of that pier."

Summer tightened her arms around him.

Walter tapped on the door. "Can I come in yet?"

"No," James growled.

"So have you two settled your differences?"

"We're working on it," Summer called out.

"Then I'll leave you to your reunion."

"Good night, Dad," James said in what was an obvious hint for his father to leave.

"'Night, kids. Kiss and make up, okay?"

"We're going to do a lot more than kiss," James whispered in her ear.

"Promises, promises, promises," she murmured.

"You can bet I'll make good on these."

Thirteen

"This is my wife, Summer," James said, his arm around her thick waist. Although she was only six months pregnant, she looked closer to nine.

"I'm so pleased to meet you," the older woman said.

"Who was that again?" she whispered to James.

"Emily Rohrbaugh, president of the League of Women Voters."

"Oh. I don't know how you remember all these names. I'm impressed."

"I'm more impressed that you can remember all your lines in *Beauty and the Beast*," he said. "But here's my little trick for recalling names. I try to tie them in with something else," James told her. "Some kind of object or action."

"Rohrbaugh is something of a challenge, don't you think?" Summer raised her eyebrows.

"Roar and baa," he said under his breath. "Think of a lion and a lamb. A lion roars and a lamb goes *baa*. Rohrbaugh."

Summer's face lit up with a bright smile. "No wonder I married you. You're brilliant."

"I bet you won't have a problem remembering Emily the next time you meet."

"I won't."

"She's a good friend of Elizabeth Manning's," James said, feeding his wife a seedless grape. It was a test of his restraint not to kiss her afterward. One would assume his desire for her would fade after all these months; if anything, quite the opposite had occurred. She was never more beautiful to him than now, heavy with their children.

"Elizabeth Manning?" Summer repeated. "I didn't think she'd be the political type."

"She isn't," James said. They mingled with the crowd gathered on the patio of an influential member of the state senate. "But the two of them have been friends since high school."

"I see."

"Do you need to sit for a while?"

"James," she groaned. "Stop worrying about me."

He glanced down at her abdomen. "How are Mutt and Jeff?"

She circled her belly with both hands. "I swear these two are going to be world-class soccer players."

James chuckled, reaching for an hors d'oeuvre from one of the several platters set around the sunny patio. He gave it to Summer.

"James, I don't believe I've met your wife."

James recognized the voice—William Carr, the president of the Bar Association. He quickly made the introductions. He never worried about Summer saying the wrong thing or inadvertently embarrassing him. She had a natural way about her that instantly put people at ease. She was charming and open and genuine. These political functions weren't her idea of a good time, but she never complained. She seemed eager to do whatever she could to aid his campaign and had proved to be the asset he knew she would be.

"I'm very pleased to meet you," she said warmly as they exchanged handshakes.

The obvious topic of conversation was Summer's pregnancy, which they discussed but only briefly. She managed to deftly turn the conversation away from herself, and soon Carr was talking about himself, laughing over the early days when his wife was pregnant with their oldest child.

After ten minutes or so, Summer excused herself.

"She's an excellent conversationalist," William Carr commented as she walked away.

James did his best to hide a smile. It amused him that Carr could do most of the talking and then act as if Summer had been the one carrying the discussion.

"It seems strange to think of you as married," the attorney said next.

"When I'm with Summer, I wonder why I ever waited so long."

Carr shifted his weight from one foot to the other. "If I'd given you advice before you were appointed to the court, it would've been to marry."

"Really?" This came as a shock to James.

"You're a fine young man, and I expect great things from you. Just between you, me and the fence post, I think you're doing an excellent job."

"I hope so," James said, but there were some who weren't as confident as William Carr. Generally those under the influence of Ralph Southworth. To James's surprise, Southworth had managed to prejudice several supporters against him.

"You remind me of myself thirty years back," Carr told him.

James considered this high praise. "Thank you."

"But you needed a little softening around the edges. You

came off as strong and unbending. Not a bad thing for a judge, mind you, but being a little more human wouldn't have hurt."

"I see." James didn't like hearing this but knew it was for his own good, however uncomfortable it might be.

"It's easy to sit in judgment of others when you live in an ivory tower."

James frowned uncertainly. "I don't understand."

"Until you married Summer, your life was a bit…sterile. Protected. If you don't mind my saying so… A married man knows how to compromise. I imagine you've done things to make your wife happy that you wouldn't normally do."

He nodded.

"In my opinion, marriage matures a man. It helps him sympathize and identify with his fellow humans."

"Are you trying to tell me I was a stodgy stuffed shirt before I married Summer?" James asked outright.

William Carr seemed taken aback by his directness, then grinned. "Couldn't have said it better myself."

"That's what I thought." James reached for a tiny crab puff.

"By the way, I wanted to congratulate you on a job well done. That multiple homicide was your first murder trial, wasn't it?"

"Yes." To be honest, he was happy it was over. The ordeal had proved to be exhausting for everyone involved. The jury had found the young man guilty, and after careful deliberation, James had pronounced the sentence.

His name and face had appeared on television screens every night for weeks. It went without saying that a lot of people were watching and waiting to see how he'd rule. Liberals were looking for leniency, and hard-liners wanted the death penalty. James had agonized over the sentence.

There were more victims than the ones who were shot during those hours of madness. Three families had lost loved ones. Seventeen others would always carry the mark of a madman's gun. Innocent lives had been forever changed.

James had delivered a sentence he felt was fair. He didn't try to satisfy any political factions, although the outcome of the election could well rest on his judgment. He'd sentenced the killer to life without the possibility of parole, with mandatory psychiatric treatment.

It would've been impossible to keep everyone happy, so his decision had been based on what he considered equitable for all concerned. Some were pleased, he knew, and others were outraged.

"Thank you," James said, "I appreciate your vote of confidence."

"The decisions won't get any easier," William Carr told him. The older man grabbed a stuffed green olive and popped it in his mouth.

"The bar will be taking their opinion poll about the time your wife's due to have those babies of yours."

James knew that whether or not the results were published was at the discretion of the bar. The vote could sway the November election.

Summer returned just then, looking tired. Despite her smile, William Carr seemed to realize this. He wished them his best and drifted away.

"Are you ready to leave?" James asked.

"No," she protested. "We've barely arrived."

"We're going." His mistake was in asking her; he should've known to expect an argument.

He made their excuses, thanked the host and hostess and urged Summer toward their parked car. Her progress was slow, and he knew she was uncomfortable, especially in the heat.

"Charlotte's due in two weeks," she said when he helped her inside. She sighed as she eased into the seat. The seat belt barely stretched all the way around her.

James paused. "What's that comment about Charlotte about?"

"I envy her. Look at me, James!"

"I am looking at you," he said, and planted a kiss on her cheek. "You're the most beautiful woman in the world."

"I don't believe you," she muttered.

"You'd better, because it wouldn't take much to convince me to prove it right here and now."

"James, honestly."

"I am being honest."

She smiled, and he couldn't resist kissing her a second time.

After they got home, Summer sat outside in the sunshine. She propped her feet on a stool, and her hands rested on her stomach.

James brought her a glass of iced tea.

She smiled her appreciation. "You spoil me."

"That's because I enjoy it." He sat down next to her. "I don't suppose you've thought about packing up and leaving me lately?"

Summer giggled. "Once or twice, but by the time I finished dragging out my suitcases, I was too tired to go."

"You're teasing."

"Of course I'm teasing."

"Speaking of suitcases, do you have one ready for the hospital?"

"Aren't we being a little premature?"

"Who knows what Mutt and Jeff are thinking." James's

hand joined hers. It thrilled him to feel his children move inside her. "And this time you might want to take more than your toothbrush, a book and your bedroom slippers."

"That goes to show you the mental state I was in."

"Never again," James said firmly.

Summer propped her head against his shoulder and sighed. "Never again," she agreed.

The day of the September primary, Summer woke feeling sluggish and out of sorts. Getting out of bed was a task of monumental proportions. She felt as if she needed a forklift.

James was already up and shaved. He'd been watching her carefully all week. To everyone's surprise, including her doctor's, Summer hadn't delivered the twins yet. She'd read that twins were often born early. But not Mutt and Jeff, as they'd been affectionately named by James.

"Most babies aren't born on their due dates, so stop looking so worried. This is *your* day." She sat on the edge of the bed and pressed her hand to the small of her back.

James offered her his arm to help her upright. "How do you feel?"

"I don't know yet." The pain at the base of her spine had kept her awake most of the night. It didn't seem to go away, no matter how often she changed her position.

"When are we voting?" she asked.

"First thing this morning," James told her.

"Good."

"Why is that good?" he asked anxiously. "Do you think today's the day?"

"James, stop! I'm in perfect health."

"For someone nine months pregnant with twins, you mean."

Summer swore that somehow, God willing, she'd make it through this day. James was so tender and endearing, but she didn't want him worrying about her during the primary.

They gathered, together with Walter, at the large Manning home for the election results that evening. Summer was pleased for the opportunity to be with her friends.

Jason and Charlotte, along with their toddler and infant daughter, Ann Marie, were among the first to arrive. Many of the friends who'd worked so hard on James's campaign showed up soon after, shortly before the first election results were announced.

Summer planted herself in a chair in the family room and didn't move for an hour. The ache in her back had intensified.

Feeling the need to move about, she made her way into the kitchen. She was standing in front of the sink when it happened. Her eyes widened as she felt a sharp, stabbing pain.

"James," she cried in panic, gripping the counter. Water gushed from between her legs and onto the floor. "Oh, my goodness."

"Summer?" James stood in the doorway, along with at least ten others, including Elizabeth Manning.

"I'm sorry," she whispered, looking at James. "But I think it might be time to take me to the hospital."

She saw her husband turn and stare longingly at the election results being flashed across the screen. "Now?"

Fourteen

"James... I'm sorry." The pain that had been concentrated in the small of her back had worked its way around her middle. Summer held her stomach and closed her eyes, surprised by the intensity of it.

"Sorry," James demanded, "for what?" He moved quickly and placed his arm around her shoulders.

"You'd better get her to the hospital," Elizabeth advised.

"I'll phone the doctor for you," Eric added.

James shouted out the number he'd memorized, and five or six Mannings chanted it until Eric found a pad and pen to write it down.

Summer felt as if everyone wanted to play a role in the birth of their twins.

"Toss me the car keys, and I'll get the car as close to the front door as I can," Jason Manning shouted.

James threw him the keys, and Jason hurried out the front door.

"What about the election returns?" Summer asked, gazing at the television.

"I'll get them later," James said as if it meant nothing.

"I'll leave messages on your cell phone," Charlotte volunteered, "and James can call us when he has an update on Summer and the babies."

Summer bit her lip at the approach of another contraction. It hurt, really hurt. "James." She squeezed his hand, needing him.

"I'm here, sweetheart. I won't leave you, not for anything."

Jason reappeared, and the small entourage headed for James's car. It was parked on the grass, close to the front door, the engine running.

"The doctor said you should go directly to the hospital," Walter said breathlessly. "He'll meet you there."

"Don't worry, Summer, this isn't his first set of twins," Elizabeth said in a reassuring voice.

"True, but they're mine," James said.

"James?" Summer looked at her husband and noticed how pale he'd suddenly become. "Are you all right?"

He didn't answer for a moment; instead, he helped her inside the car and strapped her in. Before long he was sitting next to her, hands braced on the steering wheel. Summer saw the pulse in his neck pounding.

"It's going to be fine," she whispered. "Just fine."

"I'll feel a whole lot better once we get you to the hospital."

"Call us," Charlotte shouted, standing on the steps, waving.

Summer waved back, and no fewer than fifteen adults crowded onto the Mannings' front porch, cheering them on.

"James, are you okay to drive?" Summer asked when he took off at breakneck speed. He slowed down and stayed within the speed limit, but there was a leashed fear in him that was almost palpable.

"I'll be okay once we get you to the hospital."

"The birthing process is perfectly natural."

"Maybe it is for a woman, but it isn't as easy for a man."

With her hands propped against her abdomen, Summer smiled. "What's that supposed to mean?"

"I don't know if I can bear to see you in pain," he said, wiping his face as they stopped for a red light.

"It won't be too bad."

"Hey, you saw the films in our birthing class. I don't know if I'm ready for this."

"You!" she said, and giggled.

James's fingers curled around her hand. "This isn't a laughing matter. I've never been more frightened in my life. No, only once," he amended. "The night I came home and found you gone."

"The babies and I are going to be just fine," she said again. "Don't worry, James, please. This is your night to shine. I'm just sorry Mutt and Jeff chose right now to make their debut."

"At the moment, the election is the last thing on my mind. None of it matters."

"You're going to win the primary," she insisted. Summer knew the competition had been steep, and Ralph Southworth had done what damage he could, eager to prove himself right.

"We're almost at the hospital," James said, sounding relieved.

"Relax," she said, and as it turned out, her words were a reminder to herself. The next contraction hit with unexpected severity, and she drew in a deep breath trying to control the pain.

"Summer!"

"I'm fine," she said breathlessly.

James pulled into the emergency entrance at Virginia

Mason Hospital and raced around the front of the car. He opened the door, unsnapped the seat belt and lovingly helped her out.

Someone rolled a wheelchair toward her, and while Summer sat and answered the questions in Admitting, James parked the car.

She was on the maternity floor when he rejoined her, looking pale and harried.

"Stop worrying," she scolded him.

James dragged a chair to the side of her bed and slumped into it. "Feel my heart," he said and placed her hand over his chest.

"It feels like a machine gun," Summer said, smiling. She moved her hand to his face and cupped his cheek.

"I need you so much," James whispered.

Summer couldn't speak due to a strong contraction. James clasped her hand and talked to her in soothing tones, urging her to relax. As the pain ebbed, she kept her eyes closed.

When she opened them, she found James standing by the hospital bed, studying her. She smiled weakly and he smiled in return.

Dr. Wise arrived and read her chart, then asked, "How are we doing here?"

"Great," Summer assured him.

"Not so good," James said contradicting her. "I think Summer needs something for the pain, and frankly I'm not feeling so well myself."

"James, I'm fine," Summer told him yet again.

"What your husband's saying is that he needs help to deal with seeing you in pain," the physician explained.

"Do something, Doc."

Dr. Wise slapped James affectionately on the back.

"Why don't we let Summer be the one to decide if she needs an epidural? She's a better judge than either one of us."

"All right." But James's agreement came reluctantly.

For Summer the hours passed in a blur. Her labor was difficult, and she was sure she could never have endured it if not for James, who stood faithfully at her side. He encouraged her, lifted her spirits, rubbed her back, reassured her of his love.

News of the primary filtered into the room in messages from Charlotte and various nurses, who caught snippets on the waiting room TV. In the beginning Summer strained to hear each bit of information. But as the evening wore on, she became so consumed by what was happening to her and the babies that she barely heard.

She lost track of time, but it seemed to her that it was well into the wee hours of the morning when she was taken into the delivery room.

James briefly left her side and returned a few minutes later, gowned in surgical green. He resembled a prison escapee, and she took one look at him and laughed.

"What's so funny?"

"You."

James drew in a deep breath and held Summer's hand. "It's almost time."

"I know," she breathed softly. "Ready or not, we're about to become parents. I have the feeling this is going to be the ride of a lifetime."

"It's been that way for me from the night I met you."

"Are you sorry, James?"

"Sorry?" he repeated. "No way!" Leaning over, he kissed her forehead. "My only regret is that I didn't marry you that first New Year's."

"Oh, James, I do love you."

Dr. Wise joined them. "Well, you two, let's see what we've got here, shall we?" He grinned at James. "Congratulations, Your Honor. You won the primary. This is obviously a night for good news."

Two months later Summer woke to the soft, mewling cry of her infant daughter. She climbed silently out of bed and made her way into their daughters' nursery.

There she found James sitting upright in the rocker, sound asleep with Kellie in his arms. Kerrie fussed in her crib.

Lifting the tiny bundle, Summer changed Kerrie's diaper, then sat in the rocker next to her husband and offered the hungry child her breast. Kerrie nursed eagerly and Summer ran her finger down the side of her baby's perfect face.

Her gaze wandered to her husband and she felt a surge of pride and love. The election had been that night, and he'd won the court seat by a wide margin. During the heat of the last two weeks of the campaign, James had let her compose and sing a radio commercial for him. Summer had been proud of her small part in his success, although she didn't miss life on the stage. Her twin daughters kept her far too busy for regrets.

James must have felt her scrutiny because he stirred. He looked up and saw Summer with Kerrie.

"I might as well feed Kellie, too," she said. Experience had taught her that the minute one was fed and asleep, the other would wake and demand to be nursed. Her twin daughters were identical in more than looks. Even their sleep patterns were the same.

James stood and expertly changed Kellie's diaper.

When Kerrie finished nursing, Summer swapped babies

with him. James gently placed his daughter on his shoulder and patted her back until they heard the tiny burp.

"Why didn't you wake me?" Summer asked.

"You were sleeping so soundly."

"It was quite a night, Your Honor," she said, looking over at her husband. "I couldn't be more thrilled for you, James. Your position on the bench is secure."

"I couldn't have done it without you," he told her.

"Don't be ridiculous."

"It's true," he said with feeling. "You and Kerrie and Kellie. The voters fell in love with the three of you. Those radio commercials you sang were the talk of the town. I'm the envy of every politician I know."

"Because I can sing?"

"No, because you're my wife." His eyes were dark, intense. "I'm crazy about you, Summer. I still can't believe how much you've given me."

"I love you, too, James." Summer closed her eyes. It had started almost two years ago in Vegas, when it felt as if her heart was breaking. Now her heart was filled to overflowing. Life couldn't get any better than it was right then, she decided.

But Summer was wrong.

Because the best was yet to come.

* * * * *